HYMNS OF THE WILD

LITURGY OF WORLDS BOOK 2

NATHAN HARTLE

First edition. 2023.

ISBN ebook: 978-1-7374114-1-3

ISBN paperback: 978-1-7374114-3-7

To my parents

PROLOGUE

AS THE GUARDIAN HURRIED away from the prison that held the gods, he felt Huire among them, watching him.

Long ago, when he was human, his terror would have been a cold tingling through his body. Not anymore. Like the gods, he could take whatever shape he wished, but the cloud of particles that made up his body felt nothing. Fear was a pure blossoming in his intellect. So was anger.

The vast crystalline hall that surrounded the prison oppressed him. Its many gateways to planets across the universe were open doors through which Huire's people could attack.

She, the greatest of the gods, had called out for rescue to her people, a kingdom of humans who had worshipped her far away and long ago. They worshipped her still, and they wanted her back. She had assured the Guardian they were coming.

As she spoke, her patient serenity driving him mad, he had known she was right.

He saw their dreams.

The palace that contained this hall had a mind of its own. It had already located Huire's people somewhere among the stars and warned him of their coming by filling his mind with images from their sleep.

The beings who built the palace had been smarter and stronger than him, and not even his considerable arrogance could convince him he was fit to take their place. The magnitude and complexity of the job tossed his mind like a sailboat in a storm. Now, with the dreams arriving faster and faster, he was truly over-matched.

But he was not helpless. He had realized he could affect the humans through their dreams. Focusing on a few of them at a time, he could draw out memories associated with certain feelings.

What a weapon human dreams could be.

He had already failed once to stop the human company. The woman whose dreams he invaded had joined the company despite his best efforts. He had played on her fears only to push her toward Huire.

He must get better at using his weapon.

As he hurried out of Huire's hall with dreams falling thick around him, he summoned all his eons of hatred for Huire. He would need it for the fight ahead.

Among the human company, he found a man on the verge of collapse. Breaking that man would break them. He would do just that.

1

—·—

SHADA

WHEN SHADA OPENED THE door to Emberly's wagon, Bishop Arumin's booming shout drove her back a step. It cut through the ringing that the bombing in Ronia had left in her ears.

"You swore to obey Huire's will, Emberly!"

The bishop noticed Shada first. Usually, he greeted her with grandfatherly cheer. Now, red with anger, he said nothing.

Captain Emberly sat behind his tiny desk, fingers on his temples. Many in the company had headaches from the bombing, which had targeted them but mostly killed ordinary Ronians instead. Between the explosions and the street battle with terrorists that followed, the company had lost three soldiers. Arumin had announced that a group called the Unheard were responsible, though he had kept the source of this information to himself.

Shada stepped out of the warm jungle night of the planet Caidfell and into the wagon's cramped confines. The captain looked up with a glare.

"What do you want?" As he spoke, he saw her for the first time. The words twisted in his mouth as he tried to stop them. "I'm sorry, Caretaker," he said, sitting up straight and folding his hands. "What can I do for you?"

Shada nodded in greeting. "I suppose you know what I'm going to say, Captain."

"Yes. Our route."

"I've heard you insist on crossing the jungle using the north road."

The captain's eyes shifted to the bishop. "We were just talking about that. Yes, I insist. The main road is more likely to be watched."

"I don't understand." She kept her tone polite. It would not do to upset Emberly more than needed. "The Lady wants us to take the main road. We must retrace the path she took on her way to Ronia."

Emberly spoke with visible restraint. "Shada—Caretaker—I'm not sure the Lady is aware of our exact circumstances."

"She's the Goddess Huire's messenger." It was not a direct response, but it was the core of the issue.

"Her messenger. She's not the Goddess herself."

The captain's boldness surprised Shada. It had the flavor of blasphemy, if not its substance. Maybe soldiers were like that.

Arumin could not contain himself. "She speaks for the Goddess, Emberly. It's the same thing."

The captain kept his eyes on Shada. "If I only knew why—"

Shada let her impatience show a little. "Because she knows the route is usable. She's taken it before."

Emberly shook his head. "Sheer luck must have kept them alive. We can't count on that. Plus we're a much larger group. If the convicts are out there, they'll certainly spot us."

Arumin stepped over to stand with Shada, facing Emberly shoulder to shoulder. He had calmed himself with remarkable speed. "You're scaring yourself over nothing, Captain. The convicts can't possibly still be alive. If anything should worry us, it's the jungle."

He was right as far as Shada knew. Caidfell's jungle had been deadly even before Ronia abandoned the prison camp. Common wisdom held that the convicts left behind after the uprising must be long dead.

Emberly glanced between the two of them, an expression crossing his face that Shada had never seen there before. He looked trapped.

His next words sounded like a painful admission. "I believe the convicts are not our only enemy."

When Shada grasped his meaning, she understood his embarrassment. The bishop's voice changed radically, hinting at a concealed smile. "My Goddess. Captain, have you been listening to the soldiers' ghost stories?"

Emberly glared. "Those stories persist for good reason."

The bishop gave him no respite. "If you believe wraiths haunt this jungle, then surely we'd be safer on the main road, out of the deepest wilderness."

"I repeat: the main road is easily watched. By anyone out there."

Shada opened her mouth to reply, but the bishop cut in. His voice rose, incredulous. "How can you—"

He stopped himself from saying whatever it was. Maybe there were measures he was unwilling to take yet. Instead, he switched tactics. "The main road is in worse condition than we feared. The north road is narrower. Imagine the state it must be in."

Emberly had regained his footing. "We'll cut through."

"Won't that take too long?" Shada asked. This matter was outside her experience, but it sounded time-consuming.

"If it does..." Emberly paused. "That's why we brought explosives."

The word "explosives" cast a pall over the room. Before that morning, Shada had never heard an explosion. She never wanted to hear one again.

Everything about Arumin betrayed disbelief. He spoke softly. "You say you're worried about being noticed. Then you suggest we start blasting."

"Won't anyone out there hear us, Captain?" Shada added.

"The girl is right. Every living thing within a day's walk would hear us. What are you really worried about, Emberly?"

"Your Holiness, I don't answer to you." The captain's voice sounded strained. "Huire will judge me. I've made my decision."

Arumin exploded. "Judge you she will, soldier!" His face was red, and his neck muscles bulged. "Tell me about the Goddess! How dare you!"

He flung open the wagon's door and hurled a last volley. "Her will shall be done. Someone will do it."

He stormed out, leaving the door open and dust settling.

Shada tried once more. Her voice was tiny in the wake of Arumin's. "You're forgetting what matters, Captain. The Lady commands—"

"I've forgotten nothing," Emberly snapped. His usual genteel manner with her had slipped. "I think you've misunderstood the Lady."

"I've heard her clearly. She traveled safely with the last caretaker because the Goddess protected them. The Goddess will do the same for us."

The captain's head had settled into his hands. When he heard her last words, it jerked up. "She didn't protect my men who died this morning."

The words hung in the air. Shada could have answered in a few ways. She could have reminded him that everyone had known the danger when they took the crusader's vow. But that would be worse than saying nothing.

"No," she admitted as she walked out.

2

NOR

As THE NIGHT DEEPENED, exhaustion had divided the travelers. Some had completed their chores and collapsed into sleep. Others lay awake in the dark, reliving the sights of that morning.

Several, finding the night terrifying, had gathered around a fire. The stockade wall surrounding their hilltop shielded them from the wailing, relentless wind. It also protected a small garrison and the gateway that led off of Caidfell.

Around the fire, the men listened to each other talk to avoid feeling alone.

The bombing had partly deafened some, and these spoke in shouts. Others twitched nervously at their outbursts. Conversation meandered. They cursed the Unheard, the terrorist group that had perpetrated the bombings. Occasionally, someone called into the night, "For Victory Park!"

Brother Nor stared into the fire, sometimes glancing away to relieve his eyes. Once again, he was imprisoned with a flame for company. Outside the circle of light, the silence waited.

It had found him in his prison cell on Ronia and followed him all the way here, to the edge of known space. It stalked him through the shadows, hoping to meet his eyes so it could pounce. He sat quietly amid the men's chatter.

In his pocket was the battered envelope that Cadmon, his abbot, had given him when they parted. Cadmon had posed a question: "What are the gods made of?" The envelope held the answer. If Nor answered correctly, he would become an elder of their order. His fellow monks called such questions "quandaries."

Promotion to elder would be unprecedented for an apprentice antiquary like him. Nor had spent his career scouring the empire for artifacts of the old world—advanced technologies forbidden to all Ronians except his order. When Nor asked why he had been chosen, Cadmon had answered evasively.

Nor felt guilty at receiving the honor over more deserving candidates. To make it worse, he had no idea how to solve the quandary.

Across the fire, a soldier named Borna cursed violently and slapped his own shoulder. "Damned pests everywhere! Is it always like this?" he asked Merin, a slightly built man on Nor's bench.

Merin straightened and nodded. Captain Emberly had conscripted him from Caidfell's garrison to replace the company's astronomer, whom a wagon had crushed during the bombing. The man's only other qualification, if it could be called that, was that he'd briefly met the Lady's first caretaker, who had passed through this fort while carrying the Lady to Ronia.

Meeting the first caretaker, a giant with a dog's face, would have left an impression on anyone, but Merin said nothing about it. He had obeyed his new orders without protest, taking the crusader's vow and exchanging his uniform for the simple, anonymous cloak and traveling clothes worn by the company.

The night was warm despite the planet's notorious nocturnal wind. Still, Merin huddled as if dredged from a river. "I'm afraid so," he said in reply to Borna. "Not as many flying pests up here on the hill, but the crawling ones can still find you. They say the jungle is worse."

"Haven't you been down there?" Borna asked. He was broad and strong from top to bottom, and his beard held the remains of his dinner.

"Never," said the new astronomer, flustered by the attention. "We only leave the fort to clear the hillside of new trees. And only during the day."

"They're still expecting an attack after all these years?" Borna's sneer suggested an apology was in order.

Merin looked into the flames, perhaps to divine an acceptable answer. "Not really. After the convicts revolted, this garrison went on high alert. The attack never came, but no one changed the order. The army doesn't like thinking about this place. Still, there are nights—"

"Why all the worry?" Borna interrupted. "If any of that rabble survived this long, they'd be living in trees like animals." This earned a laugh from the older man next to him. Borna turned to him. "Eh, Elisar? They'd beg us to march them back here in irons."

"It's not just the convicts that scare the army," said Elisar. "It's the whole bloody planet. Who ever saw a night like that?"

Beyond the stockade, the dark pressed in. Clouds blocked the stars, and the heavy, moist air raised beads of sweat on the men's faces.

The land below their lofty perch was black as a cauldron of pitch. Despite the ringing in his keen ears, Nor heard a river of fast-moving air, wide as a city, moving through the valley. Hell itself, the Outer Dark, could scarcely be as formless as this night.

The silence crept up on Nor again. He turned back to the firelight, eyes aching.

"They're expecting to find someone alive down there," said Robir, another private. He sat up straight, cloak folded under him, blond hair hanging over his eyes. "That's why we did away with our uniforms. No use advertising who we are. Emberly learned that on Gallobraith if he learned nothing else."

Chuckling at Robir's courtly manner, Borna replied, "Not likely." His eyes lit, and his face reddened. "Huire's sake, I'll say it plainly. Emberly cracked on that planet."

Discomfort was palpable. A few glanced toward the wagons. Robir watched the fire thoughtfully.

Seeing their reactions, Borna protested, "There's no shame in it, mind you. Everyone gets their turn. Sometimes the mind can't reckon things." He swatted another insect.

"I wouldn't talk that way in this fort," said Merin. "The captain is a hero to these men." He blushed. "And to me."

Borna stared at him. "What's your name, friend?"

Merin told him, stumbling over the syllables.

Borna repeated the name. "Can't blame you, I suppose. If Emberly had been in charge here when the convicts escaped, things might've been different. This place is for lunatics." He captured a flying pest in his hand, crushed it, and flung it into the fire. "That's why the bishop couldn't handle it."

A few people muttered at that.

Borna was defiant. "His Holiness admitted it. He wasn't cut out for the army. He's a coward."

"That's enough," Nor snapped, surprising himself. Borna was right, and Nor enjoyed hearing someone say these things aloud. But as Cadmon insisted, his feelings were unimportant.

Borna looked stricken. "Begging your pardon, Brother Nor. I forgot a holy man was present."

"It makes no difference," said Robir before Nor could respond. "These judgments aren't ours to make. The Goddess chose the bishop to lead us. She's listening to us, and so is her messenger."

More glances toward the wagons, this time to the wagon where the Lady and her caretaker stayed. In Nor's experience, the Lady knew only what she saw and heard. She could not be everywhere at once. But he saw no reason to discourage rumors to the contrary.

As the men watched, the door of Emberly's wagon opened, and Shada stepped out. When the bishop had left moments ago, he had gone in a huff, but Shada moved unobtrusively. She noticed the men around the fire watching her, and Nor imagined she met his eyes. Flinching under their collective gaze, she disappeared into the wagon she shared with the Lady.

Giggling, Borna spoke first. "Bad idea, that."

Elisar seized this lighter topic. "A few weeks on the road, she'll make things ugly. They'll be knifing each other over her."

"They would have," said Borna. "Looks like the bishop beat us to it."

"I doubt he's interested. That man of his, Brin, is taking care of him. And the captain doesn't have enough sense to see what's in front of him."

Borna spat into the fire. "Well, that's to my benefit."

"She'd never have you."

"Just you watch."

"Shut your mouth," said Nor. "Think hard before you speak again." He heard his voice and realized how angry he was.

Borna returned Nor's stare. Nor's milky-white eyes, so alien to most, did not seem to bother him. "What's the problem, Brother?"

"Stay away from the caretaker."

Borna's face was relaxed. "Brother Nor's been shut away in a temple. Away from women. Maybe away from jokes, too, since he's forgotten what they sound like."

Nor said, "Don't even look at her."

A smile touched the soldier's lips. "I can't promise that. Meaning no disrespect, Brother, but you can't scare me, not even with Scripture. The Goddess forgives. I've angered her before, but she always takes me back."

"She might spare your soul, but she won't protect your body. If you get near the caretaker, you'll regret it."

Elisar broke a silence that grew heavier by the second. "Doesn't talk much like a monk, does he?"

"Borna," Robir barked before Borna could answer. "Brother Nor is one of us."

From the shadows beyond the fire, someone said, "I'm afraid that isn't so, Private."

It was Orund, a sergeant who had argued with Nor that morning. He knew things about Nor's past that the monk wished were secret. As the dancing firelight revealed his face, Nor felt sick.

"Brother Nor feels no love for us," said Orund. "After all, we're Ronian soldiers."

Robir protested. "Sergeant, we don't know this man."

"I know enough."

Nor wondered how long Orund had been waiting in the shadows. "Sergeant, I can see you want to say something. Say it or leave."

"Nothing will save you from judgment," Orund replied. "Not even your Temple."

"I'm already saved," said Nor.

Orund ignored him. "Huire blesses those who punish sinners. They save her the trouble."

It was a doubtful interpretation of Scripture. "I'm certainly a sinner," Nor replied. "If you are too, go away and reflect. If you aren't, go ahead and try to punish me."

"Some sinners are below the rest."

Robir asked, "Are you sure you have the right man, Sergeant? What could this monk have done?"

Orund spoke softly. "I heard your name, heard about your eyes. Unnatural, they said. When I saw your face, I knew."

Borna looked from Orund to Nor and back. "What do you mean?"

"This man is our enemy. He brawled with some of our fellow soldiers. One of them, a boy, he mangled forever."

Nor said, "Dorsy." The name haunted him, as did the face that went with it. He tried to take a breath, but the air seemed thinner. "Do you know him?"

"No," said Sergeant Orund. "But he's one of us. For some of us, our brotherhood is our only family. That's all I need to know."

Nor swallowed. "It was complicated."

"Are you going to tell me he deserved it? I don't care if he's the filthiest swine who ever lived. I'd still take him over ten of you."

Robir interrupted. "Listen to me, Sergeant. We have no right to judge people's worth."

"No, the sergeant is right," said Nor. "In these clothes, without my robes, I'm just a man. He can challenge me anytime. Is that what he's doing?"

Orund breathed deeply, perhaps reconsidering. Attacking a monk, robed or not, was a dreadful sin. The Goddess would forgive the sins of anyone who took the crusader's vow—as long as they completed the crusade or died trying—but Orund might still fear for his body, which his superiors could punish.

At last, the sergeant said, "Someday soon, you'll pay for what you did. You and all offworlders. You're all the same."

Nor picked up a twig and prodded the fire's ashes. "What about all the offworlders you've killed? Wherever your empire goes, it makes slaves and corpses. My people—"

"Your people were too busy killing each other to notice us!" Orund spat. "We civilized you, and now we defend you."

"My people kill for home and honor," said Nor. "Yours kill for profit."

Orund softened his voice. "How would you know any better? Killing's bred into you. That's how it is with the lower orders."

Nor dropped the twig.

"You can't hide what you are," Orund said. "If you had honor like Dorsy, you wouldn't have tried."

The silence that stalked Nor faded into the night. It knew when to leave him alone, when he could hurt himself most. "I knew Dorsy better than you. He wasn't brave at all, or honorable, when I took out his eye. He begged, in fact."

He shook his head. "And you call him family. It's a wonder your empire has lasted this long."

Soldiers leapt to their feet. Orund rounded the fire.

Nor did not think much. He stood and backed away from the flames. Three men advanced on him: Orund first then Borna and Elisar. Others followed, less committed to the fight. Nor's back neared a wall. They would quickly surround him unless he ran, and running held no appeal.

In any case, where would he go? The jungle?

Orund charged, and Nor raised his fists. Whether he survived or not, what happened would be simple.

3

—·—

NOR

EVERYONE STOPPED IN THEIR tracks as a scream rent the night. It hung in the air, wavering, a sound to freeze the breath.

It came from Hulgar, a private in Emberly's company. Stumbling into their midst, he screamed himself breathless and fell to his hands and knees, hacking and panting.

He was a giant man, nearly as large as any two others combined. His muscles trembled and shone with sweat. As his coughing subsided, he began to sob, loudly and unreservedly.

For a moment, no one around the fire said anything. Among the tents, voices called out, and heads emerged from openings.

Orund knelt next to Hulgar, the fight apparently forgotten. He spoke gently. "What is it, friend?"

Hulgar's grief continued as if no one else was there. Orund placed a hand on his back. Others tensed as if expecting an outburst, but Hulgar smothered Orund's hand with his own then held it to his face, wetting it with tears.

Orund gulped and put his other hand on the private's head. "You're here with us."

In the firelight, Hulgar's eyes were beads, and his tears ran gold down to his beard. He sniffed and shook his head. "No, and I won't be ever again."

Squatting, Orund laid his arm across the man's back. His fingertips did not reach Hulgar's far shoulder. "Can you feel this? Hold on."

The private nodded. His face distorted with his inner struggle.

"What's happened, man? What have you taken?"

Hulgar snorted and shook his head again. Strands of saliva hung in his beard as he looked at the ground. "Nothing, sir. I just... Something happened to me, sir. I don't know what to say. It was like a dream, but it was real. Dreams are confusing. This felt as real as you do."

The soldiers who had come from the tents and the nearby barracks were drifting away. The scene was painful to watch. The man must be unhinged if he unabashedly admitted being troubled by nightmares, which Ronians saw as the products of a poorly disciplined mind.

The gap that separated Nor from the Ronians, his adopted people, never stopped growing. He had learned as a boy that denying one's feelings separated one from the group. Dreams were echoes of the soul, and keeping them secret deprived one's family and clan of their lessons.

Hulgar rose to his knees and stretched his arms toward Nor. The monk remembered the suffering faces of those whom he had given the last rites before death—a teenage boy's, an old woman's, many at once.

The big soldier collapsed awkwardly and groveled at Nor's feet. "Brother, speak for me. I'll keep my vow. Let me prove it."

Nor's skin crawled at the man's worshipful pose. He knelt and spoke with the calm assurance expected of a holy man. Here was a problem he could confront without fighting. "Your vow is intact, Private, and you'll surely prove yourself. Your sins are forgiven unless you abandon the crusade."

"But what I saw..." Hulgar looked sick. "We aren't worthy." His voice grew louder, carrying across the yard. "We've been judged, and Huire has abandoned us. There was a man there, watching, a man made of diamonds—"

"What is this?" shouted an officer emerging from a tent. He advanced on the men with barely restrained force, his tied-back gray hair stretching the corners of his face, which was not yet old. His eyes bounced from Orund to Hulgar.

Orund replied, "Lieutenant Roark, the private here is ill. His suffering got the better of him, but he's recovering."

Roark shifted his barbed gaze to Hulgar, still on his knees. "What do you say, Private?"

Unaffected by the officer's menace, Hulgar answered mildly. "Our sins have returned to us."

Roark glared. "You had better start making sense, now."

Hulgar straightened and spoke loudly enough for all to hear. "Our fate is sealed. It was decided there." He pointed out into the lightless gulf of the jungle.

Roark absorbed this and knelt by the private. He spoke with great reserve.

"I hear that once in a while, soldiers vanish from this fort at night. Something takes sentries during their watch. It happened in the old days, too, at the prison camp. Ask the bishop or the captain; they'll tell you. Private Hulgar, are you listening?"

Hulgar turned his head partway to Roark, keeping one eye on his private visions.

"We probably don't know half of what lives out there. Some even think the jungle itself takes them. It sneaks into your mind first, grows inside you. Then one night, you climb over the wall and vanish."

Hulgar shook. Roark said, "I don't know if it's true. But if you keep crying, I'll hang you by your arms from the wall, and we'll find out."

Bishop Arumin had come out of his wagon and was watching from a distance, out of earshot. The captain had also appeared. Scarcely dressed, he looked around as if unsure where he was. Lucky for him, few noticed his confusion.

Hulgar's lip trembled, a surreal expression on his powerful features. "I did it again. I was there, and I did it all over again." A whine escaped his lips, and he wept loudly.

Roark stood with a sneer. He gazed down on the private, but he spoke to Orund. "Is this how you lead men, Sergeant?"

Dazed, Orund murmured, "He's a good man. Fearless. He's just confused. He must be ill."

"He's cracked, and he's not the only one." Roark looked at the others. "Did those bombs this morning really frighten you all so much? Let me tell you, worse is coming. Pull yourselves together, or you'll end up like Hulgar here. A sad mess." He pointed to Borna and Elisar, whose eyes were wide. "Get him on his feet."

"Sir," Borna muttered. He and Elisar did not move.

Roark caught a whiff of disobedience. "This man has blasphemed, ignored orders, and sacrificed his honor. He will—"

"Wait!" cried Nor.

This lieutenant hid his annoyance poorly. "Brother Norhim?"

"The private may have had a vision," Nor said. "His dream may be a message from the Goddess." He had no reason to believe this, but it could be true.

Roark stared at Nor as if he had sprouted wings. He pointed to Hulgar. "You think the Goddess spoke to *this*?"

"She speaks in strange voices," Nor said agreeably. "The dreams she sends can be overpowering." He wanted to save Hulgar, though he did not know why. He pitied the man, but there was more.

"But what he said... It was sacrilegious. He said Huire abandoned our company. That can't be true." Alarm rippled through the others.

Nor improvised. "It's likely Hulgar saw what awaits if our mission fails. It was surely terrible for him, but it was necessary. Now he can remind us what we stand to lose. We face a world without our Goddess, for all time."

His words released tension. Someone sighed. Arumin would probably have approved of Nor's handling of the situation. But he wondered what Cadmon would think of him manipulating these people like puppets. Or what the Lady would think of him lying in her name for unidentifiable reasons. For the moment, it was fortunate that she only spoke to Shada, who was not here.

Hulgar's face was a spasm of emotion. "I felt it all. My hands..." He clenched a fist and opened it.

"You've survived," Nor said, offering his hand to the private. "You'll be stronger for it. You must show your strength to your friends. Can you control your tears for them?"

A few seconds passed, and Hulgar nodded. He took Nor's hand and stood, towering over him. A few onlookers whispered that the monk had miraculously lifted the giant. Nor let them talk. He could not tamp down every rumor.

Reaching up, Nor put his hand on Hulgar's shoulder and guided him toward the tents. On the way, he locked eyes first with Lieutenant Roark, who glared, then with Sergeant Orund, who turned his head away.

He wondered what his own expression was telling others. He thought the bombing that morning sufficiently explained Hulgar's outburst, and he feared his face would show his lie.

Hulgar's face held no deception, only fear and a desperate need to trust. Nor did not think himself capable of surrender like that. He remembered the blind beggar at the temple doors in Ronia, whose empty eye sockets had fixed Nor as surely as living eyes.

When Hulgar had begged for his help, Nor would have stepped in front of a rifle to save the man's faith from Roark's brutal discipline.

There were worse ways to die. It might even be cowardly, a quick escape from the terrifying future. At least it would have freed Nor from the staggering weight of the envelope in his pocket, the mystery that he could not penetrate. He asked himself again, what were the gods made of?

4

SHADA

"THE CAPTAIN WILL NOT obey?" The Lady sounded unfamiliar with the words. "My child, you accepted this?"

Shada's cheeks burned. She stood before the Lady, still reeling from the soul-piercing shriek they had just heard from outside. The Lady, anxious for Shada's report, had forbidden her to go out and see what was happening. "It's probably a nightmare," she had said, her voice like a thousand voices speaking as one. "If the others need us, they will come to us."

The Lady understood people only as a subject she had observed from outside, but she might well be right. The explosions in Victory Park and the battle afterward would haunt many people's sleep, in this company and in Ronia.

That left Shada with no choice but to admit her failure. "I did. I told them you want to move straight ahead. But the captain will not back down."

"I'm surprised you found that acceptable."

The burning in Shada's cheeks spread across her face. "Emberly was stationed here before the uprising. So was Arumin. They know more about this world than anyone. I can't hope to—"

"Hope has nothing to do with it. The Goddess wills that we follow the path of my journey to Ronia. Debate is worthless."

Shada was trapped. She would never measure up to this situation. "My Lady, I want to obey you. But I have no authority with these men."

"You certainly do. You must realize you speak for the ultimate authority. The Goddess chose you, so the others must bow to your words."

"Emberly's troops obey him, not me." Shada's voice betrayed her embarrassment. "If I try to—"

The Lady interrupted with firm assurance. "Why do you think men like the captain and the bishop command obedience?"

Life had given Shada little reason to consider such things. "Because they're confident."

"Not just that." The Lady shook her head, an unpracticed motion that was only recognizable in context. "They have turned their wills into weapons. Take the captain. With only a ribbon of rank, he controls dozens of armed men. Anyone who opposes him must do it secretly. And you have something far more powerful: the word of Huire, to whom all other gods pay tribute. He cannot stand against you."

"I see," Shada said, hoping her tone conveyed at least a little authority. She had stopped short of saying she understood. How a person could wield power she did not feel inside her was a mystery. If it was as easy as the Lady said, every pauper would be a king.

The Lady smiled. "No one can do it but you. You accepted a terribly hard role, and it will get much harder. You may soon long for the day when you compelled a famous warrior to change his mind."

Shada nodded. Her mouth opened, but her thoughts drowned whatever sound emerged.

"You must speak to the bishop tonight," the Lady said. "He will take your side. The two of you must plan for the morning. You'll speak Huire's will to Captain Emberly until she restores his faith."

From outside came the sound of unabashed weeping.

"The poor man," said Shada. "You're right. He must have had a nightmare. He'll feel humiliated tomorrow."

"Perhaps," said the Lady. "Though he needn't. What about your nightmares, child? Do they shame you?"

Shada froze. Her throat constricted. "What do you mean?"

"Last night, you spoke and turned in your sleep. No one else heard it, rest assured. But I hear very well, even when I'm in my box."

"I..." Shada stammered. The truth she had concealed was going to come out now, before she was ready.

She had been having odd dreams since the night before she met the Lady. They were haunting, spectacularly vivid, and she had suspected they were visions from Huire. But their meaning had been unclear, and she had finally decided the Goddess would not be so cryptic.

She was sure the Lady would want to know about them. The Lady could be rabidly curious, particularly when it came to clues to Huire's will. Despite being Huire's messenger, the Lady had no automatic knowledge of Huire's mind—a fact that would surprise many people if they knew it.

Shada should have told her about the dreams weeks ago. She did not understand why she hadn't. Yes, she was afraid of seeming fragile and unstable, but there was more.

The Lady continued, "When you woke up, I heard you crying, but you said nothing about what you had seen."

Shada remembered the dream keenly. A shining face made of crystal had rushed toward her, commanding her in an awful scream to *Stop*. She had thought it meant she should not take the crusader's vow—that she should flee the Lady, run into the streets of Ronia, and disappear.

Since her previous visions had pushed her toward the crusade, she had decided in her confusion to ignore them all. They would do her no good if their messages conflicted.

She recalled waking up crying, closing her eyes briefly, and opening them to find the Lady looming over her. The Lady had worn her true shape, that of a gray, twisting cloud. She only favored her current shape, that of a pleasant old woman, because it made people comfortable. Shada had comforted herself by remembering that amid that shifting, humming mass lay the divine.

Since the Lady had not mentioned her crying that morning, Shada had assumed she had not noticed.

That had been foolish. Since appearing to Shada in Ronia, the Lady had shown she could see without eyes and hear without ears. Shada could keep few secrets. Her beating heart and rapid breathing betrayed her. Had Bishop Arumin not assured her otherwise, she would have suspected the Lady read her thoughts.

Not that Shada normally hid her feelings well. They took control of her face and manner, and fighting them made it worse. It was happening now—she was shaking. The Lady could hardly miss it.

"What did you dream about, child?" The Lady's affectionate tone and pet name reminded Shada of her own smallness.

It was long past time. Shada told her everything.

Each of the visions she remembered and the memories they contained. How their meanings eluded her. How they stayed with her during the days, their images hanging before her and their moods clinging to her. How one of her eyes opened on the waking world and the other on the land of sleep.

She spoke in one long sentence, afraid of what would happen when she finished. But to her surprise, she felt mostly relief. Her sin was confessed. Now she had only to face the consequences.

"How odd," the Lady answered after the longest pause she had ever left before speaking. Another pause followed.

The Lady's body contracted, the familiar golden shape and elderly features dissolving into a cloud. "It is not yet midnight," she said. "Some of the others are still awake." There was indeed chatter outside.

A face formed in the cloud and spoke to Shada. "I let you see me like this because I have faith in you. As you have faith in Huire. Many people would not understand."

She returned to her matronly form, hovering over a small chair as if sitting on it. She reached out, her arm stretching an unnatural distance, and covered Shada's hand with hers. Shada's fingers prickled. "While I am hidden," said the Lady, "you must be my eyes. I hope you will learn you shouldn't fear telling me the truth."

"You're right, Lady," said Shada. "I was afraid of what you would think. The dreams have been so bizarre." She had described how the people in the visions did not look quite right. They were larger than life, with overly expressive faces. Time's distortion of memory was both literal and visible.

Those people's appearance had reminded her of the Lady's, how her face trembled with energy, warping to show joy or sorrow without a natural sense of those feelings.

"May I ask you something?" said Shada. Stunned that the Lady was not angry, she wanted to move on. If the Lady had any thoughts about the dreams, she was keeping them to herself.

The Lady smiled with vast patience. "Yes, dear."

"Why won't you help the company when we're in danger?" The bishop had warned her not to ask this, but the Lady's assurance against fear inspired her.

The Lady answered readily. "I rarely leave the box because the cosmos is dangerous for my kind."

Shada had heard this already, though she did not know what the Lady meant by her "kind." "What could threaten someone like you?" she asked. "If you tell me, I'll watch out for it."

The Lady's face remained neutral. Maybe her range of learned expressions did not cover every emotion. "I am repeatedly surprised by how little you know about the Scriptures. Especially for someone born in Ronia. Though from what you have told me of your life, you cannot be blamed. Perhaps I should get used to these kinds of questions. My last caretaker didn't speak."

Shada thought of that other caretaker, the mute giant with a canine face. On the day he introduced her to the Lady, he had found a private moment and knelt down to clasp Shada's hand.

He had held it with great care. The look in his eyes transfixed her. He had wanted to speak, badly. His pleading gaze had stayed with her, coming to mind the next night when she fled the temple back into temporary obscurity.

That man had led a torturous life, right until the end. Mortally wounded while protecting the Lady, he had limped away, determined to die alone. The soldiers in this fort had encountered him not long before that, when he walked out of the jungle, carrying the Lady's box. They had almost shot him. It shocked them to see anyone come out of the wilderness. She wondered how that fight would have ended.

Maybe she should have studied the Scriptures before agreeing to become the new caretaker. But as she kept reminding herself, the Lady had chosen her, and refusal would have meant a life of hiding. Shada would have to trust the Lady's judgment, and Huire's.

The Lady brushed Shada's cheek with her fingers. "You're right to ask. But you must accept this: I won't tell you everything, and I won't always explain why. In the end, my word must be enough."

She withdrew her hand and gathered herself over the chair. "Is your mother dead?"

"No," Shada said flatly. Cold gripped her. She would answer the Lady's questions, but there were things she hoped not to relive. "Not as far as I know."

"I see." The two watched each other, and the Lady dropped the subject. "In any case, the Scriptures say that darkness descended on the worlds of humanity after Huire and the other gods left them."

Shada knew the outlines of this story. She waited.

"It was an age of horror. Forces moved among the worlds—things the Scriptures describe as demons. They disappeared long ago, but they may lurk out here in the reaches of the cosmos."

Shada heard laughter outside. Soldiers, cheery again after the tearful disruption, carrying on like a pack of dogs.

"If they still exist and they find me or one of my kind, they will devour me. Not even the Goddess could face them and survive, and I am but an ember of her power."

The idea of an enemy that could outmatch Huire was new to Shada. The wagon grew warmer, and the walls closed in.

"Thus," said the Lady, "I must remain hidden. All hope depends on my survival. I wish it was not so."

Having broached this subject, Shada hurried to change it. "I'd better visit the bishop before he goes to bed."

She meant to change her clothes first, but the Lady showed no sign of offering her privacy. Determined not to be afraid, she stepped toward the chest where she had stored a few pieces of clothing.

Before she reached it, she stopped. Silence stretched. The Lady watched. Shada picked up her boots instead.

"The Goddess has blessed you above all others," said the Lady, and Shada caught the shadow of a smile on her face. "I cannot express what that means."

The words were so vast and vague that they meant little. Shada's chest ached in a hollow spot where she had made room for a wealth of feeling.

Wrapped in her cloak, she left the wagon at a brisk walk, hoping to leave pointless thoughts behind. The Lady was Huire's servant, and Huire was part of the very nature of the universe. The Lady's simple presence must fill a room with truth and meaning. It was hard for a mere human to know how to feel about that.

Like everyone everywhere, Shada would have to try to appreciate things as they were. Perhaps in time, she would no longer wish the Lady's eyes would turn away.

5

—·—

EMBERLY

HULGAR'S OUTBURST HAD WOKEN Emberly from strange, vivid dreams, the same memory-filled kind of dreams he'd had for several nights now. Each contained a piece of the captain's past, and overlooking them all was a solitary figure, a man who shone like faceted glass.

Emberly had stepped out of the wagon but, ashamed of his frazzled state, had only watched from a distance as Nor comforted the soldier.

Now, returning to the wagon, he found his brother, Rayan, waiting.

As he stepped into the vehicle's dark interior, Rayan whispered in his ear, "Would you like to see me again? Do you even hope I'm still alive?"

Emberly jumped at the voice, to his brother's certain pleasure. But he did not bother to look at Rayan, knowing he would see nothing. Real or imaginary, Rayan's ghost had no visible form that Emberly had ever seen.

The captain muttered, "If you had survived in this jungle for all these years—if you and other convicts were still out there—then you couldn't be here, speaking to me. That would make me a madman and you a hallucination."

"Not necessarily." Rayan sounded in high spirits. "Maybe I decided to project myself across space. Have you ever seen me fail at something I put my mind to doing?"

Answering the question honestly would give Rayan too much satisfaction, so the captain changed the subject. "Would you want to see me?" he asked, walking to his cot. Floorboards creaked behind him, but he still refused to turn. There would be nothing to see, and he would feel like a fool.

His brother's voice replied, "Certainly. I never repaid you."

The words made Emberly stiff and uneasy. Sitting on the cot, he growled, "You owe me nothing."

"Of course I do. My struggle goes on, thanks to you."

The captain's chest hurt. "You're wrong."

"You're my finest soldier," said Rayan. "You set—"

"Shut up!" Emberly broke in. "I don't want to hear about that."

"Ah, fear of the truth. You haven't changed."

"You want the truth?" Emberly swallowed. "I don't know what to hope for. Are you alive? Dead? Do I hate you? Do I..."

Seconds passed, and Rayan snorted. "I'll spare you the agony of saying it: 'love.'"

Emberly lay on the cot, not bothering with blankets. Sleep was far away. A few lungfuls from a pipe would have let him rest, but all pipes were now out of reach, perhaps forever. He had left that vice behind, but it had yet to leave him.

"Why are things so damned hard?" he asked. He lay in the dark, his brother watching. The scene was almost companionable.

When he finally slept, the dreams overtook him again. He saw Rayan in prison.

⸻⸻◦⸻⸻

A row of cells. A single weak lantern somewhere. Behind bars, a squatting figure shrouded in darkness.

Emberly remembered this evening well.

The prisoner was Rayan. He was pale, and bruises from the guards' abuse stood out on his skin in the jail's biting cold. But he was enduring spitefully, as he did in any trap.

He could wait so long without speaking that Emberly always said the first word.

Emberly was not a captain yet. He ran his hands over his face and felt its youth. He finally said, "I passed Imperial Hall on my way here."

Rayan waited several seconds before replying, "And?" He could make Emberly wonder if his own words made sense. Though Emberly knew of the tactic, it still worked.

"It's always been there," Emberly continued. "I can't imagine what the city would look like if the hall were gone, blown to dust. What about the people inside? When I saw the hall, I tried to picture it."

"What did you see?"

Emberly shook his head. "I never thought you were capable. Even you."

"There isn't much I can say, Cyril, except you were wrong."

Emberly rubbed his hands up his oddly smooth temples and into his hair. "How could you do that? How could you even conceive of it? I knew you and your rabble were planning something, but that?"

"You knew there was something, but you didn't try to stop me. Why not?"

"I didn't want to believe it."

"Refusal to accept facts. That's always your mistake. The things our city has done—in the name of defense, of progress—have sickened it to its soul. That hall is the heart of its evil and decay. Without some cataclysm to change everything—"

"I can't believe they haven't killed you!" Emberly cried. "If only Mother and Father had the courage to let you suffer the fate you've earned..."

"They don't deserve your scorn. They've made a stand for what they believe."

"You've got them so turned around they don't know what to believe. Mother's sun rises and sets with you, and blood means more to Father than anything."

"Father is right about that. Family over money and ti-tles," said Rayan. "Our parents have shown their devotion to us."

"To you, you mean."

That struck a nerve. "Excuse me?"

"What about my life? You have no future, so you've taken mine. Halting your execution has cost us everything. I obeyed Father's rules, and he threw it all away."

"You're only thinking of yourself."

Emberly slammed his forearm against the bars. He observed the pain from a distance, refusing to wince. "You've ruined us with your revolution. But I'll save us."

Rayan's eyes dropped. "I was wondering about the uniform."

"Soldiers of exceptional courage are sometimes granted titles. I'll win fame in the wars and win back our name and position. Tell me now that I'm only thinking of myself."

Emberly cringed at his younger self's naivete. How could he have expected that plan to work? That it had indeed worked was no excuse.

Rayan did not attack his ambitions. Perhaps they aroused his pity. "Well, if the ruling families have their way, there will soon be enough wars for everyone."

Emberly would not be distracted by politics. "Mother has asked me to volunteer for a tour on Caidfell so I can make sure they treat you well."

His brother's eyes narrowed. "Oh, no. I wouldn't do that, Cyril. That prison is no place for you."

"Do you think I'm weak? That I couldn't survive there?"

"It's not just the planet that would grind you down. It's the things they would make you do. I hear the commandant is a monster, a perfect beast. When you see how the convicts live and know you're to blame... You don't have the spirit for it, Cyril. You're too kind."

"I can do whatever I choose. You aren't the only one who can get what he wants."

"As always, you follow in my footsteps."

Emberly struck out again, punching one of the bars. His knuckle hurt so much it might be broken, but he refused to show it. "Never again! Whatever you do, I will undo. In this uniform, I will be your opposite."

The earnest surprise in his brother's laugh was its most maddening aspect. "When we were younger," said Rayan, "my friends and I mocked you. How you followed me everywhere. I longed for you to grow up. But somehow, you're more pathetic as a man."

Emberly spit at him. In the darkness, he could not tell if he hit his mark. When Rayan's voice emerged again, it was colder. "Your wife must be proud."

Taking a long breath, Emberly calmed himself. "Charlotte will always be a reformer. But she respects tradition. She will stand by me, whatever I do."

"What choice does she have? But it's no wonder Mother loves her."

Neither spoke for a while. Emberly lapsed into the exhaustion that accompanied conversations with his brother.

"Cyril," said Rayan, "someone might kill me before the morning. If they don't, I'm going to a place that tears people apart and swallows them. I expect you to take the role that would have been mine. Lead this family and care for it."

"I'll care for it above everything. And I actually mean it."

Rayan did not take the bait. "No doubt you do. That comforts me."

Emberly wasn't finished. He still thirsted for blood. "It's more than you deserve. Soon, I will command troops of my own, and I'll protect decent people from men like you."

Rayan's eyes widened. He cackled. The laugh grew until he slid to the floor, a writhing shadow.

Emberly leaned his forehead against the bars and bared his teeth. "I should kill you myself, you..." He had no words equal to the moment.

Turning to go, he said, "The rest of your life will be brief and miserable. I will leave you to it." He stormed out, and laughter followed.

⚊⚊◆⚊⚊

Emberly shot upright in the dark. "Are you here?" he whispered.

"Of course." Rayan spoke right into his ear.

Emberly jumped yet again, as he always did. He couldn't stop himself.

Rage swelled like fire. "Get away!" He threw an arm, touched nothing, of course, and leaned away to distance himself from the voice. He leaned too far in the small cot and fell to the floor.

Rayan cackled.

Emberly scrambled to his feet. He faced the wall. "We're finished! Get out! You're a monster."

"Perhaps," said Rayan calmly.

"Imperial Hall. How do you always make me forget it? I try to hold on to it—so I can remind myself of what you are—but somehow, you make it slip away. Well, I've remembered. Get out of my sight!"

"You send me away, brother, but you always call me back. I visit at your invitation, do you realize that?"

"Not this time." Sweat ran down Emberly's face. "I don't care if you're alive or not. I'm taking the north road, nowhere near the prison. Get out."

His brother spoke in his ear again. "If I'm a monster, so are you."

"Don't say it."

They both knew what Rayan's next words would be. "You set me free," he whispered. A vague, cryptic phrase.

Hearing it, Emberly whirled, fists up. Searching for that grinning, knowing face. He saw no one. He would have screamed if there weren't others around to hear him.

For the rest of the night, he slept badly and dreamed much.

6

— · —

EMBERLY

THE DESCENT FROM THE fort the next morning was perilous. The hill's bare slopes were loose and eroded, and the switchback road threatened to give way under the wagons. With each turn, the company came closer to the tumbling ocean of jungle below. No one liked the looks of it. The load beasts' muzzles tightened, and their ears flicked.

The song of the wind in the trees, so violent at night, had softened to a distant chorus. The canopy was a wild array of colors that gave the overall effect of deep red. Here and there, a tree towered above the others, casting shadows across acres.

Emberly had ordered everyone to be silent, but he suspected this was futile. The forest knew they were here.

No babble of birds and insects or rustle in the underbrush reached the company. The day held a bewildering stillness that the captain remembered well. Only the trees themselves shifted, and one wouldn't notice at first glance.

Limbs and branches pushed against each other, wrestling for dominance and sunlight.

As the party reached the crossing of the old imperial roads, the wagons' rumble echoed from the walls of foliage. Emberly's boot sank into moss that swelled through gaps between the broad flagstones. The moss responded by belching a cloud of particles. He imagined spores entering his lungs, burrowing, growing.

Bishop Arumin dismounted and joined him. "We seem to be alone," he muttered.

Emberly stifled a chuckle. They had served here together, and returning had spawned a feeling of comradery that neither of them wanted. The captain offered a reluctant joke. "The jungle must be sleeping."

He recalled a bit of rhyming advice popular among soldiers here. Arumin remembered, too, and recited it with distant sarcasm. "Move in the light, hide in the night."

Emberly had not expected their interactions this morning to be pleasant, let alone to involve jokes. Either something was amiss, or the bishop had been replaced by a changeling. Surveying the canopy's heights, the captain resisted a sense of fatalism.

The company could not wait here long. The roads were apparently in deplorable condition. The main road stretched away in front of them, leading straight to the ruins of the prison. On it, bursts of tangled flora had driven apart the flagstones and crumbled their edges. Tree-filled swamp lurked on either side. The north road would be worse. The men would work hard with axes today.

Both roads ended in the same cluster of logging outposts where Emberly and his fellow guards had once supervised prisoners on overnight work details. There, prisoners and guards alike had spent sleepless nights huddled in windowless barracks, praying for morning. The north road was a little shorter, passing several similar logging sites. The main road led straight to the prison before swinging dramatically to arrive at the outposts.

According to the Lady, somewhere in the jungle beyond the outposts lay an undiscovered gateway.

Maybe three days' journey, given the road conditions—and the need to take shelter before dark. The sturdier the shelter, the better.

If Rayan and any other convicts still lived, they would likely be at the prison. But Emberly was determined to never find out. There were multiple reasons to take the north road, and though he told himself he valued them equally, the assertion rang hollow.

Emberly passed word for Private Merin to join him. When the young man arrived a few long minutes later, he was out of breath.

The captain said, "Private, ride in the front with me."

"Yes, sir," Merin said. He paused and squirmed before gasping, "I apologize again, sir, for my poor impression."

Emberly suppressed a groan. Merin was an unasked-for gift from the fort's commander—a replacement for Emberly's dead astronomer. The captain did not really want a new astronomer. The company was bound for uncharted planets, where the role would be a formality and star charts useless.

But he certainly wanted someone who knew more about Caidfell's wildlife than he did. Surely someone had studied it since Emberly left this planet—though life here evolved so quickly that such efforts were dubious.

The commander, a smarmy drunk, had offered Merin as a learned scholar, and the captain had gullibly accepted. A quick interrogation of the stammering private showed Emberly had been duped. He now had one more mouth to feed, and the commander had one fewer. Merin brought the company's total to forty-six people. Unless one counted the Lady.

There was still hope regarding the wildlife. Some-one—not Merin—had sketched some local life forms in a book, with descriptions alongside. It was better than nothing. Merin, who was at least literate, would keep it and read from it.

Emberly said, "Apology accepted. Stay close and be ready to consult that book."

"I would, sir. But..." Merin floundered.

Emberly let him struggle until he emerged with "It's the book. In all the hurry, I'm afraid I've left it behind." It sounded like a deathbed confession.

Silence was reply enough. Merin looked at the ground until the captain dismissed him.

As the private trudged away, Arumin said, "Men were never at their best here."

Emberly shook off the setback. "We'll set out at once, Your Holiness. Will one of your priests ride in front with me?"

"'I'll do it myself, Captain. The company will like seeing its leaders side by side. And who knows these jungles better than us?"

Emberly nodded. Whatever its cause, he would enjoy the bishop's agreeableness while it lasted. "No one, apparently. So be it. Fathers Nor and Brin will be safest in the wagons."

"A small correction, Captain. Nor is no priest. If I was as powerful as everyone thinks, he wouldn't even be a monk."

The captain surveyed the column. Nor sat atop the priests' wagon. "Did you speak to him about last night?"

"I've tried," said Arumin, "but I can't get through to him. Watch him, won't you?"

"I'm authorized to punish anyone here. Provoking a fistfight is certainly reason enough. But I'd rather not test whether my soldiers will lay hands on a holy man."

"Norhim tested your soldiers last night. They aren't afraid of him."

"No one even threw a punch. If something must be done, I'll need your public blessing. I won't undermine the authority of holy men. Fear of the Goddess will hold this company together when all else fails."

The bishop nodded. "I think we understand each other."

Disliking his conspiratorial tone, Emberly changed the subject. He gestured to the branch of the crossroads leading north. "We should start soon. The north road is an hour's march at least."

Arumin's pause was slight but portentous.

The bishop shook his head. "We mustn't take the north road, Captain Emberly. Our path lies straight ahead, on the main road." His tone remained conversational even as his words threatened to destroy their company.

The captain's chest tightened and ached. He fell silent too long to pretend their talk was still amiable. "The decision is made, Bishop."

"You must unmake your decision," replied Arumin, "unless the Lady has changed her mind or Shada misunderstood her. Shall we see what the caretaker says?"

"She already..." Emberly began, but he trailed off. Shada was approaching, led by Father Brin.

Arumin dipped his head with a knowing smile. "Caretaker."

The girl kept a wary eye on the trees. Tiny amid the forest, she displayed her lifetime of domestic servitude with every step. Keeping her alive would require attention Emberly could hardly spare, and if Arumin had made her his pawn, the dangers would multiply. The captain wished he could slap the bishop's smile away without endangering his soul.

Though the captain's fears centered around Shada, the sight of Father Brin was somehow worse. He had met Brin once before, on Caidfell, when the priest was only a boy. That child's face burned in his memory, pale and sick in a landscape of death. Its gaze was blank, accepting, and terribly peaceful.

Shada stepped forward, and Emberly gratefully looked away from Brin. The caretaker's arms cradled the alien vessel where the Lady dwelled. Emberly had not fully accepted that any box could contain a divine being. It defied understanding. It was easier to believe that everyone—maybe the whole world—was playing a vast ongoing joke on him.

When he spoke to Shada, he spoke also to the thing she carried. "Is something the matter, Caretaker?"

"I'm afraid so, Captain," she said. "We must take the main road instead of the northern one."

Emberly had expected this, but still a cold pit opened in his stomach. Nearby, the main road opened like a maw, with the prison waiting in its belly. "I won't ask why, because no reasoning will change my decision. We will take the north road. The Goddess may punish me if she sees fit."

"Bishop Arumin and I will forbid your men to obey," she said. "Though I don't know what will happen then."

"Do you know what the punishment is for mutiny?" Scaring her might shake Arumin's hold on her. The bishop had surely drilled her on what to say, but if Emberly could reach the shy woman underneath, he might change her mind or even free her from the bishop's clutches.

"Captain Emberly," she said.

The simple words took him aback. His name and his rank. Unwilling to actually threaten to shoot her, he countered with a hard stare that cut through her to the trees behind.

Her eyes widened slightly. Still, her voice was steady enough. "We have a choice to make. We must decide where our faith lies."

Emberly waited.

"We cannot believe in ourselves," she continued. "We're so often wrong. There's so much we can't see."

"I understand that," said Emberly. "But Huire chose each of us. She must value our judgment."

"I know," Shada said curiously. "I don't understand it. But I'm realizing it doesn't matter. The decision is not ours. She has taken that burden from us."

"Does she want us to walk into an ambush?"

"If necessary, yes."

"Impossible. There has been some mistake. I must protect my soldiers and you. That is my duty."

"If we stray from Huire's path, she'll return our sins to us."

"I will take them all." Emberly's blood ran cold. The weight of his own wrongs was terrifying. But there was no other way. "The responsibility is mine alone."

Before she or the bishop could reply, he shouted orders to the column. They would set out at once, down the path to the north road. The soldiers moved, and Shada did not forbid it.

Emberly had reached the head of the column when a sergeant called to him. The man pointed to a figure on the main road, approaching the open jaws of the forest.

He cried out. Shada was walking into the jungle alone—alone except for the Lady's box in her arms. The bishop stood where Emberly had left him, watching her go.

"Caretaker!" The captain called again to her shrinking form. She would disappear into the trees at any moment.

Mounting, Emberly caught up easily and stopped in her path. "Where are you going?"

She stopped. "I don't know. Only she knows. But I'm still afraid."

"I could strap you to a wagon."

"That alone would drive your men to mutiny. If it didn't, I would slip away the first chance I got. They won't let you lock me away."

He gritted his teeth, eyes watery. "If you go alone, you will die. The crusade will fail."

"Then it will fail regardless." She looked down at the road. "Or else the Lady is a liar, and we are all fools."

"There is no need for this," he said. "I can't accept it."

They were quiet for a moment. Finally, she replied, "I killed someone. At least, I think I did. He was my employer, but he wanted to be more. He would never have left me alone. If I had to, I would do it again. I suppose that makes me a murderer."

She met Emberly's eyes and said, "I don't know why you joined this company. Maybe you feel guilty about something. Whatever it is, there is only one escape: we have to follow the Lady without question. If we don't, this is all for nothing."

If she was a murderer, she was not the only one. Emberly also needed forgiveness—for things he had done, things he planned to do, and things he knew that he wished he did not. What he would give to keep his secrets was something he was still learning.

He let himself give in. "I trust you."

Like that, almost before he knew it, the issue was settled. He and his company would follow Shada down the divinely ordained road toward whatever waited there. Dismounting, he walked at her side back to the crossing, where the bishop still waited.

7

— · —

BRIN

STAUBEL, THE COMPANY'S DOCTOR, had brought an ailing soldier for Brin and Nor to watch over. He said they could help the man more than any medicine. His name was Carrowy, and he had collapsed after feeling sick all morning. With the crimson jungle closing in around them, the holy men had laid him in their wagon and removed and folded its peaked wooden top to give him fresh air.

Through countless layers of vegetation under the canopy high above, a precious feathering of light reached the sick man's face and glistened in the fluids running from his eyes and nose. He had not spoken much.

Brin sat in the wagon's front corner, as far as he could get from everyone. His head rang where a mysterious attacker, now dead, had struck him not two days ago. The nauseating pain rose and fell, and he was sure his skin was turning yellow. If Carrowy vomited, Brin would quickly follow.

At the wagon's rear sat Nor, gazing with concern at Private Hulgar, who sat across from him. Since his outburst last night, the giant man had fallen silent. His face twitched, and his mouth moved as he kept some inner counsel. Even sitting, he was tall enough to see over the side of the wagon.

"What do you see?" Nor asked him. The monk spoke softly, as they all had since entering the forest. He had failed a few times to draw Hulgar into conversation. As before, the soldier shook his head and turned inward.

The wagon's other occupants were its driver, a quiet man older than anyone in the company but the bishop, and Witerin, a thickly bearded private with wide eyes who filled the quiet with frightened murmuring. The latter was clearly unwell, having complained of extraordinary dreams much like Hulgar's. Unlike Hulgar, Witerin was anything but silent.

Nor said to Hulgar, "If you have anything to say, don't be afraid. Talking can help you think."

Brin bristled with rage at the monk. He knew nothing of anyone else's heart. He could not give them permission to speak. Hulgar was big enough to snap Nor's neck with one hand. Brin reveled in the poisonous taste of that thought.

Only someone who knew fear like Brin did should speak of it. Someone who had faced death on a rooftop, had watched a friend die, had begged for his life, as Brin had.

Arumin made no secret of hating Nor. Brin had reserved judgment, knowing the old man often let personal gripes get under his skin. But now, he would reserve it no longer.

The fine chain around his neck itched as the day grew hotter. The vial on the chain beat on his chest with each bump of the wagon. It would hang there until the end of their journey, where he would use it to kill the gods in their own realm.

Sylvana had ordered him to do it. So had her friends—hooded men with snakes' eyes who had rescued Brin from death.

But they had not really rescued him. They had only delayed his execution. If he failed to kill the gods as they commanded, he would die. An agent they had placed in this company would kill him.

And that was that. The crusade would inevitably fail. Its objective was laughable, a task for a philosopher. Brin would be murdered by someone whose face he had already seen.

Hulgar did not share Brin's outrage. He looked around, his eyes showing little understanding of their surroundings. In that respect, he was no worse off than anyone else.

The road twisted, dodging trees too huge to be easily removed. Smaller trees and vines pushed up through gaps in the road to block the company's path. Several men worked to clear the road and place thick planks to bridge dangerous gaps.

The largest trees were of dizzying width, their heights unguessable. Brin had been a child when he last saw them, but they seemed no smaller now.

"What do you see?" Nor asked Private Hulgar again.

Hulgar stood, loomed threateningly over the monk, and vaulted out of the wagon. He walked toward the rear of the column as Nor's milk-white eyes watched him go.

On the floor, Carrowy laughed. It sounded like a coughing fit. "The man cries in his sleep. But still, nobody messes with him."

Witerin's muttering quickened and grew louder. There was no escape, Brin thought. No matter how far they traveled from the nearest temple, priests were still damned nursemaids.

Nor smiled at Carrowy. The expression was unnatural on him. "He'll handle his own trials as he chooses."

"D'you see the burn marks on his arm?" asked Carrowy. "The small ones, bunched up like flowers?"

Nor nodded.

The private shut his eyes, which still ran with tears. "He does it to himself. He's collecting them."

"I've seen other soldiers do things like that," Nor replied. "When they're haunted by past battles."

"We all have our ways," said Carrowy. He shifted his body, seeming uncomfortable in each new position. "I have mine, Brother Nor. But I've left them behind now."

Nor listened.

"Someone said I'm brave for joining this crew," Carrowy continued. "But I don't think so. I joined to escape from my demons. I could never've left them behind otherwise." He squeezed his eyes shut against some private agony. "But all will be forgiven, eh?"

The monk's face was even stonier than usual. "That's right. You've done what Huire asked. Just keep the faith."

"Yes, the faith," said Carrowy.

The column slowed as it approached a thick mass of trees and smaller vegetation blocking the road. As Nor looked ahead, Brin saw his eyes up close. They were drab and featureless, with no pupils or irises.

Brin said to Nor, "I think his Holiness is wrong. You're not so bad." His anger had cooled, and he almost regretted his venomous thoughts.

Nor gazed at him. You never knew his eyes were moving unless his head moved as well. "Lets you have opinions, does he?"

"He's learned he can't stop me." Brin smiled, a practiced motion. "He didn't want you in this company, you know. Neither did the captain."

Nor put his palm on Carrowy's forehead. "And yet here I am. Funny how things turn out."

"Your abbot pushed you on them. The bishop respects the abbot, though they are old enemies."

"He must respect him a lot if he took me on board. There was a price, wasn't there?"

"Only the two of them know that. But I daresay you're right. You cost Cadmon dearly." Brin pulled his sleeve away from Witerin, who had leaned over to toy with it. "But it convinced the bishop you're worth something. No one can doubt you're brave enough."

"Is this what he sent you to tell me?" Nor's eyes were soft and, in Brin's mind, free of judgment. "What an inefficient way to communicate. What kind of plot does he want me for? Is he planning a mutiny?"

Brin dropped his smile. "I'm his man, but that's not all I am. Not everything is a plot."

"Not a good one."

"Goddess, you're difficult," Brin spat. "By all means, avoid making a single friend."

But the monk had stopped listening. He and everyone else were watching the road ahead.

The knot of thick, towering trees in their path was much wider than it had appeared, stretching away from the road in both directions. It was a living wall.

Through gaps, they saw the other side, where another kind of tree dominated the forest. These were wiry and numerous, with leaves like sleek red blades, and they were unmistakably attacking their larger neighbors. In a scene like a still painting of a cavalry charge, they crashed against their outnumbered enemies, coiling around them as if to choke them and pull them down.

The battle would destroy the road someday soon. Already, a fallen tree lifted and tilted the stones dangerously.

The column halted. Emberly and Arumin conferred on their mounts, their simple clothing making them look entirely too ordinary and vulnerable.

Murmurs passed through the ranks. Soldiers glanced around, searching the shadows. For men who had survived Gallobraith, the jungles of this otherwise unexplored planet must stir unwelcome memories. When Emberly ordered a detail to carve a path through the trees, Brin wondered if the men chosen were grateful for the distraction.

"I guess no one expected this," said Nor.

Brin was scared and wanted to share the feeling. "Think about what that means. It's only been a decade since the convicts' revolt, but the entire landscape has already changed. I never saw those smaller trees back then."

If Brin's imprisonment here was news to Nor, he did not show it. "How can that be?"

Brin shook his head. "This jungle fights with itself. No one knows why, or at least they never told me."

Nor watched the men battling the underbrush. Ember-ly was among them. "The captain must enjoy being back here. More than the bishop, at least."

"I doubt it." The monk's statement was shockingly dimwitted. No one wanted to visit a graveyard where they had been prematurely buried. "If anyone had fond memories of this place, it would be him. The Hero of Caidfell. Yet he rarely speaks about it."

"And he usually doesn't mind talking about himself."

For the first time during the conversation, Brin smiled accidentally. "You have plenty of reasons to dislike Ronian soldiers. Yet here you are, comforting them when they're sick. Saving their souls."

"What else should I do?"

"Nothing! That's just it. They're one arm of the empire, and we holy men are the other. The planets Ronia has conquered would be our rulers if we weren't theirs. The world is what it is."

Soldiers shouted. They had broken through the trees. A few slid through the gap to attack the trees from the other side. When the way was clear, they would have to guide the wagons across the tilted road.

Now and then, a soldier returned to the wagons, clutching a small wound on his arm or leg. Doctor Staubel examined them.

While briefing the company that morning, Emberly had emphasized that little was known about the stings and venoms of this wilderness. If he had his way, this company would add nothing to that body of knowledge. They must avoid injuries. That hope was already proving futile.

In the briefing, Emberly had talked about Caidfell's dangers to the exclusion of almost all else. He had barely mentioned the bombing of Ronia or Huire's blessing of their journey:

"You all know that many have died here. Those who survived, like his Holiness and I, don't say much about it. In truth, there's little to tell. The local plants and animals change so fast it's hardly worth naming them. Science met the same fate here as many other visitors. It was broken.

"His Holiness and I will offer advice where we can. So will Father Brin."

Arumin must have wished the captain had not mentioned his shameful service. Brin had desired the attention even less. Many pairs of eyes had turned to him. One of them belonged to the man who would kill him.

Emberly had continued, "For now, I'll say this. Don't touch anything unless you must. Stay together, and stay on the road. Finally, trust your eyes and ears over your intuition. This place will toy with your mind. Many have died here because they lost their wits. Good luck."

He had dismissed them after Arumin led them in prayer. Brin had fled to the wagon, away from the staring men all around him.

Nor and Brin did not speak again until the company passed the barrier. While soldiers manhandled their wagon over the tilted section of road, the holy men supported Carrowy.

Afterward, they sat waiting for the rest of the company. Gazing at the twisting sea of dagger-tipped trees, Nor said, "Abbot Cadmon is not my friend. He's made that clear. Whatever intrigue Arumin is planning, leave me out of it."

Brin stared. "Did you and Cadmon fight about something?"

"He cares about his own ends. They matter more to him than any person. I've known too many people like that."

"The bishop doesn't want to conspire with you," Brin said. "You're not subtle, and he knows it. He only asks you to support him toward mutual goals."

"So you *are* speaking for him."

Brin's head was a burning ulcer. Witerin's muttering wore on his nerves. "Arumin gets what he wants. Make sure you're on his side when the time comes." Brin did not know what "time" he meant, but it would come. "I hope you will be there."

Nor did not answer. Like a flower closing its petals, he had sealed himself off.

The landscape sank quickly into the swamp. The trees thinned, leaving broad stretches of empty mire, and soon, the road dropped into the murky water and out of sight. Clusters of plants lurked there, sending up stalks and vines.

Brin jumped when Nor spoke. "Do you love him?"

Off balance, Brin stumbled into the trap. "Who?"

"Since when have you tried to hide it? You know who."

Brin smiled. Despite all his practice, smiling was difficult. His special relationship with Arumin was common knowledge, but fear kept people from talking openly about it. Now, someone was confronting him directly and leaving him no clear escape.

He pretended to misunderstand. "Of course. I've been with His Holiness since I was young—since he rescued me from this cursed planet. How could I not love the person who's given me everything?"

The deepening water had reached the men's ankles. The corners of Nor's mouth twitched. "I don't mean the love of a son. I mean the love of a mistress."

Brin wanted to believe Nor had misspoken. That hope kept him from bursting into a storm of rage and shame. He answered slowly. "That's a careless question, Brother Nor. And a baseless accusation."

"Why must it be an accusation?" Nor said. "It's admirable. You would never engage in physical love, of course. That's forbidden to holy men. The bishop shines with love for you, yet he restrains himself. I only ask, are you burdened with such feelings for him?"

Brin jumped up. "Insolent misbreed!" he shouted, a startling sound in the quiet jungle. "I offer friendship, and you..."

He stopped as a wave of dizziness swept over him. They were all staring again. He felt himself fall then realized he was still standing. He sagged onto the bench but slipped off of it.

Thin arms wrapped around him, slowing his fall. It was Witerin, who shrieked in Brin's ear as his beard engulfed Brin's face.

Instantly, Brin forgot the man had saved him from a bruise. He thought only of the last man to save him. The man who had struck him on the head, giving him the bump that kept hurting and hurting.

Every bit of him needed to escape Witerin's arms. He tore away and threw an elbow but missed the man's face. Scrambling onto the bench, he would have jumped from the wagon had the jungle not waited outside.

The wagon passed under a cluster of vines that had grown up from the water to dangle from a tree.

One of these grazed Brin's arm. He shivered at its light touch and stepped down from the bench, but now the vine had wrapped around his arm.

It stuck and pulled him toward the back of the wagon. About to fall out, he yanked on the trapped arm and yelped at the feeling of a thousand tiny fishhooks cutting his skin.

Others tried to help. The wagon's driver called for a halt.

Nor pulled on the vine while Witerin tried to wedge his shaking fingers between the vine and Brin's arm. Both men gave up quickly, gasping in pain. Brin glimpsed a few drops of blood on their palms.

Panicked, not thinking, he grabbed the vine with his free hand. He tore that hand away with a cry as countless tiny barbs pricked it. The vine quietly embraced his arm.

The driver had reined in his team, but the wagon stopped too late. As the vine stretched, the tree bent, bringing an entire tree's worth of dangling vines down on their heads.

The passengers brushed at them in annoyance then in confusion. Gentle tendrils stuck to wrists and shoulders.

The vines moved on their own. It was so fluid and natural, Brin felt no shock. One of the wagon's pair of load beasts bellowed as a vine snaked around its hind limbs.

Nor shouted to clear the wagon, but it was too late. Two vines now held Brin, and others quickly caught Nor and Witerin. The driver fought to control his frightened team. Only Carrowy, now asleep, was untouched.

The rest of the company had realized something was terribly wrong, but their commotion was meaningless to Brin. He was tangled and hurting. Ahead, the vines crawled up the body of the thrashing load beast like an awakened nest of spiders. Wounds of striking red opened in the beast's hide.

A vine took the animal's neck in a calm embrace. Mindless with terror, the beast tore its head away. This jerked the wagon toward the edge of the road, and Brin and the others tumbled amidst the cutting vines.

The beast paid dearly. It quieted as its blood splashed in the ankle-deep water on the road.

A soldier reached the wagon and jumped on board. Armed with a saber, he hacked away to free the passengers.

The vines contracted defiantly, pulling wagon, animals, and men into the swamp with irresistible might. The wagon stayed upright thanks to the other load beast, a thick and stubborn elder that set its hooves and pulled. Its companion followed gently, its will fading as it bled. The driver had lost all control.

The man with the saber had fallen onto the road, dropping his blade. He had managed to cut a few of the thick, tough vines. Stretching, Brin reached the blade.

Of the two vines holding him, only the first touched his skin. The second draped over his shoulder. After a few fruitless swings of the saber, Brin slipped out of his robe, escaping the second. Then, shielding his hand with the robe, he held the first to the floor and hacked away. To his delight, he freed himself in seconds.

The pulling beasts had stretched some vines out to their full lengths. The plants held on, and the animals dragged the wagon sideways, away from the road.

The tree holding the vines gave way, coming up by the roots. It landed in the water and sent a wave onto the soldiers on the road. The wagon lurched forward and finally stopped, caught by something on the bottom. Brin fell again. The few vines not yet severed were stretched to the limit, too weak to pull in their prey but too strong to release it. The unharmed beast strained and cried out.

The passengers were strewn about the wagon's floor. They rose, gasping and bleeding. They'd had little time to be scared until now.

The company swarmed on the road, which lay across a watery expanse. Trees rose around the wagon, and shapes lurked below. Carrowy, moaning, finally sat up.

Under the water, things began to move.

8

—·—

BRIN

THE SABER SHOOK IN Brin's hands. The water rippled as something moved beneath.

The passengers grew quiet. Nor and Witerin stopped fighting the vines that held them. Only the old load beast that had dragged them here still struggled.

An ugly thump came from under their feet as a heavy object scraped the wagon's underside. The wood sounded paper thin.

Brin, giddy, wanted to swing the sword at something. Even useless action was better than waiting.

Nor caught his eye and pointed toward the road. Brin saw it. Shapes softly churned the water where the wagon had left the road. It was more of the vines that had dragged them here. The tendrils were spreading out, moving generally toward the wagon.

"They know where we are," whispered Brin. His mouth was dry.

But it got worse. Other clumps of vines were waking into action, spreading in all directions from points along the road.

Private Carrowy, rising painfully, grasped their predicament. "Holy Mother."

"We can't stay here," said Nor. A vine still held his wrist.

From atop the wagon, Brin could see the front of the company, where several soldiers had plunged into the water. By starting there, they might wade out to the wagon while avoiding the vines. But between them and the wagon stood an expanse of straight, thin trees into which they would soon vanish from sight.

Witerin nudged Brin, and he turned.

Silently, a tree had sprouted from the water near the wagon. It was as thick as a man's waist, covered with rusty bark but with no leaves or branches, and it ended in a point. As it rose from the water, it bent toward the wagon, curving like a snake despite its girth.

No one spoke. The noises from the road faded. Even the load beast stopped struggling, sensing the strangeness of the newcomer. The tree hung over them, bowed like a hook. Its tip pointed at them, sharp as a raptor's claw.

Brin jumped as a hand landed on his shoulder. He huffed in relief and anger when he saw it was Witerin, who had hoped to comfort him but done the opposite. The man's eyes were wide. His mouth, almost lost in his beard, twitched with silent muttering.

The injured load beast bellowed. Brin thought it was the loudest thing he had ever heard. The driver had cut the animal loose, and it had fallen, its blood spreading with the water's lazy drift.

The tree whipped forward and down. Its claw stabbed through the beast's head.

The tension on the wagon burst. The men scrambled to free themselves from the vines. The surviving load beast writhed in blind panic, nearly toppling the wagon.

The old driver fired his pistol. The shot only chipped the tree's bark.

The tree rose with leisurely swiftness and turned to the driver. The dead load beast hung from the tree's narrow end, dangling by its pierced head. The tree lifted the carcass and wore it as easily as Brin wore the vial around his neck.

In one motion, the claw rose as high as a two-story house and whipped down at the driver.

The old man expected the strike. He dodged the claw, but the hurtling body of the load beast smashed his bottom half. Wood splintered as the claw stabbed into the floorboards.

The floor jumped under the impact. Brin fell, and it knocked the wind out of him. He landed on someone, and someone else landed on him. The saber lay under them all. He could not tell if it had cut him.

With a shriek of strained wood, the claw wrenched itself from the floor. The load beast stayed where it fell, having crushed the driver's seat and much of the driver.

The tree rose and turned its claw toward the pile of humans. Brin thought clearly, *Please, not me.*

A commanding shout pierced the air. It was Emberly, ordering his men to fire. On the road, the company's rifles thundered. The volley sent chips of the tree showering into the water. The shots did not hurt it much, but they drew its attention from the wagon. The claw turned toward the road but did not move. It was rooted in place.

But it somehow knew what was happening around it. It had no eyes, but maybe it could hear.

While it was distracted, Brin and the others untangled themselves. Brin snatched up the saber as Nor hissed at him to cut the vines. Only one tendril each held Nor and Witerin, but the fibrous stalks resisted their knives devilishly. Brin must have gotten lucky, freeing himself so fast.

He went to Witerin, whose vine was closer to breaking. He swung the sword as hard as he could. The strike did little, and Brin couldn't have hit the same spot twice on his best day.

The wagon shook. The surviving beast had pulled it almost free. Nor twisted his trapped wrist, trying to unwind the tendril, which tightened as the beast pulled them farther from the road. The vine came away slowly, raising droplets of blood on his skin. Tears and swamp water wet the monk's face.

Rifle fire kept coming. Emberly had his soldiers firing volleys in groups, keeping up a steady pounding. For the moment, the trees focused on the road instead of the wagon. The captain paced behind the men, his shouts resounding despite the shooting.

Brin hacked madly at Witerin's vine. The soldier, oddly calm, crouched and laid the stalk over the wagon's back wall. With a few more swings at this steady target, Brin finally freed him.

The monk's progress had been slow. His fingers slipped in his blood as he worked. The trapped arm was the same one that had worn a sling when Brin met him. The vine had grown tighter as the beast gained distance with its efforts. Frantic with hope, it was dragging them farther from the road.

The rest of the vines were getting closer. Within a few minutes, they would find the wagon.

Nor's fingers slipped in his blood. "Here," he said to Brin, offering his knife. His face was pale. "Give me the sword. Cut the animal loose."

The tree was still distracted by the fire from the road. But the company's ammunition was finite. They could not keep shooting forever.

Brin would have to free the beast without drawing the tree's attention. He looked at the open space between him and the front of the wagon and sank to the floor.

His body tried to refuse his commands. Only the thought of others watching from the road moved him. He slipped out of his cloak, as the others had already done. Gripping the knife's handle hard enough to crack it, he bent low and crept forward.

Two steps later, a second tree emerged from the water almost in arm's reach.

It rose with horrible speed. Thick bundles like muscles covered its base. Its claw-tip bent to point at Brin accusingly.

Brin had nowhere to hide. Impossibly, he kept moving. Sliding over the dead beast, he saw the driver crushed under it. The man was still, but his eyes were open, following Brin as if from a painting.

The live beast was tiring. Its noise had not yet attracted the trees, both of which now pointed toward the road.

Their hearing must be duller than a person's, or the men on the wagon would be dead already. Maybe facing multiple sources of noise confused them.

The animal was held in place by a thick yoke and U-shaped bow enclosing its neck. This might be easy after all. Brin put the knife into his trouser pocket and climbed off the wagon, sinking into the warm water. On the bottom, he felt muck and tangled branches.

He approached the beast and reached for the pin holding the bow in place. The animal roared and thrashed. The wagon jumped forward, knocking Brin over. He reached again, but the beast lurched away.

Brin's mind reeled. He was stuck. The claw-trees had not attacked yet, but they surely would.

Then he realized why Nor had given him the knife. Pulling it from his trousers, he wondered which vein on the beast's massive neck he should cut.

The animal's eyes were wide with fear and hatred. If he tried to kill it and failed, it might attack him.

He lunged weakly. The creature reared as the blade touched its skin.

Brin also recoiled from the feeling. Suddenly, the thought of pushing the metal through flesh made him sick. He was trapped as surely as the animal. He could not kill it, even if it dragged them away from rescue. He wanted to cry.

As he bent, gagging, he put his hand on the yoke. Then he looked at it and told himself he was a stupid bastard.

He could forget the bow and detach the yoke. Within seconds, he did so. The beast fled like its tail was on fire. Yoke and all, it bounded through the swamp, away from the road.

He turned to the wagon. The shooting from the road had finally lessened. Emberly must be conserving ammunition. The claw-trees pointed here and there, indecisive.

Brin sneaked onto the wagon, pulling himself slowly from the water. The trees didn't notice. He was perversely proud to find Nor had still not freed himself. The monk had cut his vine three-quarters through, but his movements were slowing as he tired.

An animal's howl reached Brin's ears. A gaping pit had opened before the fleeing load beast, which slipped toward the precipice. Water thundered into the gulf from all around, and Brin thought he glimpsed twitching and glistening in the pit, hints of a vast anatomy.

The water's force overpowered the beast. It tumbled in with a scream, as human a noise as Brin could imagine. The rim of the pit contracted, and the opening swelled shut.

With a spout of rejected water, the beast's last whimper was lost.

Brin opened and shut his mouth. He stepped toward the wagon's rear. A plank snapped under him, loud as a gunshot.

The claws turned his way in a blink. He threw himself forward, but his foot broke through the floor, and he fell in a sprawl. The claws reared to strike, and he curled like an infant, wondering what he would feel.

A pistol fired. He thought he was dead. The driver dropped the weapon, which had taken a chip of bark from one of the trees. Still lying on the floor, the man rested his head back as the two claws came for him.

They struck simultaneously and met in his chest. Their force capsized the wagon. Amid screams, Brin tumbled until the water swallowed him.

His legs struck rocks and limbs on the bottom. Shouting in pain, he surfaced to find the wagon on its side and partly submerged. Nor still battled the vine, which hung over the vehicle's upward-facing side.

Brin and the two surviving soldiers huddled near the monk. Here, under the wagon's side, they could not see the claw-trees. No one had a knife to free Nor. They searched their belts and pockets, the bottom of the wagon, and the ground nearby but found nothing.

They looked at each other, and the rest looked at Brother Nor. He said softly, "You need to leave."

"No," Carrowy whispered. Witerin shook his head. Brin did not answer. He had started to like the monk, but they could do little to help him. If they all died trying, no one would benefit.

Nor might have read his thoughts. In the same hushed tone, the monk said, "Father Brin serves the bishop. He is above me in life and death. Save him."

Speaking in urgent whispers, they reached a compromise. Witerin took Brin and waded toward the patch of thin trees where the rescue party would appear. Carrowy stayed with Nor, and together, they worked to free the monk. Glancing back, Brin wished he had understood Nor better.

Soldiers on the road cheered as Brin and Witerin started out. Emberly's voice called urgent commands. Brin was grateful, as any distracting noise might save him and Witerin from attack. Then the men's cheering turned to shouts of alarm.

Resting his aching legs in the muck, Brin glanced up warily to see the men pointing behind him. Witerin's hand touched his shoulder, and he turned. Forgetting to be quiet, he cried out.

Nine claw-trees now stood above the wagon. Some could reach Brin easily. It was horrible how they loomed together, judges of a false trial.

As Brin and Witerin absorbed the sight, the first claw stabbed down between them. It sent up a geyser, and Brin's limbs grew lighter. He plunged toward the capsized wagon, the closest shelter. Claws splashed behind him with flashes of shadow and rushes of air. He'd lost sight of Witerin. Water erupted as they struck again and again, endlessly.

He dove into the cover of the wagon. Nor and Carrowy shrank back inside. Witerin arrived last, colliding with Brin.

Brin forgot to be angry. Their survival was unbelievable. The men blinked at each other in the waist-deep water.

A claw punched through the wood above them. It winked into existence before they could move, piercing the wagon's side and front in a single blow, lodging itself in place. Everyone ducked belatedly, then dove underwater as more claws struck in response to the noise.

As the claws dug to reach them, something moved the wagon. The stuck claw was trying to withdraw but could not. The tree's monstrous strength was pitted against the weight of the wagon and everyone in it.

Brin and the others tumbled to one end of the wagon as the tree hoisted it into the air. The swamp fell away below. Striking claws glanced off their moving target.

The water in the wagon rushed out, nearly taking the men with it. Brin clung to a bolted-down bench with one arm and Witerin with the other.

Nor fell out. His vine saved him from a fall. Still not severed, it clung to him and he to it until Carrowy grabbed his hands. It hung from the wagon's axle. Its other end had been uprooted and hoisted with all its offshoots like a ruined fishing net. Below, the other vines were still spreading through the swamp.

Having lost their prey, the claw-trees struck the water for a moment and straightened to their full heights. If anyone fell from the wagon, the splash would surely attract them. They could wait forever.

The wagon stopped rising. The tree that lifted them could go no farther. It was still bent in a hook by the vehicle's weight.

Things were quiet in the wagon. Shots from the road echoed across the swamp. Brin's hands and wrist burned anew, trickling blood under the vine's remains. Carrowy and Nor struggled to quietly pull the monk onboard. Witerin was growing frantic. Teary-eyed, he rocked back and forth, mouthing a private diatribe.

He wept. Nor's peril aggravated him. Getting louder, he was bound to draw the trees' attention. Brin wished he could move farther away. He wondered if he could bring himself to shove the man from the wagon.

He touched Witerin's arm. "Be at peace," he said. "The Goddess awaits us." He wished he could hear those words from someone else.

Witerin stared at him. "Father."

Brin liked the title even less than usual. "Yes?"

"Father," the man said again. "Come home now. Now." His voice rose with urgency.

Confused by his words, Brin did not reply soon enough.

"Now!" Witerin screamed. He snatched Brin's wrist, yanked it across his own body, and shoved Brin from the wagon.

The water hit Brin flat on his back and drove the air out of him. He surfaced to thunderous motion as the claws struck the wagon from all sides, again and again.

Someone fell nearby. Carrowy surfaced, face down, bleeding from his middle.

Debris rained. The wagon was falling apart. Nor hung again, still held by the vine.

One tree pulled back with Witerin speared on it. The soldier cried out, which brought the claws to him. They struck and pulled. As their competing forces distorted his body, opening a hole in his center, Brin glimpsed his face. It was awed, transported.

Brin shut his eyes as the trees pulled apart. What he heard made him sick.

Weight fell on him, and he dove under the water. When he came up, it clung to him. He touched it haltingly, as if it was red-hot, and peeled it away. It was most of Witerin's shirt.

He flung it away and ran. This was beyond courage or cowardice.

The water held him back, and he slowed to a trudge. He stumbled over debris on the bottom. He had forgotten his headache, but now he remembered.

The spreading vines had come close enough to spit on. They blocked him from the road, leaving him nowhere to go but toward the trees. They were likely moving faster than him now.

He saw a small gap in the trees ahead. A soldier stood there. Was this the rescue party? Brin raised his arm and shouted, but the man ignored him. He was struggling with something.

The man died in a blur of splashing water and blood. Brin could not help watching, grotesque as it was. There was no warning.

When it was over, Brin sank to his knees. He bent until the water covered his face.

He wondered how he would die. Most of all, he hated Witerin for abandoning him.

9

—·—

ARUMIN

As soon as the pointed tree rose from the water, Arumin knew he would plunge into the swamp to save Brin.

He saw it from near the front of the column, where he and Emberly had ridden together. When the first frightened shouts reached them, Emberly rode back in a rush, ordering the bishop to stay where he was.

Arumin tolerated the order briefly, even when he saw Brin among those in the stranded wagon. He could not help, and he would only get in the way if he tried. He watched as a small rescue party ordered by the captain set out into the swamp.

Starting near Arumin, at the front of the column, the soldiers would cross a thicket of narrow trees to reach the wagon, avoiding the clutching vines in the water. They were younger, stronger men than the bishop, and he told himself he would be a fool to follow them.

Until the tree rose from the water. He did not know what it was, but he knew this planet. It had marked him and everyone who lived here. When he saw that tree, he knew he must reach Brin at all costs.

He threw his cloak aside and plunged into the swamp, following the rescue party. Warm water rushed into his boots. He had not stopped to shed his robe, and it was quickly soaked. The jungle tainted whatever it touched.

He was unsurprised when, over the thicket of narrow trees before him, he saw the tree strike down at the wagon. The company had pleaded to Caidfell for safe passage, and the planet had refused.

He plunged ahead, eager to catch up to the rescue party. The water deepened, reddish detritus piling its surface and hiding its secrets. The thought of growing exhausted, of being forced to watch and wait, was un-bearable.

The five soldiers sent to rescue the wagon had ad-vanced slowly. The bottom was slippery and uneven, and terrors might lurk there. Each man gripped a pistol with both hands.

Arumin caught up as they reached the thicket. The trees were the same basic strain that had overrun this part of the forest, but their branches were unique. Each tree had only a few, and they ended in a single round knot tipped with a long thin leaf. The trees looked undeveloped, even diseased.

The soldiers' eyes widened when they saw Arumin. They could hardly be pleased. The old fool they were bound to protect had rushed into mortal peril. After a moment's confusion, they circled the bishop and advanced in a protective formation.

In front was a boyish, handsome private named Cay. He had come to Arumin earlier and knelt to receive his blessing. When he stood to leave, his eyes had met Brin's so briefly the bishop almost had not noticed.

The instant was carved into Arumin's mind. He had seen it again and again, feeling by turns sure he had imagined it and sure he had not. When Emberly formed the rescue party, Cay had volunteered instantly. What should he make of that?

As the water reached their waists, they stumbled over unseen branches and trunks of dead trees. One of the submerged objects caught Arumin's foot.

He fell slowly, cushioned by the water but no less helpless for that. He shut his eyes as the swamp enveloped him, its floating debris tickling his cheeks. Something stung his exposed hands and face repeatedly, like an angry insect. As he fought to stand, he reached for the branch that had trapped his foot.

He blindly traced the object's shape and opened his eyes. It was a femur, the remains of a human leg. Before he could stop himself, his hand met the grimy sphere where something had torn the bone from its missing hip socket. On the other end, the knee joint was wedged under a pile of bones.

Below the surface, the water was clear. Pinpoints of light pierced the algae and cast everything in a bloodred glow. The eyes of the dead watched him from skeletons strewn around. Most had been dismembered and lay in fragments. Their skulls sloped on top, like no breed of human he had ever seen.

The soldiers reached him. Hands pulled him up, but he resisted. He had lain in this quiet so long. His initial horror was gone. The dead things watching him were miracles, and he thanked the Goddess, whom humans had created to work miracles.

The stinging got worse, erupting on his face and neck. Looking around for his attacker, he could not believe what he saw: movement within the water itself. Empty spaces, writhing transparent tubes. One stung the corner of his eye, and he thrust himself above the surface.

The soldiers held him and spoke soothingly, as if he were an invalid. Gunshots rang out from the road.

Cay begged to know if he was injured. Tearing himself free, Arumin snapped at him to make for the wagon. Cay appeared surprised and hurt, and that made Arumin want to hurt him more.

Over their heads, a whistle sounded. It was cheerful, like a songbird. A bright strip of blood appeared on Cay's shoulder under a clean tear in his shirt. As the wound grinned at them, another whistle sounded.

There was a weighty splash as one soldier's arm fell off. The man saw it waving in the mire and grunted in confusion.

Everyone lurched back from the sight, sending waves in all directions. Each man would regret the action in his own way.

More whistles. From the trees overhead, vines were whipping down. Bunched in tight clumps at the end of each branch, they uncoiled at fantastic speeds to cut through anything in their path. One snapped across the chest and face of a third soldier, leaving a deep red groove.

Two soldiers were still unhurt. They moved in to protect Arumin with their bodies. One shoved Arumin into the water and hunched over him as the bishop spat and cursed.

Cay panicked. He fled toward the wagon, arms raised in pitiful defense. Whistles like birdsong followed him, and water erupted with the lashes of vines, but so far, he remained intact. Maybe the trees could see him some-how, or maybe they felt the waves he made.

The soldier whose face and chest were cut stood in a waking dream. His flesh sagged. He stumbled away into the trees, ignoring the others' calls to come back.

The man who had lost his arm retrieved it. He examined it end to end as if considering it for purchase.

One of the men standing over the bishop shouted over the din, "Your Holiness, we must go back."

Up to his neck in water, with invisible things stinging him all over, Arumin surveyed the scene. The rescue party had come well into the thicket before the trees attacked. The vines on the trees around them hung loose, having already struck. The vines on the trees behind them were still coiled and ready. They could not safely return to the road even if the bishop had wanted to.

Back where the rescue party had left the road, more soldiers were entering the water, either to rescue the rescue party or to replace them when they died.

Most of the thicket still lay ahead. Cay was nowhere to be seen, but he had triggered many of the vines as he fled. These now hung listless, short enough that they didn't cut the other trees. How long until they could strike again?

Grasping a soldier's arm, the bishop pulled himself to his feet. "We absolutely will not go back. Draw your swords, and let's move."

The man replied with strained reverence. "Your Holiness, we can't reach the wagon. We won't live long enough."

"Some of us won't," Arumin admitted. "But some of us might."

The man absorbed the fact that he'd been sentenced to death. He nodded. "For you, Holiness."

The man who had lost his arm shivered. A comrade held and comforted him as a dark circle spread in the water around them.

"We're leaving," Arumin said. "He must wait here for help."

"He hasn't got long, Bishop."

"None of us have long, you damned fool! If you still honor your vow, draw your blade and move."

Sinking low in the water, Arumin and the two remaining soldiers set out for the wagon. They could see it now, overturned. Vines were spreading through the water between it and the nearest part of the road, so no one could reach it from that direction. Several soldiers had apparently tried, and they were now fighting for their lives among the vines.

By the time Arumin and his guards reached the mid-point of their trek, one of the men had been slashed across the leg. The other had lost several fingers and now gripped his sword with the wrong hand. Should he ever return to Ronia, his career in the army was over.

The invisible underwater attackers were stinging Arumin viciously under his shirt and trousers. The soldiers kept twitching. They felt it too.

They found Cay's body, recognizable only by its red hair. It jerked and bobbed as the invisibles helped themselves. Cay had done the others a favor by triggering many vines along their path. But the trees and vines ahead waited, tensed and undisturbed.

Arumin decided he must sacrifice one of the remaining soldiers, sending him ahead to clear the way. He was trying to choose when another idea struck him.

"Underwater," he said. Faced with blank stares, he added, "We'll stay under the water from here on. Leave your guns and swim. Come up only to breathe."

Maybe it would hide them from the trees. No one knew, but no one argued. One after another, they inhaled and dove.

Arumin kicked off from the bottom and swam with one soldier in front and one behind. The plan worked. The vines left them alone, though many were long enough to reach underwater. But the invisibles swarmed over him, gathering wherever he bled. They filled his undergarments. He paddled madly.

Finally, they reached his eyes. When they slipped under his eyelids, he leaped out of the water.

As he broke the surface, his chest exploded. The pain astonished him. Putting his hand over his heart, he touched a narrow trench in his skin where the vine had hit him.

The soldier behind Arumin collided with him. The bishop dove again, swimming against a tide of exhaustion that tempted him to lie back and float away. His chest wound burned as if held to a flame.

While above water, he had seen that the thicket ended close ahead, and the wagon lay not far beyond it. A nest of coiled vines overhung the thicket's edge.

The soldier in front slowed as his wounded leg bled. Underwater, Arumin saw the man's cut widen. The invisible things tugged its edges, eating away the skin. The man clawed vainly at them.

The devouring wisps massed around them all, nearly invisible and too many to count. Perhaps blood attracted them. It no longer mattered. The man ahead stopped moving, overwhelmed. The others crowded behind him, trapped and afraid to surface.

Arumin had no idea what to do. He could think only of saving himself.

The attackers were tearing apart the man in front. Through the water, the bishop saw the little squirming tubes filling with blood and bits of swallowed meat.

The things found the tear in Arumin's chest, and he cared about nothing else. For ages, he struggled, out of his mind. He heard the others gurgle and scream, and he screamed too, bubbles tumbling to the surface. Finally, he planted his feet amidst the bones on the bottom and sprang from the water, praying the vines would end him quickly.

Eyes closed, he waited several seconds, aware that he was still alive. He opened his eyes to a nightmare.

The water was a soup of human remains and scraps of clothing. The vines above him hung limp with gore. Red brighter than the trees splattered their trunks.

The man with the leg wound, unable to endure any longer, had surfaced just before Arumin. The thick horde of vines above had greeted him.

Mumbling a prayer, the bishop helped the remaining soldier to his feet. "Great Mother," said the man when he opened his eyes. He held the stumps of his lost fingers close.

"Move," Arumin ordered.

They waded through the dead man's shredded remains. The hanging vines had spent their fury, though they tore at Arumin's clothes. As the two men moved into the open, the invisibles' attacks tapered away. Maybe they had eaten their fill.

Brin's wagon hung from one of the awful snake-like trees that stood in the swamp. The other trees were still for now. Figures floated under the wagon, a load beast and at least one man. Another body hung from the wagon, caught on something.

The scene was too alien to be real. The bishop moved through clay.

When he saw Brin hunched in the water, he breathed again. He recognized the young priest's vulnerable, familiar stance.

"Brin," he called. The word sounded forbidden.

Brin stood and stepped toward him hesitantly. Arumin charged on, tripping over bones and dragging some with him, until they met and embraced.

The bishop held his charge close, leaned back, and peered into his eyes. Brin spoke first. "There you are."

Feeling reckless, Arumin pulled their faces together and kissed his cheek. Brin stiffened, surprised at the intimate gesture.

Behind the bishop, the surviving soldier coughed and said, "Your Holiness." It sounded like a question. Worry tugged at Arumin, but he kept kissing Brin's cheek, because they were alive.

"Bishop!" the man shouted. Arumin turned to curse at him and saw the true reason for his distress.

"Oh," he said stupidly.

The water between them and the road was alive with choking vines. They were the same type that had pulled the wagon off the road.

They were closing off the path back to the trees. The soldier struck at them with his knife, trying to keep their escape route open.

It was hopeless. Brin's face showed terror. These men were counting on him for an answer. Brin had done so for many years now. The bishop would provide, as he always did.

"Hold me," he said.

Brin wrapped his arms around the old man hesitantly, perhaps wondering how this would help them escape. He trembled violently. A piece of a vine still clung to one of his wrists.

The bishop took a long breath and emptied his lungs. His fears fell away, and a smile crept onto his face. He asked the soldier, "What's your name?"

The man was in no mood for conversation. "It's Tabard."

"Private Tabard, your vow is fulfilled," Arumin said. "When you pass, it shall be into Huire's arms."

The man understood that the bishop was pronouncing them dead, but he would not accept it. As the vines surrounded them, he struck them faster and harder.

The bishop whispered to Brin, who had stiffened like a day-old corpse. "The same goes for us. I love you, and I'll see you very soon."

Brin struggled in his arms, caught between panic and resignation. Off in the swamp, the wagon finally fell from the tree, sending waves across the water.

As vines crawled up Arumin's back, his spirit soared. Though he would die, he had not failed. He had given his last to Huire's cause, of which he was a small part. The other crusaders would have to carry her banner from here. He would rest now in her full glory.

Brin had frozen. The vines groped between them and around them, binding them together.

Tabard fought like a bull. The din of his struggle slipped far away.

Arumin pressed his cheek against Brin's. They were such different ages. The vines toppled them like an upright stack of kindling. Brin fell on top of Arumin as the water closed over their heads.

Arumin wondered what form the Goddess would take when she came. Once, he had doubted he would join her in the next world. The memory of that fear embarrassed him.

With tremendous effort, he let water pour into his lungs. Sooner would be better.

She appeared, glowing in the mire. She was as beautiful as he had expected, familiar but strange. She stood over them, and he closed his eyes. There could be no doubt.

10

NOR

NOR HUNG FROM THE wagon after everyone else had fallen. The vehicle shook like a toy on a string as daggers pierced it from every direction, tearing pieces away.

When the attack ended, he strained to climb into what remained of the wagon. Exhausted, he kicked his legs and hooked the fingers of his free hand over its edge. That took the weight off of the vine's cutting barbs. From there, he hauled himself up.

Catching his breath, he searched for some knife or sharp edge. There would be no escape without cutting the damned vine, which was still held together by a fringe of fibers strong enough to support his weight.

Finding nothing, he bit down on the fibers and ground his teeth together. As he worked, the tree spasmed, tossing him and the vehicle up. He clung to the wagon and managed not to fall, but seconds later, the tree jerked again. It wanted to be rid of its burden.

He saw no way out. Even if he escaped the wagon, the trees would kill him when he hit the water. He was sure they could hear somehow.

He kept grinding the vine between his teeth, biting so hard his jaw ached, until only a few strands held the vine together. He tried to pull it apart with his hands, but it held. He pulled again with all his might.

The tree jerked again. Caught off guard, he flew from the wagon without a struggle. The vine finally snapped as his weight pulled it.

He hit the water flat on his back. Shocked by the cold impact, he surfaced to see the wagon falling toward him.

He had no time to think. It crashed down, and the world turned dark.

Blurred light reached his eyes. Fragments of sky hung overhead, holes in the wagon's bottom. The vehicle had fallen upside down on top of him, and he was alive. Pressing his face into the thin gap between the water and the wagon's floor, he gulped air and went under, waiting for the trees to attack.

Under the water, he heard massive splashes in the distance. A distant roar of voices. The vines must have dragged more wagons into the swamp.

He waited. Time became immeasurable.

When nothing happened, he tested his limbs. Finding himself intact, he tried to accept that he was alive.

Another splash. The waves of the first splash had reached him, rocking the wagon with agonized creaks. The entire swamp had risen against them.

If the Goddess had decided he would survive this, then he would survive. If not, he would die soon. Trapped under the wagon with the trees waiting outside, he could only escape by breaking the floor, and the noise from that would bring the trees to him.

Still, they should have killed him already. What could this reprieve mean? He could think of only one possibility: the letter in his pocket.

Maybe Huire had let him live so he could finish his test. Abbot Cadmon would call him an egomaniac for considering it. The Goddess had taken several lives already today, Brin's probably among them. Holy men got no special protection.

But Nor had a specific duty on this journey—to answer his quandary. He was obligated to try, whether the Goddess kept him safe or not. Since he would certainly die soon, barring a miracle, he had better try now.

He whispered the quandary. "What are the gods made of?" His wrist tingled where the vine's severed end still gripped it.

The quandary made no more sense than it ever had. Had Cadmon meant him to take it literally, metaphorically, or some other way he hadn't considered?

The test's difficulty was its entire point. The ability to pull water from a stone was what made a priest an elder. Meanwhile, Cadmon would not ask him a question if it was truly unanswerable.

So be it. Before letting himself die, he would answer the quandary, rightly or wrongly. Then he would open Cadmon's letter and see if he was correct. A right answer would make him an elder, if only for his last moments of life.

Opening it might be difficult. Cadmon had made him promise not to open it before he found an answer. He had spoken a secret word designed by their order to compel Nor's obedience.

Nor doubted the word could really stop him from opening the letter. That had not stopped him from feeling betrayed and insulted when Cadmon used it.

But here he was, about to prove the old man's suspicions correct. He would open the envelope without giving the answer proper thought. He told himself he had no choice.

Outside the little world of his wagon, seconds had passed. Still the voices rose, and more impacts rocked the water.

He thought of something. His jaw dropped. He sat up, hitting his head on the wagon.

He grabbed the envelope from his pocket. It was underwater, and as he peeled it out, his breaths became little cries.

He cradled it, a pulpy mass with no obvious top or bottom, and squeezed his eyes shut. He tried to sob, but despite the water, it sounded dry and dusty like a fake laugh.

The envelope's contents must be unreadable. The quandary would remain unanswered forever.

The thought defied reality. Huire had called him to be tested and saved his life so he could complete the test. Now her reason for both had evaporated.

An awful thought gripped him. Huire might have arranged the events that led to this moment as a punishment. Or as a joke. The silence he had sensed waiting in the jungle, that had followed him since his imprisonment, might be the Goddess's wrath pushing him toward this fate.

Another thought formed and grew. If Cadmon's letter had been destroyed, then everything Nor knew about the Goddess was wrong. He could not yet accept that.

The only alternative was that the letter was not ruined—that inside the soaked envelope, Cadmon's final words for him were still readable.

It was impossible. But he had seen the impossible happen before. The Lady's appearance in Ronia was a literal miracle.

In his thin layer of air, he held the envelope before his eyes. Light from overhead highlighted its wrinkles. He only allowed himself a glance. If light shone through and he glimpsed the answer, it would be disastrous.

The sight of the waterlogged envelope gave him no encouragement. He would simply have to believe the letter had been preserved. Which left the critical step of solving the quandary.

He whispered Cadmon's question over and over. "What are the gods made of?" He could no longer find meaning in the words.

The answer must come soon. So many minutes had passed since they left Ronia—he wished he had spent more of them thinking about this.

He would not live long enough to approach the question rigorously. An especially gifted candidate for eldership might enter a trance in which he transcended logic and mathematics, darting through clouds of information under the guidance of reflex.

Nor would need to rely on instinct. Even in ideal circumstances, he was not good at that. Doubts and conflicting voices filled his mind constantly, and the voice of instinct was like a single stranger in a crowd.

Outside, where the turmoil still raged, the trees waited. He began to shiver. He lifted his wrist from the water, vine still attached, and stared at his wounded hand.

If he blurted a false answer simply to complete the test, he would fail by default, even if his answer happened to be right. A candidate who lied to the order in such circumstances and became an elder would earn Huire's wrath. She knew the truth.

This raised a question. What if Nor decided not to answer the quandary now? If he could not properly contemplate the mystery, maybe he should wait until he could. If he burst from the wagon without opening the envelope and the trees killed him, it would mean he had been wrong about everything. The test would have been a punishment or a joke.

The Goddess had saved his life minutes ago when nothing else could have. She would not do that only to watch him die with his purpose unfulfilled.

Warmth filled his chest. Huire would protect him. If she didn't, the universe would lose all coherence.

This was a test. It must be. He wondered what would happen when he burst forth. Maybe Huire would stop the trees from attacking. Maybe he would be torn apart, only to rise again. His heart quickened at the thought of the suffering that might lie ahead.

But he would suffer regardless. It was a choice of fates, and he knew which end would come quickest. Feeling above his head, he found a hole through which he could fit if he broke a few weak boards.

Once he made his decision, his fear diminished, and he felt lighter. Answers were coming.

He broke through the boards and rose from the wagon. Water fell from him in torrents, and the light was stunning.

The claw-trees were falling. Some floated in the water already, each sliced halfway up its trunk. Others whipped and struck haplessly as something, a silver-gray cloud, attacked them one after another. It struck each in the shape of a whirling disc and cut through it with a deafening buzz.

Through the swamp toward him strode Shada. She glowed with a silvery aura that hummed and swirled. As the disc whipped back and forth across her path, cutting down everything in front of her, she stared straight at Nor. Her face showed the self-possession of someone walking on a wire. Around her feet, the trees floated, twitching as they died, their whiplike ends splashing.

The men on the road were cheering, but Nor quickly forgot them.

He was amazed to be alive but not shocked. He felt the same way about Shada wading through the swamp to him. Standing by the wagon, she offered her hand.

She smiled. Pain and fear lost their importance.

"Come with me," she said. "We'd better be going."

He took her hand. From that moment, she never left his thoughts.

11

SHADA

DESPERATE TO ESCAPE THE men's awed faces, Shada stepped into her wagon and shut the door. The tingling cloud surrounding her fell away and reformed as the Lady, her face gently concerned.

"My dear," she hummed, "you frightened me. I wish you had warned me before you went into the swamp."

Now that she was back in the wagon's familiar confines, Shada's heart slowed to its regular pace. The rush of energy drained away, replaced by illness and sleepiness.

"I apologize, Lady," she replied. "I don't know if I did the right thing. The trees were about to attack the wagon when it fell. I didn't want anyone else to die."

"Of course not, child." The Lady's tone was a pat on the head. "It's only natural for a kind soul like yours. But I don't think you realize the danger you were in."

It was a strange thing to say. Shada could hardly have missed the danger unless some of it was invisible. "Perhaps not," she said.

"They are good men. I love each of them more than you know. But not all will return from the road we are taking."

Still dripping wet, Shada undressed. It was getting easier to change her clothes in front of the Lady. As she pulled on dry trousers, Shada asked, "But why not save them if we can?"

"Save them from what? From entering the womb of the Goddess? They have already been saved in the most important way. When they return to Huire's embrace, this world will be an unpleasant memory."

The wagon shifted as the column started moving. Shada sat on her cot. She was close to the heart of something, and her desire for an answer overcame her fear. "But you didn't let me die."

The Lady frowned. "That should not comfort you. Your purpose is harder. Unlike those who died today, you have much more suffering in store."

Shada remembered seeing the bishop and his priest dragged from the water, half-drowned. She thought of Nor emerging from the overturned wagon and desperately grasping her hand, his pale eyes intent on her face. After they reached the road, she had excused herself curtly from his presence, uncomfortable with his profuse, reverent thanks. "I don't know what I meant to do. Those trees would have killed me if you hadn't stopped them."

"I intervened because it is important that you stay alive for now. The men we saved were meant to die here. In dying, they would have accomplished their purposes and avoided the horrors that await those still living."

"I was so afraid for them," said Shada. "I didn't think I was brave enough to do what I did. I felt like a different person."

"We have many faces," the Lady replied. Her frown stretched to the size of a tragic theatrical mask.

"When I asked you to help them..." Shada paused. Watching the men fall from the tipping wagon, she had not just asked, she had begged. When the Lady refused, Shada had watched until she couldn't bear it. "I didn't understand why you did nothing. I'm afraid to tell you all the things I felt. Though of course you'll guess them all."

"And when I did not obey your wishes, you tried for yourself."

"Yes." There was no way around it.

"What you did was brave, and you had the best intentions. But you lack faith. Do you think I would let those men die if they would be better off alive?"

"You mean, they had served their purpose," Shada said.

"They would have had they died. Meeting their natural ends would have completed the circles of their lives. Because I intervened—for you—the men are now unfinished, adrift. The Goddess's hand has come only to point the way, not to carry her people through their ordeals. Next time I refuse to help the company with some threat—thus endangering my existence by leaving my box—it will be harder for the men to accept. They will wonder why I made this exception."

The scum of the swamp dried and itched on Shada's limbs. "I didn't know."

"Didn't you? I told you of your place in the plan. You are indispensable. When you entered the swamp, did you expect to die?"

"I don't remember."

"I doubt it. I think you knew I would help you."

"It... occurred to me," she admitted. "I wasn't sure. I thought..." Her mind turned. She had thought more things in those moments than she could recall.

The Lady filled the silence. "You hoped to help them. If I helped you—"

"I didn't see how it was wrong," Shada interrupted.

"You didn't trust me."

The skin of Shada's face shrank against her bones. "I..."

"You committed a pair of sins today, my dear." The Lady placed her buzzing, immaterial fingers under Shada's chin. "First, you believed that you, above Huire, knew what was right for your fellows. Second, you took advantage of your own importance to force me to intervene."

Sickness churned in Shada's belly. "That wasn't my intention."

"Our goals are not always conscious. Ignorance of your feelings shows a lack of self-reflection."

Shada could barely squeeze words out of her throat. "I just didn't want them to die."

"Your desires are not paramount," said the Lady with finality. "Neither are mine. We are each playing parts in a larger story, and none of us know its true shape."

"I'm sorry."

"Remorse is the first step. The second is change. Will you take my words into your heart and use them?"

"I can. I will." Shada forbade herself to think otherwise. The truth was, part of her wished she had entered the swamp sooner. She and the Lady could have saved more lives. Maybe if she told herself she was wrong enough times, she would believe it.

The Lady's frown almost vanished. Her eyes swelled with sympathy. "Don't be discouraged. This morning, you behaved remarkably. You convinced the captain to change his plans. You're showing I was right to choose you as caretaker."

"It was like stepping off a cliff," said Shada. "I did it because I had to." She paused. "When you asked me to be your caretaker, I ran away because the role was too big for me. I didn't think I was capable."

"I remember," the Lady replied. "The bishop asked me to forget you and find someone else. He hoped to take on the role himself. But I knew you would return."

"Every bad thing that happens to me or my family starts with being noticed." Shada had forgotten if she was answering a question or what the question had been. "I wanted to hide until everyone went away. But hiding felt worse. Poisonous. I won't do that again."

"Do not confuse courage with righteousness. No one likes pain. But when it is our duty to face it and we fail, we must at least embrace sorrow. Through remorse we scour ourselves of impurity.

"You are discovering your power. You can create change. But change brought about through evil turns to evil."

"Forgive my boldness," said Shada. Even the wagon was no longer safe.

"Your boldness needs no forgiveness. But you must direct it with pure motives." The Lady's ghostly mouth bent up at its corners. Shada looked away without meaning to.

Nearby, the box where the Lady dwelt sat partly open. As Shada pondered it, someone knocked on the wagon's door. Before she could turn away, the Lady hummed past her, collapsing into the box like an explosion in reverse. The box's door shut.

Shada had never seen the Lady enter the box up close. She took a breath to compose herself after the bizarre sight, then she answered the door.

It was Nor, soaking and haggard. He still wore the tatters of his robe. His wrist had been hastily bandaged, but it would take a blanket to cover all his scrapes and bruises.

Shada so dreaded enduring more adoration—especially from someone she admired—that she almost shut the door. Instead, she opened it wide enough to admit her face and blurted, "You're very welcome, Brother Nor."

His brow furrowed in confusion, and she realized she had miscalculated. He responded slowly, in his serious way. "I don't want to bother you, Caretaker. But I think I did after you saved me. I said too much. I was feeling a lot of things. By all rights, I should have died."

This was not what she had expected. She shifted her weight, no longer determined to close the door quickly.

He mistook the action for impatience. "I'll be brief. I'm sorry I acted so strange. Gripping your hand like that and thanking you over and over. That's all."

He shivered. He had been shivering all along, but she had not noticed. The sight reminded her what a terrible experience he had been through.

She wanted to hug him, reassure him, but thought better of it. A man like him would hate being pitied. "No apology is needed, Nor. I did what was right."

A little knot of worry formed in her belly as she remembered the Lady was listening. What Shada had done wasn't right. She should have stayed out of danger and let Nor die. But she could not yet make herself believe that, much less say it to Nor. She knew being the caretaker could mean distancing herself from the others. Maybe this was why. It made honesty impossible.

Feeling trapped by the conversation, she began to excuse herself. "Well—"

He said the same thing at the same time, and they both paused so the other could continue.

During the pause, she noticed a sound. It was a high note, faint but impossible to ignore once heard.

The noise grew painful. It came from outside, where voices were rising, and from above. Nor stepped back to look as nearby timber shattered with a crash. Shada jumped out of the wagon.

The trees had closed in on the road as it left the swamp. To one side behind the column, dust settled where a strip of wiry trees had fallen. Several men stood there and peered into the woods. As more gathered, they held their arms to their faces.

She and Nor trotted over to join them. As they approached, she buried her nose in her sleeve. The odor was stunning—sweat, blood, and unwashed bodies.

An object as flat and broad as a hut's roof rested on trees it had mowed down. It was a leaf of incredible proportions. The howl it had made swooping over the trees was now a wavering, grating mewl.

The captain rode up at dangerous speed. He regarded the leaf grimly but without surprise.

"Emberly!" someone exclaimed in a harsh croak.

Shada turned to see a bloody half corpse standing on the road, wrapped in a shawl. It was Bishop Arumin, his face gaunt, chest bandaged. Behind him stood Dr. Staubel, unable to control his patient.

The bishop's appearance alarmed Shada. He did not appear capable of standing, but there he was.

Emberly's eyes widened. "Bishop?"

"Do you know what that is?" Arumin's shout ended in a coughing fit.

"I know."

Arumin's voice cracked. He looked like a lunatic ranting about the world's end. "You must destroy it!"

"We will."

On the captain's orders, several soldiers walked out into the deep mud. They dragged the leaf toward the road by its stem, a rotted shaft as thick as Shada's thigh. The leaf seemed surprisingly light given the damage it had done.

As the men pulled, the leaf wailed louder. Opposite its stem, its edges flared out like wings from its pointed apex. The cries came from there.

The soldiers hoisted the leaf onto the road. Its smell thickened the air. At Emberly's direction, the men carried it away, down the road toward the edge of the swamp nearby. The leaf moaned.

Emberly finally noticed Shada and Nor. "Caretaker, please return to your wagon."

Nor whispered to Shada that they should go. But Shada was transfixed.

The apex of the leaf now pointed at her. At its tip, the leaf's sharp edges met its primary vein and swelled to form a vertical edge like a hatchet.

There, facing her, was a set of bumps and creases that looked like... She denied it. Her mind, seeking order, saw a face. But it could not be. She could forgive herself an occasional hallucination.

Yet from a small cavity in the structure came a voice.

The captain blocked her view with his shoulder and ushered her toward the wagons. Nor followed.

"What is it?" Shada asked.

"I don't have time to explain," Emberly snapped. His voice softened. "It's a signal. It will attract things we do not want to meet. We must leave, though it may be too late." He shouted to his soldiers, "Quickly!"

Cringing at how comparatively gentle he had been with her, Shada hurried toward her wagon. With a glance and a nod, she parted ways with Nor. She needed to think about how to explain this to the Lady.

She mounted the step into the wagon to see farther down the road. The soldiers carried the leaf into the swamp, where the water submerged the road. Nearby, the writhing vines that had almost drowned Arumin still drifted outward, seeking prey. The men shuffled, turning the leaf so its apex faced the water, and heaved it in with a shout.

It glided briefly on its winglike curves and landed among the vines. Shada's mouth tasted coppery as the vines found the leaf. Their tendrils sneaked across its broad back and fixed in place. They pulled in all directions. Dark brown fluid spurted from the leaf as it began to tear.

As the vines pulled it under, ripping it apart, the leaf's cries became a series of shrieks. The sounds were raw and brainless, an expression of pure suffering.

Shada dove into the caravan, slammed the door, and covered her ears. The noise still reached her as surely as the leaf's smell had.

She did not see the Lady watching her until she dropped her hands. The Lady's face was blank like a doll's as she asked, "What happened?"

Shada wished she did not have to talk about it. If only she could rest first. "I don't know. I..." She stopped. At least it was the truth.

"My dear, there must be more. I know it is difficult, but you must try harder."

In a jolt of anger, the words slipped from Shada's mouth: "If I am failing you, go and find out for yourself!"

She stopped, shocked at what she had said. Anger still simmering, she added, "Stop hiding and go out there."

The Lady was never really silent. The hum like distant insects followed her everywhere. Now it grew louder, though she said nothing. Shada's face tingled and flushed, but she said nothing either.

The Lady slowly formed a cloud and drained away into her box. Her feet disappeared first. As they went, she said, "I cannot spare you, child. I have already explained that."

"I know," said Shada. Her outburst had felt true, and she could hardly hide her feelings from the Lady anyway. But still. "It's just... something is wrong with all of this. I don't know what. Maybe it's me."

Only the Lady's chest and head remained. "I will leave you and your monk friend to decide that."

"Wait," said Shada. She had been wrong. Always wrong.

The Lady disappeared without another word. Shada was alone. The screams of the dying thing floated over the rumble of wheels.

12

— · —

EMBERLY

THE DEAD WHO COULD be recovered lay atop the gear in a wagon. They would get no proper interment. The company could spare no one to transport them back to Ronia and her holy mountain.

As daylight waned, Emberly stayed at the back of the column, watching behind. He spotted the shape as it groped its way over the trees. Wide as a river delta, the swarm lay thick on the canopy as it passed.

Maybe the company had moved far enough from the spot where the leaf fell. If not, he hoped the swarm would do its work quickly.

Lieutenant Roark's curses echoed from the front, where soldiers rushed to clear trees and other obstructions from the road. They could not afford more delays.

The swarm was a pale, gentle blue, striking against the red jungle. Emberly had never seen a swarm that color, which meant no Ronian likely had. He did not know what it would do if it landed on them, and it was no use imagining. All that mattered was that they probably would not survive.

Few could have understood his belief that the jungle itself had sensed the company's presence. Perhaps the battle in the swamp had turned the wilderness against them, but Emberly suspected it had been waiting to devour them since they set foot on the planet.

As dark came, the wind quickened, whining through the trees. It sounded like an orchestra of broken instruments playing a dissonant theme that was not quite a song.

During his first nights stationed at the prison, the trees' music had kept him awake hour after hour. He had learned to plug his ears with wax, but he still heard it. It spoke to him directly at times, asking how long he really meant to resist its will. Later, he wondered if the convicts' revolt had in some sense saved him from the music.

The company moved quickly. The thin, twisted trees that filled this part of the jungle were surprisingly brittle, often falling to a single axe stroke. In a moment of stupidity, Emberly grabbed with his bare hand a tree the axes had missed. It crumbled in his grip, but its trunk was woven around several others, so it did not fall on him.

"Not long now," said a voice in his ear. His heart missed a beat. No one was watching him, and no one would see

Rayan anyway, but the nearest soldiers might hear Emberly if he spoke.

"People are watching," he whispered, moving his lips as little as possible.

In life, Rayan had read Emberly's mind with infuriating accuracy. Death had not lessened this talent. "Do you think they'll hear me?" he asked with a chuckle.

Emberly clenched his teeth. That sarcastic tone wore on his temper as much now as when they were children. He would have answered, but he did not wish to be heard conversing with the air.

He turned in his saddle. Not far behind them, a river of delicate blue was pouring like molasses from atop the canopy and onto the road.

Rayan saw it too. He said with a touch of awe, "Ah, yes, a swarm. We knew you might meet one. Your options are decreasing. Time has that effect."

"What will it do to us?"

It was a useless question. Rayan seemed to know nothing that Emberly didn't know. But he seized on the captain's show of ignorance. "I have no idea," he said, incredulous. If he were alive, his head would have tilted in disbelief. "The swarms are always changing. What does its color say to you?"

Emberly snarled. "What must I do to make you go away?" It was louder than he intended. He glanced ahead, but no one had heard him.

His brother was calmly smug. He had wanted an outburst, and he had gotten it. "Back to that, are we? If your mind created me, drive me out of it."

The captain gripped his head with both hands. Thank the Goddess no one was watching. "This will end soon," he whispered. "I'm going to rid myself of you."

"Nonsense. You keep calling me back."

"Say what you will. Soon you'll haunt me no longer."

"How? Are you going to pray harder?"

"I don't know, but I'll do it."

"That's what I've always wanted, brother. For you to abide by your word."

The sun had set. Wind tugged Emberly's cloak, easing the day's heat. It came from the direction of the swamp.

He had feared this. The wind was against them. Caught by it, the swarm would rush this way, guided by the road like a flood in a riverbed.

"I'll see you in the waytower, I hope," said his brother.

Emberly felt him depart.

He galloped to the front of the column, shouting all the way.

He reminded the men to cover their faces and skin with any extra clothing they could find. He told the men cutting down trees to work knowing all their lives depended on it.

Only someone who knew what was coming would think they weren't working fast enough. But Emberly would not yet tell them to flee on foot—abandoning their supplies would only mean a slower death.

There was one option he had not tried. The Lady. Since she had emerged to lead Shada's courageous but insane rescue mission, Emberly had hoped she might be softening in her refusal to help the company through peril. Maybe her stubborn reclusiveness was simply the result of Arumin's excessive fear for her safety.

He cherished the thought but let it pass. The Lady could not be so naïve as to be shoved into hiding against her will. Her refusal to help must have come from her, at least partly. If Emberly challenged her on that or on whether she knew Huire's will with certainty, Arumin would fight for her—verbally and maybe physically.

It would be a hard conversation and one requiring time. If it came, the captain would learn how defiant he dared to be and what offers or ultimatums he dared to make. It could be so cataclysmic, such a risk to lives and souls, that he would only risk it when death and the crusade's failure were looming and certain. Then they would all learn Huire's true will.

A scout returned with news Emberly had hoped for. Just ahead, hidden by trees, stood the waytower, a shelter for travelers. The company might reach it if they hurried. The captain would delay his confrontation with the Lady for another time.

Moments later, he regretted his optimism.

The sky filled with soft, drifting blue. The swarm obscured the road behind them.

As the last trees blocking their path fell, blue flecks like flower petals danced and swirled on the wind. The wagons rolled toward the waytower, which was set off the road on a stone foundation.

Reaching the tower, the company halted, and the drivers leaped out to unyoke the animals. Emberly sent a few men running to open the doors.

The tower's square, windowless exterior was coated in toxic pitch to protect it from wildlife. When Arumin had overseen its construction as commandant, he had made sure it was sturdy enough to protect high-ranking visitors—a luxury not afforded the barracks at the logging outposts.

Arumin had specified the place should have no windows. Any gap in the building's armor would admit invaders, some of them too small to see. The tower had three exits: one in the front, one in the back, and a weighted hatch at the very top.

Several wooden troughs sat in front of the building. Coffin sized, they were coated with pitch and fixed to the ground. They had lids, some of which were missing.

The tower's heavy front doors leaned back, so anyone entering had to lift and swing them. Emberly's soldiers were struggling to open them. The pitch had run into the hinges.

The drivers lined up the animals to enter. Other men hurled food and supplies from the wagons. Emberly looked over his shoulder and told everyone to run.

Leaving bags where they fell, the company raced for the doors, more hands helping to pry them apart. As the air filled with specks of fluttering blue, the opening slowly widened. The doors' hinges squealed and bent.

Billowing flakes were filling the wagons and piling on the ground in drifts. They gathered on shoulders and hoods.

The doors opened. The caretaker entered first, box in hand, and the holy men followed, Brin and Nor supporting Arumin. They hurried down a stone ramp to the floor below ground level.

The company pressed into the dark room as quickly as it could, people and animals shoulder to shoulder. The captain went last. He and Lieutenant Roark each held a door open with his back. The road and sky disappeared behind the advancing thunderhead of the swarm.

Emberly and Roark looked at each other and scrambled down the ramp. A door thumped against the captain's head as it fell shut.

Clutching his head and cursing, he glanced around. With the doors closed, the room was too dark to see. A few candle flames sprang to life, revealing a high wooden chamber filled with soldiers watching him. He had more decisions to make.

"Take your outer clothes off carefully," he said. "Don't let the flakes touch your skin. If they do, see Dr. Staubel at once."

In a far corner, Staubel shook his head. What he could do against this unknown threat was anyone's guess. He was already tending wounded. Private Carrowy lay at his feet, maybe dying from his wounding by the tree. Next to him, Private Tabard sat miserably. He had lost several fingers, a career-ending injury.

Six soldiers had died or gone missing in the swamp, all privates. It was a terrible loss for this small company of a few dozen people, only two days out from Ronia.

More would have died had Shada not entered the swamp. Emberly had watched, too late to stop her, recognizing that he was witnessing a miracle. Her glowing, protective aura had been fantastical, the sort of thing that only existed far away and long ago.

Having seen what the Lady could do, Emberly had to accept that the world he knew had changed. He would accept it like a soldier, with little hope of understanding.

Lanterns flared, and the room glowed. The ceiling was several stories up, reachable by a wide ramp that wound its way around the walls to a hatch set in the ceiling.

"Emberly," said Brother Nor. The monk was upright despite the beating he had taken. Staubel had bandaged his wrist. The monk rarely addressed Emberly by rank, though what he hoped to prove by this was unclear. He pointed to the ceiling.

The captain saw nothing unusual and shook his head irritably.

Nor snapped, "In the corner."

Emberly looked again, and there it was. A patch of blue flakes clung to the ceiling and walls.

"Damn." Emberly sent men up the ramp to find and block the hole in their defenses and others to search the upper rooms for similar breaches. They were fortunate to have a solid place to hide. In the rare encounters with swarms at the prison, he had heard of people hiding under tarps.

He gave his orders as efficiently as possible. Still, there was more. Sleeping arrangements, checking on the wounded, sweeping blue flakes from the floor...

His thoughts dispersed as a sergeant approached. It was Feng, a graying army lifer whose short, hefty stature was unmistakable. "Captain, we're missing one."

Everyone heard him. The room fell silent as they looked around. Emberly's chest tightened. It was obvious who was absent.

Tonelessly, he asked, "Did anyone see what happened to Private Hulgar?" The question was painfully futile.

No one had seen. Hulgar must be outside. The swarm must have caught him.

The soldiers went back to work with a new trudge in their steps. Emberly asked Nor to wait by the doors in case Hulgar returned. He had heard the monk's people had sharp eyes and ears. The swarm might be less aggressive come nightfall, so they could risk opening the doors if it meant saving a life. The monk agreed without complaint.

The captain spoke and acted mechanically. Best to keep everyone busy. Few had much affection for Hulgar, whose size and temper made him feared. He had acted especially strange since his outburst last night. But he was one of them, and he'd been taken from under their noses.

Emberly imagined all those who died today joining the soldiers he had lost in the past. In his mind, they were tossed on a stinking pile with everyone who had ever died for Ronia. Never buried, simply rotting.

Early in his career, he had vowed to remember the name of every soldier he lost. During the fever dream that was his tour on Gallobraith, the promise had slipped away. He had never decided to give it up. He simply realized one day he had long ago stopped trying.

Shouting came from the hatch in the ceiling. Men carried someone through the hatch and down the ramp.

It was Merin, the astronomer. He must have hurt himself somehow. Emberly, who doubted the man's competence already, was annoyed.

But the others' faces told him this was serious. When he saw blue residue covering Merin's face and neck, he called for Staubel and ran to meet the group.

He leaned in and spoke to Merin. "Private?"

Feng held one of the man's arms. "He hasn't said much, sir."

Dazed, slathered with blue, Merin looked like a grim clown. The flakes had melted into his skin. No one knew how they worked or even what they were, but Emberly had seen this before. He remembered entire labor details found dead in the jungle, convicts and guards alike. It was too late for Merin.

"What happened, Sergeant?" he asked.

"We opened the hatch to the top floor," said Feng. "He volunteered to do it. Turns out, the roof caved in a while back. The room must be piled with the blue stuff. Spilled right in his eyes when he opened the hatch."

Staubel arrived and stepped in front of the captain without a thought. "Is this what I think it is?"

Emberly nodded. Staubel told the men to place Merin with the other wounded. As they carried him away, the private tried valiantly to use his feet.

The captain and the doctor watched. Staubel said with detached interest, "Captain, do we have any chance of escaping?"

His tone made deception futile. Emberly said, "It depends on what happens outside."

"What about Merin's chances? You've seen attacks like this."

"Only their aftermath. The swarm could devour him, poison him, transform him. It's different every time."

"But it's always fatal."

Emberly murmured, "Usually."

"I'll clean him and watch him. We'll find out soon."

As the doctor walked away, the captain replied, "Let me know when it starts."

13

— · —

ARUMIN

CLAIMING AN EMPTY UPPER room for themselves, Arumin and Brin spread their cloaks on the floor. The bishop settled onto the coarse fabric, handling himself like old pottery. The gash in his chest felt ready to split with each breath. Other, smaller hurts dotted his body.

A solid man for his age, he had counted on his heartiness to aid him against whatever came along. Especially Brother Nor or Captain Emberly, if their rebellious natures threatened the crusade. But his heartiness had left him for now. A flick of a tree's limb had rendered him simply an old man.

More than ever, he needed allies. Most of all, the young man next to him.

Brin lay close to the lantern. Someone had pried the vine from his wrist and bandaged it. He was still shaken and quiet, but his injuries were minor, and he was young. He rolled toward Arumin and propped himself on an elbow.

"What does it feel like?" he asked, leaning close to the bishop's wound.

"It hurts." The wound made Arumin pay each time he spoke. He closed his eyes.

"You're lucky the vine missed your eyes. Though if it hadn't, you might have the second sight by now." Brin made jokes few others dared.

He pointed to Arumin's chest. "I wonder what Huire will give you in exchange for this. When she takes, she also gives."

Either he was speaking sarcastically or he had misunderstood the saying. "She is no haggling trader," Arumin reminded him and sighed at the pain.

He recalled their moment in the swamp, wrapped in each other's arms and the choking vines. He had been ready to die together. "There is less of me now. That's all."

That silenced both of them for a moment.

Brin watched him and fidgeted. He had awakened from his shock, and now he would not remain still. "You've added to your collection," he said, running his hand over other parts of Arumin's chest, where far older scars lay in ridges that would never fade.

The hand felt strange to the bishop, a light touch amid a patchwork of past agonies. In some places, he could not feel it at all.

"Wherever these came from," said Brin, "it could hardly be a better story than today."

Arumin stared at the ceiling. Brin had pressed him to talk about his scars before, and he could hardly have picked a less agreeable time to try again. The bishop blamed himself. He usually gave in to Brin sooner or later. But not on this.

There was a memory he did not let his waking mind recall. It stood in plain sight, but he had learned to look away.

This was not weakness. He had little trouble picturing other terrible things he had witnessed. But when Brin searched for that one forbidden place, Arumin's mind reeled.

They had spoken of it too much already. If the bishop slept tonight, he might dream of the tunnel.

The pressure of Brin's hand on his chest connected him to the rest of the world. It moved toward his stomach, and he grunted in protest. Misunderstanding, Brin slid his hand farther down.

The bishop snatched the hand. "No."

"Fine."

To avoid an evening of angry silence, Arumin needed to say more. "You don't have to."

Brin snorted and lay with his arms crossed. "I know that. Do you think that's why I do it?"

Arumin swallowed. "Of course not."

"No one commands me," Brin spat. "Not even you."

"Of course they don't," the bishop said. His chest stung a little less. Maybe he was getting used to being in pain.

To his surprise, Brin did not shout back. Instead, he looked away. "I hoped it would make you happy."

"Look at me," replied Arumin softly.

Brin did, slowly.

"Every part of me is crumbling," said the bishop. In an urgent whisper, he added, "Why are you here? What do you want?"

Brin shook his head. "Do you really not understand? Why must I 'want' something, while you're the hero?" He sighed. "You almost gave your life for me today."

Arumin thought of their embrace in the swamp, of accepting the water into his lungs. "Yes. It wasn't so hard."

"Not to you," said Brin. "But to me... It's like a language I don't speak."

"We've lived different lives. You're always reminding me of that. Mine has been less terrible than yours."

Brin rolled over to face him again. "So many years, and we still can't grasp each other. I'm afraid we never will."

The bishop looked down. "We only need to accept each other. I accept you."

"You too. But I'd feel better if I could do something for you."

"It's already enough."

Brin snorted, frustrated but resigned. "Someday, I might learn to be like you."

"Lean on my shoulder," said Arumin.

Brin obeyed. The old man kissed his hair.

Silence fell, and the bishop became aware of their surroundings: the bare walls, someone moving in the next room, and the howling wind, which faintly penetrated even the thick hide of the waytower.

Brin must have been listening too. He asked, "What is this place? This planet, I mean."

Arumin's mind was hazy. The pain was returning. "I wish I knew."

"And the blue cloud outside? What is that?"

Arumin spoke slowly, pushing through the sting in his chest. "It's a swarm, composed of living things. They wander the treetops until they catch a scent."

"What about that giant leaf, if that's what it was? Where did it come from?"

The bishop pursed his dry lips. He was tired. "From the trees. The largest ones. Do you know which trees I'm talking about?"

Brin nodded. Looking out over the jungle that morning, they had seen a few lonely, colossal trees that towered over the rest. "I think the rumors are true. This jungle is just evil. It's ruled by demons."

The bishop closed his eyes. "Do you really believe that?"

"I don't know, but... something sent the swarm to attack us. Isn't that what you're saying?"

Giving a single nod, Arumin heard Brin take a deep breath.

"I'm scared to ask, but why didn't it catch us?"

"My guess is it was only partly aware of us. It is sleeping now. When it wakes in the morning, we should pray it leaves. By tomorrow night, we must reach the prison."

Upon Arumin's mention of the prison, Brin changed the subject. "I spoke to Brother Nor. He was not amenable to your friendship."

"So we feared."

"But he's predictable," Brin quickly added. "I can steer him. Also, he fell out with his abbot before we left Ronia. I foresee no need for drastic action."

"We must contemplate what may be required. If we act, we cannot hesitate."

Brin shifted uncomfortably. "When will we know it's time? If, I mean."

"Anyone who stands between this company and Huire—and refuses to budge—is Huire's enemy. And we are her soldiers. Nor and Emberly are dangerous, and I trust neither to back us against the other."

"We're in a bad spot." Brin sounded a little relieved. He feared violence more than he should.

"Only for the moment. We need friends with muscle. Disgruntled soldiers, especially anyone angry at Emberly. There must be some. Their tour on Gallobraith was rough. Meanwhile, Nor has made enemies enough on his own. Finally, we'll seek soldiers who have great faith in Huire. They'll believe in this crusade more than anyone."

Brin's face was somber. "Do you really think we'll have to remove Emberly?"

Getting closer to sleep, Arumin replied, "I hope not. We can still influence him. For one thing, he wants to be a hero. We can make him feel like one. Or not."

Brin made a noise in his throat. Arumin pictured him frowning thoughtfully. "I don't think he's that simple. There's more to him than we've seen."

"We'll watch him. If there's something worth knowing, we will know it."

"He tried so hard to take us on the north road. Maybe... maybe he's afraid to return to the prison."

Arumin smiled. "He and I have that in common."

"Me too," said Brin softly. "I thought I'd left there forever."

"We escaped once. We'll do it again. It'll be easier now that no one's alive to keep us there."

"No matter what, we have the Lady." Brin said this rhythmically, like an incantation. "Not that she's obligated to help, of course," he added, maybe hoping to avoid that argument.

Dozing, the bishop remembered something that woke him. Though his eyelids stayed closed, he could not help turning his eyes to Brin. "When the vines in the swamp pulled us under, did you see anything strange?"

Brin sounded half asleep. "I mostly saw your chest. I couldn't move."

Arumin recalled the vines cutting him and Brin's weight pushing him down. Dying, he had felt cares and consequences fall away. His part was done, and he had dropped all his planning and scheming, the details his mind exhaustingly clenched. Having set a great work in motion, he would move on.

The pieces of a misshapen life, seen anew, formed a picture of beautiful symmetry. He had not struggled. Though afraid, he had not cared.

The Goddess had appeared, glowing and radiant. Next to her, the physical world was astoundingly ugly. Every doubt in his life had been quieted.

Brin moved over and rested his head on Arumin's shoulder, breathing slowly. The bishop decided once again that they must sleep.

After Emberly's men dragged them from the water, the feeling of completeness had melted to nothing, like the remnant of a dream. His memory of Huire's appearance felt like a well-crafted lie. He tried to convince himself he had only seen Shada and mistaken her for a vision. But he would need a lot more convincing.

Someone had carried him to the doctor's wagon. Had he been alone, he might have lain there, trying to recover the dream until he died.

Brin's exhales warmed his chest. The tower was quiet. Even the forest wind sounded fainter.

Here they were, inexplicably alive and left to continue. To keep scheming.

Though speaking still hurt, he mumbled the answer to his own question. "Neither did I."

14

—·—

EMBERLY

IN ONE HAND, A candle. In the other, a bottle. A letter, pinched between fingers. A man made out of glass.

A voice stirred Emberly from his dream. "Brother."

He woke with a gasp and the anxiety of a guard who has fallen asleep on watch. He raised his head from the desk that filled much of his tiny room. Sleep must have claimed him swiftly after he sat to clean his pistol, which lay dismantled in the light of a stubby candle.

He cursed. He had meant to check on the company again before he slept. His imagination made wild promises of the chaos that had ensued in his absence.

"I was worried, Cyril," said Rayan behind him. "You were crying."

"Ha. I doubt that." The denial was a brotherly reflex. He hoped he hadn't been crying. The thought of someone walking in and seeing that curdled his blood.

"You'll believe what you want," said Rayan with an accepting sigh.

Emberly promised himself Rayan would not draw him into a fight. "How long was I sleeping?"

"Not long, I think. Time is strange for me. What were you dreaming about?"

The captain recalled the dream with instant, unnatural clarity. Like his other dreams recently, it could barely be called a dream. It felt as solid as Rayan's voice sounded.

He had promised to be rid of his brother, but until he learned how, these visits would continue. He dreaded hearing what Rayan would say about his dream. But if Emberly kept it to himself, Rayan would needle him until he broke down or they fought about something else. Best to get it over with.

He spoke warily. "I was in the prison's dungeon. The last night I visited you."

Rayan jumped at the chance to upset him. "Do you mean the last night before—"

"Let me *talk*. I won't have your interruptions."

"You brought me a drink that night. And that letter."

"They'd been rough with you." Angry at Rayan, the captain allowed himself a cruel chuckle. "You were floating in that little hole up to your neck. How did you keep from sinking?"

"I braced my legs inside the hole. You figure it out quickly when you're trying not to drown."

Emberly peered down the barrel of his pistol. Deep inside was a black smudge he'd been trying to reach when he fell asleep. If only he had his gun-cleaning brush. The company had left almost everything in the wagons. No one knew what state their supplies were in. Their food might be gone or ruined.

But right now, he mostly missed that brush. Nothing else could reach the smudge.

Trying vainly to reach the spot with a handkerchief, he said, "I had a right to be drunk. A certain commandant named Arumin was about to kick me out of the army. Years of mediocrity left him no choice, or so he'd said. I wrote to Charlotte to prepare her. She'd have to tell our boy something." The memory hurt, but the words kept coming.

Rayan said, "You weren't much for killing lazy convicts, even when ordered. You dreamed of military glory, but you lacked the stomach for the dirty work. I'd predicted it all when I learned you'd enlisted."

Emberly huffed. The moment he entered this room, he had known Rayan was here. His brother's mad bastard essence permeated the small space. Now their conversation was turning into a fight, as it always did.

"I've decided you're dead," he announced.

To his dismay, Rayan was not hurt. "Are you sure?"

"No. But until I know otherwise, I'll pretend you are. I can't go chasing ghosts."

"Indecisiveness weakens the spirit. That's why you always think you're a victim."

Emberly swore. Looking down the barrel in the candlelight, he saw that the pesky smudge rose above the curve of the metal. A lump. He tossed aside the handkerchief and attacked it with his finger, saying, "You always made up your mind quickly. And now look at you. A ghost."

"If I'm a ghost, you should envy me," said Rayan, his voice rising. Had he been standing there, he would have swept his arms wide. "A ghost is a spirit, unbound by time or space."

"That's not what I've heard about ghosts."

"While you are a prisoner. Of circumstance, of weak will, even of this accursed tower I helped to build."

Emberly sneered. "I'm no prisoner. I have the power to act and much to lose. What do you have?"

"Not much, I admit. If I'm a figment of your imagination, then I come and go as you please. I know what you want me to know, and I speak the words you give me."

Emberly closed his eyes. "They say this planet drives people mad. Maybe that's where these dreams are coming from—the planet itself. Maybe it sent Hulgar's dream too."

"No. This planet is a clever place, but here's a free bit of wisdom: these dreams come from something else. Somewhere else."

"How do you know that?"

"I don't. Just a feeling."

"What about you? Did this planet send you to visit me?"

"You've had all the wisdom you'll get out of me."

"Now that, I agree with." Emberly grunted in satisfaction. "If you've come from my own mind, what does that mean for me?"

"It means you should be locked in a cell. But if I'm not your creation... If I'm really a ghost..."

"Then my brother is dead."

"Maybe. But isn't that too easy? Too easy for our family, anyway."

Emberly glared at his gun. "Our family? Do you still call this a family?"

"You should be happy. Just down the road, at the prison, so many questions will be answered."

"You can keep your answers. I don't need them."

"Do you listen to yourself? Scrambling to avoid any scrap of responsibility for your choices."

Sweat rolled into Emberly's eye. "My choices led to—events—I didn't expect. I acted in ignorance, which is worse than doing nothing."

"I'm close to giving up on you, brother. You're the most spineless revolutionary who ever lived."

"I am no revolutionary!" Emberly shouted. The noise echoed through the tower. He tasted blood, and his heart raced. "You and the beasts you call friends taught me all I need to know about revolution."

"We're beasts, are we? What are you? A civilized man, I suppose."

"Yes! Absolutely damned right!" Emberly pounded the desk.

To the captain's pleasure, he felt Rayan simmer with anger. "We never finished talking about your dream. I want to know what makes a civilized man cry."

"Don't bother asking. You already know."

"I can guess. It's why I woke you just now. I remember that night too, and I knew you couldn't endure finishing that dream."

Emberly scoffed. "I've had every kind of nightmare you can imagine. I shouldn't admit it, but it's true. They haven't hurt me."

"Not this one, because it's real. I'll say it again: you don't have the stomach."

Emberly took several deep breaths. To calm himself, he thought of Charlotte. She was the only person Rayan liked too much to disparage. "I never finished writing that letter. Soon, everything changed, and there was no need."

"She wouldn't have been angry."

Emberly wished he had that contraband alcohol he'd been drinking in his dream. "No. She wouldn't have said a damned word. Just that little sad smile."

"It was you who deserved to be damned, consorting with demons like the commandant. Or the bishop, as they call him now. Goddess, do you remember his flute? How he'd stand up on the wall and play? He played well enough, but the same damned song over and over. If he meant it to torture the prisoners, well done. It probably drove the wraiths away from the camp."

Their conversation was following similar lines to the one they'd had in his dream, adjusted for time and events. They were even repeating whole sentences here and there. Maybe Emberly's dreams had gotten so thick with memory that his sleep could not contain them.

He closed his eyes and ran a fingernail over the pistol's carved grip. "When I first came to Caidfell, I thought it was the beginning. Of my career, of my life beyond you. And it was. But looking back, it feels like an ending too."

"You missed something, Cyril. This planet is a punishment, no matter who you are. The killers and rapists imprisoned here, who poisoned everyone around them, belonged here. They're dogs. Take it from me—I'm a dog. But you refused to kill them."

"They didn't all belong here. What about the political prisoners?"

"We were the worst of all."

Emberly gripped the neck of his imaginary bottle. "Why can't you speak plainly?"

"If you don't like it, you can always stop summoning me." Rayan sighed. "You have a gift, Cyril. Like me, you feel others' pain. But instead of using that to get what you want, you let others' feelings control you. You must change if you're to survive. You must become *less*."

"You sound like Arumin sounded when he told me I was finished."

"You should have gone home. Left this planet. Now it's too late—it's got you. We've got you."

Emberly froze. Only his arm moved, lowering the pistol into his lap. "'We'?"

Rayan's voice lowered conspiratorially. "Do you know what you said in your sleep? It was while you were crying, just before I woke you."

Determined to avoid distractions, Emberly parried the question with his own. "Are you telling me that you and the convicts are still alive? You're not a ghost after all?"

Rayan ignored him. "You said it that night too. We were drunk, you pouring drinks in my mouth while I treaded water. Then the shooting started outside. The screaming. I told you to stay with me. The empire's troubles weren't yours anymore. But you—you had a duty. 'I'm one of them,' you said. Then you ran from the room."

"It was true." Emberly emphasized each word. "It still is. The empire is my life. While terrorists like you and your friends are my enemies."

"Say what you will about me and my friends. You're one of us."

"Leave me. Get out, and never speak to me again."

"You're the best friend I ever had. You set me free."

For an instant, the captain lost his mind. He spun, pistol in hand, to face his brother.

He could never be fast enough. Swinging his dismantled gun at an empty room, he pulled the trigger. When he regained control, he clenched his teeth and tossed the gun onto the desk.

With nowhere to go, blood boiling, he sank to the floor.

If anyone heard the noise, no one came to check on him. He was still on the floor when his brother returned. Boots scratched the floorboards.

"I'm sorry," Emberly whispered.

Rayan's voice was gentle. "I shouldn't have woken you. Go to sleep. Finish the dream."

"I don't want to finish it." Emberly's voice went high like a child's. "You're right, I don't think I can."

"I'm too harsh sometimes. You can finish it, and you must. How else can you put yourself back together?"

"I can't. When I sleep, I see it all. I don't know what will happen. I'm close to something terrible, and these dreams keep pushing me..."

He felt Rayan's hand on his head. "I shouldn't have left," said his brother. "After all that's happened, you need me."

Emberly choked. "Stay if you like."

"I will. We're a family."

Emberly returned to his seat and found his pistol. He reassembled it, ignoring the smudge on the barrel.

As he worked, his brother spoke words of encouragement. Emberly nodded along, determined not to sleep. Soon, their conversation would turn sour, and they would fight again.

15

NOR

LEANING ON THE RAMP by the entrance, Nor dozed through the burning in his wrist and the aches in his body until Merin stirred. Jerking awake, the monk saw Merin on the floor in the corner, tossing in the candle-light.

Doctor Staubel sat by the suffering man, watching with his elbows on his knees. He had wiped most of the blue residue from Merin's skin.

Merin writhed, baring his teeth. Sleeping bodies filled the space between him and Nor. Soldiers lay on the floor and propped themselves against walls, using their cloaks as blankets. The animals huddled in the back. Everyone feared the stray blue flakes that kept turning up, having melted into thick liquid at nightfall.

Nor stood and looked for a path to reach Merin and Staubel.

Outside, a large weight hit the slanted doors behind him. He whirled as more impacts followed. None of the sleeping men stirred.

Nor leaned close to the doors. Beyond the pounding and the wind, he heard a far-off, dismal wail.

He called, "Hulgar?" More pounding was the only answer.

Emberly had posted Nor here to let Hulgar in despite the danger of opening the doors. Nor was not sure it was Hulgar doing the pounding, but the thought of abandoning the man convinced him to take the risk. He lifted the bar from the doors.

One door swung open before he could touch it. Instinctively, he jumped back and raised his fists.

A vast shape toppled through the opening, and the door slammed behind it. Hulgar staggered and slumped onto the ramp. Nothing else came through the door.

Nor stepped forward.

Hulgar stared with the eyes of a trapped animal. Blue flakes dotted his skin and clothing. "Brother Nor."

"Are you hurt, Private?"

Nor had to repeat the question before the man answered with a stiff shake of his head.

"We were worried," said the monk. "Where have you been?"

Hulgar gagged and sank onto his back.

Soldiers were waking up. Staubel reached the doors and kneeled to examine the private.

Nor asked, "What happened out there?"

Hulgar shook his head. He waved at Nor to come closer. When the monk crouched beside him, he whispered, "Brother Nor, I'm scared."

"Of what?"

"I hid in one of the troughs out there. I don't care about these." He smacked the blue spots. "I'm thinking about so many things. Too many. I had to be alone."

"When did this start?"

"Last night. You remember."

"Yes."

"But I didn't tell you everything. I keep seeing my wife in dreams. Last night, I watched her leave. She yelled and swore at me, but I couldn't hear her over my own yelling. I let her leave. I just wanted quiet." His lip trembled.

"Now, listen," Nor began. "It was only a dream."

"That's not what you said before."

Damn it. Nor cast about for a response. "Are you sure this was part of the same vision? These things can run together."

"It felt the same. A dream so real it was like a memory. She never came back. Someone took her, and I never found her." Hulgar's tears flowed.

"I see. I'm sorry. But why did you stay out there so long?"

"I felt peaceful. Never felt anything like it. The swarm piled on the ground, and I heard something calling."

His eyes glowed. "I prayed but not to Huire. She's left us, Brother Nor. You can't tell me otherwise. I know why she made me watch my wife leave—that was the moment I was damned."

He was speaking faster, and Nor struggled to keep up. He should hear what Hulgar had to say, but he must not let him talk himself into further delusions.

Hulgar continued, "We're outside Huire's kingdom, Brother. Other things rule us here, and I prayed to them."

Nor glanced around. If the others had heard Hulgar admit to heresy, Nor could not escape punishing the man. Fortunately, the private's voice was still low. Only Staubel was close enough to hear. Nor pressed a finger to his lips, and the doctor nodded, agreeing to keep the secret.

Now, to correct the delusion—if he could. "Hulgar, that's not true. Huire's domain has no borders. All other gods are her vassals."

Hulgar grimaced. "Bless you, Brother, but you won't survive thinking like that. I can feel that you're wrong. The peace I felt, lying there."

"But when you came in, you sounded scared."

The private's face fell, caught in tight, pale lines. "I went into the forest. To meet my new master."

"Hulgar, no."

"Oh, yes. I did. I walked, no idea where I was going, and saw a glow ahead. It was coming toward me, so I stopped and waited. The light was gold then red then green, every color. It was shaped like a man, a skinny little man, and its color kept changing. It swayed like a drunk as it came to me. I was peaceful still... so peaceful. But I wanted to run too."

Nor prayed this story wasn't real, and not only for Hulgar's sake. "What did it want?"

Hulgar shook his head. He looked on the verge of crying again. "I don't know. I knelt before it. 'I'm here,' I said. 'Show me your ways.' But it said nothing. Just stared at me, those dark eyes. Smooth hair all over its body. That peaceful feeling started to go away.

"Why would it call me out there for nothing? Did it hate me too? As well it might, Brother Nor. I'm the worst man you've ever met." He started crying.

Nor swallowed. "You were deceived, Hulgar. It's better that it didn't speak to you."

"What does it take?" the private demanded. He tore back the sleeve of his undershirt, displaying the clusters of burn marks on his arm—raised lines arranged like flower petals. "I showed it these. 'Don't they prove I'm sorry?' I asked.

"Its mouth was a slit. It twitched, but no words came out. Then it fell over. Stiff like a board, it fell to the ground. Its colors went away, and it turned all brown."

"It died?"

Hulgar might not have heard him. "I was walking away when I heard something. I spun around. I'm touchy like that since Gallobraith. Things were creeping around it, lanky, dark things. It had been a lovely creature, strange as it was, and seeing them surround it... it was worse than any dream."

He sounded haunted. "I wanted to find out who rules this world. But this couldn't be the answer. Couldn't be. Those things lifted their heads—and howled."

He sighed. "That howl, it struck me senseless. I don't remember anything more."

Nor struggled to understand it all. No one knew all the things lurking in this wilderness. The story was coherent enough to be true. But after Hulgar's outburst last night,

Nor had to wonder if this had been another dream. The man showed no embarrassment at his terror. If he was lying, he was doing it expertly.

Someone pushed past Nor, almost knocking him over. It was Sergeant Orund, who had been upstairs. He dropped to his knees next to Hulgar. "What's happened?"

After listening to a short version of Hulgar's story, he stood. "Let's wake the captain."

Though Nor longed to return Orund's shove, the sergeant was right. "I'll get him."

"Wait for me," Orund hissed.

The monk left without waiting.

He reached Emberly's door before Orund caught up. The sergeant leaned close.

"Careful, Brother Nor. It's dangerous here. If you don't listen when I speak, who knows what might happen?"

Inside, Emberly was talking urgently to someone. When Nor knocked, he fell silent.

The door opened to show Emberly alone in the room. "What is it?" the captain snapped.

A moment of resounding silence passed. Emberly would brook no discussion of what they had heard, so no one mentioned it. "Hulgar's returned, sir," said Orund.

Emberly picked up a few small items from the desk. "Where was he?"

"In the forest. He claims he met some kind of spirit, a thing that changed colors."

Emberly's hand stopped while reaching for his pistol. "Did it hurt him?"

Orund eyed the captain doubtfully. "Luckily, no, sir. Hulgar may be confused."

Emberly glared. "I'm surprised to hear you talk that way, Sergeant."

"Sorry, Captain. I meant to say, I don't think Hulgar was deserting us."

"Words like 'confused' can ruin a soldier's career if they're used wrong. Don't use them if you're not sure. Brother Nor, did you talk to Hulgar?"

"Yes."

"Do you still believe his dream in the fort was a divine vision?"

"I do," Nor lied.

Orund cut in. "Shouldn't we wake the bishop, Captain?"

"Not yet. Until we know whether Hulgar is insane or inspired, we won't judge him publicly."

Emberly marched past them, and they followed. Nor walked behind the others, afraid to turn his back on Orund. He had lied to save Hulgar, and now Hulgar would have to live up to his lie. He hoped for the man's sake that his dreams were truly from the Goddess.

Downstairs, Merin was getting worse. He had stopped thrashing, but the effort of holding still showed on his face. His breaths were huge and leaping. When Staubel spoke to him, he responded only by shaking his head.

The doctor had found no injuries on him. Whatever the swarm was doing to him, it was happening under his skin.

"We'll make him comfortable and wait," said Emberly. "It's not over, I'm afraid."

Downstairs, everyone was awake. The captain questioned Hulgar carefully.

On second listen, Hulgar's story was nearly impossible to believe. Nor prepared himself to contain Emberly's anger. If the captain decided to shoot or hang the man, Nor would have to stop him somehow.

After all, it was Nor who had convinced Hulgar his dream was a prophecy. In trying to protect him from his superiors, he had led him astray. Of course, Hulgar might be lying to hide an attempted desertion, but that seemed least likely of all.

Finally, Hulgar might have lost his mind. He would not be the first person Ronia had driven to insanity.

Emberly's final question surprised Nor. "Could you find this clearing again?"

Everyone was listening. Hulgar closed his eyes and said, "I... don't think so, sir. Before, I followed where *it* led me. But it's gone now. It won't say anything." He squeezed his eyelids together as tears ran down his cheeks.

The captain nodded thoughtfully. He put Hulgar in the doctor's care and watched him walk away.

Orund opened his mouth to speak, but Nor cut him off. "Why did you ask if he could find the place?"

"For one thing," said Emberly, "I kept him talking because I hoped, if he was lying, I would see it."

"What will you do with him?"

The captain's face darkened. "I don't know yet. If I need your involvement, I'll tell you."

There was little need to speculate. Emberly was simple: to him, Hulgar was either lying or mentally unstable. Caring for him in that state would take resources that Emberly could hardly spare. He already had holy men and the caretaker to protect.

Unless Nor intervened, Hulgar would never leave Caidfell.

He remembered the wailing sound. He could still hear it outside. His ears, though battered by the explosions in Ronia, were still sharper than the others'.

"Emberly, stop! I can hear those things he saw. I hear their screams." His call reverberated in the quiet room.

The captain asked, "Are you sure? I can barely even hear the wind." The question implied he was willing to believe. Maybe he hoped Hulgar would be vindicated.

"His people have a knack for it, sir," Orund reminded him. The sergeant had been watching Nor since their words outside the captain's room. "Sharp senses. It's one of their gods' gifts." He snickered. "Look him in the eyes and guess another."

Rarely had Nor been more aware of his foreign-looking eyes than now. His rage at Orund rushed back even as he strained to control it.

Emberly defused the sergeant's comment with a withering stare. He said to Nor, "If you can hear the creatures through these walls, then you can follow the sound."

Nor nodded.

"Put on some extra clothes," the captain continued. "We're going outside."

"Why?" Nor was too stunned to feel properly frightened.

Emberly strode to him and leaned in close. Anyone watching would have thought he was scolding Nor. Instead, he said in a low voice, "I believe I know what Hulgar saw. I hoped he was wrong, but if you hear them, it must be true."

"What?"

"They're called wraiths. We don't know much about them. But we need to find them, quickly. I don't know what they'll do, but we'll be better off that way than if they come to us."

Nor nodded.

A series of cries broke the quiet of the hall. Merin's suffering was overwhelming him.

16

NOR

One of the waytower's doors opened bit by bit. The blue residue had piled onto the doors like sticky snowdrifts, making them heavier.

Five men left the tower. Nor was the last to go. Outside, the swarm had fixed to the ground ankle-deep, and its millions of half-melted flakes shone under the moon.

The alien screams Nor had heard, which he hoped came from Hulgar's alleged visitors, were trailing away. They disappeared before he could be sure of their direction. He reported this to Emberly, and the others grumbled under their breath.

Before the captain could answer, someone spoke. "There." It was Private Robir, whom Nor had met by the campfire before Hulgar's first nightmare. Nor recalled the private staying out of his fight with the soldiers.

Robir pointed to the tracks Hulgar had left when he walked away from the tower and, later, returned at a run.

His boots had torn pieces from the gelatinous mass of the swarm, and the swarm had not yet flowed into the holes.

Emberly nodded. "We'll go that way and see if Nor hears anything."

In the tower, they had covered themselves head to toe with mud and ashes. These came from a pair of hidden wells the captain uncovered in the floor. Lifting the hatches, they had drawn water from one and ashes and dirt from the other.

At Emberly's instruction, they had mixed the wells' contents and slathered themselves. The thick mud hung on them in clumps, masking their natural odors. Emberly hoped this would help them go undetected.

Now the captain looked at each of them. "Quiet from here on."

They set off on Hulgar's trail, Emberly in front, Nor after him, and the others behind. The holy men did not see them off, and neither did the caretaker. Nor wondered if Arumin knew about this odd mission. The bishop would not take kindly to being overlooked.

The other two men, Borna and Elisar, worried Nor more the jungle did. From what Nor had gathered during their argument, they put little value on the lives of non-Ronians. The two men had said nothing since Sergeant Orund had called their names.

Orund's choice could not be coincidental. He had seen Borna and Elisar argue with Nor. Now he had picked them to follow Nor into the forest. His other choice, Robir, would be unlikely to interfere with whatever happened.

To Nor's dismay, that left Emberly as his only likely ally. He doubted the captain would help murder someone under his command. He would find that beneath him, even if that someone was a nuisance like Nor. But what if the others threatened to kill him too?

They followed the tracks across the road and into the trees. Blue residue stuck to their boots, gathering dirt and leaves as they walked.

Before they left the tower, Emberly had told them what little he knew about the beings he hoped to find. Few living people could claim to have seen them as closely as Hulgar. Now and then, convicts laboring in the jungle had disappeared. Others blamed the disappearances on "wraiths."

The guards, protected by the convicts' fear of the jungle, let the rumors run wild. Eventually, they had come to believe in the wraiths too. The jungle was deadly and ever present, and it was natural to give it a form and a name.

The plan Emberly presented was vague. They would cautiously approach the wraiths and negotiate for the Ronians' safe passage through the wilderness. The captain suspected some convicts still survived at the prison—a great many convicts, if he feared them enough to contact the wraiths. He did not say what the Ronians could offer in exchange or how he planned to communicate with the creatures. From Hulgar's account, they were not talkative.

As the group walked, the wind rose. Shadows swayed.

Nor listened. The screams began again, hoarse and wheezing. There were many voices. He wondered how the others could miss the sound. Thankfully, they were downwind of its source.

They were moving in the right direction. Nor took the lead. Their path twisted among clusters of wiry trees that played with his senses of time and distance. He tried to memorize distinctive whorls of trunks or knotted branches, but there were too many. Luckily, the walk was not long.

As Nor led them uphill, the wind reached terrible new crescendos. The men bent low and covered their heads to ward off thrashing branches. The screams also grew more powerful.

He saw a glow. The trees ahead reflected strange colors. The screams faded again, but now he could follow the light. The others finally saw it too.

They crept to the edge of the clearing, hiding behind trees. The wraiths had once again taken up their unnerving song. Its volume was heart-stopping.

A fire roared in the center of the clearing. Whipped by the wind, the shuddering pillar of flame almost reached the treetops. A small hill of wood formed its base.

On its far side, many wide eyes shone red in the flame. The creatures' heads and bodies were wisp-thin shadows. Each stood several meters from the fire. As one, they turned away from it to face the jungle. Their screams dragged on, each creature bending wildly backward as it expelled the cry.

"Goddess help us," whispered Robir.

The captain gestured menacingly for silence.

Nor seconded the prayer. They were witnessing the perversity of a world created by an alien god.

Outside the ring of ghostly figures lay a row of large, rolled leaves. Each leaf was wrapped around an oblong shape as tall as a person.

Nor shivered. These wraiths' strangeness defied all he knew. But they must be human. Back when the gods expanded through the cosmos, transforming worlds for human habitation as they went, they had also transformed humans in countless ways. Thus, they had created the Changed.

Never in the gods' voyages had they discovered beings as intelligent as humans. They found primitive life forms, but these often had not survived the gods' changes to their native planets.

This was an important moment. Nor must remain calm, for the others' sake if not his own. He should not assume the wraiths were wicked. To many Ronians, Nor's eyes made him alien and frightening. Until he knew more, the figures in the firelight were simply offworlders like him, the tainted children of lesser gods, entitled to adoption by Huire. He must always hope.

The screams—now he thought of them as a song—faded again. Still, Emberly watched.

One of the wraiths walked toward the wrapped leaves, dropping to all fours as it moved. As Nor's eyes adjusted to the light, he saw that its front limbs were longer than the back ones and ended in hands.

It grabbed the stem of one of the leaves and dragged it toward the fire. There was something heavy inside. Nor's suspicions deepened.

The figures gathered around the leaf as the song died away in their throats. The smoothness of their motions suggested great strength and control. Nor struggled to see the details of their appearance. They merged with their background, whether fire or shadow.

The one who had brought the leaf crouched and pulled it open. As it unfolded, the leaf broadened to a teardrop shape that framed its contents. It was the corpse of a wraith.

Unlike the live wraiths, it was clearly visible. Its upper body was robust and muscular, its waist and back legs small. Its head was blocked from view, but its body was covered in smooth slate fur.

The song ended. The wraiths stood still as wind thrashed the trees. They leaped on the corpse and tore it to pieces with tooth and claw.

They moved with almost invisible quickness. Some ripped muscle and skin from the limbs. Most dove for the belly, tearing it open and shoving their heads in or pulling out innards and devouring them with lustful urgency.

The air left Nor's chest. His companions mouthed curses and prayers.

The wraiths in the clearing seemed far away and his earlier thoughts foolish. Who was he to offer the Goddess's forgiveness?

What he saw fit no story that ended in redemption. As a boy, he had seen his clan's dead burned on pyres, delivered to the lords of the sky. They would join their ancestors in eternal war to rule the heavens. It was the only natural way.

The Ronian way, laying their embalmed dead underground to await the Goddess, had sickened him at first. Though he accepted it as Huire's will, the thought of being forever hidden from the sky still brought him creeping dread.

Every culture Nor knew of took one path or the other—burial or cremation. But here was something new, a third way. This was primal theft, robbing the dead of passage to the next world. Only lunatics or starving people would do it.

Nor did not look away. The act of watching was both painful and life-affirming. His heart raced, and not only with fear.

Voices spoke to him, those of old Cadmon, of Arumin, of every holy man he had known. Their message was simple: it cannot be. This abomination must be stopped.

The wraiths ate the dead man quickly. They piled his bones in the open leaf, and the wraith who had opened it dragged it away into the trees, returning moments later.

Nor thought of the bones left in the woods, rotting and picked over by vermin. In the clearing, other bodies awaited the same fate.

What could he do? He was a sworn instrument of the Temple's will, and its will here was obvious. But acting to stop the wraiths could cause his companions' deaths and the failure of their crusade. What would become of the Temple? And hadn't the Lady already showed she would protect them?

He should wait for Emberly to act. But Emberly, infuriatingly, was doing nothing.

The wraiths' song began anew. It was slower now, and the voices were less harmonious. The first wraith pulled another leaf toward the group. This bundle seemed lighter.

Nor froze, unable to think. He watched as the song faded and the wraiths opened the leaf.

When he saw what lay inside, he jumped to his feet. His companions did the same. The body in the leaf was small. Under a tangle of black hair, blood, and dirt was the face of a child.

A Ronian boy.

Hands on their weapons, the three privates marched forward. Emberly stopped them before they stepped into the clearing.

Robir, Borna, and Elisar looked incredulous. They clearly could not fathom leaving the dead boy to be eaten.

The wraiths' meal would begin any second. Nor rose and whispered, "Emberly, let them go."

"No. Not yet," the captain hissed viciously.

Nor pointed. "If they eat that boy, he may lose his soul."

"We will show ourselves when I say. Not before."

Robir pushed in, speaking in the same hushed tones as the others. "Sir, you can't ask us to just sit here."

"I'm not asking anything. I am ordering, and you will obey."

"We are Ronian. If we don't save that boy's body, we're nothing."

Emberly's rage was an awesome sight. "You took an oath. You are what I say you are."

Nor said, "And the boy? What is he?"

"We've lost him already."

The boy had been thin and undeveloped, not yet a teenager. Wounds covered his body. He was too young to have been a convict at the prison camp.

"Of course," Nor said. "Your empire didn't care about him before he died. Why would it care now?"

He never learned what Emberly would have said to that. As he spoke, the wraiths sprang onto the boy.

Borna and Elisar both turned away. Robir and Emberly watched the things eat. Robir's face was contorted; Emberly's was dull.

Nor watched too. He had let the boy come to this.

"That child couldn't have lived on Caidfell alone," said Borna. "Did you see his wounds?"

For Nor, it was too familiar. "There was a battle."

Emberly nodded. "Some convicts must still be alive. They've been fighting with the wraiths."

The first wraith dragged away the leaf that held the child's bones. He returned with another leaf.

Robir said, "Well, he's gone. Captain, you got what you wanted. We have no business here."

"Listen," said Emberly. "We're going to wait until they've finished with... this. They're in the middle of a meal. Their blood is boiling. When it's over—"

Nor had lost all patience. "All you know is based on rumors. We can't befriend them. We look exactly like the convicts they are fighting. If you won't stop this 'meal,' then we must leave before they spot us."

"We have to warn the others," added Robir.

The wraiths gathered around the next bundle.

"Fuck this," said Borna. He rose to his full height. "I'm leaving. You can hang me."

He grunted like someone had punched him in the gut. He pointed to the clearing.

The leaf was open. Inside was a member of their own company. Nor did not know his name, but he had gone missing in the swamp. He was pale and filthy, and his clothes had been stripped away, revealing a gash down his face and his chest.

"It's Keesin," someone whispered.

The man was dead, but that would soon be the least of his troubles. The wraiths would devour his body, leaving him no vessel in which to meet the Goddess. He had taken the crusaders' vow, so his sins were forgiven. But dwelling in Huire's presence might feel hollow if she could not embrace him.

Everyone was quiet. Robir, Borna, and Elisar exchanged meaningful looks.

Emberly guessed their plan. "Stay where you are, or I will shoot you."

Robir could endure no more. His calm veneer disappeared. "What will we tell the others? That we let them eat him?"

"Be silent, or you won't live to say anything."

Elisar muttered something inaudible and likely treasonous.

The song of the wraiths had died away again. The figures stood around the corpse of Keesin, waiting for the unknown signal to feed.

The body moved. The man tilted his head and twitched his torn lips. He was alive.

Nor gasped. The three privates raised their rifles and advanced. Emberly blocked their path, hand on his saber's handle. He and Robir stood nose to nose as they cursed and threatened in whispers swept away by the gale.

Borna shoved the captain. Emberly's hood fell as he staggered. He pulled his sword from its sheath in a fiery arc and swung its point from soldier to soldier, driving them back a step.

Without thinking, Nor stepped in front of the blade.

Aiming its tip at the monk's heart, the captain paused, twitching.

"Let them go," said Nor. He must have been more scared than he knew, as the words came out in a whisper.

Emberly might not hear him, but the meaning of his action was clear. The captain's expression was opaque as he slowly lowered the blade.

Nor was exhaling in relief when Emberly punched him in the jaw. The others gasped as he fell. Through bleary eyes, he saw Emberly standing over him. The captain had drawn his pistol and pointed it at the men.

"Back up," he said.

Robir stared at him, eyes wide. Keeping his eyes on the captain, he offered Nor his hand.

Glad for the help, Nor stood and leaned on Robir.

Emberly watched, alone among the trees at the clearing's edge. At any second, they would hear the wraiths eat a living man.

Turning away, Nor came face-to-face with Borna and Elisar. They had been waiting, and both of them stared at him. He had forgotten Orund's threat. If these men really meant to kill him right here, he certainly could not count on Emberly's help.

They all jumped as gunfire rumbled over the trees. It came from the direction of the tower. Piercing screams followed.

The wraiths whirled toward the noise. The five men stood directly in their sight.

Nor caught a last glimpse of many pairs of eyes touched by flame. When the wraiths charged, they were too fast to see.

17

—·—

SHADA

SHADA GAVE UP TRYING to sleep and opened her eyes to the pitch darkness of her tower room. The bishop had left her a lighted candle, but she had put it out when she lay down to rest.

She reached across the floor for the candle but found nothing. A wave of fear struck her, and she swept her arms, searching the rough boards. The dark felt like a void in which she was floating, and she wanted proof that the world still existed.

Her hand located the candle, but she had no way to light it. She stood up and groped for the door. By luck, she guessed the right direction and reached it. The hallway was dim, but when she opened the door, its light was like a flood. With relief, she saw her room, dusty but solid, and the Lady's box near the far wall.

The box was closed and inert. Since Shada's moment of defiance, the Lady had not emerged or spoken. Though her presence had been overwhelming, her absence was worse. For all Shada knew, she might emerge from the box and banish Shada from her presence. She might demand a new caretaker. She might never appear again.

There was nothing to do but wait for morning. Shada left the door ajar and lay down again. With her ear to the floor, she felt the man approaching before she heard him.

She closed her eyes and turned her face up toward the ceiling. Whoever it was, he entered the room with soft, deliberate steps and closed the door.

Her mind spun at the implications of the sound. He had not simply come to check on her. She lay still and tried to breathe evenly. The footsteps stopped.

A boot nudged her leg. "On your feet, Caretaker. You are not asleep, and you will want to stand for this."

She opened her eyes. A lantern in his hand lit the room. He was one of Captain Emberly's soldiers. She had seen his face before but not noticed it. He watched her intently.

Rising slowly, she tried not to think for fear she would panic. There were only a few likely reasons for his visit.

He gazed at her without speaking, his stance casual. Though she was terrified, his aloof study made her angry. "State your business," she said.

"My business need not harm you, Caretaker. Though it may harm you greatly if you wish." He placed the lantern on the floor to one side, freeing his hands. "I ask only that you stand aside and stay quiet."

"You mean to take the Lady?"

"I am going to take her." The man's voice tightened with nerves or annoyance. "Go and stand against the wall."

She was between him and the box. He was large enough to move her without much trouble, but he had not. She stayed where she was. "Who are you?"

His casual manner returned. "Nobody. Just a pair of boots from the ranks."

She took a guess. "The people who bombed Ronia—the Unheard. Are you a friend of theirs?"

"That's not your business." His voice tensed again.

Shada kept talking. Surely the Lady would wake up soon, and she could deal with this intruder like she had the trees in the swamp. She would fight for her own safety if not Shada's. "What about the men dressed in black—the ones who fought the Unheard while we fled Ronia? Are you one of them? That's it, I'll bet. But why are you stealing the Lady now? You won't survive in the jungle alone, not even on the road."

The nervousness he was trying to hide burst into the open. "If you hope to live, Caretaker, you should not wish to know these things." He placed a hand on a knife that hung from his belt. On his other side hung a pistol. "Get out of my way, or I will open your throat."

Her chest ached as her heart pounded against her ribs. "That would be unwise," she told him. "The Lady won't let you take her."

"You're wrong," he replied. "I am her caretaker now. But I won't serve her like you. I'll be her master, and she will protect me through whatever perils I meet, human or otherwise." He reached under his shirt collar.

"I can see you're nervous. Maybe you're in a hurry. I don't blame you. What happened in the swamp would panic anyone."

He drew the knife with his free hand and pointed it at her face. He grinned, a forced and brittle expression. "You don't want me as a friend, girl."

She answered, "The swarm might still be outside. We're trapped here. Your only hope is that the Lady hasn't bothered to come out yet."

"She will wait. And one who commands her cannot be trapped." He replaced the knife and pulled a necklace from under his shirt. On its thin chain hung a small vial. Its thick glass contained a fine, dark powder. He raised his voice, which shook a little. "She is listening, but she senses danger. Don't you, Lady? Your kind protect only themselves."

"Her kind?" asked Shada, momentarily distracted. "Who are her kind?"

"Quiet," the man snapped. Grabbing the stopper on the vial, he observed the container's contents with something like affection. "Hear this, Lady. I am holding a small bottle. Inside is something you haven't seen for a long time—if ever. But your Goddess knows of it, and she fears it. So do any other gods who still live."

He stepped around Shada with the cagey speed of a cat. He approached the box warily, a step at a time. "Lady, you know what I speak of. Unless you want it released into the world, you'll stay in your little cage until I tell you otherwise."

The box remained inert as he picked it up and put it under his arm. "I was planning to lock us in here for the night, me and my two hostages. Then I could give you to Emberly in exchange for a riding beast. But I think not."

He bounced on his heels, his nervous energy palpable. He looked on the verge of an outburst. "I need fear nothing. I'll leave tonight—but first, there's someone I must kill."

He faced Shada and sighed. "What shall I do with you?"

Shada leapt at him.

She had little chance of success but for one thing. As she bent her knees to lunge, an eruption of gunfire shook the building.

The man's eyes flashed toward the floor. She grabbed his free arm, meaning to immobilize it, but he stepped back and wrenched it away.

Shada fell to her hands and knees. She knew the blow was coming but was not ready for its force. His fist struck the back of her head, and she fell on her side, not quite believing any of this. Her arm went numb. Her foot kicked the lantern, and it shattered against the wall.

She looked up as he pulled his knife. "So be it, Caretaker," he said.

She rolled onto her stomach to get up. He kneeled on her back and drove her to the floor. With a butcher's calm he raised her head by the hair and brought the knife across her neck. Feeling its cold, she begged for the Lady's help with a wordless scream.

The knife left her throat. She covered her face, overcome with gratitude, and lay on the floor. The man shouted, and a plague of insects buzzed. Where the lantern had broken, something crackled.

She peered over her hand. The man reeled and coughed. The Lady had shaped part of her cloud into a hard, sharp edge. She was cutting him all over, too many wounds to count. She sliced any limb or extremity he raised to defend himself.

The vial rolled away, close to the growing fire. Its glass was too thick for a short drop to break it. But flame might be different.

The small fire already vomited smoke. Its heat stung Shada's skin where she was closest to it. Meanwhile, her blood collected on the floor. The man's knife had cut her neck a little.

She might have lain there, dreaming, had his screams not jostled her.

Through the bitter smoke filling the room, she saw him thrashing on the floor. His shoulder lay in the fire, which licked him greedily. The Lady was holding him there, against the floor. Soon, he stopped struggling and fell silent.

Shada watched dumbly. Her head still rang from his blow. The fire spread across the dry floorboards. Waves of scalding heat brushed her, burning her eyes and lungs. She dropped to the floor, coughing, and squeezed her eyes shut. She crawled forward, and the air got hotter. She crawled the other way and hit a wall.

The fire's glow pushed through her eyelids. It came from everywhere. The door, if it had ever existed, was hidden far away. She was a bit of meat on the bottom of an oven, boiling, peeling, turning black.

Though overwhelmed, she refused to be a prisoner even now. She started crawling again. She would keep moving until she could not.

18

BRIN

By an evil twist of fate, Brin was the first to sense that something was wrong. He woke up next to Arumin and stood without knowing why.

All sounded quiet in the tower, which meant little given the thickness of the walls and floors. Maybe the aches throughout Brin's body had awakened him. He was surprised his stinging wrist had let him sleep at all. Together, his injuries hurt enough that he forgot his headaches now and again.

In that dark room, the nightmare his life had become was omnipresent. There was no Ronia, no life before this crusade, no world at all outside this room. His recent brushes with death were veils draped over his eyes to torment him.

Hoping to prove there was more to life than this tiny room, he lit a candle and sneaked out the door. The hallway greeted him, reassuringly solid. But he wanted still more proof. Though the waytower still existed, maybe the larger universe outside its doors had vanished.

He could not go outside until morning, of course, but he could check on the sleeping company downstairs. At least he would know that others were trapped in this little hell with him.

The ground floor was dark except for a few scattered candles. The men were still and quiet. Brin stopped on the ramp and scanned the room. Dozens of people, all pulled into one mad scheme together.

He recalled the night attackers had invaded the temple on Ronia. The Lady had killed two effortlessly, manifesting a pair of sharp appendages to stab them both through the head.

It was an image he brought to mind whenever he was sure she was a fraud who was leading this company to its doom. Her power was real, and that meant she was real.

Arumin was also real. One could say what they would about his blind faith, but he had tried to save Brin in the swamp, calmly accepting death when it seemed inevitable. Though part of Brin resented him for agreeing to this mad journey, he was no fraud.

Crowded as the room was, it was easy to forget people were missing. The death that had missed Brin by a hair in the swamp had claimed almost everyone with him.

Among the dead was Cay, who had noticed Brin the way men and women alike often did. Brin had thought little of the flirtation, but the man's loss hurt. It was one fewer pair of arms to shelter him from danger. Cay's death meant death had inched closer to Brin.

Coming to the ramp's bottom, Brin wondered what he had expected to find. The others existed, all right. One of them out there, snoring and farting, was the man sent to kill him if he failed in his mission. His unbelievable mission to kill the gods.

So Sylvana had promised him. She whose delightful, sexy cynicism had matched his so well he'd grown attached to her. Who, of all people, was so seduced by a set of mysterious, powerful strangers that she had given her life for them. For their cause, whatever nonsense it would surely turn out to be. If he lived to find out.

His assassin lay in this room, slumbering and vulnerable. If only—

A shape crept through the gloom. A chill tickled Brin's spine, and he stifled an embarrassing gasp. He had retreated a few steps up the ramp before he realized the shape was moving away from him, toward the doors.

He let out a breath then held in another as the shape's importance struck him. This must be why he had awakened. To see this. Whatever was wrong, it was before him now.

He surprised himself by setting out toward the doors, keeping his steps quiet and carefully stepping over sleeping men. If they were all trapped here together, then what was good for one was good for all. He would make sure his hunch of danger was imaginary.

The figure approached the doors. When it passed through the glow of a candle, Brin stopped and peered. He was not far behind the figure, and he knew its face. It was Private Merin, the astronomer who had managed to get himself covered in the swarm's flakes.

The man walked hunched over, as if into strong wind. He had recovered remarkably. When Brin last saw him, he could do little but lie, shaking, in the corner. Private Hulgar, the swarm's other victim, still lay there, his massive shape recognizable from across the dim room.

Brin caught up as Merin reached the short ramp that led up to the tower's doors. Two guards lay there, asleep. Whispering Merin's name, Brin touched his shoulder.

Merin whirled and slapped the hand down. "Stay away!" His shout was a clap of thunder in the silent room, startling even him. He snapped his head this way and that.

Brin tamped down his surprise and annoyance. He tried to speak kindly, as a holy man should. "Going for a walk, soldier?"

"You won't understand."

"Understand what, Private?"

"It's leaving. I can't... I can't let it..." Merin turned toward the doors, which had been closed and barred after Hulgar returned.

People were waking up. The guards stirred and raised their heads. If Merin meant to open the doors, Brin might need help stopping him. Merin was a slight man, but he was a trained soldier, and Brin was not known for his strength.

Brin used his favored trick when called to help or advise others. He acted as a better priest than him would act. "Let me help you find 'it.' We'll find it together as soon as you're feeling better."

Merin sank into a defensive crouch. He shook his head sadly. "You don't know what this is like."

"Tell me," said Brin.

"What is this?" Lieutenant Roark's icy voice cut through their exchange. The officer's long silvery hair was down.

The private stepped toward the doors. Brin cried, "Merin, don't."

Roark knew all he needed to know. He pointed his pistol at Merin. "Has it all been too much for you, Private?"

Merin glanced at the gun and returned his attention to the doors. He put his hand on the wood as if feeling the outside.

Roark continued, "Life in the fort should have hardened you. But this planet is where they send the dregs of society."

"Lieutenant," snapped Brin, "that's not helpful." Brin had been sent to this planet once too. In a way, Brin was from this planet.

"This is a military affair, Father," said Roark. Raising his voice, he addressed the room. "Anyone who wants to live, point your weapon at Private Merin."

Everyone was awake. Some were sitting up, others standing. They hesitantly reached for their guns and raised them, a glinting candlelit forest. Behind them, the beasts lowed softly.

Gaping, Brin wondered if this could all be a dream. Seeing the door guards scamper out of the line of fire, he hurried after them.

But someone else stepped between Merin and the guns: Sergeant Orund. "Lieutenant," said Orund, "he's sick, sir."

"Desertion," Roark said, "is a special crime. Only the weakest commit it. What we do to them reminds us of the cost of betraying our brotherhood."

"You can't do this," pleaded Orund. "You can't."

Cursing the impulse that had brought him downstairs, Brin interjected, "Lieutenant, be reasonable."

Doctor Staubel spoke from nearby, his young face pale. "This is not how we do things, sir."

Unmoved, Roark said to Orund, "Step away from Private Merin unless you wish to die with him."

Merin examined the doors' surface, rubbing his hands across the grain.

Sergeant Orund called for all to hear, "He's done no harm! That blue cloud poisoned him, but he's fighting it."

"He should have fought harder," said Roark.

Brin summoned the courage to intervene one more time. He blurted, "I declare that the Goddess forgives Merin for his sins."

Roark took aim. "She is more forgiving than me. Ready, Merin?"

Brin's bandaged wrist stung. His head throbbed. He smelled something acrid. He looked around miserably, wishing for Emberly, for someone to make things safe. The room had gotten darker.

He did not see Hulgar attack Roark. Only dim chaos and shouting, then the giant soldier lay atop the lieutenant, pinning him to the floor, fists pumping. Others wrestled to pull him off while the rest wondered where to point their guns. "Open it!" Hulgar shouted.

A faint red glow from somewhere—the hatch, up the ramp. That acrid, toxic smell again. Brin's thoughts converged. "The tower's burning," he moaned, his voice pitiful, lost in the din.

Things happened quickly.

First, a weighty thump behind him. Merin had lifted the bar from the doors and dropped it. He shoved one open with desperate strength and fled outside. The door landed with a boom in the open position.

Wind blasted through the open doorway. Brin reeled at the night's fury, which felt strong enough to carry them all away. It blew out all the candles.

"No, Merin!" yelled Orund.

Facing the wind, Brin glimpsed the outside world. It still existed after all. The light from inside the tower fell on the trees. Their leaves and branches were bare. The night was still. The swarm was gone.

Everything changed for Brin. The world outside the tower was a real place, a place of comfort, of solid ground.

Away from this crusade and this band of lunatics. A place that wasn't on fire.

Brin ran for the open door, fleeing this awful tower and everyone in it. He passed Orund, who was on the ground. The sergeant looked up, wide-eyed, at Brin and shouted something. Maybe he was hurt. But Brin could spare no time to help.

It had all happened in an instant. Then he realized his danger. He dove to the floor as gunfire erupted. Shots struck all around the door, too late and scattered to stop Merin.

Deafened and panicking, Brin scrambled up and out the door, running for his life against the wind that was trying to push him back inside.

A short distance outside, Merin lay on the ground, his arms and legs spread wide.

Something held him down. A shadow come to life.

A flurry of motion. Something knocked the wind out of Brin, who found himself on the ground.

More shadows pulled him to his feet, stretching his arms painfully. They were everywhere, and they held him with strength he dared not challenge.

All at once, they glowed. The woods were full of their lanky, primal shapes lit softly like reflected starlight. Their eyes were dark pools.

Brin said the only sensible thing. "I surrender."

19

EMBERLY

THE INSTANT EMBERLY REALIZED the wraiths had seen them, he knew what he had to do.

They charged on four legs, moving so fast the eye caught only flashes and afterimages. Emberly had time to deliver two simple commands. "Drop your weapons! Get on your knees!"

The order went against every instinct for self-defense, and his men might not obey. For Emberly, throwing away his gun despite the oncoming attack was one of the hardest things he had ever done. But he did it, so he might survive.

Guns fired around him, and he realized not everyone would.

The wraiths struck in a storm of teeth and muscle. Thrown backward, Emberly hit the ground and rolled. Claws tore at his face and arms but spared his eyes. He heard anguished screams.

The tide battered him, and he could only wait and endure it. When it ended, he opened his eyes. Claws dug into his arms, pulled him to a sitting position, and held him in place. They stabbed a little deeper each time he moved, and he quickly learned to hold still.

Two of the wraiths crouched in front of him, silent and inscrutable. They began glowing, like Hulgar had said. It seemed impossible to be so near them. Their closeness made them real. They had not blinded him, thank the Goddess.

That left him alive to witness his plan in tatters. He had not relished the plan to begin with—the price of success was so grim, the wraiths were so unpredictable—but it had been something.

The fight, if one could call it that, was over. He needed to learn who had survived. His job held him together, as it often did.

He dared not turn his head for fear of the wraiths' claws. So he turned his eyes, scanning the edges of his vision. A dark-red patch stained the dirt to one side.

The wraiths watched him, still and wordless as spiders. He was too scared to look squarely at them. His breathing quickened, and he wondered if he was dying. For a time, panic took him away. He paid little attention to his surroundings until a pair of boots ground the dirt in front of him.

A man stood there, a Ronian. He had walked among the wraiths like he was their friend.

He was middle-aged, his face timeworn under a wild beard and mane. He wore a skirt sewn from some other garment and a shirt with its sleeves torn off. He stared at Emberly. "I wasn't expecting guests."

Emberly's voice was hoarse. "We mean no harm. We came to speak to *them*."

"Them?" The man glanced around and seemed to remember the wraiths. "You must know something I don't."

"Are you their friend?"

"No. They have no friends, not among offworlders. But they haven't killed me yet."

"They must like you."

The man's thoughts had moved on. "You've made them nervous. They were in a ritual frenzy when you sneaked up, or they would have noticed you sooner. I'm surprised they spared any of you."

"So am I," Emberly admitted.

"But they only spared you for the moment. If you want them to keep on sparing you, tell me how many soldiers you have."

"Are my men alive?"

The man touched his beard. "Some."

"Who?"

"Emberly," said Brother Nor with a grunt of pain.

"Anyone else?"

"One more," said the stranger. "Yellow hair. I don't think he likes me."

"Traitor," spat Private Robir.

The man smiled, amused. "Ronia betrayed me first. I keep the company I must." He told Emberly, "Your other two men disobeyed your order to surrender. They died fighting. I suppose the empire would be proud."

He frowned. "While we're on the subject, why did you surrender?"

When he looked at Emberly, his eyes gleamed. He might have recognized the captain. He must have been a convict after all.

Emberly again felt something like panic. This time, it was different, a surging pressure in his heart. "Just a feeling," he said. "I've heard rumors about the wraiths."

He hoped the stranger would leave it at that, but no such luck.

"Have you?" said the man. He let the silence stretch. "It's true they have a strange streak of mercy. They're more than animals, regardless of what you've heard. It troubles them to kill a helpless enemy, though they often kill him anyway. When Ronia invaded this planet after the prison fell, the wraiths were known to kill everyone at an outpost except the patients in the infirmary."

"Ronia... invaded Caidfell?" asked Robir. "An invasion? What are you talking about?"

A smile touched the stranger's lips. "Must be a secret. If your leader here knows, I'm sure he'll tell you."

The hair on Emberly's neck stood up as his fears were confirmed. A man like this, who had lived through the prison revolt and the times that followed, would know damaging secrets and wouldn't hesitate to mention them. The captain would face difficult questions from his men.

The stranger dropped the subject for now. "To business. No travelers have come out of the gateway since Ronia's troops left. Your group is too well armed to be anything but soldiers. Can I assume those guns we heard a few minutes ago were also yours?"

The pressure in Emberly's heart had grown to massive proportions. Members of the crusade were forbidden to reveal their journey's purpose to outsiders. On the chance they encountered surviving convicts, they had a cover story. They would claim to be a force sent to offer the convicts amnesty.

In the light of day, the story was flimsy at best. No one had seriously thought it would be needed.

He did not reply immediately. His answer should not come too easily.

The man shook his head. "They must have been your soldiers." He chuckled. "Who else has that many guns?"

He glanced downhill, in the direction of the waytower. "It doesn't matter now. The enemy has them, which means they're done for."

"What do you mean, 'the enemy'?" asked Emberly. "I thought they'd been attacked by wraiths." It was useless to pretend ignorance. If everyone at the tower was dead, there was nothing left to hide.

"They probably were. Just not *my* wraiths. Ronia's wars have come to Caidfell, my friends, and everyone is taking sides. We'd better be going now, or they'll find us."

The wraiths moved as one. Emberly gritted his teeth as clawed hands pulled him up. Other wraiths gathered Borna and Elisar's remains.

As they forced Robir to stand, he growled, "Are we going to the prison?"

"Certainly not," said the stranger. "The prisoners still live there, but they're no friends of mine. That place has turned upside down. The prisoners are now the wardens. The luckiest people in your company are the dead ones."

He smiled grimly at Emberly. "That's how it goes around here."

It was that smile, not any before or after, that told Emberly he was looking at his brother. Recognizing Rayan, the pressure in his chest exploded and faded with a slow rumble. It had not been panic but the growing recognition that he'd been avoiding.

The things he'd done to avoid this meeting. He'd risked contacting the wraiths, tearing apart the company, angering a Ronian bishop. And the things he'd been prepared to do...

He heard Rayan's voice often but never saw his face. He had assumed Rayan, if he still lived, would look like Emberly remembered him plus a decade. He had not anticipated how profoundly the jungle would shape his brother. Rayan was filthy and hollow, a creature of the wilderness.

Yet now that he had recognized Rayan, Emberly wondered how he had failed to know him sooner. His expressions and gestures were unmistakable. How frightened Emberly must have been of Rayan to avoid knowing him. He could not imagine what Mother and Father would think of their sons overlooking each other like that.

But he need not imagine. Rayan recognized him. That smile said it all. Rayan had toyed with him his whole life, and no matter where Emberly went, he would always find Rayan there, waiting.

20

— · —

SHADA

RETURNING TO THE WORLD was cruel. Shada woke to pain that reached from her throat into her chest. She tried to lie still, but the wagon's bouncing would not let her.

She heard a noise. A young soldier lay in a cot next to hers. It was Private Merin, the astronomer. Between them knelt Father Brin, murmuring a prayer.

"What…" she began then did nothing but cough for a while. Putting a hand on her throat, she touched a small bandage in the spot where her attacker's knife had cut her. Her head ached where his blow had landed.

Brin had jumped a little when she spoke. He replied softly, "I'm glad you're alive, Caretaker. What would we do without you?"

His greeting lacked spirit. He looked pale and haunted, older even. She had hardly spoken to him before now. Usually, he followed in Arumin's wake, his piercing eyes assessing everything for its use. He struck Shada as profoundly selfish. She wondered what had happened to produce such a change in him. That raised the question of how long she had slept.

Her throat stung from her first attempt to speak. She was not yet brave enough to try again. Filling much of the wagon's interior was the unconscious form of Private Hulgar, whom Shada knew only by sight. On the floor sat the Lady's box. Its door hung open, displaying its empty interior.

Shada sat straight up and gasped, "Where is she?" Coughing less this time, she looked around for her boots. Her voice was hoarse.

Brin put a finger to his lips. "They don't know about her."

She lowered her voice, grateful to speak with less pain. "Who doesn't know?"

He gazed at the sleeping soldier. "Some people no one expected to see again. The convicts from the old prison camp."

Shada tried to stand in the cramped space. Dizziness nearly toppled her. Compromising, she waddled to the wagon's small window on her knees, refusing the priest's offer of help. She rose, braced herself, and looked outside.

The company's wagons rolled along a jungle road, probably the same road the crusaders had traveled the day they arrived. Some of the Ronians trudged beside the wagons, unarmed. Others sat huddled in the vehicles. A larger group of shabbily dressed men and women held them captive, walking alongside with weapons that included the crusaders' own rifles.

Some of the Ronians' faces were desolate. Others showed violent terror like that of trapped animals. Shada lowered herself to the floor. Brin had gone back to prayer. When he stopped for a moment, she asked, "What happened?"

His sigh was less annoyed than resigned. "Something attacked us at the tower last night."

Throat still stinging, she attempted a longer sentence. "You don't know what it was?"

"The men call them wraiths. I didn't think they were real. All I know is that there were a lot of them. They captured the company and handed us over to the convicts. I'd never believe it if I hadn't seen it."

Shada leaned against the wall. A thought struck her, and she cried through the pain, "Where is Nor?"

Brin's eyes widened a little at her disproportionate concern for the monk and her familiar use of his nickname. She blushed. But his answer was grave. "We don't know. He, the captain, and a few others left to find the wraiths and speak to them. We haven't seen them since." Maybe he realized how grim that sounded, because he added, "But apparently, they weren't gone long before the wraiths arrived. They might have returned after the convicts took us."

Shada breathed deeply and clung to that hope. She had no idea why the captain would wish to contact those beings, but if that contact had gone badly, it could have caused the attack on the tower.

"Speaking of that, keep your eye on these two." Brin's voice was flat as he nodded at the two soldiers. "They betrayed us. Let the wraiths in. We'll be lucky if our own men don't knife them before they can face proper justice."

Shada stared at Merin and Hulgar. Blue crust dotted the skin of each man.

Traitors? She could not imagine what they could gain by turning the company over to enemies. There must be a slim possibility that it had been an accident.

Then again, another traitor had tried to steal the Lady last night. Privately, Shada had taken to calling him Boots, since he'd mentioned his boots, and naming him something silly made his memory a little less terrifying. She would have to tell the others about him. There could be other spies in the company.

But her immediate duties lay elsewhere. "What's happened to the Lady?"

"I don't know," he answered. "The waytower burned down."

That would be the fire her attacker had started. The Lady could not have been destroyed by it. She could fly, slip under doors, go wherever she wanted. Shada didn't know if the Lady could be destroyed. All of which made her disappearance stranger. It was Shada's duty to find her, all the more so if Shada's rebelliousness had driven her away.

Shada had to get more out of Brin, who seemed eager to stop talking. "Hasn't anyone seen her?"

The priest shook his head, distracted. "I haven't. Maybe someone else has. The convicts are always watching, so no one's had much chance to talk. A lot happened last night, but I only saw pieces of it."

She nodded impatiently. "Go on."

"The wraiths surrounded the tower. But it was burning, and they mostly kept their distance. Then the convicts arrived—they must have befriended the wraiths somehow. Most of the company was still in the tower, but everyone would have burned inside it if they hadn't surrendered.

"I heard one man disappeared completely. You were the last person they carried out. Someone found you in a hallway."

His voice held a question. She answered, "I don't know what happened to me. Maybe the Lady saved me." The

Lady had certainly saved her from Boots. Mere hours after the Lady had stated her reluctance to intervene in the company's affairs, she had been forced to help Shada again. Now she had gone.

A surge of fear took Shada, and she stood up. "I've got to find her." Talking was getting easier.

Brin's mouth opened as he searched for words. "You can't go out there."

"I have to. I'll ask the others if they've seen her."

The priest stood and leaned in close. She wondered if he would physically stop her from leaving. "Don't call attention to yourself," he whispered. "When we get to the prison, you won't want these people to notice you if you can help it. Not for any reason."

"I've got to try," she replied. "I've got to do something while I have a chance."

"There is no chance!" His intensity startled her. Without trying, she was getting close to whatever had so upset him. Part of it must be simple fear for his life, but that was not all.

She waited and listened, expecting him to go on. If he proved himself too distracted to reliably judge danger, she would feel like less of a fool for leaving this wagon.

But instead of saying more, he knelt to return to prayer. Only when she kept watching for a few minutes did he speak again. "I didn't want to shock you after what you've been through, but I can see it's no use." He paused self-consciously. "Here it is: the convicts despise Ronian soldiers. When we get to the prison, unless there's another miracle, they'll probably kill all the soldiers in our company. They may spare me and you if we're lucky."

Chills ran down her spine. She had known death was possible, of course, but Brin's reminder made it real and made her feel powerless.

She wanted to keep talking more than ever. That could make what awaited down the road feel farther away. "Father Brin, may I tell you something?"

He nodded. Since he did not seem to care about formalities, and the two soldiers slept on, she sat on the bed near him and spoke, keeping her voice low to save her throat. Coughing here and there, plowing on despite the pain, she told him about her dispute with the Lady: how Shada had disobeyed her, talked back when corrected, and challenged what she was told. She told Brin this might be why the Lady had disappeared.

She wished she was talking to Nor, though one hardly had a right to choose in these matters. She did not fully trust Father Brin, but he listened without complaint.

Until she told him about Boots. He grew still as she related the attack. When she told him Boots had meant to kill someone before he left, Brin grunted and bent as if he was concealing a punch in the gut.

This surprised her. She had assumed her attacker meant to kill her, but perhaps Brin thought otherwise. She was deciding whether to broach the subject when a voice startled her.

"I keep hoping it was a dream," said Merin. He stared into space, talking to no one in particular.

Brin did not answer. After Shada's story, he had turned to stone.

Shada filled the silence. "If you mean last night, I'm afraid not."

He raised a hand and examined the blue residue on it. "I can't feel it anymore. Its effect has faded, thank the Goddess. But I remember how it felt. What it made me do."

Shada watched him pull a speck of blue from his hair and roll it between his fingers. She asked, "Did that stuff hurt you?"

Merin's face reddened, and his mouth twisted. Patches of blue residue stood out on his face and in the corners of his eyes. "Yes, though not how you might think. It led me to betray everyone."

Shada moved and sat on the floor in front of him. "It must have given you no choice. Did it cause you pain? Torture you?"

"In its own way." He did not meet her eyes.

"You couldn't help it, then."

"Who can say?" His voice became wistful. "I'd never imagined a feeling like it. Once I felt it, I would have done anything to feel it again."

Shada gulped. She tried to put her hand on his, but he pulled it away. "It's still on me," he said, his lip trembling. "Its effect fades with time, but you don't want to feel it even once."

"Well, it's over now," said Shada. "You can try to forget it." The words were inadequate, and she wished she could take them back.

He shook his head but replied, "Yes." His voice was dutiful. "We'll get to the prison soon. You and Father Brin should tell the convicts that we're holding you by force. If they think you're friends of the Ronian army, they won't be kind to you."

"Do you think they'll kill you?" Her head ached where her attacker had struck her.

"I've tried to think of reasons why they wouldn't. They could hold us hostage to force concessions from Ronia. But the empire won't bargain with the likes of them."

The wagon's interior was suffocating. Shada said, "But they didn't kill us last night. So there's hope."

"A quick death may not be what they have in mind. Especially for the bishop." Embarrassment flashed over Merin's face as he glanced at Father Brin, kneeling between them.

Shada, too, had forgotten that Brin was more than an assistant to Arumin. Everyone knew it, though of course no one mentioned it to them. Their relationship apparently brought them no trouble, maybe because of the bishop's power.

Brin must have sensed the others watching him. If he blushed, it was overshadowed by his fearful pallor. He sighed, a despairing release of tension. Maybe he was glad someone had mentioned the real cause of his distress.

"The bishop knows his duty," he told them in a low voice. "To spread Huire's word. He must simply do it. If he does, all else is secondary."

Shada tried to sound hopeful. "When I see him, I must tell him about my trouble with the Lady. He'll know what to do."

Brin swallowed audibly and nodded. "Yes. He'll hear your confession. He's wiser than me."

"And he needs to know about the man who attacked me. He might know what it means."

Brin closed his eyes. A moment later, he nodded.

He fell into opaque silence. The others joined him for a time, listening to the bouncing and creaking of the wagons. Soon, Brin moved to pray next to the sleeping Hulgar.

After a while, Merin spoke. "We need the captain. But I dread seeing him after what I did."

Shada put her hand on his knee, and this time, he did not protest. She was comforting herself as well as him. The Lady was gone, she did not know why, and she could not begin to search for her because she was trapped in this wagon. Her throat still itched and stung. Meanwhile, all of them were rolling toward an unknown fate. For the moment, she felt beaten.

"Well," she said. Not wishing to leave it there, she added, "Nor and the captain are very determined men."

"Yes," Merin replied. "They have courage. More than some of us."

Shada remembered a cold knife on her throat. "They do. Then again, how much difference can courage make in a place like this?"

21

EMBERLY

EMBERLY STOOD AT THE bottom of a great red bowl. The floor was split into sections that curved up on all sides to form a rim several times his height. Above was the open sky. Realizing he was inside a giant flower, he swayed, took a few steps, and fell.

The surface he struck was soft as a mattress. Many thick stalks stood clustered at the center of the flower. Topped with cones of startling green, they all leaned in reverence toward an emerald-colored spire in the center.

Emberly could not remember ever feeling so peaceful. He easily accepted the strangeness of his surroundings. As an insect, his only obligations were to wander inside the flower, live briefly, and vanish.

He laughed, and the sound surprised him. He remembered nothing after the wraiths took them from the clearing. Now he was here, in a world of fantasy that he did not want to leave. He had utterly failed in his mission, but it did not matter. It had never mattered. The joy and relief of that thought struck him with almost physical force.

The truth was wonderfully simple. Things were only good or bad if he decided they were. If he refused, the universe would be at peace.

It was sad that he had taken so long to learn this. But sadness was not real! Epiphanies accumulated until he grinned and kicked out his legs like a child, cracking the bits of dried mud still clinging to his skin and clothes.

"Cyril," said Rayan.

Few people used Emberly's first name. He rolled his head until he spotted his brother standing on the bowl's rim, where the petals suddenly stopped rising and curved downward. Yesterday, the sight of Rayan would have summoned emotions of terrifying power. But in his new state of acceptance, it barely stirred him.

"Hello, brother." When he spoke, the intervening years were nothing.

Rayan smiled. He dropped onto his back and slid down the petal to the center of the flower, where the stalks gently stopped him.

He stood with a lazy groan. His younger self shone through in the sound, and Emberly laughed again. It was a blessing to be free of old grudges.

Rayan strolled over to him.

The captain placed his hands behind his head and took a deep breath. He wondered what his brother would do. Help him to his feet? Stomp his head in?

Rayan did neither. Settling to the ground, he lay on his back next to the captain. As he did, he scanned the rim of the flower, but he saw nothing that interested him.

They stared at the same sky. Rayan said, "Brother, I'm not surprised to see you. Does that make me insane?"

The captain shook his head. "I'm not the person to ask."

Rayan laughed. "You're the sanest person I know."

"It's been a long time since you knew me." Emberly smiled at how simple the truth was. "I've changed."

"No. I can already tell that you haven't."

The statement sent ripples through the quiet of Emberly's mind. He wanted to be believed. "It's true. I've heard your voice. You've been speaking to me, more and more often."

Rayan stared at him.

"Have you heard my voice too?" Emberly asked hopefully.

"I suppose I have. I had a feeling you and I were not finished. Time never rid me of it."

The captain's heart quickened. He met Rayan's eyes. "Was it really you? Were you visiting me across all that distance?"

Confusion flashed across Rayan's face and disappeared before Emberly could think much about it. His brother was slow to answer. "Of course."

"Goddess," Emberly gasped. His eyes grew misty. "I thought I was losing my mind."

Rayan's eyes fixed on something. Several wraiths perched on the flower's rim. In the sunlight, they appeared as a dark-gray mass tinged with blue.

The captain spoke in a hushed voice. "How did you speak to me? How did you manage it?"

"I don't really know," admitted Rayan, sounding frustrated and deep in thought. "It's this jungle. Things flow here. Some places are like that. They're clever—they have wills of their own. Maybe something here lets you travel to far-off places. Really clever places might take you places without you ever knowing it." As he spoke, his voice faded with wonder. "Do you know what I mean?"

He had never sounded so spiritual. Emberly looked at the man he had so recently hated. Mischief took hold of him.

"No," he said squarely and fell back, roaring with laughter.

Rayan's face hardened, and he drew his knees to his chest. The laughter had stung him, and the newly carefree Emberly felt demonic glee. In a lightly mocking tone, he asked, "How, in all the worlds, did you fall in with these creatures?"

Rayan glared. He would try to take his power back. "I'll tell you, but only if you tell me something first: what are you doing here, Cyril?"

Emberly squinted at him. "Don't you remember? If we've been speaking—"

"I do. Of course I do!" Rayan snapped. "But... why did you leave that tower and come into the jungle last night?"

The captain gazed at the sky, where his thoughts lay open. "I told you. I was searching for the wraiths."

"Why, for all that is holy? Did you want to die?"

Emberly chuckled. "I don't think so. I hoped to convince them somehow to let us pass through the jungle so we could get off the road. The road leads to the prison."

Rayan nodded knowingly. "You hoped to avoid the prison. How did you know the convicts still live there?"

"I didn't," Emberly answered slowly. "But I was afraid they might."

"But... your company was heavily armed. Surely you didn't fear the prisoners that much. Weren't you afraid of the wraiths in the jungle?"

"Of course."

Rayan's eyes narrowed. "Were you hoping to avoid battle?" He was in sight of something he wanted, and he would push until he got it.

The pressure was unpleasant, and Emberly answered to make it stop. "No. I hoped to avoid you."

That silenced Rayan for a minute. Then he sat up, eyes alight.

"Of course. Of course you did. You didn't know what I might say." He smiled, and Emberly saw the predator that hid below his skin. "Here you are, with a little army of your very own. Who would have thought?"

Emberly's stomach ached.

"Perhaps you were right, Cyril. You have changed. You must have if Ronia made you a leader. You've figured out how the world works, haven't you?"

"Where are my men?" Emberly asked. The question nagged at him.

"The wraiths have the two we captured with you. I'm afraid they devoured the man you tried to rescue. As for those at the tower, the convicts have them. You'd better forget about them, brother."

The captain sat up, his peace shaken.

"Have they hurt Norhim and Robir?"

"I can't say. It's out of my hands."

The captain stood up and turned in a circle. The flower's only clear exit was a round hole someone had cut in its floor. Dizzy, the captain staggered as he said, "I have to see them."

"They can wait. If there is damage, it's already been done."

The top of a ladder poked through the hole, lying against its rim. Emberly swayed as he marched toward it.

Something moved in the corner of his eye. A wraith descended the slope with masterful agility. As it moved, its fur turned soft red like the flower.

It was upon him in no time. He tried to step back and raised his fists, but his movements were slow and stupid in comparison. It grabbed his face and drew him in. Its eyes gaped like pits as it exhaled a thick musk into his mouth and nose.

It smelled like clay, grass, and body odor. He relaxed and studied the fine, tight fur on the wraith's face. It pulled away, and he watched it return to its companions.

It was beautiful, how it moved. He laughed, blessed for what he had seen.

A hand fell on his shoulder, and he looked into Rayan's smiling face. His brother embraced him. The captain hugged him in return.

When they let go and faced each other, Emberly said, "What's happened to me? I don't understand."

Renewed serenity lay over him, an unmovable haze. Through it, he heard Rayan say, "They are drugging you, brother. I'll bet you don't even care, do you?"

"No." The plain syllable amused the captain.

"I never needed any such potion to make you follow me," said Rayan, his teeth bared in a grim smile. For a moment, the predator surfaced. "But I'll take no chances. Not now. By the time you're free of it, there will be no going back."

"I'd like that. I want to understand." Emberly put his hands on his brother's shoulders. "Is all of this real? Flowers are supposed to be small. Don't you know that?"

Rayan's smile faded. He shook his head and patted Emberly's hands. "I'm sorry, Cyril. No, flowers don't have to be small. Not here. This is a land of giants." He gripped Emberly's fingers. "Soon, you'll understand why I'm doing this."

The thought seemed to excite him. "Maybe you'll even be *glad* I did it. Can you imagine? You'll understand me. For now, know this: you were fated to come here, and your arrival changes everything. We're going to be kings together. We'll make things as they should be. Come with me, and I'll take care of you, as I always should have."

Emberly nodded. His happiness was unshakable. He would accept whatever came. It didn't matter, and it never had.

⸺⬦⸺

A land of giants, indeed. After descending the ladder for a long time, they walked among enormous trees that twisted and collided, diving below the soil and surfacing to race for the sky. Trunks as wide as streets met in knotted burls. Rayan approached a doorway in one of these.

Wraiths were everywhere, on the trees and peering out from the underbrush. Not one of them spoke.

Something blotted out the sun. Nearby, many trees met to form a trunk prodigiously larger than any other. Even in Emberly's reverie, its girth shocked him.

"I told you," Rayan said.

Emberly could not remember what Rayan had told him. His brother had been talking since they left the giant flower, but the captain was too tranquil to pay attention.

Luckily, Rayan repeated himself. "The biggest trees are like kings. They rule their kingdoms and watch over them."

"One of them sent a swarm after my company," Emberly said. A thought threatened to curdle his inner peace, which had already faded a little. "My men might all be dead."

"You're an invader here," said Rayan. "It's a miracle anyone survived. You were among the thin, tangled trees, yes? That was a different kingdom. Its ruler is one of the most feared. Its territory encompasses the prison, sadly for those who live there."

They climbed, using rough handholds, to the burl's entrance. When they passed through the eye-shaped bole that formed the doorway, Emberly blinked in darkness.

"We'll wait here until our eyes adjust," said Rayan. "I've learned to endure the dark. The wraiths caught me building a fire once—I've never been closer to death."

"They don't like fire?"

"They hate it. And they hate us. But they respect it as a destroyer, using it for pyres like the one you saw. They're like us in a way. They hate what they fear. You should be familiar with that feeling."

Emberly felt his brother's smile, though he could not see it. "What do you call them?"

"The wraiths?"

"Don't they have a proper name?"

"They don't even have words as far as I know. That wailing you heard is the only noise they make. They speak in other ways. They're an odd strain of humanity."

Emberly recalled the wraiths' silence as they'd held him down. He'd been scared to death, though he could no longer fathom what that felt like.

His eyes adjusted. The faint light from the doorway fell on shelves that covered the walls. The burl was hollow, and the shelves stretched from the rough floor to the invisible heights overhead.

"They speak in other ways," Rayan repeated, pointing to the shelves. They were lined by objects, each shaped like a ceramic vase that had collapsed as its maker shaped it.

"I don't understand," Emberly said. He buzzed with pleasant curiosity.

Rayan lifted one of the crumpled objects gently, as if the mere weight of the air might crush it. Its surface was a rippling, faded pink. Rayan presented it to Emberly. "Open it slowly."

Starting from the top, Emberly peeled away part of its velvety surface.

"That's enough," Rayan said. He tipped the object so light spilled through the opening.

Peering inside, Emberly saw delicate stalks, pistils, and filaments. The object was a closed flower, a smaller specimen of the kind he'd woken up in.

Rayan held it to his nose and inhaled. He moved it close to Emberly's face. Its scent was dusty and unremarkable.

"This room holds only one collection," said Rayan, closing the flower. "The tribes serving the other trees must have ones like it."

"What is it?"

"What did you smell?"

"Not much." The captain chuckled.

"I agree. To us, it's nothing. But to them, it's an entire world. The scent stored in this flower contains what you or I might learn from a book. From a shelf of books."

"What does it say?"

"I have no idea," Rayan answered. "Things we wouldn't care about, most likely. The path followed by a single insect on a single day a century ago. The sounds and feelings of a moment when one of their warriors killed another."

Emberly's mind could not penetrate this idea. "Why?" he asked, hoping the question was appropriate.

"I can only guess why they care about these things." Rayan smiled. "It's good to talk to someone. I look forward to being among people like us again."

The buzz in Emberly's head was slowly receding. His thoughts were increasingly his own. "What people? Where are we going?"

Rayan was about to place the flower on the shelf. He turned. "Don't you remember our agreement? We made it as we walked."

"I forgot," said the captain.

Rayan's composure slipped. "We're going to the prison," he snapped. "The person who rules it stole it from me and controls it with cruelty and violence. I fled here to save myself. You will help me take it back. For us."

"My soldiers are there."

"Of course. That's why you must come. If we do it right, with a little help from the wraiths, the takeover will be quick and simple. We both know the prison inside and out. We're the only chance our friends have—assuming I still have friends there." Rayan put the flower down a little too hard, and it collapsed. One of the dried petals had split down the middle.

Emberly watched the flower topple with dreamy slowness. A shadow appeared in the doorway.

"Are you listening, brother?" Rayan demanded.

Emberly heard him as if from a great distance. He nodded absentmindedly.

"Cyril, I need you," said Rayan. "Events are moving quickly, and the story of this land is being written. The revolution has come. The one I always talked about."

Emberly smiled. "Yes. I remember that one."

Rayan's face was wild. That face had frightened their parents. "I need you to be the man you were on the night you set me free."

Emberly's inner quiet shattered like thin ice hit by a rock. He put his head in his hands.

"I never stopped hoping," his brother continued. "I knew you were no slave, no imperial lapdog. I taught you all I could, and you proved me right. You unlocked the door to my cell."

Emberly's eyes grew foggy. If he tipped over, the fall might break him to pieces.

"You were a hero!" said Rayan. "The prison fell, its evil ended, thanks to you. Do you realize that?"

Emberly choked. "I didn't expect you to free all the prisoners. And what you did afterward..."

"I don't believe you. You unlocked my cell *because* you expected it. For a short time, you faced what your empire really is."

"I just wanted to free you. I couldn't watch you waste away in that cell anymore."

Rayan looked down and said, "That warms my heart. I almost wish it was true."

The dam had burst. Emberly babbled. "How could you...? All the guards you murdered. I knew all those men."

"It wasn't me. Once I freed the other prisoners, I couldn't have stopped them. They collected a debt they were owed."

"Goddess. If I had known…"

"Would you honestly take it back? From what I can tell, the false story we told of your bravery made you a hero in Ronia."

"Yes, I would take it back."

"You sound desperate, brother. In the final tally, hundreds of people were freed from brutal servitude. Many soldiers of a tyrannical empire died. And we returned you safely to your masters, telling them you had fought us so bravely we couldn't bear to kill you."

Emberly closed his eyes. "No one in Ronia knows how the revolt started. But some have guessed there was a… traitor. The rest of the convicts—do they know it was me who freed you?"

"No. Your secret is still a secret. They only know I protected you because you were my brother."

Tears tickled the captain's face.

"You've hidden your betrayal for a long time, Cyril. Your life has surely depended on it. I can't remember all that we've said during my… visits, so forgive me for asking: have you never been tempted to confess your crime?"

Emberly closed his eyes. "It's not about temptation. It's about necessity. People need me."

"Well, it's for the best," said Rayan. "Look at what's happened. Fate has brought you here, at *my* moment of need. You and I will take back my kingdom, and it will be ours. What do you say?"

"Thank you for saving me. It feels perverse to say it, but I'm grateful."

"I need more than your gratitude, Cyril. For now, I need your help too. Do I have it?"

Emberly shook his head. "You always did the thinking, Rayan. I don't know what to say."

Rayan stepped back and spat. "Is this what you've become? Is this why they made you a captain—because you asked for permission? Maybe Ronia should be pitied instead of hated."

He was quiet for a while. Then he said, "They've got your men. I know where they're keeping them."

Emberly could hear his own heartbeat.

"The wraiths have learned how to talk to us. They speak to each other using smells their bodies produce. Our noses are feeble compared to theirs, but they've learned to make scents potent enough to affect us. They can make you feel happy, sad, anything. They can't control your mind outright, but they can influence you. Do you understand?"

"Yes." Emberly wasn't sure he really understood, but he didn't want Rayan to be angry.

"They've worked on it for years, as a weapon to use against us. They test it on any Ronian prisoners they take. They did it to me, and I nearly lost my mind."

He frowned. "I convinced them to spare you. But your men..." He let the sentence trail away.

Emberly suddenly understood. He shut his eyes.

"What do you think of that?" asked his brother.

Emberly shook, and his chest rose and fell. "You're torturing them."

"The wraiths are, yes. Don't you have anything to say?"

The captain bent over and cried out. "I don't know what to say! Tell me!"

The shadow in the doorway slipped inside, moving toward the captain. Rayan held up a hand, stopping it.

Emberly's fingernails dug into his scalp. "What have you done to me?"

Rayan's face twisted. Roaring, he raised a boot and shoved the captain to the floor.

He marched back and forth for a moment and petered to a listless halt. Hands on his hips, he stared at the ground. "I planned to guide you for a time. Keep you under the wraiths' spell so you'd have to listen to me. So when your head cleared, you'd understand what we'd done and why."

Emberly raised himself to a sitting position.

Rayan came and put his hand on the captain's head. His eyes were far away. "Why can't I go through with that plan? After all the things I've done. Why can't I do this?" He waved dismissively. "Lie down, Cyril. Rest."

Emberly obeyed with gratitude. He lay near a wall. In his exhaustion, even the solid wood floor welcomed him.

But he could not sleep. Several times, Rayan stopped the wraith from approaching him. Finally, it tried to rush around Rayan, but he jumped in front of it and lunged at it. To Emberly's amazement, it darted from the room.

Rayan turned to him, looking deeply weary. He waited and watched the captain from across the room.

After a brief restless interlude, Emberly sat up and stared at his brother.

A few minutes later, he jumped up. He tackled Rayan in a few strides.

"Where are they?" Emberly howled. He punched Rayan in the face, shook him, and heard his head strike the floor. "Where are they?"

Rayan smiled sadly. "You can't escape, Cyril. The forest is endless."

Emberly hit him again. "I can escape if you're my hostage."

"The wraiths have no love for me," said Rayan with a choked laugh. "They've only kept me alive to use me.

Even so, those guarding me had to fight off others who wanted me dead. And those are just the ones who dared to approach me or you. Offworlders are nightmares to them. Our presence is an abomination. Their superstition is so strong it's kept them from attacking the prison."

Emberly took a knife from his brother's belt and held it to the man's chin. "We're leaving. We're still going to the prison, like you planned. But we'll go now, while Nor and Robir might still live."

"Cyril, we'll be lucky if the wraiths allow us to leave at all, especially after I chased that one away. By freeing you from their potion, I've altered the plan, and they won't like it. We need their help."

"And it seems they need ours. They want you alive. Me too, or I wouldn't be here. Why? What use are we to them?"

"We are their chance to be rid of an infection threatening their world. They will no longer tolerate offworlders dwelling on Caidfell outside of their control. Unless you and I take over the prison, acting as their agents, every Ronian on this planet is doomed. That means your friends and mine. To do it, we must combine forces, and that will take both of us. Your men won't follow me, and the convicts won't listen to you."

"You sound like a valuable hostage to me. Get up."

They rose. Emberly kept the knife at Rayan's throat.

Rayan sighed. "If you insist on hauling me around at knifepoint, you'll get us both killed."

"We can't stay here." Emberly stopped to think. "This would be so much easier if only I could trust you."

"You don't have to trust me, Cyril. Just remember that each of us is lost without the other."

"And you remember this: I wish I'd left you to rot in that cell."

22

NOR

Nor hung naked against the lumpy bark of a tree, his arms spread wide and his feet brushing the ground. The bark draped in loose rags over his bruised neck and shoulders, dripping with sap that had dried and stuck him to the tree trunk.

The trunk was thicker than he was tall. It lay on the ground, curving around him to form an enclosure that he could not see over. There was only one exit, a tunnel through the trunk at ground level, as tall as a wraith and guarded by two of them.

The wraiths were everywhere. Those on the ground appeared rust colored like the wood, while those atop the enclosure had made themselves pale like the sky. He jumped when he saw one moving close to him. He wondered if it had touched him while he slept. If he could not believe his eyes, he did not know what to believe.

He had to get out of here, but the dried sap would not budge.

Someone whispered. It was Robir, who hung nearby, crooked as if they had tossed him there carelessly. His body, like Nor's, was bruised and filthy.

His whispers sounded menacing. His dry lips clicked in a rhythm, like a chant. Maybe he was praying to the Goddess, but it sounded like no prayer Nor knew of.

The air grew thin, and he gulped it in alarm. Something was coming for all of them, human or not. It was coming through the trees, under the ground, beyond the sky.

He called to Robir to stop chanting before he summoned whatever it was. Robir twitched and whipped his head around, squinting as if he could not see. He resumed his chant with new fervor.

Nor convulsed in the grip of the yellow sap. He shouted at Robir again, even wishing in his panic that the wraiths would silence the man somehow.

The wraiths watched them both. The stillness and silence of the audience made Nor wilder. The fit of panic passed, but another came, and another. Between them, he panted, wondering how many he could withstand.

He did not see the approaching wraith until it put its hands on his face. Its little mouth flexed, and a jet of air entered Nor's mouth and nose.

Its breath was thick with the smell of mold and stagnant water. Nor's terror left him instantly. He sagged, breathing easily again. If the sap had not been holding him, he would have fallen on his face. Another wraith had breathed on Robir, and the two returned to perch near their fellows.

Nor's fear subsided, leaving him momentarily lucid. He called to the wraiths, "Why are you doing this?"

The still forms gave no answer. Perhaps they were as confused by him as he was by them. Nor reminded himself the wraiths were as human as he was, though he could not imagine why an alien god had twisted people into such forms. They must be doing this for a reason. An experiment, perhaps.

"Monk," Robir muttered.

"What?" Nor prayed he would not spend his last minutes of life conversing with a lunatic.

"Pray with me," Robir said.

Surprised, Nor obliged. "Holy Mother," he began.

And emptiness froze his insides. The words were mere noises. Their power and meaning were gone.

He dropped into an abyss. It swallowed him, Robir, the wraiths, even the Goddess. It had waited underneath them all.

"I can't help you," he said to Robir. Anything he said might infect the private with his emptiness.

"Do you feel it too?" asked Robir. He looked as dead-eyed and helpless as Nor felt. Stillness without rest.

Nor's fear had vanished, replaced by an absence of—anything. Time slowed to a crawl. Escape from this place meant nothing. Color drained away, leaving only lines and shapes hung out for the void to mock.

With his last glimmer of energy, Nor thought of Shada. When her face entered his mind, he briefly mistook her for the Goddess. Simply forming and maintaining her image and knowing it was her was a triumph.

This victory opened a space amid the oppression. He focused on his gratitude that Shada was somewhere else, somewhere better.

As for him, he saw the truth, the final meaning of every-thing, and it was too terrible to endure. But his heart kept stubbornly beating.

Time trudged on in that horrific calm, passing in drips. He clung to Shada's face as if he was sinking in quicksand and she was a fraying rope.

A flare of sensation. Someone was touching him. The wraith had returned, and it breathed on him again.

The exhilaration of wild rage filled him. His will re-stored, heart pounding, he strained to free himself from the tree-wall. He pulled furiously, willing to do anything to get his hands on the beasts tormenting them. To his surprise, the sap broke with a crack. He fell to the ground, caught himself with his hands, and jumped up.

The wraiths fled the ground except for the two guarding the exit. The rest climbed to the top of the trunk and sat watching him. Cowards. He roared and spat at them. They did nothing. Vibrating with fury, he spun back and forth, teeth bared, until his eyes fell on the pair of guards.

They squatted, motionless, before the tunnel's entrance. His ferocity didn't move them in the slightest. Behind them was his only conceivable means of escape.

From the wall, Robir cried out for help. Despite his thrashing, the sap still held him. But Nor could spare no attention from killing the creatures in front of him. Fear was a memory.

He charged the wraiths at the exit. One of them planted its hands on the ground and kicked him in the chest, sending him flying and rolling across the little arena. He stopped underneath Robir.

Though his muscles ached and the wind had been knocked out of him, his anger pulled him to his feet. The sap holding Robir finally broke with a wet crunch. The man fell, driving Nor to the ground with him.

Nor cursed and shoved him off. The Ronians did nothing right. His fury turned away from the wraiths and toward the man in front of him.

Robir rose, and they faced each other. Nor scoured his mind for an insult, some reason to fight.

The soldier spoke first. "Thanks for the help. Some holy man you are."

Nor gasped in his anger. "You don't deserve help. You're just one of Emberly's lapdogs."

"To hell with Emberly! You know nothing about me, you savage," the soldier yelled.

They squared off, hands up, eyes wide, ready to lunge. Nearly out of his mind, Nor thought primal, brutal things. His bandage had fallen off, and his wrist was bleeding again. He hardly understood Robir when he spoke.

"Stop!" the man cried, visibly calming himself. "We mustn't do this. I'm not your enemy, monk."

Nor's mind reeled. "You're a Ronian. That's all I need."

"We didn't sign up for this. We're here because of one man." Robir was resisting the wraiths' spell better than Nor was. "It's my fault. I should've done more to stop him."

"Who?"

"Emberly! I should have stopped Emberly from commanding the crusade. I knew what he was like. But I didn't know how to stop him."

Taken aback by the confession, unrelated as it was to their present situation, Nor growled. His anger diminished, and in his warped mental state, he did not like that.

Robir looked at him with unnerving vulnerability. "You have to understand in case you survive. Emberly isn't who you think. He's a madman."

Nor scoffed. "Pull yourself together."

"If you live through this, you have to protect the company. From him."

Nor's chest loosened, and he breathed easier. The soldier's effort at peace was defusing his anger. He mastered himself, ashamed at being the voice of irrational rage. Not all soldiers were puppets.

And what he had seen of Emberly did not contradict Robir's claim. That conversation Emberly had had with himself in the tower...

"We'll both survive this." Nor declared this firmly. "I don't know how, but we will."

He offered Robir his hand. "Let the wraiths witness the failure of their spells."

But Robir's eyes widened, and before Nor could react, wraiths grabbed them both. Nor's mouth filled with the creature's heavy breath, sickly sweet this time.

The wraith released him, and he looked around. More wraiths had gathered on the tree-wall. Robir lay shaking in a fetal curl.

The private was laughing. When he saw Nor, he melted in hysterics.

Nor chuckled, not knowing why. With that spark, laughter consumed him like fire in a parched forest. He collapsed and laughed until he could not breathe. Everything was funny.

His laughter went on and on, wringing all worth from everything. It was a living thing that would destroy him and move to a new host. He closed his eyes, afraid he would see something so funny it would kill him.

He was going to laugh himself to death. Of all the ends he could meet, it would be this. He realized with terror how funny that was.

Movement distracted him. The wraiths were on their feet, hopping, circling the enclosure. Even the guards leaped up onto the wall. They stared down at the exit, where Captain Emberly had appeared.

Next to the captain was the man who had accompanied the wraiths last night. A scuzzy jungle dweller, he looked no more appealing or trustworthy in the daytime. He said nothing, only held out his hands, palms forward, then placed his arm around Emberly's shoulder.

He was declaring the captain to be his friend. Nor, his mind in tatters, decided that Emberly had betrayed them somehow, made a deal with this scoundrel to save himself. The idea grimly amused him, and he laughed some more.

The stranger gestured to Nor and Robir and brought his hands to his chest, claiming them for himself.

The wraiths only watched.

Emberly whispered to the stranger, who shook his head. Emberly whispered again, fiercely this time. The two men started slowly toward Nor and Robir.

The wraiths did not hesitate. As one, they rushed Emberly and his companion from all sides, fast and silent.

A knife appeared in Emberly's hand. As the wraiths closed in, he grabbed the stranger, putting the blade to his neck. "Back! All of you, now! Do you understand me?"

They did, well enough. They stopped all at once, an instant consensus, and crouched. They appeared both relaxed and ready to pounce.

The commotion had dragged Nor from his vortex of deadly amusement. He kept laughing, but his laughter lost its poisonous intensity. With an effort, he sat up and watched what was happening.

"I'll do what you want," Emberly called to the wraiths. He turned, maybe looking for a leader. "I'll carry out your plan. Just give them to me." He nodded to Nor and Robir.

"Why even try?" said the stranger, sounding resigned. "You know they don't understand."

Emberly sighed as if admitting the man was right. "Fine." He spoke softly to the stranger. The man looked bewildered, but Emberly continued, insistent.

Understanding grew on the stranger's face. Using the tip of his boot, he began scratching out a large, unfamiliar symbol in the dirt. Emberly directed him, still holding him at knifepoint.

They had the wraiths' attention. The creatures watched intently, stepping back to give him room.

When the stranger finished, he stepped to one side, Emberly following awkwardly, and traced more symbols. Nor giggled at their dance.

As the man finished tracing, a wraith emerged from the crowd. It peered at the symbols and turned to the others, exhaling audibly from its mouth.

To Nor's amazement, the wraiths withdrew a moment later. Though many sat on the wall, none remained in the enclosure. Emberly released the stranger and walked over to Nor, offering his hand.

Nor accepted, and Emberly pulled him up. Even now, the monk could not stifle every laugh that tried to escape his mouth. The fact that he and Robir were still naked did not help. Between chuckles, he said in amazement, "You came for us."

The captain was strangely unfazed by his laughter. "Let's go, before they change their minds."

The stranger glowered but nodded.

"Go where?" said Robir. He stood alone, arms crossed. Though he was still laughing too, his tone was dark and rancorous. His shifting facial expression threatened to send Nor into fits of amusement.

If Emberly noticed Robir's hostile tone, he did not acknowledge it. "The prison. We're going to free the others and capture it."

"Is that so, sir? Our last mission didn't go so well. We failed to rescue one of our own from these fiends, and we lost a couple more trying. What makes you think you'll do any better this time?"

The captain fixed him with a glare and opened his mouth to answer, but the stranger interrupted. "We must leave. Now," he said, walking out of the enclosure.

After a final glance at Robir, the captain followed.

Trailing them, Nor and Robir still emitted occasional giggles. Nor's were tired but elated. Robir's were grim and hollow.

23

SHADA

THROUGH THE THICK GRATE overhead, Shada saw occasional watching eyes. The pit was round and walled with stone, too narrow to lie down in and deep enough to break her legs if she tried to climb out.

Every surface she touched marked her skin or clothing with the filth of decades. She had no privacy to use the refuse bucket they had given her.

When the grate finally opened with a metallic groan, she thought it was falling in on her. She had curled up and covered her head when the man laughed. "It's only me, love," he said. She did not know him. "Time to climb out."

He dropped a rope and hoisted her up without much effort. Coming out of the pit, she saw the field of tents and simple structures that filled the grounds of the prison. They surrounded thick stone walls, inside which stood a squat, robust keep. It was built like a castle from centuries past.

The man smiled through a scarred face and dropped the grate. Its clang startled two small children who were waiting to glimpse the stranger.

He waved Shada along, and she followed him toward the wall. His clothing was heavily patched but clean. The others dressed similarly. Around them, men and women went about their morning routines. Children played in dirt lanes.

Those who saw her stopped chattering. In her wake, the only sound was the dying night winds.

The people's hush was her first clue that their captors thought she had a special role in the prisoners' company. Then again, they might be watching her because they never saw strangers.

She'd had little chance to talk to the other crusaders, and she had learned nothing more of the Lady's whereabouts. The convicts had taken the Lady's box along with their weapons and supplies.

"Where are my friends?" she asked the man. Her head and throat still hurt.

"Close," he replied. "Not very restful, is it? That hole, I mean."

"I would've slept except for the wind. How do you stand it?"

He chuckled. "The wind wasn't the worst part in the old days. Try sleeping down there with soldiers pissing on you."

They entered the walls through an open set of sturdy wooden doors. The walls were wide enough to walk on top of. The stone courtyard bustled with activity. People watched her. She kept her eyes on her guide's back.

Straight ahead were the doors of the keep. The man lit a candle before stepping through and into a corridor. They climbed a set of spiral stairs.

The place was dark, with few windows. Shada could not have retraced their steps. They finally entered a shrine, where carved stone reliefs on one wall surrounded a smooth, blank patch of stone. Like many spaces devoted to Huire, its floor was covered by a worn prayer rug.

A figure knelt on the floor, facing the blank stone patch. A hand drew back a hood, revealing the face of a middle-aged woman.

"Kneel with me," the woman said.

Shada's guide had disappeared.

In no position to refuse, Shada sank to her knees next to the stranger. Clasping her hands behind her back, she shut her eyes.

"The Goddess hears everything we say," said the woman. "That's no less true outside of holy places, but inside them, we are always reminded. For this conversation, we should both keep her in mind."

"I agree," Shada replied. If the woman was trying to frighten her, she had succeeded.

"Your companions are alive for now. I hope you can give me a reason to keep them alive. If you fight me, I'll show you how little any of your lives mean."

"What do you want?"

"Tell me who you are—your little army first then you."

Shada didn't know what to say. This woman might have already interrogated the others. There was no telling what she knew.

No one had expected to find convicts alive on Caidfell. But the company had arranged a cover story just in case. Shada began, "The men are Ronian soldiers."

"We could hardly have missed that. Continue."

"We've come to offer you forgiveness," Shada told her. "The empire wants you and your fellow prisoners to come back to Ronia."

The woman stared at the smooth patch of wall where Huire would someday be.

Uneasy with the silence, Shada continued. "There are conditions. The bishop will—"

"Stop," said the woman. "I've told too many lies to fall for such a poor one. If you lie again, I will start killing your friends."

Shada grew weak. Her knees already ached from kneeling. "You won't believe the truth if I tell it."

"Are you their slave? It's hard to talk about, I know."

"No," replied Shada forcefully. "I chose to be here."

"What is your name, free woman?"

"Shada."

"And what is your role among these men?"

"Nothing. I serve the Goddess."

That startled the stranger. "A holy woman? Of what order?"

"What is your name?" Shada asked. Knowing the woman's name would make the conversation feel a little fairer.

The woman answered casually. "Belith."

Shada braced herself. She was a poor liar, and if she kept trying to deceive this woman, people would die. She would be as honest as she could, as dangerous as that might be. "I belong to no order, Belith. I directly serve a messenger of the Goddess."

Belith stared at her. "You seemed sane until now."

"It's true. I care for a servant of the Goddess, a being we call the Lady."

"Do you speak to her?"

"Yes."

"What does she sound like?" Belith asked. The captured soldiers were forgotten for now.

Shada suspected she was falling into a trap. Her answers might convince Belith that she was truly mad. "She sounds like many voices speaking all at once."

"Can you see her? Does she show you things? Visions?"

"Yes to the first question. I've had visions, too, but I don't know where they came from. And I think they've stopped." It was true. She'd had no visions last night, but more importantly, she no longer felt them waiting to seize her when she slept.

"So it goes," said Belith with a smile. She pointed to the edge of the floor, directly below the Goddess's emptiness. There sat a small vine plant in a clay pot. Several bright-red vines had crept from the soil. Some reached up the wall toward the carvings while others stretched across the floor toward their knees.

"Can you summon her? If what you're saying is true, I want to meet her."

"No," said Shada. "I know I sound insane, or like a liar."

"Maybe. But most holy people are neither. I should know."

"Did you belong to an order?"

"Long ago. I still do, I suppose. I will always be Sister Belith, all the way to the Outer Dark. These things can't really be undone." She paused. "So. You can't prove your claims, and I cannot disprove them. I'm afraid I must err on the side of caution."

Shada swallowed. "We aren't your enemy."

"Our enemy is anyone who's not one of us."

"We are only passing through." She would not mention the crusade's mission unless pressed. If she and the company were to survive, let alone find the Lady, they would need to satisfy Belith's curiosity somehow, and to have the needed conversation, Shada would have to appear sane.

Belith frowned. "With a 'messenger' sent by Huire?"

"Yes."

"Where are you going?"

"We don't know exactly. A lost gateway, somewhere in the jungle."

Belith glared. "Your story grows steadily more fantastic." She leaned down and picked up the potted plant in both hands. Her right hand and wrist were swollen and pockmarked.

"Maybe you don't know the truth about Ronia. That city's soldiers have killed many friends of mine. And none killed more than the miserable old man leading your company."

"The bishop?"

"We knew him as the commandant. When he ran this prison, he was a butcher."

"I only know what everyone knows," Shada said. "That Caidfell is a terrible place."

"Terrible, and the empire made it worse. You must know what I mean—you don't look like a Ronian."

"I was born in the city," Shada said, correcting the common mistake. "I got the marks on my face from my mother. She was an offworlder."

"Still, you're not a true Ronian. I can tell." Belith stroked one of the plant's vines with her swollen fingers. The stalk twitched. "I wish you could show me this 'Lady' you claim to serve. I wish I could trust you."

"She hasn't spoken to me in a while." Shada looked at the blank space on the wall. "I would not let myself trust her, and I may have driven her away." She had no idea what she would do if the Lady never returned. As frightening as the Lady could be, so far, being alone was much worse. The Lady couldn't leave them. Not over a single rude remark.

"When you've been damned, there's some solace in knowing why," said Belith. She pushed back her hood to reveal long, graying hair and a hollow, once-pretty face. "Some of us don't even have that."

With her swollen hand, she pinched the vine between her fingers and palm. She gasped and threw it down. A small barb withdrew into the vine. Her hand was bleeding a little. Her breath caught, and her face reddened.

"When your people captured me, I had a metal box," said Shada. "If you bring it to me, it might help me summon the Lady."

"How?" Belith gasped the word, clutching her hand.

"I won't say."

"Then I have no reason to search for it."

Shada hesitated but decided to risk revealing the box's importance. "It's where she spends most of her time."

Belith's eyebrows rose. She spoke haltingly. "Are you... insane? I must be. But I'll watch out for... this box."

She closed her eyes and breathed heavily. When she spoke again, her voice was more even. "Since you confessed a sin, I'll confess one to you. I executed a man yesterday for betraying his wife."

Her wounded hand had clenched into a shaking fist. With great effort, she opened it slightly. A drop of blood fell to the floor.

"Weakness is poison," she said. "We can't survive it any longer."

She picked up the potted plant and held it toward Shada. "Now, you."

Shada looked at the nearest vines, which hung loose on the floor. Her insides tightened. "What is it?"

"It has no name. I found it in the jungle."

"What will it do?"

"I don't know. It may help to prove you're telling the truth. But I know this: unless you let this vine sting you, I'll start killing your friends right now."

Shada did not think any more about it. She grabbed the vine and squeezed it in her palm.

The agony knocked her flat. She lay on her back, her head ringing from hitting the floor, shaking her hand to escape the burning.

Belith stood slowly. "I hope this will give you a vision. I wish I could stay and find out, but there are things I must see to. Don't try to leave this room. We'll talk when it's over."

She stopped at the door. "Whatever happens, your 'bishop' will never leave this place. This planet should have been his grave long ago."

The pain spread up Shada's arm like fire. She barely heard the door slam. The Lady had never felt farther away.

24

— · —

BRIN

THE GUARDS DRAGGED BRIN to an underground corridor. There, they made him try to walk on his own. Unable to see much, he slumped against the wall. His knees buckled, and he sank to the floor.

They pulled him up by the armpits and forced him to stand, wrenching his bound wrists painfully behind him. He didn't dare protest.

Soon, they stopped by a tall, heavy door. Voices came from inside. A few minutes after his guards knocked, the door opened, and rough hands shoved him forward.

The first thing he recognized in the dim candlelight was Arumin's face. The bishop's head protruded from a small hole in the floor. Water filled the hole, and the stone around it was wet and mossy. For an instant, Brin feared Arumin was dead, and he was relieved to see him struggling to stay afloat, eyes bulging.

A cloaked figure stood near the bishop. Its head turned to reveal a woman's face. Her age was probably midway between the bishop's and Brin's. When he saw her, he breathed a little easier. Women had hurt him less than men, and he felt little attraction to her.

She stalked toward him and said, "Kneel."

He obeyed.

The bishop stared at him with urgent meaning in his eyes.

"What's your name?" asked the woman. Her breathing was heavy, as if she had been shouting.

"Brin," he replied. He had not spoken in many hours, and his voice squeaked.

"Mine is Belith. Judging by your bishop's expression, I believe you're the man I want to see. Do you know why you're here?"

Brin looked at Arumin. The bishop's hands must be tied. How long could he stay afloat?

"You have questions," he said.

"That's not all," Belith replied. "Mostly, you're here because your bishop needs to learn that his actions have consequences."

"What is this?" said Arumin. His voice was strained, almost unrecognizable.

Brin's head and chest tingled. "The bishop is wise." It sounded like a prayer.

"I hope you're wrong about that," said Belith. She moved toward the bishop with the same stealthy gait. "If he's wise, what kind of world is this?"

Against all judgment, Brin was defiant. "This is a world where the winners are those who choose the winning side."

Her eyebrows rose. "I suppose you're one of the winners."

Brin glanced at the bishop and knew what to say. "Yes. I'm on the side of the Goddess."

She stared at him until he met her eyes. "Do you know who I am?" she asked.

"I know your kind."

She laughed, a raspy sound. He thought of her odd step and realized she was hiding intense pain. "I won't ask what kind that is. It's clear you don't remember me. Why would you? I'm a fading old thing. Ten years have passed, and none of them have been kind."

Brin swallowed. "You knew me at the prison?"

"I knew your face. Everyone did."

Arumin said, "Touch him, and I swear I will kill you."

She ignored him. "You were so young, and you drew attention. There was nothing I could do to help you."

Brin looked at the floor. "I've mostly forgotten those days."

"It's a blessing to be young. Since you're still with the commandant, I assume you've stayed with him all this time. Did he take you with him when he ran away?"

"Yes."

"What did you think of him? Watching him flee his post, leaving his men to die?"

Brin didn't answer.

"Has he taken good care of you?"

"He taught me about Huire. Thanks to him, my soul belongs to me."

"What did he want in return? What could a handsome young man offer such a decrepit creature?"

"Nothing!" Brin snapped. He could hardly control his anger. This woman would not toy with him.

Belith spoke in a kinder tone. "I believe you." She knelt close to him. "I'm sorry I asked about those things. They're not mine to know."

She stood again. "Brin, have you realized yet that I brought you here to kill you?"

The bishop growled from deep in his throat.

"You will die to make a point. The bishop refuses to answer my questions, and that decision must cost him dearly. What do you think of that?"

Brin cried and despised his own weakness.

"I would feel the same," Belith said. She pulled a gun from under her robes. "This will be a painless transition."

"Stop," gasped Arumin. "I'll tell you what you want to know."

"It's too late, Commandant," Belith replied. "If you only answer me now, under duress, you will defy me again when the danger is gone. I must leave a mark in your mind, as you've marked so many others."

"It's true!" shouted the bishop.

Belith paused. "About the Lady?"

"Yes, all of it."

"Where is this being?"

"I don't know. I haven't seen her since we left the waytower."

"What about your company? How many remain?"

"You've captured everyone."

She pointed the gun at Brin. "I'm afraid I don't believe you."

"What more can I say?" Arumin cried.

"The truth."

"I've told it!"

"Brin, I hope you've relieved yourself. When we die, we lose control of our bowels."

"No!" croaked Arumin. His head slipped under the water.

When he surfaced, she said, "We have fewer Ronian soldiers in our pits than entered this jungle yesterday."

He glared. "Have you been watching us?"

"Around a dozen are missing. Where are they?"

"We lost them in the swamp."

"Not all of them."

"You weren't there."

"You know, I don't have to kill this man quickly."

Choking, the bishop said, "Some left the waytower before your wraith friends came. They left without my knowledge, and they never returned."

"How many?"

"Five, I heard. I was asleep."

"Why did they leave?"

"There was a noise—howling, outside. They went to investigate. It must have been your wraiths."

She thought for a moment. "Who led the group that left?"

Arumin answered slowly. "Emberly."

Belith looked stunned. She almost dropped the gun. "Rayan's brother?"

Arumin gave no reply.

Though her mind was clearly busy, Belith shook off her surprise. "Do you think he will come here?"

The bishop spat a mouthful of foul water. "He has no choice."

She nodded. "Brin, you're going to live a bit longer. Do you want to return to the pit where you slept?"

Brin nodded, sniffling.

Belith lowered her gun. "Tell me one thing." She knelt beside Arumin, grabbed his hair, and forced his head underwater.

"What are you doing?" Brin gasped.

"Tell me what this is." She opened her free hand, which was red and swollen. In her palm was the vial.

He had almost forgotten they had taken it. The sight broke what was left of his nerve. He cried again.

"You tried to hide it from my men. It's a curious little thing. Why is it important?"

Dark water lapped her wrist and the rim of the hole. Tension in her arm hinted at the struggle under the surface.

Brin stammered. If he told the truth, he might be killed—if not by this woman, by a member of the Ronian company. When Shada had told him of her attacker, Brin had felt overpowering relief, sure that man must be the assassin Sylvana's friends had placed in the company. But betting his life on it was another matter.

"He hasn't got long," Belith assured him.

Brin decided to lie. "They are ashes. My father's."

"You had a father?" Belith sounded doubtful. She examined the powder in the vial. "It's black. I've never seen ashes like that. You're lying, Brin."

"I'm not," Brin whispered.

Seconds passed. The water churned as Arumin began to drown.

Brin shut his eyes as hard as he could. Above all things, he wanted to survive. And that wasn't all. If he told this woman about the vial, he would have to reveal its purpose. She had no reason to keep his secret, so she might tell others. Everyone would know that Brin had conspired with enemies, yellow-eyed men like reptiles, to kill the Goddess Huire and all the other gods with her. Arumin would know.

"He's almost gone," said Belith. "What is worth this?"

He wished he was brave, so he could tell the truth, save the bishop, and let himself be shamed. But the words would not leave his mouth. His desire to survive would not allow it. In his paralyzed state, he waited.

The water had calmed.

Brin couldn't watch anymore. He stared at the floor. Nothing made sense through his wet eyes. "Please..."

"Well?"

He opened his mouth, closed it, and turned away.

He heard a splash and a gasp. Belith had pulled Arumin up by his hair, letting him breathe. The bishop sputtered and moaned.

Belith looked at Brin, who did not meet her eyes. "That's good to know," she said. "I'll talk to you both soon." She left.

Brin went to Arumin. Alone in the room, they cried, Brin lying on the floor with his face near the bishop's. Brin wondered if the pain he felt was love.

The door opened, and Belith's men entered. They picked Brin up and shoved him toward the door. Arumin called, "What did you tell her?"

Brin was halfway back to the pit before he answered. "Does it matter?"

25

SHADA

Somehow, Shada slept despite her pain. When she woke, the burning in her hand had faded somewhat, becoming bearable.

Her dreams had not been orderly memories like the other dreams she'd had lately. These, too, stayed with her after waking, but instead of making her mind cloudy, they clung to her like nettles. She blamed the plant's poison.

She would have traded all her previous baths to take one now. Her throat still stung from the smoke last night. Ache piled on ache.

When she sat up, the Lady was in the room. Shada jolted forward like a catapult.

"You're still here!" she cried.

The Lady had assumed her golden, matronly form. She knelt on the floor in front of the shrine. "Still?" she said in her familiar chorus of many voices.

"I don't know why I said that," Shada admitted. Nothing she said was right. "You were here while I slept, weren't you? Or was that a dream?"

The Lady's head snapped around to face her, twisting far enough to break a real human's neck. "Were you listening to me?"

"I didn't mean to. I think I overheard you in my sleep." She remembered now. Through visions of blood-soaked vines circling her throat, she had heard an argument. It had started as begging, turned to threats, and then turned back into begging.

But the Lady was the only other person here. "Was someone yelling at you?" Shada asked.

The Lady hesitated minutely then replied with a question. "What did you dream about?"

"It was a nightmare. Poisonous vines were tearing me to pieces. My body swelled like a balloon." Fear of it still clung to her. "There were other things too. Lots of things, all jumbled together."

"Did you relive any more memories?" asked the Lady.

"No. I think the visions are over. Strange as this sounds, it feels like they've finished with me. Actually, my head hasn't been this clear in days."

"Let's hope they're not over. We must learn what we can from those visions and the memories in them."

They hadn't spoken about the visions since Shada had first reported hers to the Lady. Shada wondered why. "Lady, where did they come from? Did the Goddess send them?"

More hesitation. "I don't know, child."

That was disconcerting to hear. Shada knew the Lady was not privy to all Huire's thoughts, but she'd hoped the Lady at least knew more than Shada did. She said, "Other people in the company are having them now. Maybe it's this planet. It's known to play tricks on the mind."

The Lady's head turned back toward the altar. "I don't think the planet is at fault here. And the dreams don't sound like Huire's doing. I sense something else at work."

"Could it be the man I saw? The one with the face that shone like crystal?"

"Perhaps."

"Can't you... speak to Huire about it? You're her messenger."

"I am Huire's will given form. No speaking is needed."

Shada was not sure if she should press the point. The Lady had just returned. It would be foolish to risk angering her again.

But Shada's newfound clarity told her it was better to be frank. The Lady could often guess her thoughts anyway. "If you are her will, then you ought to know whether she sent these dreams. Is it something you don't want to talk about? If so, I'll understand."

The Lady stared at the space on the wall reserved for the absent Goddess. Her ability to see without eyes made even ordinary actions strange. "I know you will. I should not forget how considerate you are. But I truly don't know where these dreams are coming from. I sense a presence behind them, an awareness of some sort, but that is all. While you slept, I tried speaking to it, but I heard nothing. I tried speaking to Huire too."

Her forgiving tone was a blessed relief. Maybe mending their relationship would be easier than Shada had feared. "Maybe it's like you said. You don't need to speak to Huire. You are 'her will given form' as you put it, so whatever you do, it's what she wishes you to do."

"I used to think so. But what if I had never come back to you? Surely she wouldn't want that. I could have disappeared."

"But you didn't," Shada countered. It was surreal, giving counsel to a divine being.

"You don't understand," said the Lady. "I can do anything I wish—laugh, scream, throw myself into a fire. It can't all be what she wills."

"Why not?"

"While we were apart, I tried many things to see where my freedom to choose ends. It doesn't." Her voice was calm, as always. "Why do I feel so free and yet trapped?"

"I don't know."

"And if I can disobey her will, how can I know what I choose is right?"

Shada shivered. "Did you say you talked to Huire while I was asleep?"

"Yes. I prayed, Shada."

"I've never seen you do that."

"It seemed appropriate."

"What I heard... It sounded like you were upset."

"What do you think you heard?"

"You sounded enraged. You shouted."

The Lady heaved a great sigh. It was as artificial as everything else about her. "I must admit something, Shada. This is all very hard. There is too much to think about."

Shada listened.

"I can't hear Huire's voice anymore. I used to be certain I knew her will. But now I wonder if I ever did. Uncertainty is everywhere. That's why I don't know where your visions came from. Being cut off from her like this is... so terrible."

Shada nodded. "Huire is bigger than we are. I suppose we might never understand."

"That is unacceptable."

"You may wish for certainty, Lady," Shada said, blinking back tears. "But for me, having someone to feel lost with is a relief. I don't even know if that woman, Belith, is planning to kill me."

"I hope you won't ask me to rescue you."

Shada swallowed. "No, I will not."

"Thank you for that. Where is my box? I left it with you when I saved you."

Jarred by this change of subject, Shada said, "I don't know. I'm sorry. One of these people must have it."

"I miss it," said the Lady. "Isn't that strange?"

"No. It's your home."

The Lady smiled. "Yes, that's right. A home. Will you pray with me?"

Shada rolled onto her belly and pushed herself up. Hurting all over, she knelt beside the Lady.

"I won't ask you to save me again," she said. "But I'm grateful you saved me in the waytower. After you fought that man, you pulled me out of the fire, didn't you?"

"Yes, and I left my box with you. Maybe I should have kept it. You can repay me by helping me now. I have never prayed before today."

"I'm not much good at it myself. In the Temple, you start by finding your remorse. Think of the bad things you've done, and feel ashamed. Take your shame and offer it up."

The Lady did not answer. Shada tried to pray, but her mind was restless. Soon, she realized why. There was a question she needed to ask.

It hung before her eyes, and she could see nothing else. Finally, she asked, "Lady, when you fought the man in the waytower, why did you kill him like that?"

"How do you mean?"

"You can kill easily. But when you killed him, you did it slowly. You kept cutting him, and you held him down in the fire."

The Lady waited. She expected more.

"Why?" Shada asked, fumbling. The question was too important to leave unasked.

Finally, the Lady said, "I could not have saved him otherwise."

"'Saved'? What do you mean?"

"He needed a moment before death to repent. Killing him instantly might have sent him straight to the Outer Dark."

"Couldn't he have repented without torment?"

No answer.

"It seemed so cruel."

"It was merciful."

"It was all so frightening. The man, the fire. I've been thinking about it ever since. What he did was terrible. Maybe when you hurt him... you were simply angry."

The Lady's head swiveled to face her. "I risked my life to save you. I faced not only the usual dangers of leaving my box but the danger of fire, which harms even me if I touch it. Do you think I risked all that because I was in a huff?"

"Of course not. But isn't it natural to be furious when someone threatens you?"

Another sigh. "Child, I am not like humans in that way."

"Are you sure?" Shada was afraid to say these things, but they were right.

The Lady's voice rose. "Because I asked you to be honest doesn't give you the right to insult me. I feel anger, but it's not like yours. The petty squabbles of the physical world don't interest me. When that man threatened us, fire filled me. It was the zeal of Huire, giving me the passion to do what was needed."

"I'm glad," Shada said quickly. "It was just in time. When he pulled the knife away, I thought he'd cut my throat." She still felt that knife. Part of her suspected she was actually dead, a ghost who would fade as soon as she was forgotten. But a ghost did not fear speaking its mind.

"Why did you wait until the last moment? Were you waiting until my death was certain?"

"I've made a mistake, girl," said the Lady. "I spoke to you about things outside your understanding."

"What was in that vial the man was holding? What are you so afraid of?"

The Lady drew herself up. "When you have the memories I was born with—when you know the things I was forced to know and must make sense of them—then you can decide the value of your hurt feelings. You might even be grateful I risked everything for you. I'm worried that being the caretaker has led you to think too highly of yourself."

That was the last that either of them spoke. Shada tried to pray, but she kept wondering how it felt to be held in a fire. How could one even think, much less repent?

Soon, the Lady disappeared. Seconds later, boots pounded the floor outside, rushing toward the door.

26

—·—

EMBERLY

EMBERLY AND THE OTHERS hid behind trees while the guards fell.

He hoped the wraiths understood the object of their attack: to quickly and silently capture the prisoners' current leader, a woman Rayan called Belith, without alerting the entire prison to their presence. So far the wraiths had been quiet as the grave, but having recently witnessed one of their blood frenzies, Emberly feared that might change.

The captain gripped his saber, found by Rayan in the hollow of a large tree. The wraiths had stored the items taken from Emberly, Nor, Robir, and their dead comrades in that hole, apparently to limit the wicked presence of offworld artifacts to a single tree.

The wraiths had watched from nearby, offering no resistance as the Ronians recovered their weapons and equipment—and Nor and Robir's clothing. Emberly had wondered if the near-fight over the two men's fates had changed the wraiths' perceptions of his little party from tentative allies to enemies. Maybe they were preparing to attack, working themselves into a frenzy.

His fear seemed confirmed during his party's hike through the jungle. He and Rayan had been pondering their slim odds of capturing Belith without the wraiths' help when Emberly spotted movement in the trees.

It had been a flash of green on green, almost the same color, but he recognized the way the shape moved. He whispered what he had seen to the others, assuming an attack was imminent.

But it never came. The wraiths had ventured steadily closer, escorting the Ronians toward the prison camp. Only a handful were present. Rayan had been first to realize the creatures meant to help them after all. The captain had swelled with elation.

They needed all the help they could get. Nor and Robir, between occasional bursts of giggling, had explained the torment the wraiths had inflicted on them. Surely neither would be up for much of a fight. Learning that the scraggly stranger in their midst was Emberly's famous brother interested them little.

Emberly had seen allying with the wraiths as an ugly necessity. But now that the creatures had so hurt his men, some guilt belonged to him.

This guilt had been worsened by Private Robir, whose plain resentment of Emberly was a problem the captain must soon deal with. He didn't know its origin, but it had worsened since his rescue from the wraiths. Surely Robir did not resent being saved from torture.

But the man had legitimate reason to feel suspicious of the captain. He and the others had seen Emberly communicating with the wraiths using written symbols, a shocking sight considering stories of the wraiths portrayed them as illiterate monsters. Soon, they would ask the captain how such a thing was possible, and Emberly would have to answer them.

But that was a problem for later, after they all survived this attack.

Night had fallen, and the wind was howling when they reached the wide clearing that held the prison camp. They stopped at the edge of the trees and looked ahead. There lay the keep, the prison's chief and most substantial building. An ugly stone lump surrounded by stone walls, it contained a maze of corridors that might have baffled less knowledgeable invaders.

The others stood and crouched beside Emberly, shifting and peering into the dark. Soon, the wraiths would advance and begin their violent work.

Robir had spoken little since they'd left the wraiths' settlement. The private rarely wasted words anyway, making it all the more surprising when his voice pierced the windy night.

"Wraiths are taking their time, eh? What could they be thinking?"

Emberly realized the question was meant for him. He shook his head.

He heard a frown in Robir's voice. "Don't you know, Captain?"

"What do you mean?"

"I mean that you can talk to them. You drew those pictures on the ground. What did they mean, by the way?"

Emberly showed his irritation. "We attack soon. We'll talk about this later."

"No. Now."

For the first time, the captain turned his eyes from the clearing. "Excuse me?"

"We'll talk now, sir."

Emberly glared at him. "Quiet down. Eyes front."

"If I wait until later, you'll brush me off again. You forget, sir, that I've served under you before. I know how you are."

The captain stared. "Do you regret my saving your life, Private?"

The man was unaffected by his gaze. "Always thankful to Huire for another day, sir. But that's her purview, not yours. I wish you'd let us save those Ronians at the wraiths' bonfire, though. A boy and one of your own men."

"That boy was already dead. And Private Keesin died soon after—as I've told you already."

"But he wasn't dead then, was he? We could have stopped them both from being eaten."

Emberly nearly lost his temper. "You saw what happened when—" He stopped himself before his voice could rise to a shout.

Robir's eyes shone with satisfaction. "Now, about those symbols."

Emberly knew he should refuse outright to say more. But he had an answer that might settle this issue right here. "Rayan showed those symbols to me. He uses them to talk with the wraiths."

But Robir did not back down. "Really? Why didn't he use them? He just waved his arms around."

An instant passed in which Emberly should have answered if he had an answer.

Rayan interjected from his other side, where he had been listening. "It's true. I invented them."

"I see," said Robir. Unsatisfied, he turned back to Emberly. "What did they mean?"

Rayan shrugged at the captain. He was out of ideas. Having lived through the prison revolt and its aftermath, he knew the history of the symbols and had saved Emberly from a stumble.

The captain had an answer ready this time. "It was a plea for mercy. It meant 'we surrender.' You might not like it, Private, but it worked." This was true, as far as it went.

Robir's eyes said plainly that he knew Emberly was deceiving him and that he was eager to learn how. "That's a simple enough message. Sounds like a job for one picture, not several. The first looked like a hand, which could well mean surrender. But the second... unless I'm wrong, the second looked like a skull. What does a skull—"

"Enough," Emberly snapped. "You have your answers." The wraiths could move at any time.

"No, I don't," said Robir. "Not yet. But I will. Borna and Elisar died because we wandered into the jungle in the dead of night to hunt phantoms. There, we just happened to run into your criminal brother. What're the odds?"

Emberly wished he could jump across the gap between them and throttle the man, but that would mean leaving his cover. "You'll never know. Because you're right—I'm brushing you off."

Robir nodded gravely. "Borna and Elisar aren't the first friends I've lost under your command. I want to know why they died. I hope it's a good reason... Captain."

Several wraiths emerged from the trees around them. Advancing into the clearing, they disappeared ahead. Soon, cries of pain and alarm sounded here and there. Emberly hoped the creatures would spare the guards' lives, but he would not count on it.

When Rayan moved, the captain followed, furiously signaling the others to bring up the rear.

A few windows glowed in the keep, but no fires burned outside its walls, where the night wind whistling through the clearing could throw sparks onto tents and huts. The men encountered no guards as they hurried across the camp.

Near the keep's gated walls, they stepped on a metal grate. Something stirred in the pit below it. With a few harsh whispers, Emberly identified his soldiers. Stifling a rush of emotion at their familiar voices, he bent with Nor to move the grate.

Rayan gripped his shoulder. "No time," he hissed.

He meant that he and Emberly must keep moving, and he was right. They could be discovered at any moment, and they needed to get as close as possible to Belith before that happened.

Following previous arrangements, they left Nor and Robir to free as many crusaders from the pits as possible. Once they emptied this pit, they would check the others, remaining undetected as long as they could. They would only fire their guns when they had to.

Emberly and Rayan continued on.

In the wind, the camp's ramshackle buildings and patchwork tents groaned and flapped. Many dated back to Emberly's time on Caidfell. Dusty paths ran between them, thankfully empty. The captain saw no one until they reached the gate.

There, motion in the shadows told him a wraith was waiting. It must be one of theirs, or it would have attacked already. It climbed the wall, negotiating the battlement with chilling ease, and opened the gate from inside.

Two guards lay dead in the courtyard. The wraith had torn their throats open. Emberly was no closer to accepting these beings' humanity.

Rayan snatched one of the dead men's rifles and inspected it. He patted the corpse's pockets and took what he wanted.

He found a key ring and, fitting a key into the keep's door, unlocked it.

Though only one wraith came inside the keep, things continued to go smoothly, making Emberly more worried than ever. The wraith quickly and quietly dispatched the few people they met in the echoing halls.

Emberly and his brother were like boys tagging along behind their much stronger elder brother. The wraith moved with an assurance beyond pride. The captain stepped over each of its victims, shaking away their grasping hands, and turned to watch them disappear around each corner.

With Rayan pointing the way, they soon arrived at a door. Rayan pulled out the keys, but it was unlocked.

Inside, a woman was curled up on the floor. The room was mostly empty otherwise except for a cot draped with blankets by one wall. The woman looked like a pile of rags with hair. She might have been dead, but in the quiet instant before madness descended, Emberly heard her breathing fitfully, asleep.

Wraiths attacked from the shadows.

Emberly fell first. Someone knocked his legs from under him, and hands stronger than his wrenched his saber away. A rifle fired, crushingly loud in the small room, and Rayan shouted.

The fight was over in a few seconds of noise and motion. When Emberly looked up, the wraiths were all gone. A thin, graying woman with a pistol stood over him and Rayan. His brother stared at her with pure contempt.

"It seems I have more friends than you, Rayan," said Belith.

"Not true," Rayan spat. "You will learn that soon."

She regarded him sympathetically, like a sick friend. "What was your plan? Did you think killing me would put you back in charge?"

"I've no desire to kill you. That's your way, not mine."

"You can't win," Emberly said. "Surrender now, and save your people's lives."

Belith laughed, a single fat syllable. "And here's another poor soul caught in Rayan's web. You're Cyril, aren't you?"

"I am."

"Rayan has aged poorly, but you still look alike. Being his brother saved your life once, long ago. That won't happen again."

Rayan started to rise, and she shouted, "Stay down!" To the captain, she said, "Where are your men? Freeing the rest, I suppose?"

"Your guards are dead or fallen," said Emberly. "Every moment, more of my soldiers escape those accursed pits. You can gain nothing by fighting us, but you could lose a lot."

"You may be right, but that's a small matter. We were all lost the day Ronia sent us here. That includes you, Cyril."

She exchanged glances with Rayan. "My wraith allies have chased yours away. Killed them, maybe. And many more are coming. I've been expecting you. You can't win."

Rayan snarled. "Still have friends among the wraiths, do you? How many, Belith? A few dozen? I have hundreds on my side."

Belith's confident expression slipped. "If that's true, why did you attack with only a handful? Was it for the sport?"

"To spare your lives. You know what they can do."

"You're lying. You can't help lying anymore, Rayan. It's who you are."

"He's telling the truth," Emberly interrupted. "I've been to the wraiths' settlement. I had no idea there were so many."

Belith replied, "I hold the word of a total stranger in higher esteem than Rayan's. But I still don't believe you."

Rayan said quietly, "Unless I take control of this camp tonight, every one of us is doomed. The wraiths will have me in charge, or they will no longer tolerate our presence."

"Have you forgotten?" she said. "Doom doesn't scare me much anymore."

Rayan gritted his teeth. "Do you care so little for others? Think of all the people here."

"Do you really think, between me and you, I'm the one who needs to hear that?"

Emberly turned his head at a small noise. A pair of wraiths stood in the doorway. Belith sighed, clearly relieved.

The captain looked at her. "These wraiths you've befriended... There can't be enough of them to save you. If you care about anyone at this prison, surrender."

"There aren't very many left to care about, Cyril Emberly. Your bishop and your empire killed most of us."

She nodded to the wraiths, who dragged Emberly and Rayan from the room. As they went, Rayan cursed her and vividly described what his wraiths would do when they arrived.

27

—·—

SHADA

SHADA HELD HER BREATH as footsteps rushed past the door—and faded down the hallway. She exhaled massively.

On a whim, she turned the doorknob. To her surprise, the door opened. With a chuckle of disbelief, she leaned into the corridor.

A dead man sprawled on the floor. He was bloodied, as if an animal had killed him. She had seen corpses before—in Undertown, many poor and sick lay unburied for a while—but few so carelessly mutilated.

Though she had no idea what was happening, she would not wait here to find out. Whatever had killed the man, she did not trust the room's flimsy wooden door to keep her safe.

As she lingered, trying to plan, a storm of noise and shadow ripped through the hallway. It ended in an instant, leaving her to duck inside the doorway too late. Whatever had passed, it had left the air rippling and sparks falling from torches.

She stepped out warily but heard nothing more. She thought the clamor had moved off to her right, so she turned left.

Her heart raced, and her chest swelled. She had little hope of finding her way outside, let alone rescuing anyone else, but at least she was doing something against her captors' will.

When the corridor split, her natural worry returned. Belith might not control everyone here. Who else might find her wandering, and what might they do?

She heard another commotion ahead, voices this time. They grew rapidly louder, coming her way. She darted around a corner and pressed herself against a wall.

The loudest voice was gruff and unfamiliar. By the time it passed her hiding place, its shouting had fallen to bitter muttering. It was a man, staggering along, held by creatures unlike any she had seen before. They were thin, strangely proportioned, and the same color as the dim walls of the corridor. Had they been still, she might have missed them.

Then came Captain Emberly, held by more of the creatures. Shada had an idiotic urge to call out to him. Here, in this twilight world, was someone she knew and who knew her.

After they passed, she followed them. If she was lucky, they might go outside.

But she had only taken a few steps when a voice called to her. "Feeling better?"

It was Belith. Shada hesitated, wondering what answer was least dangerous. "I heard something outside the room. Then I saw a body—someone is dead—and something passed—"

"And you thought you'd escape?"

"Not really," Shada admitted. "Where would I go? But whatever you do with me, just—"

Belith silenced her with a dismissive head shake. She stared at Shada, hands on her hips, and sighed. "There are any number of things I could do to punish you. I probably *should* punish you. But I can't. Not if I want this 'Lady' of yours to help me. If she's even real." The last bit sounded like a private thought spoken aloud.

"She's certainly real." Shada decided not to mention the Lady's visit yet. She had not recovered the Lady's confidence, and she could not prove the visit had occurred.

Putting her fingers on the bridge of her nose, Belith asked, "How is your hand?"

"It hurts. Though the rest of me hurts more."

Belith opened her own swollen hand. A bloodstained welt filled her palm, bright and new. "It doesn't pain me as much nowadays. Maybe I'm used to it."

Shada's hand had started bleeding again. "I can't imagine going through it even once more."

Belith smiled, weary but relaxed. "That's the voice of inexperience. I can't yet risk hurting you, but I also have no idea if you're lying. One factor in your favor is that I want your Lady to be real. I want it badly. I probably should not admit I need guidance, but you've arrived during a moment of weakness." She pressed her lips together.

"Very well. Until I know for sure, you can help me in another way. Come with me." She walked away.

Shada followed at a distance. She did not yet believe her escape attempt would go unpunished.

Soon, Belith opened a door at the end of a hallway and stepped back, inviting Shada to enter first.

Keeping her eyes on the woman, Shada stepped into the room.

Coming in after her, Belith closed the door and sat on the floor near a cot. Stretching her legs, she pulled her cloak tighter. "Sit."

Shada glanced around the bare room with its one small window. Her eyes fell on the cot. Belith noticed and misunderstood. "I wouldn't sit there, love. Not yet."

Resigning herself, Shada sat down cross-legged in front of the other woman.

Belith rested her chin on her good hand. "What did you see after the vine stung you?"

Shada had no desire to relive those nightmares. "A lot of things," she said. "It was very violent, and none of it made sense. It reminded me of dreams I had as a child, when I got fevers."

Belith nodded soberly. "It's not the same now, is it? You can't force true visions. But we have to keep trying. There's so little time left."

"What visions?" asked Shada. "What are you trying to do?"

"I'm repenting." Belith leaned over and reached under the bed. Blankets draped to the floor, hiding her hand and wrist. She pulled out a crimson vine, a larger version of those in the shrine. It came out easily, hinting at considerable length.

Shada's chest ached at the sight, and her hand throbbed. She thought of the plant growing there, under the bed, alone. Raised in constant darkness. The thoughts it might have.

"Doesn't it need sunlight?" she asked.

"She received little in the wild. Bigger things overshadowed her. Yet she clung to life."

The vine twitched in her hand. Shada leaned back.

"She's grown since I brought her here," said Belith. "The one in the shrine is her child. The bigger they grow, the more they move."

"We saw plants like it in the swamp," replied Shada. "They didn't sting like these, but they dragged a wagon off the road."

"I've no doubt. A cousin of these, perhaps. I've treated these well—I don't want to find out how nasty they can get. The forms life takes are endless here. This planet's god may have left, but a new god took its place: change."

Though she was hesitant to mention the Lady, Shada wished to take Belith's mind off of the plant. "I should tell you, the Lady spoke to me again."

The ploy worked, perhaps too well. "She did?" Belith cried then glanced around as if suspecting the Lady might be listening. She continued, softer. "Why didn't you tell me immediately? You said you'd had no visions."

"It wasn't a vision," said Shada. "When she appears, others can see her too. To be honest, nothing came of it. I keep failing to accept her will, and I'm afraid she's losing patience."

"Find a way to summon her!" Belith croaked.

"I can't. She's not my servant; I'm hers."

Belith took a deep breath and nodded. "Try opening yourself to the experience. That's what I used to do when I could." She raised her scarred hand, dangling the vine in front of Shada. "Take it again. In the same hand."

"No," said Shada. She might be able to endure the sting again, but she would not if she had a choice.

"Why? Can't you see what's at stake?"

"All I felt after it stung me was pain. Pain and nightmares. Since the Lady first appeared to me, my life has been like a dream. Now my visions have stopped, but that plant has replaced them with poison." She laughed. "They might be gone forever anyway, and I don't know if I should be relieved or scared."

"You realize, don't you, that I can hurt you badly if I want?" Belith asked.

"Please, don't."

"Maybe that would draw your Lady out of hiding."

"Please, no," Shada said. "The last person who tried to hurt me died terribly."

Belith frowned. "So, here we are. We need the Goddess more than ever, but she won't speak to either of us."

"Why do you want a vision, anyway? Pray to her. That's all most people ever get."

"I've never been content with prayer, Shada." Belith sighed. "Huire used to visit me in person."

"When you were a holy woman?"

"Starting when I was a child, I had fits. Without warning, things around me would look different. I would smell and taste things I couldn't describe. Then Huire would come, cradle me in her arms, and tell me things that hadn't happened yet. When I woke, my mother would say I had acted strange and fallen asleep.

"It scared my parents. Each time I woke, I told them things. As I grew, the dreams came more and more. It was exhausting—for all of us. Finally, my parents sent me to a Temple convent. They thought the sisters would use my gifts for good." She flicked her fingers. "I learned a hand-sign language there that I've used to befriend some jungle creatures."

"Did joining the order help you?"

"No. My dreams became more frightening. Visions of the end times. The end of the empire, of humanity, of the stars themselves." She chuckled. "My mother superior thought I was insane or possessed. She told me the local bishop wouldn't tolerate such tales—that I should keep them secret to show my loyalty to Huire."

"Our bishop is different," Shada said. "He believes very much."

Belith shook her head at the reference to Arumin. "At any rate, I was unconvinced. The dreams were more real than life. I worried I was betraying the Goddess's generosity by not sharing her gift."

Shada could guess how this story ended. "Is that why you're on Caidfell?"

"Mostly," said Belith. "I could have kept the dreams to myself, though I might have truly lost my mind. Instead, I fled the convent and lived on the street, ranting to passersby." She laughed at the memory, not without fondness.

"I should have tried that," Shada said. She had forgotten that Belith knew almost nothing about her. That was easy to forget, the way they were speaking now.

"The sisterhoods are powerful on my birth planet," Belith continued. "They're a remnant of what that world was like before Ronia came with its Temple. Our gods spoke through women, and not even the Temple could convince us any god would do otherwise. Of all the Temple's hierarchy, my people loved the sisterhoods most. We even formed orders of our own."

"But you still had a bishop."

"We accepted our limitations. My people were few, and Ronia was next door, a single gateway from us. By the time I left, we were practically part of the city."

"Ronia took over my mother's planet. My father says she always missed her old ways."

"My people did too," said Belith, "especially when they heard me speaking. I didn't know what my visions meant, but I thought if I told others about them, the Goddess would accomplish her designs."

She opened and closed her hand. The vine waved but did not sting her. "Any time I spoke, crowds gathered. They loved it. Some believed me; some wanted to. They sensed it, like I do... Ronia will not last forever. We think it's mighty because we've seen no one mightier. But we will. Nothing stays the same. Who knows that better than me and you?"

She shook her head. "It didn't last long. Once the crowds got big enough, Ronian soldiers came for me. I hid in people's homes until someone gave me up. The bishop wanted me off the planet even more than the Ronians did. So here I am."

"Was it worth it?" Shada asked.

Belith looked alarmed. "Worth it?"

"You told the truth. You had a gift, and you tried to do the right thing."

"The right thing," the woman said tonelessly. "You've missed the point of my story, Shada."

"Which is?"

"My mother superior was right. It was a test, and I failed. Everyone told me. Everyone. But I thought I was special."

"Aren't you?"

"Aren't *you*?" Belith said with a growl.

"I... don't know."

"Some people have great tasks to accomplish." Belith's gaze drifted up to the wall over Shada's head. "Other people are tested to ensure they know their place. I'm the second kind."

"I don't believe that," said Shada.

"You're not listening. My mind was diseased, but I had the nerve to think I was some kind of prophet."

"You don't know for sure. Who are we to judge? I've done little better than you, but Huire still chose me."

"She chose you, yes. But you sound convinced you are failing her."

Shada looked at the place where the vine had emerged from under the bed. "I think I am."

"If she gives you another chance, remember me. Think of what's left when the thing that makes you special is taken away. When I was arrested, the visions stopped. They'd been nightmarish at times, but then my life became a nightmare that did not end.

"Prison was hard. But that wasn't the end. They sent me here, a place where nothing was sacred. You worked, you starved, and sooner or later, you died. People kept others as property. Children too. I saw one..." She shook her head and shut her eyes.

When she opened them, she looked at Shada.

"When your Lady shows herself again, I must speak to her. I need her. If I have to keep you here until that happens, so be it."

"You don't need to 'keep' me," Shada replied. "I'll stay. But I'm warning you, she comes only when she wishes. If you anger her, she may not come at all. She may be listening now. In the meantime, you must do something for me."

She was in a poor bargaining position, but Belith was taking her seriously. "Go on."

"The men in my company must be safe. I don't know where those shadow-things took the captain, but they must not hurt him." She didn't bother asking for their release. Without the Lady, they could not get far. She doubted either Arumin or Emberly would willingly return to Ronia. Freedom would have to wait.

Belith gave a single nod. "I'll abide by this within reason, for now."

"And something else: I will not touch that plant again."

"Why would I agree to that?"

"Because I've never felt farther from my true dreams than I did after that vine stung me. If you think the Goddess sent them, then don't poison my mind with that. I won't touch it, and neither should you."

Belith grinned. Shada could follow the lines of her teeth up to trace the outlines of her skull. The woman said, "You've lived among the Ronians all your life. You must know what penance is. I have to show Huire I'm ready to listen. If she speaks, this plant's venom is no match for her voice."

She dropped the vine. Once free, it stopped moving. She stood with a grunt, using her good hand. "We have an agreement until one of us says otherwise." She took the stained pillow from the cot and tossed it to Shada. "Sit on this. You're too young to give yourself an aching back."

"Are you going to sleep?" Shada asked.

"I doubt I'll sleep much. I haven't slept in my bed in a while—it's not really mine anymore. But I should tonight. We have so little time."

She pulled down the blanket on the cot. Shada shrieked.

Belith gazed steadily at the nest of vines covering the narrow bed. As the blanket fell away, they moved a little. Thick and mature, they grew from under the cot, where there lay a malformed mass, potato red.

Belith turned to face Shada and lowered herself toward the cot, supporting herself with her good hand on its edge.

Shada jumped up. Before she was halfway to her feet, Belith snapped, "So our agreement is ended?"

Shada sat again. Her heart pounded.

"Don't move from that spot, no matter what," said Belith. "I'm going to need you."

She lay down on the cot. As her weight settled on the vines, she twitched and whimpered. The older, stronger vines curled up to embrace her. Amid her screams, she called out Shada's name.

28

— · —

ARUMIN

ARUMIN'S STRUGGLE TO STAY afloat grew easier once he braced himself against the walls of the little hole. Pushing his back and knees against the algae-covered stone, he sank more slowly. The wound on his chest burned, and he hated to think of the filthy water seeping into it.

He would keep hoping for survival as long as he could. In the swamp, he had prematurely accepted his death, and he could not bear the pain of doing that again.

When Belith returned, he was relieved. She would bring the end closer, whatever it was. She murmured to someone in the hallway and closed the door behind her.

He was aghast at the sight of her. Welts and dried wounds spotted her face, trickling blood here and there.

As she tottered forward, he held in his curiosity. He had lost track of time since she left. It might have been minutes or hours ago. She sat down near him, nearly collapsing to the floor.

He had meant to let her speak first, but he soon lost his patience. "I thought you'd come to finish me off. But from what I see, you may not last long either."

She spoke with a tremor. "I don't know what to do with you."

"Did you think seeing me would help?" asked Arumin. Braced against the wall, he could speak easily enough.

"Maybe. Your missing friends came to save you, but they failed. Knowing that and seeing you, I hoped I would feel that you'd lost."

By "missing friends," she must mean Emberly and the others. The news of their capture was hard to swallow, and Arumin couldn't hide his bitterness. "What about this arrangement favors me?"

"Commandant, you've finally destroyed us. Years ago, you ruled us from this building—your palace." She waved a hand at the ceiling. "From here, you watched us and played that damned flute of yours. When you tired of that, you could strike us down on a whim. Now you've finished what you started. We won't survive this fight."

"I know your face," he said, "though I don't remember your crime. But tell me this: were you innocent of the charges?"

"No, certainly not."

"Did you hurt people?"

"Yes. Not their bodies but their souls."

"A false prophet. Few crimes are worse in Huire's eyes."

"I've tried to make up for it." She leaned to one side and rested on her elbow. "I've kept these people together. I've put myself through agony. But she hasn't forgiven me."

"You may not deserve forgiveness," Arumin said. "Look at what you did in the uprising. How many men did you and your brethren kill? Those men obeyed the law. They had families who depended on what little coin they earned."

"Those men served an empire without a soul. They knew its cruelty, but still they served it."

"Violence with a rational purpose is not cruel. Tell me, what was your purpose?"

"I wanted to help these people!" she snapped. "It wasn't supposed to be cruel."

"Did you truly want to help? Or did you want to be special?"

"I wouldn't respect your judgment either way."

He sniffed. "Then why are you here? To ask me to pray for you?"

"I don't need your prayers. I don't know why the Lady accepts you unless she doesn't really know you."

"Everyone knows me," said Arumin. He had slid until his face was almost underwater, and he paused to recover.

"I've been a coward and a killer. But after I fled the uprising and faced public disgrace, I threw myself at the Goddess's feet. I asked her to make me better."

As he spoke, he missed Brin with painful sharpness. "I asked her, if she would not change me, to use my flaws for her purposes. If I must be a monster, I will sin so others don't have to."

"I see." Belith smiled whimsically. "If you think she would accept that, you lack faith."

Arumin's jaw ached. He realized he was clenching his teeth. "Why are you here?"

"Don't be angry. I lack faith too. I've put several people to death. We both lack faith in kindness and forgiveness. We think the Goddess's strength is not enough—that we must apply our own. We think she needs us to rescue her."

She laughed. It echoed from the walls, a beautiful sound. "We drove you out only to replace you. First with Rayan then with me. We woke from a nightmare but created our own."

"Faith is not enough," Arumin spat. "We cannot win in this world if we ignore how this world works."

"Your Scriptures wouldn't approve of such talk."

"Here's a secret, from one leader to another: the rules are not for us."

She leaned forward, amused. "Who are they for? The little people?"

"Yes. For those whose biggest sins are stealing from their neighbor or sleeping with their brother's wife. We who shape the world are different."

"You think we're better than them?"

"No!" It was Arumin's turn to laugh. "We're worse. We tarnish our souls for their sakes. We even take their lives when we must. Then, when we die and meet Huire ourselves, we hope we made the right choices."

"Do you think you will meet her today?"

"That's up to you."

Belith lay on her side, propped up by her elbow. "I wish you could live long enough to watch everything you've worked for collapse. But I can't spare your life that long."

"Then accept your defeat and do whatever you mean to do."

"Do you know what your handsome young friend told me while I held your head under water?"

A knife stabbed Arumin's insides. He refused to show her how badly he wished to know.

"Nothing," she continued. "Think about that for whatever time you have left."

The knife sank up to its hilt. A wet chill washed over the bishop. Brin had told her nothing. Brin, who had fled the burning waytower without a thought for Arumin. Had the boy asked, the bishop would have told him to do exactly that. But that made no difference, because Brin had not asked.

Belith's voice became slow and aimless. "I pray you will die knowing you are damned."

She drew a breath and called Shada's name. The girl entered. Her eyes widened when she saw the bishop, but she said nothing. Arumin, caught off guard by her presence, returned her silence.

She knelt next to Belith.

Breathing heavily, the older woman grunted, "It must be now. Hurry."

Shada nodded. She rose to leave but stopped partway, her eyes lingering on the bishop.

Arumin found his voice. "Shada, help me out of here! Lift me up, quickly!"

Belith's head had sunk to the floor, her eyes slitted. She appeared semiconscious.

Shada told her, "I have to help the bishop. He's going to drown."

The woman did not answer.

Wrapping her arms around Arumin, Shada managed to lift him until he could throw a leg over the rim of the hole. He thrashed and squirmed his way up onto the floor.

"I'm sorry, Bishop," said Shada. "I promise I'll untie you soon. But right now, I have to hurry." And she did, out the door.

Arumin looked around for his clothes, saw them lying in a bunch in a corner, but his body was too heavy to move. He could have melted into the cracks between the stones.

He did not think to call after Shada. During this creeping, eternal day, he had dreamed of being free from the constant fear of drowning. He had remembered Belith threatening Brin and fantasized about what he would do if he got his hands on her.

Now Belith lay there, vulnerable. Shada had foolishly left them alone.

But though he was partly free, Arumin could not think clearly. He could hardly breathe. He was disintegrating, no longer a man. He looked at the watery hole, saw it was terrifyingly close, and tried to crawl away, sure he was going to tumble back in, this time forever.

29

SHADA

SHADA LEFT THE BISHOP'S cell with relief. She tried to remember Belith's directions, but images of Arumin fighting to stay alive distracted her. By letting herself relax in Belith's presence, she had nearly forgotten what the woman was capable of.

She was feeling lost when the distant roar of a crowd reached her. Following the noise, she emerged into the courtyard.

It was night outside. Torchlight revealed blood drying on the stone floor. It was enough blood to have killed whoever lost it. Amid the gore stood a pair of haunted-looking guards. In a community this small, they must have known the victim.

They raised their weapons at the sight of her. She jumped and shouted Belith's password, and they stopped short and exchanged glances. She delivered the message Belith had given her and urged them to hurry. Convinced despite their confusion, they left through the great wooden doors in the wall.

A crowd was gathering outside. News of the night's events must have reached everyone who had managed to sleep through them. Waiting for the guards to return, Shada shifted her feet and heard her boots snap in the sticky blood.

The noise outside swelled. Rayan entered through the gates, flanked by the guards, who closed the doors behind them. He ignored the blood. She knew it was him by his resemblance to the captain.

When he saw her, a parade of emotions crossed his face. The strongest was relief. "I wondered if we would meet," he said.

"Do you know who I am?"

"I know a little, Shada. There is much more I'd like to learn if you'll allow me a few words."

"There's no time now. We must hurry."

"Why, and where?" His voice turned harsh in a blink.

"First, I should tell you Belith agrees to your terms."

His mouth opened but formed no definite shape. "Terms?"

"You will lead this camp again. In return, you'll call off the wraiths' attack."

Rayan stared daggers at her, searching for the trick. "Why?"

Belith had not told her to expect this question. She had told Shada of Rayan's leadership—his lies, abuse, and manipulation. It sounded hellish, but it wouldn't do to share that opinion here. Shada replied, "It's not for me to say. You should ask her. She wants to speak with you."

He sprang forward. "Where is she? In her chamber?"

"No. I will take you to her."

"Just tell me."

She hesitated. The guards had looked as surprised at Belith's surrender as Rayan had. His eagerness to see her clearly alarmed them.

"She asked me to come with you," Shada said.

"I know this place better than anyone," he said. "I don't need a guide."

"Of course not. I wouldn't suggest otherwise." This was her usual method with hostile strangers—relentless politeness.

It worked. Maybe he realized he had been overeager. "Forgive me. I know you wouldn't. But I have something very important to tell her."

"She has things to say also. But she's ill. She'll need me to speak for her."

"Dear Shada, I have known Belith for a long, long time. I will understand her perfectly."

Shada was tired of this game. "That's not what she wants."

"But I am in command, am I not?" He edged closer.

"Not yet, you aren't. It's up to her."

"She knows she has no choice!" His courteous facade dropped again. It came and went with dizzying speed. "What right does she have to set terms? And what power do you have to enforce them, girl?"

"They have us," said a guard. "So mind your words."

Rayan turned to him in a flash. "Should I? Should I indeed, Neery? Do you miss that witch so much already?"

Neery's face was stony. "I haven't missed you. I know that."

"Careful." Rayan's eyes were bright. "Let's not start on poor terms."

"Do you hear them?" Neery asked, tipping his finger toward the door and the rumble of the crowd outside. "Do they sound happy to see you?"

Indeed, they did not. Rayan glared.

The guard continued. "If you're to have any chance of getting on here, you'll need more friends."

"Fine." Rayan looked at Shada. "Let's go to Belith. Quickly."

Shada met Neery's eyes. The man had intervened as much as he dared. Rayan had the wraiths on his side. Ultimately, Neery, his family, and everyone in the settlement needed Rayan more than they needed Belith.

After a moment's thought, Shada said, "Now that we've met, I don't think you should see Belith after all."

This struck Rayan dumb for an instant. "What?" he said finally, quietly.

"I've changed my mind. I think, when you see her, you'll kill her."

He smiled. "I didn't hear that. Think very hard, and say it again."

"You heard me."

"You will take me," he said. "I promise."

She was mute. Her throat had closed.

"It was your leader's command. Do her words mean nothing to you?"

"She's my friend, not my leader."

Rayan laughed as if charmed by a precocious child. "I have no desire to force you, dear, though I easily could. Let me appeal to your mercy instead. An army of monsters is on its way to this very spot. Only I can stop it, and only if you let me do what I must. If you want any of us to survive, there is no other way."

Shada swallowed. "You must swear not to hurt her."

Rayan's face tightened. "If you knew the things she's done, girl, you wouldn't ask me that."

He frowned thoughtfully then darted between the guards. Shoving open the doors to the camp, he shouted, "My friends, I have returned!"

The crowd's roar softened at his boldness. People seemed to wonder if their anger was misplaced. He raised his hands and shouted, "I wish I had time to greet each of you. However..."

But their confusion did not last. Perhaps it was his tone, some familiar turn of phrase, or the way he raised his hands as if accepting adoration. The crowd's angry rumble returned with new intensity.

Still, his voice boomed over the noise. "We have no time for this!"

A lull followed. Calling over their heads, he continued, "The wraiths could be here at any time. They might even be listening now."

The mob's babble became unsure. Shada heard one voice shout in protest.

Rayan yelled, "We can stop them, but you must listen to me."

The naysayer shouted again. "How do you know that?"

"I'll explain, I swear it. But first—"

"No!" the voice cut him off.

Rayan gestured to the speaker. "Come forward."

A man pushed his way to the front. He was the same man who had pulled Shada out of the pit to meet Belith. That felt like years ago.

"Didn't you hear me?" the man asked. "I said no."

"I heard, Drucin. I wish you would listen."

"There's some things I want to hear," Drucin replied. "Such as, where have you been? And why did you come back?"

"I'm here because I saw a chance to help. To prove my love for you all and to restore the trust damaged by my differences with a few of you."

"A few," said Drucin. "That's putting it kindly. Where were you all this time?"

"I've been in the jungle," Rayan answered. He surveyed the crowd, meeting people's eyes. "The wraiths held me prisoner."

The crowd grew louder again. This time, it was Drucin who cut through it.

"A prisoner? Why didn't the wraiths tell us?"

"These weren't the wraiths you know. Belith's tame allies are but a small clan among nations. They committed a terrible heresy in befriending offworlders. The vast majority of wraiths are wild, like those who recently attacked your foraging parties. They marked the tame ones for death years ago. They've marked us for death too."

The crowd's faces were doubting but afraid. Rayan might be right. This world was still alien, even to these people.

Drucin shook his head. "We've been here for a while, Rayan. If they want to kill us, they've had plenty of time."

"They were too afraid—until now. Their god was a minor one, an outcast. It designed this world to repel invaders and the wraiths to be its guardians. It instilled fear of outsiders in them. But when their god left, the wraiths' fear conquered them."

He paused dramatically and looked around. "When the Ronians came, the wraiths fought only when desperate or when they caught one of us alone. They didn't fear our strength of arms. They're too powerful for that. They feared our very essence—being infected with our demonic, alien nature."

Drucin's face was somber. "What's changed?"

"What has changed..." Rayan turned to stare at Shada. "Is that the Ronians have returned."

30

—·—

NOR

SQUINTING IN THE DARK, Nor felt for handholds in the pit's wall as the soldiers behind him watched, nonplussed. He found nothing, but he could not bear to sit still and listen. The confrontation above must be happening near to this pit, as the words of each speaker sounded clearly.

Rayan's voice rang out again. "These invaders, led by our old commandant, have stirred up the jungle's wrath. Before, the wraiths mostly left us alone, sure we would slowly die off. Now, they are convinced we're here to stay. By capturing and studying a few of us, the bravest among them have begun to fear us less. Only their fiercest warriors will dare attack, but they'll be more than enough to wipe us out."

The man he had called Drucin spoke. "How do you know what they're thinking, Rayan?"

"They learned to speak to me. Knowing their plans, I begged them to spare you all. They agreed, but on one condition. A condition that stunned and baffled me. They wanted me to return and lead you."

Scoffs and groans arose. Nor did not know if this claim was true. Putting himself in charge seemed like the kind of idea Rayan would dream up. At least he was distracted from threatening Shada.

"That's quite a tale," said Drucin. "And you've told me many. So, when you murdered our friends on guard duty this very night, you did it to rescue us. Is that right?"

Rayan's voice shrank. "To my absolute shame, I couldn't save them. The wraiths cannot be reasoned with once they make up their minds. When they brought me here, their savagery was uncontrollable."

Drucin laughed. "I suppose we'll never know what really happened. I don't know why you think you're so smart, Rayan. Maybe you'll never learn. Maybe we should give up on you."

"I know my past decisions upset some of you," Rayan replied. "I hope I can restore your belief in me, but we must survive first. You don't need to like me to trust me."

"We'll do neither," said Drucin.

Hearing this, Nor was relieved for the convicts' sake but worried for the crusaders, who would only be freed if Rayan took charge.

"Let's speak to Belith," said Rayan. "She will support me. I don't know where she is, but this girl does. We must convince her to tell us."

Nor pictured him looming over Shada. He clawed at the wall. "Stay away from her!" he shouted at the sky.

The crowd's rumble had softened on hearing Belith's name, so Nor's cry sounded all the louder. In the quiet that followed, Rayan said, "Ah."

Drucin soon collected himself. "Belith has not been herself lately," he said, sorrow clear in his voice. "We've decided she needs rest. It's us you must convince, Rayan."

"I've had an idea. Let's talk to the men I came with. They will confirm what I've said."

"You can't ask us to trust Ronian soldiers. Especially if one of them is your brother."

"No, I can't," Rayan said. "Forgive me. But maybe you'll trust a holy man."

That got their attention. "What are you talking about?"

"The pale-eyed one is a monk. Not one of these Temple priests, like Arumin and his lackey. This man owes no one anything. He's as pure as they come. He'll tell you that what I say is true."

Nor almost bounced with eagerness to get out of the pit. How he would answer their questions was another matter.

A holy man's word carried weight even here. Several people lifted the grate overhead, dropped a rope, and hauled Nor up.

As the convicts helped him to his feet, Rayan spoke to the crowd. "There's something I need before I can call off the attack. It's a flute that belonged to the commandant. He used to play it sometimes as we worked. When he fled, I kept it. Playing it will signal the wraiths that I've taken charge. Check Belith's chamber—she may have taken it."

Nor's eyes stung when he saw Shada safe. She returned his gaze, her face strained with some emotion.

Rayan continued, "If you decide you believe me, I'll need that flute. Please."

A man stood at the front of the crowd, facing Rayan. This must be Drucin. He glowered, impatient with this odd request, but called, "Neery, get it."

A younger man nearby raised his eyebrows but grunted and trotted off.

"This is Brother Nor," Rayan announced. "A truer man you will never meet. Ask him what you will."

Drucin went first. "Are you really a holy man?"

Nor imagined how battered and bedraggled he must appear. He smiled. "I am."

The floodgates of their curiosity opened. Nor replied to one question after another, too many to keep up with.

He recounted, in pieces, his experiences since leaving the waytower. The story was incredible, but he told it without wavering so they would see he believed it. He tried to catch Shada's eye once or twice but did not want to draw attention back to her.

When his account reached his capture at the prison, they had heard enough. "Your story helps Rayan somewhat," said Drucin. "It matches his when you were present. But what should we think of you, Brother Nor? You and the rest didn't think twice about the people who would die in your attempted coup. You have a strange attitude toward human life, holy man."

"It's true," Nor told him. "If I was in your place, I wouldn't know to do with me. My only defense is that I believed you were hardened killers."

"What do you think now?" Drucin asked.

"I don't know anymore."

"Rather modest for a holy man, aren't you?"

"I'm not a good monk, sir."

Drucin's eyes narrowed. "If you could repeat your actions earlier tonight, would you act differently?"

"No."

The crowd buzzed, a deep and perilous sound.

Rayan looked dismayed by the conversation's direction. "Brother Nor doesn't know the wraiths' true ferocity.

They do as they want, kill as they want. But he knows that our mission is utterly essential and that we had to do what we did."

"From what I've heard," replied Drucin, "I trust him over you, regardless of what he knows. Brother Nor, on your honor, should we follow Rayan? Can we trust him to help us, if only to help himself?"

Caught between sympathy for their captors and necessity, Nor's mind raced. The silence grew uncomfortable, and people murmured.

Finally, he found an answer he could live with. "He saved our lives. Those wraiths—those people—would have killed us if he hadn't been there. I don't know what he did to you or if he'll do it again, but this much is true: the wraiths are coming."

Drucin scoffed. "So, because we're desperate, we should give him what he asks for? Yet again?"

"It's not about giving him anything. If you hope to live freely, you must accept his presence. The Goddess forgives us our sins, so long as we forgive each other."

He did not get to see whether his words made an impact. Neery returned. "The flute is gone!" he shouted.

Rayan paled. "Did you search in my chamber?"

"Didn't have to," Neery reported. "That room is mine now."

Rayan shoved his hands through his tangled hair. "Belith put it somewhere. She must have. She took everything that was mine."

One by one, everyone looked at Shada. Nor could not protect her, though he would try.

"Time to tell us where she is, love," said Drucin.

Shada was defiant. "I don't want her hurt."

"That's up to me," Rayan snapped.

"We'll find her regardless," Drucin said. "Without your help, it'll take longer. You're risking our lives."

It was true. Nor wondered why Shada put such value on that brutal woman's life.

Shada said, "Swear she won't be harmed."

"That won't be necessary," said a pained, powerful voice behind her. Arumin stood inside the courtyard, at the keep's door. His wrists were raw where rope had bound them. Belith leaned against him, nearly lifeless. He had a knife at her throat.

A hush fell. Someone said, "It's you."

31

ARUMIN

ARUMIN KEPT THE KNIFE against Belith's skin. He had half expected the crowd to charge at him, but so far, no one had moved. "I've brought you what you need," he called. "Let's discuss what you can do for us."

The people watched, breathless. Many had seen the bishop since his capture, but they still looked as if they were watching a ghost.

"What if we're not interested?" called Rayan.

"I'll carry out the sentence this heretic deserves."

Rayan smiled. "I think you've been deceived, Commandant. Has Belith been telling you she's important?"

"If she isn't, do what you will to me." Arumin kept his tone casual. "She'll die, but no matter. Then you can kill me however you choose. You've all dreamed of it, I'm sure."

No one moved.

"Bishop." Shada spoke softly, commandingly. "Let her go. This is not the way."

"Be at peace, Caretaker," said Arumin. "These people have twisted your mind. It's not your fault. They held your life in their hands. But that's over now. You're free."

Shada appeared baffled. "You've got this wrong. Please, stop."

"I know what I'm doing."

"So do I!" She stepped forward. "I speak for the Lady, and I'm telling you—"

"Stay back," Arumin shouted, "or I'll give your new friend what she deserves!"

Shada halted.

The bishop gentled his voice. "Dear, you speak for the convicts right now, whether you think so or not." He was not sure that was true, but the Lady must be on his side. She must. "You have to trust me."

"Bishop..." she began, but she glanced at Belith and stopped. Bold as she was becoming, she would not risk this damnable woman's life.

Rayan interjected, his tone agreeable. "I suppose she must live for the moment. She has something we need. You need it too, Commandant, though you don't know it. Do you remember your old flute?"

A ray of memory struck Arumin like sunlight through storm clouds. He remembered the flute, all right. He forced himself to laugh. "My flute?" But his mocking tone sounded forced, even to him.

"Of course you remember. We all do. Its music, drifting down from up on these walls. So many lived and died to that sound."

"I recall it." The bishop was confused and off balance. "A trivial thing to fight over."

"You couldn't have liked it much, since you left it behind," said Rayan. "Then again, you fled this place in a hurry."

Arumin did not flinch. That barb had pierced him many times. "Why that flute, of all things?"

"Its sound will call off the wraiths," said Drucin. "It's a long story."

Arumin's eyes jumped around and landed on Shada. At first, she looked afraid for his safety, but then he realized she was actually afraid for Belith.

"It's true," she said.

Despite his suspicions, he had little choice but to believe her for now. He lowered his head to Belith's ear. "Whisper it to me, old woman. Where is the flute?"

Belith gazed at him, her eyes unfocused. She whipped her head away and screamed for all to hear, "It's under the vines, you bastard!" She sagged, exhausted.

"She's lost her mind," Rayan concluded. "You said it yourself, Drucin. She isn't the same."

Shada gasped. "I know where it is! She keeps a vine plant in her room. Is that it, Belith?"

The woman did not answer. She might not have heard.

"I saw the vines," said Neery with a grimace. "She's been poisoning herself." He looked at Belith mournfully.

"If you know where it is, get it!" Rayan demanded.

But Neery showed no intention of leaving. He sent the other guard, a thin boy who thought better than to argue.

"That's that, Commandant," said Drucin. "You can gain nothing more from Sister Belith except our favor for letting her go."

Arumin tightened his grip on Belith. She had nearly drowned him, and now they wanted him to release her. "Why would I trust a convict's word? You fancy yourself taking charge next, I'll wager."

Drucin grimaced. "Nothing would please me less. Release her, and you might live. That's all."

"I haven't finished. If you value her life, release me and my company. Give us our wagons and supplies and set us free. You'll have no more to fear from us."

Rayan giggled like someone much younger. "Do you really still hope to leave? Your company may survive if I allow it. But you are finished, Commandant."

Cornered, fighting panic, Arumin shook Belith. "Not before I send this pitiful old thing to the dark."

Rayan tensed, bending his knees, ready to rush at Arumin. "Do what you must."

The bishop saw no way out. He would face whatever came. Trembling, he said, "Come on then. Let Huire's will be done."

Before Rayan took two steps, Neery knocked him down. Springing up, Rayan found Neery standing in his way.

Eyes blazing, Rayan called to the crowd. "This one has made his choice. He has defied me, his leader."

Neery replied thoughtfully. "When we took over the prison, you said we'd have no leaders."

Finding no support in the crowd, Rayan shouted, "It's not my fault that dream ended. It was all of you. You chose *her*!"

"The dream ended with you. Belith has killed, but she's never lied," said Drucin. "I've found I prefer that."

Rayan stepped here and there as if the ground was giving way. "Let's see if she's honest now. Belith, who should they choose, you or me?"

Belith didn't move.

Arumin could not feel her breathing. "I'll have to speak for her, I'm afraid," he said grandly. "She's been feeling a little—"

Belith gasped, "Forget me!"

The bishop pulled her head back and pushed his knife.

"No!" Drucin cried. His voice cracked. "What do you want?"

Arumin drew the knife back a little. Belith's neck bled, but the cut was not deep.

Rayan stared at Drucin in unabashed horror.

Drucin said, "You and your people can leave, Arumin. You're a monster, but I think your time is nearly over."

Arumin was triumphant. "Get my men out of those pits."

"In a moment. First, we need to find the flute."

"Bring them up. Now!" The last word rang like a gunshot.

Drucin exchanged glances with his neighbors. "What do you say, Brother Nor?"

"The bishop won't trouble you again," said Nor. "You can trust him that far."

Drucin spoke quietly to the others. People dispersed to arm themselves and open the pits. Rayan had been watching in silent disbelief.

"This is insane," he cried. "You're going to release the man who worked our friends to death, who stalks in our nightmares." He stabbed a finger at the bishop. "He's right there! Revenge is ours. The only price is the life of another killer. Belith has earned her fate."

"Haven't we all?" asked Drucin softly. "You have, Rayan. But we're still here."

The young guard returned with the flute. He walked unsteadily, bent over, his sleeves ripped and his hands and forearms swollen and bloody.

"Bring it here!" said Rayan.

The boy walked across the courtyard toward the gate, passing Arumin and Belith. His pace was meandering, and his face was red with pain.

"Stop right there, boy," Arumin called. "Come to me."

The young man halted and looked back at the bishop. His will seemed hardly his own. Seeing his hesitation, Rayan strode toward him. This time, Neery followed.

"No! Back!" The words tore from Arumin's throat, and his knife twitched.

Neery stopped and held Rayan back with his arm. His eyes darted, assessing the distance to Arumin.

"Give it to me," Arumin commanded in a voice that could shake a temple.

"You're winning, Commandant," said Drucin. "Don't spoil it now."

"I won't spoil anything," the bishop replied. "I want to play a few notes." His old Gallobrethi accent had slipped out.

"Damn you," said Rayan, still behind Neery's arm. "No more. You've had your mercy, but no more."

The young guard held the flute in both hands. Tears ran down his face.

Arumin spoke gently to him. "Do you want her to be safe?"

The boy's head bobbed up and down, making him appear even younger.

"She's been hurting herself, you know," Arumin said. "Judging by your hands, you know how she feels. Don't you want her to get better?"

"Fool," said Rayan, "she's already dead."

The young man took heavy breaths. Arumin continued. "Of course you wish to help her. Bring the flute to me."

The pain in the young man's arms must have flared. He bent and cried out, then touched one hand gingerly with the other. Seeing Shada, he gasped, "How long has she done this to herself?"

He turned to Arumin. With a few quick steps, he offered the flute to the bishop.

Arumin snatched it, dropping Belith. The woman fell to her knees and slumped until her forehead met the ground. He put his boot on her neck.

"Stay back or I'll snap this in half." Gripping his knife with two fingers, the bishop held the flute with a hand on either end. "I'll play one last song. What notes will call off the wraiths?"

"Anything," muttered Rayan. "They remember its sound."

Amid desolate silence, Arumin stowed the knife and raised the flute's lip plate to his mouth. Its body pointed to his right, where his fingers fell naturally on the proper holes.

Chest aching with the effort, the bishop played his favorite tune. He had learned it long ago as a ballad. Over the years, he had altered a note here and there and slowed the tempo. The tune had become a creature of his own creation, graceful, relaxed, and endlessly cruel. Recalling it, Brin had claimed he could not hold the entire melody in his mind at once.

By the time it ended, the crowd had huddled closer together. Drucin had crossed his arms and turned his face down to the mud.

Arumin lowered the flute. "No one has cleaned this," he said.

Something pushed the back of his legs. He looked down with surprise as he fell to the courtyard floor. Belith lay with her arms around his ankle, her shoulder resting on his calf where she had pushed him.

Neery reached the bishop first, followed by Rayan and many others. At first, they tried to hold him in place, but the action quickly became violent. Arumin curled under a rain of boots and fists.

"Enough!" cried Belith. The bishop opened his eyes to see people lifting her clear of the melee. She struggled against the reassuring hands and voices.

The attack on Arumin ground to a halt as others echoed her call. Belith shook her head and tried to laugh but only coughed. She managed to say, "This won't work."

Looming over the bishop, Rayan sneered. "Oh? What do you suggest?"

"Shut up," said Drucin. "Sister Belith, what should we do?"

Belith turned her head this way and that, smiling faintly. Her smile faded. She was looking at Shada, who had come to stand over the bishop, staring down at him with sad eyes and open mouth.

"Bring up the captain," Belith said. "It's time to talk."

Stone pressed against Arumin's cheek. Nearby, flies buzzed over puddles of drying blood. As one last boot fell on him, he wondered where Brin was.

32

—·—

EMBERLY

"HELLO, CAPTAIN EMBERLY. HAVE a seat." Belith's voice was hoarse but reasonably hospitable.

Emberly took the only other chair, which sat facing her with nothing between. Her chamber was mostly empty otherwise except for two guards who had brought him here and a small cot covered with a blanket. A cane leaned on her chair.

She asked, "Has anyone told you what happened by the gates?"

"I've heard a little. I know the attack by Rayan's wraiths was called off. Speaking of my brother, where is he?"

Sinking low in the seat, she pushed herself straight with a grunt. She seemed likely to fall off the chair if she leaned the wrong direction. The guards tried to help, but she waved them away.

"Rayan's off somewhere, brooding," she said. "I asked them to hold him, but he slipped away. So, you've heard what Arumin tried to do?"

"Yes. Would you like an apology?"

She cackled. "You make a poor prisoner, Captain. You wouldn't have survived as one of us. No, don't apologize. I'm no more doomed than I ever was. But you, I pity you." A coughing fit occupied her for a moment. "You're still tied to Arumin."

"The bishop did what prisoners do. He tried to escape. As a Temple elder, he takes threats to Huire's will seriously."

"Do you really feel kindly toward him?"

"I believe in him because my soldiers must."

"No, then?"

"I think the Goddess is on his side. It's not my place to question her choice of tools."

She smiled. "Did the Goddess tell you this herself?"

"No. But I've seen her at work."

Belith's face was lively. "I think you're right that Huire favors him. Your company made it here mostly alive, and even in defeat, you're at the mercy of a woman who lacks the stomach for more killing."

She coughed again and put a hand on her chest. "Here's the problem. I want to change, Emberly. I keep hoping for miracles and visions when really, I should be doing Huire's work right now. If my people and I hope to keep our souls, we've got to act better. We can't do that if our answer is always death.

"I wish to release you all, even Arumin. Given certain terms. But if I do, I can't ensure my people's safety."

"What if you release us unarmed?"

She shook her head. "In that jungle, with the wraiths, it would be as good as killing you. Rayan lied when he said he would release you, or else he wants you dead. I don't know if you heard, but most wraiths out there are not our friends. I've befriended only a small group—'tame wraiths,' we call them. Not a flattering term or an accurate one, but it has stuck."

She fingered the top of her cane. "Most wraiths out there, like the ones who held you, are hostile. We call them 'wild wraiths,' and they've attacked our foraging parties recently. Even armed, I'm not sure how you'll make it to your hidden gateway. Does the Lady really know the way?"

She mentioned the Lady and the gateway so casually that a few heartbeats passed before Emberly remembered she should not know about them.

His face must have betrayed his shock, which she dismissed with a shake of her head. "Shada told me about your... crusade, is it? Be grateful to her. The story you arranged to hide your purpose was pitiful, and she saved your lives by telling me the truth."

Still reeling, Emberly tried to think. He should have expected this. The cover story had been an afterthought, and the fault for that must be his. In retrospect, the crusade's attempt at secrecy seemed like a lost cause.

If she knew about this, she might have learned he had freed Rayan. He did not fully trust Rayan to have kept that secret.

Watching him, Belith continued. "A fantastic story, one I have yet to see proven. But I'll entertain it because I've seen things nearly as fantastic. And, frankly, I want badly to believe it."

Emberly frowned. "Assuming those things are true, it's in your interest not to defy the Lady by keeping us here." It was a bluff, of course. She might not know the Lady refused to protect his company.

Belith raised her hands in mock surrender. "I won't argue. As I said, your release is my goal. The last thing I need is more mouths to feed. But if I must keep you here, I will, until we're all old and gray. Let the Lady do what she will. To win your freedom, you must help me."

"Go on."

Half a smile crossed her face. "I want to meet the Lady."

His mouth opened. "You what?"

"If she's real, if you're really on a holy quest to save the empire, this is a small request. I want to see her, speak with her, and receive her guidance. I'm in desperate straits here, Captain, and my sources of spiritual wisdom have all dried up or failed me. No longer can I function without them."

He collected himself. He had expected demands, vows, and safety to be her priorities. Instead, she had asked for something simple but, maybe, impossible. The Lady would not help the company through danger, so she would probably not help here either.

"First, I don't command her," he said. "I don't even speak to her. All her communication comes through Shada."

"So I hear. But Shada can't summon her, or won't."

"None of us can. She is not some servant who comes when called."

Belith clasped her hands. "But she will emerge from hiding to protect you, surely."

"Meeting her by threatening us might be the last thing you ever do."

She sat back slowly. "What if I merely keep you from your mission? It seems worth a try."

"It isn't." He sighed. "She won't emerge. For reasons of her own, she refuses to interfere in our affairs unless at the uttermost need." His instincts rebelled against admitting vulnerability, but he must.

Neither of them spoke for a while. She looked deep in thought.

Finally, she nodded. "I'm willing to risk it." She smiled and breathed deeply as if released from a burden. "Yes. You will live in those holes forever. Unless you've got a better option."

He forced himself to be calm. "I will talk to Shada. But I don't know. What you're asking I cannot guarantee. You must be prepared to compromise."

She stretched and sank into a relaxed posture. "I've already compromised, Captain. Before you sat down, I intended to demand that all us convicts receive actual pardons from Ronia. Wouldn't that have been a fitting punishment for your lies? Demanding that you make them true?"

She chuckled. "Don't worry, I know it's impossible. I might as well ask you to pull the stars from the sky for me. And yet." Her mouth curled playfully. "Is it really so insane? We have lumber here and minerals. We could trade with Ronia for things each of us lacks. If the empire only forgave us, we could—"

"It will not happen." Emberly spoke flatly. Her voice had contained a spark of hope. To proceed, he must stomp it into the dust. "Forgiving a betrayal as vast as yours would make betrayal less costly. It would poison the empire."

"Fine, fine." She waved his attack away. "Consider the idea withdrawn. I just wanted someone to hear it once." She pursed her lips. "Let's set aside my miracle for a moment. You must still reassure me about Commandant Arumin."

"Wait." Emberly gulped, though he tried to be still. "I've got a condition of my own."

"Is that so? Right after you refused mine? Very well. I'll at least hear it."

He paused to prepare himself. "How much control do you have over your people?"

"They listen to me. I let them know where they stand."

"Will they keep a secret for you?"

A lovely smile spread across her face. "A secret? Maybe. Go on."

"After the prison fell in the revolt, Ronia sent a military force to take it back."

"I know this. We all know it here."

"Well, my soldiers don't."

Her eyebrows rose.

He continued, "It's one of the empire's embarrassing secrets. After the prison fell, the Ronian army had been humiliated, and it wanted its honor back." He scoffed at the memory. "An army came to retake Caidfell. Only a few high-ranking officers knew it. When they consulted me, I advised against the whole thing, but that made no difference. They entered the jungle as if it was a garden they meant to trample."

"We never even met them in battle," said Belith, sounding awed by the memory. "We only heard their guns and, much later, ventured out to see the aftermath."

Emberly shook his head. "The army refuses to learn. No one respects this planet until they serve here."

"Indeed." She frowned. "The jungle had seen enough of those uniforms. It tore your men apart. We only found remains. I'd never seen anything like it. I was amazed your company came here."

"The chance of Huire's return convinced important people to authorize the crusade. Everyone involved in the failed attack is sworn to secrecy." It was an amazing relief to talk about this with someone who understood. "I knew the same thing wouldn't happen to this company, because I know what that army did wrong. They met the jungle head on instead of bowing and entering humbly. I didn't make the same mistake."

She said, "None of your people know about the failed attack? Not even Arumin?"

"A couple suspect something. They saw me talk to the wraiths using symbols developed during that campaign. The army stumbled into their lairs and scared them enough to actually fight us. The soldiers who survived the first encounters learned to talk to them."

She laughed darkly. "If your men didn't know how smart the wraiths are, they know now."

"The wraiths were a ghost story to them until we came here," said Emberly. "This whole planet is a ghost story. Some of them believed, but seeing is different."

She straightened in her seat. "Well. And I thought Shada's tale was hard to believe."

"The part with the wraiths strains credulity, I know."

"Not that. I'm thinking of the part where Rayan let you escape his control. As for the wraiths, we convicts learned long ago that they can talk. Their mouths aren't shaped for speaking, but there are other ways. You know a couple—their vapors, your symbols—but the best is right here."

She raised her hands and flicked her fingers in a series of formations. "After the uprising, I was the only person in the camp who knew a hand-sign language. When a small group of wraiths came around, hoping to befriend us, I realized they could learn to sign. That made me very influential." She smiled. "I've never taught anyone else, least of all Rayan."

Emberly shook his head, impressed. There were benefits to respecting the jungle. "It's good to know I'm talking to the right person. But I have to know: can your people keep my secret? I never planned for this. I thought if surviving convicts captured us, this would be the least of our concerns."

"I think I can accommodate you, Captain. Assuming you accommodate me."

"As I said, I'll try."

"Of course, I can't promise Rayan won't tell."

"I'll handle him myself," said Emberly. "He was willing to release our company, so I think I can convince him."

Belith's face had fallen when she mentioned Rayan's name. Emberly heard dread in her voice. "Captain... we need to discuss him."

"What more is there to say? He's not in charge anymore."

"No, but he's still dangerous. I don't believe he meant to release your company. I'm afraid he may reveal your secret because you tell him not to. You should never trust him, Emberly. He acts and speaks well enough to get what he wants, but his loyalties change as often as his ambitions."

"He's too smart," the captain concluded. "Why are we talking about this? Who are you to tell me about my brother?"

"I'm someone who knows him well, maybe better than you. He forgets any promises he makes. If you remember them, he makes you feel ashamed for remembering."

Emberly's impatience was overcoming his diplomacy. "Your opinion is your own. Otherwise, none of this is your concern."

"It *is* my concern. I wish you would listen. When Rayan ruled this place, he did it mostly without violence. But there are other ways to crush the spirit, and he used them all. And he won't stop just because I let him live today."

"Enough." Emberly leaned forward. "If you will release us, my men and I will vow not to harm you. I'll do what I can regarding the Lady."

She sighed. "We come to the final obstacle. I might believe you, Captain, but you can't expect me to trust Arumin. Not after all he did here. Releasing him could be the death of us."

"You're wrong. The bishop cares about our company's mission more than anything. He'll trade peace for freedom."

"And forgo his revenge? This man forced my people to give him his old flute then played the song he played when we were slaves. That's how far his forgiveness goes. Now he has a company of soldiers whose souls are in his hands."

"I won't claim he's a good man," said Emberly. "But believe it or not, he doesn't care enough about any of you to risk our crusade in a pointless fight. Since you've allied with a group of wraiths, you'll be even more protected."

"Those wraiths don't always come and go as I wish," she replied. "What about when your quest is over? You'll march back through this planet in triumph. What's to stop him then?"

"Huire won't let him," said Emberly bluntly. "If that time comes, injustice will disappear."

She smiled. "I can see why you're a war hero. You served under Arumin and saw what he was capable of—you even carried out his orders—but you're still devoted to him. It makes me wonder if, under your decorum, you're a monster too. After all, you survived the uprising."

Anxiety stabbed at Emberly. She might, after all, know he had freed Rayan. "I survived because my brother saved me from all of you."

"Yes. He said you were off limits. So we returned you to Ronia and told your people we couldn't murder a man who'd fought so bravely. It seems they believed us. And I believed Rayan spared you simply out of love until I came to know him better."

The captain's chest ached with fear. "How can this possibly matter now?"

"I don't believe Rayan is capable of pure generosity. There was more to your survival than brotherly affection, wasn't there? And now, ten years later, you've come back."

"What are you suggesting?"

She squinted at him like an elderly woman who'd lost her reading glasses. "I don't know. I only know that when you leave, you'll likely never see him again. I, however, must live with him for the rest of my life. That scares me."

Her face became teary, and Emberly could guess what she had looked like as a girl. "He's a nightmare," she said.

Emberly's fear began draining away. Without it, he was merely sick and exhausted. "You seem like a nightmare yourself."

She laughed through her tears. "It comes back to that, doesn't it? I deserve this. We've survived here for so long, only to be crushed between the jungle and Huire's army. If we let you go, we risk putting ourselves at Arumin's mercy. If we keep you in those pits forever, we'll have rebuilt the prison. If we kill you, we'll lose what remains of our souls. And who knows when your Lady may return and wreak vengeance on us?"

Watching her, Emberly felt pity that soured instantly. "Your options are limited."

She said nothing.

Emberly pushed his advantage. "I'm not some puppet in Rayan's schemes. He released me because, no matter what, he's my brother. My return to Caidfell was simply bad luck. It's one step on a larger errand."

She gazed intently at him. "If I release you, can you control Arumin? In case his devotion to your cause falters."

"Yes."

"I must know how. I cannot risk his wrath."

"I command the company. That's why he asked me to join it. To command."

"Will your men obey you over him? Even if he threatens their souls?"

"Yes." The word echoed, and Emberly thought he had answered a little too quickly.

"And my miracle..."

"I'll do what I can." He ground his teeth. "You must accept that. Or don't if you still imagine you have a choice."

Her stare was icy. "I guess we're all prisoners. Very well. We'll release your company in the morning. If you wish, Captain, you may stay in the keep tonight. Under guard, of course."

"No. Return me to the pit."

33

NOR

Guards hoisted Nor from the pit again in the dead of night, after the commotion had died down. Brin waited among them. The guards led the two captives into the keep, treating them more gently than before.

They came to a downward stair. Before they descended, Nor saw Brin take a deep breath. Beneath the keep, they entered cool, damp hallways. Nor clung to one of the more hopeful possibilities, and he was right. The guards ushered them into a cell in which Arumin sat against a wall like flotsam washed up on a beach.

The bishop's chin rested on his crossed arms over bent knees. The beating he'd taken from the convicts showed in bruises on his face. Brin and Nor joined him, and the three battered holy men sat, each with his own wall, in what an onlooker might have mistaken for pious silence.

Brin and Arumin had greeted each other with a stiff mumble. Though Nor wondered what had passed between them, he enjoyed the quiet and groaned inwardly when the bishop spoke.

"I heard you find me trustworthy, Brother Nor. I'm honored." Arumin's voice was gravelly, as if he hadn't spoken in some time.

"I told our captors what they wanted to hear, Your Holiness. What would you have preferred?"

The bishop sighed. "A joke, Nor. You did well." His voice was strained, without the knowing arrogance that so irritated Nor. He fiddled with a small object—a shard of his flute. The convicts must have trampled it when they attacked him.

"I'm surprised to hear you say that, Bishop," said the monk. "I've done little more than stay alive."

Exhaling, Arumin tossed the piece of flute away. It clattered into a corner. "It's your duty to survive if you can. The faith and hopes of our company rest in the three of us. If we die, it should be for a greater purpose."

Nor didn't care to listen to Arumin opine on duty. "I don't think everyone in the company feels that way about me. Their comrades died in the jungle, and I didn't."

The bishop shrugged. "That's part of mourning. When soldiers lose their brothers, they want to fight. We both know what that's like. We're soldiers in our own way."

"It's more than that," Nor replied. The bishop did not usually associate the monk with himself, let alone compare him favorably. It made Nor uneasy. Maybe a sound beating had improved the old man's temperament. "I argued, loudly, with a couple men on our first night on Caidfell. Then they died while away in the jungle with me. That must have made people suspicious."

The bishop asked casually, "Are their suspicions correct?"

Nor knew Arumin thought poorly of him, but he was still surprised. "Of course not. Sergeant Orund picked them to come with me and Emberly. I'll bet it was me who was supposed to die out there."

"Ronians have long memories for perceived injustices. A man with your history will always have enemies among them."

"My history," said Nor. His throat was dry. "It was months ago, and it was only a fistfight."

"Not to the man you fought," said Arumin. "He relives it every day, I'm sure. You hurt him, so you've been hurt in turn, and you have more hurting ahead. That's the nature of ill-considered violence. You have nothing to complain about."

It was a harsh judgment but hard to dispute. Hearing it in a reasonable tone from a man who detested him, Nor found its truth easier to accept. "I'm not proud of it," he reflected. "But I'm not ashamed, either. I wonder why."

"It's pride," said the bishop matter-of-factly. "You are deeply infected with it. Believe me, I recognize it because I'm thoroughly guilty myself."

Nor shook his head. "I feel like I'm under attack. Not just now but always."

"Exactly."

Arumin's assessments, stated without his usual sardonic edge, made Nor want to keep talking. "I feel like something is stalking me," he said. It was a strange, frightening admission, but he suspected the bishop would know what he meant. The room shrank, or maybe he was growing larger. His inability to tell which dizzied him. "It's silent, and it wants to strangle me. Whenever I turn my back to a shadow, I feel it. Sometimes, it won't even let me speak."

"Have you wondered why?" asked Arumin.

Nor looked at Brin, who was hugging his knees and staring at his lap. Nor had thought the posture showed exhaustion or despair. But maybe it showed simple indifference. The young priest might be untouchable even now.

"Sometimes I do," said the monk. "But I tell myself it's all my imagination."

"No doubt it is. But sometimes, forces outside of ourselves use our imaginations as tools."

Nor said, "It won't leave me alone. I forget about it sometimes, but it comes back."

"That's because you haven't listened to it." Arumin's tone suggested this should be obvious.

"But it doesn't speak!" Nor cried. Hearing his voice echo out in the corridor, he shut his mouth, embarrassed.

For once, Arumin was not bothered by the monk's disrespect. "By not speaking, it sets an example. This is harsh, Brother Nor, but you're a fool. You are brave, and you can even be wise, but you can hardly speak without creating chaos. I suspect you do it on purpose."

Nor lacked the spirit to deny it. "What can I do?"

Arumin's eyes pierced him. "Accept the pain. The empire abused your people, as it did mine. But where would we be without it? Ronia is a beast, but it's not the only one or the worst. Revenge is not our right. We are not wise enough, and it's arrogant to think otherwise."

Nor was tempted to mention the bishop's reputation for vengefulness, but despite himself, he hoped to keep the old man's approval a little while longer. "I don't think I can accept that much pain."

"Of course you can." The bishop pointed to one of his own bruises, wincing as his finger tapped the sore spot. "This crusade is the first step. You've joined forces with Ronian troops, your former enemies, for the good of everyone. Together, we'll find the one who will save us."

"I don't think I'm worthy."

"None of us are," said the bishop. He stared at Brin, who shriveled. "We don't deserve honor or forgiveness. But Huire offers them regardless. Even prideful men like us have our uses."

"Such as?" Nor asked.

"Guarding against dangerous pride in others. Do you know whom I mean?"

Nor looked at the ceiling as disappointment washed over him. He should have known the bishop had an agenda. "Emberly."

"Exactly right. On Gallobraith, the captain behaved recklessly. Though he gave my kinsmen there a well-deserved thrashing, he put too many lives in too much risk.

"Some of his soldiers saw it, and so did his superiors. They removed him before he could do real damage. It wouldn't do if the hero of Caidfell crumbled in front of everyone."

Nor thought of Private Robir's warning about Emberly. He replied, "I don't like the captain. And he may have a reckless side. But I can't think too badly of a man who saved my life a few hours ago. I feel like... I owe him."

Arumin ignored this. "The man is a mystery," he said. "It will come clear, sooner or later. When it does, I must know I can count on your loyalty."

Nor avoided refusing outright, which might make Arumin his enemy again, by asking a question. "Why in Huire's name did you enlist him for the crusade? I heard you pursued him for the job."

"Because the crusade would not have occurred otherwise. The Temple elders and the army's high command doubted the whole affair. We needed a hero, even an imaginary one. Like the rest of us, the captain is being given a chance for redemption."

"Well, Huire must have meant him to be here," said Nor. "We ought to accept that." He had more questions for the bishop. They had not even mentioned his and Robir's torture by the wraiths.

But the door opened to reveal Shada, with a guard behind her.

"Brother Nor," she blurted. "I heard you were here." Only when she entered the room did she see its other occupants. She stopped and said, "Oh." The syllable hung in the air as the guard shut the door.

"What is it, Caretaker?" Nor asked.

Her gaze reflected anxiety at the other men's presence. She might keep some things to herself. "I have a question and a confession to make, and I—" She seemed lost. "But you're busy."

"He is not busy, my dear," said Arumin. "Please go on."

Her eyes locked on Nor's, and he saw a plea there.

"Shada," he said, "the vows we took as crusaders promise the forgiveness of our sins. It's not really necessary to confess them."

"I disagree," said the bishop. "A confession can ease the soul, whether it's 'necessary' or not. Especially if not confessing means keeping a secret that harms the crusade. That may anger the Lady and the Goddess."

Shada nodded. "I..."

Seeing her nervousness, Nor interrupted. "Do you need more time to reflect before we talk?" He was happy she had hoped to see him, but there was something she was not ready to say.

She nodded eagerly. "Yes, I think I've been too hasty. We will talk soon."

Arumin's eyes darted between them. "Nonsense, dear. Huire already knows our hearts. We confess for our own sake. We gain nothing by delaying but further self-deception."

"I..." Shada stumbled.

"Confess yourself now, to Brother Nor." The bishop spoke kindly but firmly. His reflectiveness had gone away in a flash, replaced by icy calculation.

"I've never confessed before," Shada whispered.

"No matter. He will guide you."

Nor noted how the bishop could sound kindly even when forcing someone to do something. One could not believe a word the old man said. "Arum—" The monk began angrily, but caught himself. "Bishop, isn't a confession a private matter? Must she speak in front of three people?"

"Ordinarily, maybe. But that is at the holy man's discretion, and our circumstances are not ordinary. The caretaker should confess now, before she faces further danger."

Nor would not yield. "How will she focus with so many eyes on her?"

The bishop stared at him, his voice once again quietly menacing. "Only one set of eyes matters a whit, Nor, and they're not ours."

"Do you really—"

"If she is unwilling to endure confession, she shouldn't have sinned."

As the men stared at each other, Shada said, "It's about the Lady. I can't please her. I ask too many questions."

They all stared at her.

Arumin spoke first. "What kind of questions, dear?"

She looked around, clearly conscious of her audience. "Questions about why she does the things she does. Sometimes it's hard to obey without knowing why."

"It can certainly be difficult," said Arumin with an air of charity. "But it must be done. Where is she now?"

Shada swallowed. "I don't know. I haven't seen her for hours."

Silence reigned. Arumin recovered his footing. "Tell me what happened." It was the least grandfatherly tone Nor had ever heard him take with her.

"We argued," Shada began. "I could not accept certain things she said. I tried, but... I think my faith is lacking. She got angry and left."

"Where did she go?"

"I don't know. They took her box from me."

"The convicts have obviously come to trust you," said the bishop. "You should have asked them to return it."

Shada would find no comfort even in Nor's face. People often saw their own guilt in his blank eyes. "I'm sorry." She flushed as she blinked back tears.

"You're not well," said Nor. "Bishop, we must give her a moment at least."

"No," Shada said with abrupt finality. "We'll talk now. But you're right, I'm out of sorts. It's everything. My throat still hurts from the fire, and my head where the man hit me—"

"Who hit you?" asked Arumin. His tone was nearly accusatory. He disliked not knowing things.

Shada looked surprised. "The man in the waytower. The one who tried to steal the Lady. When we fought, he—"

"Stop." Arumin leaned forward slowly. "What did you say?"

"The man who started the fire, he hit me."

"And..." Arumin's eyes were wide. "He tried to take the Lady?"

Nor had sat up straight when Shada mentioned the Lady. He pitied the caretaker, who had obviously gone through more than he knew, but a threat to the Lady overshadowed all else. "In the waytower?" he asked dumbly.

"Yes," said Shada. "One of Emberly's men. I thought Father Brin would have told you by now. Didn't he..."

She seemed to realize as she spoke that no, Brin clearly had not. They all looked at the young priest, who shrank into himself, face dark with rage or, maybe, shame.

Momentarily speechless, Arumin licked his lips. He spoke slowly, like the creep of death. "Since my assistant failed to inform me of all this the very instant he saw me, I must ask you to tell me, dear. Sit down."

"Let her collect herself," said Nor.

"Sit *down*," Arumin snapped, removing all dispute. "And tell me exactly what happened. Don't leave anything out, and don't lie. If we can't find the Lady and guard her, our souls could be lost. More than one of us has something to confess."

Shada sat down by the door, as far from any of them as she could get. Meanwhile, Brin rocked in place. Nor shivered, wondering which of them in that room felt the most alone.

34

EMBERLY

DISTANT GUNFIRE RESOUNDED. SMOKE and blood filled a small room. Insects swarmed in silent tyranny.

The small, pale face of a boy waited.

Emberly found upon waking that the shooting was not only in his dream. From the predawn sky above the pit's grating, screams echoed down. People sprinted past, shouting, raising an alarm.

The captain leaped to his feet amid his stirring men, calling to the sky, "Hello? What's happening? Let us out!"

He raised his voice each time a set of racing feet passed. His soldiers rose, glancing from him to the grate in confusion, needing answers Emberly did not have.

Only when he stopped for breath did faces appear above. Sets of hands shifted the grate and threw down a rope.

The captain pounced on the rope and called at his captors to hurry. "Wait here," he told his soldiers, who, to their frustration, had little choice.

Two men dragged him up as he dug into the wall with his boots to climb faster. Belith waited at the top.

Her health appeared worse than it had last night. She leaned, trembling, on her cane.

He began to ask her about the commotion, but she pointed past him. Some distance away, beyond the edge of the camp, lay butchered carcasses.

"Dear Goddess." He hustled toward the scene of violence. From a distance, the bodies looked like animals, but a close view of their anatomy showed otherwise.

"Wraiths." His mind raced.

Belith, hobbling, caught up a couple of minutes later. When she saw his eyes, she nodded grimly. She waited as he reached certain unavoidable conclusions.

"The wild wraiths attacked us after all," he said.

"Yes."

"Why aren't we dead? How many are hurt?"

"None that I know of. My tame wraiths defended us. I've asked them to keep a lookout lately." She scanned the distant tree line. "We had guards posted also, but the fight was so short and fast, it ended before they could get involved. Luckily, the enemy's force was small."

Despite the grim sight of the battle's aftermath, images from Emberly's dream still burned in his mind with the clarity of a holy vision. Quickly sorting it all, he decided what to do. "I'll find Rayan."

She understood. "Hurry. I don't know what my people will do when they catch on."

"I have a guess." He leaned in and whispered, "Will you free my men? They'll need to be armed."

She matched his tone. "No guns yet. But we'll start bringing them up. It will distract my people."

She told Emberly how to reach the hut where he would most likely find Rayan. Then she embraced him. The feeling was alien in its pleasantness. As her arms circled him, she wrapped him in her cloak, concealing her hand as she gave him a knife.

He hid the blade and set off across the camp, careful to walk without urgency. A few people stared, but no one confronted him. Amid the dead wraiths, a captive walking free was a mundane sight.

The hut where Rayan had lived was small and bare. Emberly had his doubts as soon as he set eyes on it, and he was right. It was empty of all but dust and rubbish.

Scanning the camp, Emberly cursed. When the convicts realized Arumin's flute had failed to prevent an attack, many would assume he had betrayed them somehow to the wraiths. They would scour the camp for him.

That meant the captain had to find Rayan first if he hoped to find him alive. If anyone could explain what the hell was happening, it was him. Emberly didn't know what he would do if Rayan really had betrayed them.

First, he had to find him. But the camp contained so many little structures, and Rayan could be in any of them. Searching alone without alerting the convicts could take hours.

Emberly's dream flashed again in his mind as another hut caught his eye. It stood out from the tents and ramshackle buildings, bigger and sturdier, a structure built by skilled hands.

Exhaling with sudden certainty, he set out for the hut. He kept his pace excruciatingly casual, making the two minutes' walk feel like years. He passed streams of convicts hurrying this way and that, panicked by the dead wraiths.

When he got close, he glanced around. Seeing no one watching him, he ploughed through the hut's door without knocking.

Rayan must have seen him coming. He sat at a long, well-used table that dominated the nearer half of the hut's oblong interior. On the table lay a few papers. Around it sat many empty chairs. Small cages lined the walls at the far end, where they had been the last time Emberly stood here. A pistol rested on the table in front of Rayan's propped elbows.

"There was nothing I could have done," he said.

"What have you done?" cried Emberly at the same instant. They said the last word together.

"Your flute trick failed," said the captain. "What the hell is going on? Why are you here?"

A high-pitched murmur drew his attention. On the far end of the table sat a small cloth bundle. A pair of tiny, jerking arms poked out of it, along with the cooing of an infant.

The sight filled Emberly with cold dread.

"What is this?" he softly demanded.

"The wraiths broke our deal," Rayan answered. "We sent the signal, but they attacked us anyway."

"Answer my question."

"I did. What did you expect? Satisfaction? There is none to be had."

"I have to know who my brother really is. Why are you *here*?" Emberly stabbed his finger at the floor. "Of all the buildings in this camp."

Rayan shrugged. "Because it's useful. It's large and well built, perfect for planning my next move. That's all, I swear."

"That you would come to this hut... after what happened here." To the captain's fury, his eyes misted over. "I don't know what to think."

"It's wood," Rayan replied. "Four walls and a ceiling, that's all. What's there to fear? If anything, putting it to use could redeem it."

But Emberly was only half listening. He pointed to the floor near the middle of the room. "That's where I found him. The boy. The night of the revolt, when I heard shooting and ran from your cell, I came here and found him."

"I'm sorry you saw that, Cyril. It must be—"

"Shut up," Emberly snapped. "You deserve to hear this, and I'm going to tell you before your own people rip you apart." For all he knew, the convicts might search this building at any moment.

He surveyed the hut. "Some guards and prisoners were running a business in this hut. When I got here..."

"What did you see? Say it."

Emberly felt ill.

"Do you still mean to play stupid after all these years?" asked Rayan. "The children who ended up in this prison—the little cutthroats in Ronia's gangs, the public menaces—did you think they all settled in happily?"

"I wondered," said Emberly, barely audible. "I knew a few went missing." He found a direction for his anger. "You knew."

"Unlike you, I couldn't have stopped it. Maybe you couldn't have, either. Many people were involved."

Emberly covered his mouth with his hand. "A convict had fought a guard over a boy. The convict threatened to tell the commandant everything, and off it went. By the time I got here, it was over. The children had run off. But there was one."

Rayan stared at the spot where Emberly had pointed. He frowned as if trying to see something. "You never told me much. Was he caught in the crossfire?"

"No, he was alive." Later that night, Emberly had freed Rayan from his cell. He had been stumbling drunk when he did it. Now, standing in the hut, he looked around for the bottle he wished was there. "The fuss was about him. A convict died on top of him, maybe protecting him. This boy was old, almost a teenager. We pulled the dead man off, but the boy didn't move. He just stared up and breathed in these little gasps."

"One of the lucky ones."

"I can't... The jungle moves in so fast, like it smells death. The dead man had a few vermin on his back, but when we turned him over—it was like looking under the deepest stone in the most stagnant creek you can think of. Shiny black things, fleeing everywhere, and blood."

His breath shook. He squeezed his imaginary bottle. "The boy didn't care. They could have eaten him up. But when we tried to lift him, he clung to the dead man and screamed."

Rayan reached out with his boot and nudged the chair opposite him away from the table.

Emberly ignored the invitation to sit. "That's how it was, everyone standing there, not knowing what to do, until Arumin came."

He placed a hand on the table. "And now that I've found you hiding here, of all places. Were you involved with those animals?"

"No!" Rayan pounded the table so hard it rattled.

A piercing wail made Emberly's heart jump. The baby had started crying.

"Never," Rayan growled. "I'm insulted that you'd consider it, whatever you think of me. I do what I must, always, and for the greater good."

"Then what is that child doing here?" Emberly demanded.

"I didn't cause any of this!" Rayan shouted, heedless of his volume. "All of it—the prison, the wraiths, Ronia itself—began long ago. The wraiths would have attacked someday, no matter what. There was nothing I could do, now or back then."

The captain threw up his hands. "You're saying this isn't your fault. Of course you are."

"It's true, Cyril."

Emberly had begun to sweat. Entering this hut had pulled him out of the present for a moment. But he had to get the truth out of Rayan.

He had planned to grab his brother by the throat and wring the truth out of him. Instead, he glanced at the infant and fumbled with his next question. "What happened outside doesn't make sense. Why didn't Belith's wraiths take the bodies away after they won the fight? Don't they eat their dead?"

He stopped and pointed at Rayan. "Maybe they left them here to warn us of your treachery."

Rayan had calmed himself. "No. They left them because they're afraid to touch them. Those wraiths out there fought and died on ground contaminated with the alien. In the jungle, it's different. They'll eat anything, even us, if they kill us on untainted ground. But the wraiths outside died too close to the evil. They're filthy with it."

"If the wraiths hate offworlders so much, how did Belith befriend some of them? Why did they protect us?"

"To keep our favor!" Irritation broke through Rayan's calm. "Belith's 'tame' friends aren't just any band of wraiths. They're outcasts, driven from their clans because they desire forbidden knowledge. The offworld, the alien, it fascinates them. They came to us because, though they fear our evil, they want power over their fellows. Power to rule this world."

The infant's cries were wearing at Emberly's nerves despite his pity for it. Thinking of his son, he considered holding and comforting the child, but he would have looked ridiculous. "Where are its parents?"

Rayan's eyes flicked to the infant. "Drugged."

Emberly cursed under his breath. "The wraiths must have been disappointed when they got to know our kind."

"Not at all. We became their fortune tellers, and they feared our anger and craved our knowledge. They even learned a hand-sign language from Belith so they could talk with us—another perversion on their part. Only Belith knew how to sign, and she would only teach her tame wraiths."

The captain tried to focus. "If we're going to fight the wild wraiths, we'll need her wraiths' help."

"After this, there can't be enough left." Rayan's calm was surreal. "The survivors may be scattered or on the run. They're terribly outnumbered, and all the supposed power of the offworlders didn't protect them."

Emberly's stomach was cold.

Rayan watched him think it over. "Cyril?"

"Yes."

"We need to leave this place. All of us. We must come with you."

The captain shook himself out of his daze. "With my company? We don't even know where we're going yet."

"But the Lady will lead you. We convicts can't survive here, and we can't return to Ronia."

"We don't have the supplies to care for everyone."

"Then take us with you and watch us starve. At least it would give us time. When the wild wraiths come again, we're finished."

"I..."

"Cyril, I don't know the answers." Rayan gave him a sad look, a winning look. "But if any exist, you and I will find them together."

Part of Emberly still doggedly wished that was possible. But he must not fool himself into thinking his brother was a good man. On the contrary, he must find out how awful Rayan was. "What happened out there? Did the wraiths really betray you? If you lied about the flute calling off the wraiths... Did you want us all to die?"

Rayan shook his head. "The deal was solid, as far as I knew. I'm only a petty bastard. I'm not a beast." He gestured to the chair opposite him. "Now, from one sinner to another, let's talk about the future."

Emberly put his hands on the chair's back. "You haven't met the boy Arumin saved. But he's here, you know."

This caught Rayan by surprise. "Really?"

"Yes. He's a man now, of course." Emberly hesitated and shot a look at Rayan. "But... I told you he would be here. When you visited me in Ronia." His heart quickened. "We've been speaking across the stars for years. You should already know he's here."

"I..."

The captain's stomach turned at the dawning realization. "I was afraid I'd lost my mind. But then I met you here. And you told me it was all real. But why didn't you know Brin is here?"

He dug his nails into his temples. "You should already know everything about that night. I told you all of it during your visits."

Rayan cast his eyes down to the table. "Cyril... these things are mysterious. Just because I don't remember—"

"Enough. No more of your mystical nonsense. You... weren't... *there.*" Emberly grabbed a chair to steady himself. All these years, he had imagined talking to Rayan.

He should be locked away. He was insane.

The baby cried harder and harder.

Rayan gazed at him, still utterly calm. "I do remember part of that night, you know. The most important part. It was almost dawn when you came to my cell, so drunk you were staggering. You babbled like a child."

"After what I saw—"

"Yes, finish. Let's hear if you're as brave a man as you think."

Still bent over, Emberly recounted the memory.

"When Arumin saw the boy, he looked stunned. Not horrified but awed, like he'd seen the face of Huire herself. He fell on his knees and slowly coaxed the boy away from the dead man. The boy let the commandant pick him up."

Rayan grunted darkly.

"Arumin looked at me. Whatever he saw on my face, he bared his teeth and said, 'Send the doctor to my quarters.' That was all. He took Brin away."

Rayan closed his eyes. "The spoils of war," he growled.

Emberly shook his head vigorously. "It can't be. Not even the bishop would do that."

"This is the man you serve. This is the system. And to this day, you believe that nothing better is possible."

Emberly threw the chair to the floor.

Rayan leaned forward to stare hard at him. "I told you that night, 'Think what you've allowed to happen.' Well, think about it now."

"I did think about it! I am!"

"No." Rayan spoke with imperial surety. "I didn't believe you then, and I don't now. Shame on you, Cyril. Go back to your masters."

Swaying, Emberly stared at the closed door of the hut.

"Or join me," said Rayan. "Prove you're not like the rest, a toy soldier. That night, you showed you could be more. You unlocked my cell, though you cried all the while. It's clear that you need me."

Slowly, Emberly picked up the overturned chair. He sat in it and faced Rayan across the table like a partner.

He pointed to the baby. "What is that child doing here?"

Taken aback, Rayan looked into his brother's eyes. "There are no answers that way, Cyril. No satisfying ones or frustrating ones. Simply none. Trust me, brother. It's a waste of time, making sense of this place. All you should know is this child is safe and will remain so unless the wraiths finish us all."

Emberly trembled. "I ask for the last time. Think carefully, because from what I see, you're a dead man. If the wraiths don't kill you, your people will when they realize they're doomed and decide it's your fault. They're out there, hunting you.

"But if you tell me the truth now, I'll protect you—for as long as I can—from this mess you've made. I know you can be better than you are. You didn't have to release me from the power of the wraiths' vapors, but you did. I think you wanted the love of a brother, not a victim."

Rayan was silent for a while. Watching him twist inwardly, Emberly said, "Please."

Staring past Emberly and through the hut's wall, Rayan took a deep breath. "The wraiths wouldn't have hurt him. The child. They wouldn't have hurt any of us."

Emberly swallowed. "Go on."

Rayan grabbed a piece of paper and a thin pencil from the table and started writing. "The wild wraiths had prepared a place for us to live in the jungle."

"With them?"

"It's a village. The clans built it together, far from here. We would have stayed there. They would have watched us and, most importantly, let us live."

"Couldn't they watch us here?"

Rayan kept scribbling, frequently pausing to speak. "This prison is diseased. They are loath to even enter it. We aliens have been here too long. Given birth and died. Our blood has seeped into the ground. In return for letting us live, we would have submitted to their dominion. In body and... in mind. They wouldn't have needed to fear us anymore."

"But why keep us alive at all? You're not making sense."

"Under their control, we're worth more alive. They hope to do more than affect our emotions. They want to put ideas in our heads. Control our thoughts, even. More offworld invaders are coming someday, and they mean to be ready."

"Blessed Huire. We were to be their slaves."

Rayan finished writing and dropped his pencil.

Emberly said, "They've tested individuals. Now they want to poke and prod a whole society."

"We would have been mostly happy."

"Happy?" Emberly gaped. "How?"

"They would have used their potions to keep us in a state of peace and bliss."

"We would have been mesmerized idiots. How could you even consider it?"

Rayan stared at him. "The alternative was death, Captain Emberly. For all of us. Those who resist the will of Ronia face an abyss."

"With their potions, why bother with you? Why do they care who's in charge?"

"I convinced them of our people's need for leaders, even in a perfect place. Their potions affect our emotions, but they don't control our thoughts. That's where I came in. To ensure their good behavior, the sheep would need a shepherd."

"Your people would not have cooperated. No sane person would."

"Sane." Rayan chuckled. "I've finally learned something from your empire, Cyril. And from Belith and from you. People must face the point of a sword for their own good."

"Goddess. I was to be your enforcer. Your thug."

Rayan smiled sadly. "I promised the wraiths I could ensure your cooperation."

"I would never have agreed," said the captain. "I would have died instead."

"Not under the wraiths' potion, you wouldn't. Between me and the potion, you're capable of anything, Cyril. They gave me a supply to keep you docile, but... when I saw how pathetic their vapors made you, I threw it away. I suppose you're right. I hoped you would join me of your own free will."

"And that baby over there..." Emberly shuddered.

"They would have taken us to our new home a few at a time, while you and your men controlled whoever remained at the prison, until the prison was empty. By the time we were all full of vapors, we wouldn't have needed your men to guard us. We wouldn't have even wanted to resist. To start, they needed a sign that I could hold up my end."

Emberly looked at the child. "Him. Those dead wraiths outside came here to meet you and accept your sacrificial offering."

"I never forgot the child's well-being. When Belith's wraiths attacked, I realized the plan had failed, and I slipped away."

A long silence fell except for the crying child. Its cries had softened. Maybe it was tired.

Emberly heard voices outside. His nerves twitched. "You would have led us. In this new world of yours."

"Me—and you. We would have been partners, kings in paradise. Our people would have loved us, Cyril. The wraiths' vapors would have seen to it."

"So much for free will. Does anyone else know?"

"That I nearly gave them a life free of endless, awful choices? No. And you won't tell them."

Someone's fist boomed against the door behind Emberly's head. The captain jumped. Rayan's gaze didn't move from Emberly's, but his eyes showed resignation. The baby, frightened anew, began screaming outright.

The captain recovered himself. "Would we have... lived there forever?"

"We would have lived our lives and passed away. No fights, no mistrust, no sick babies crying all night. Just love, peace."

"Forced peace. We wouldn't have even loved, not really."

"We would've had the fleeting part of love. The only part that's worth a damn. They planned to pair us, rotating pairs, you see, and whenever one of us spawned, they would take it away."

The voices outside grew in volume and number. They could probably hear the baby—an alarming sound, especially considering the building's history.

"The torture wasn't over, then," Emberly said. "Would your descendants have thanked you, do you think, for dooming them to a counterfeit life to save your own?"

"All life is counterfeit," Rayan shot back. "You've always doubted my ideas for a better world, and you were right. But you are a fool too. When the wraiths tortured me, I learned that no idea matters a damn in the face of pure experience. They made me ecstatic, despairing, anything they wished. Thoughts and feelings are delusions, Cyril, and we are puppets. All we can hope is to be played kindly."

"What about your revolution?"

"This would have been the revolution! Its crescendo. I realize now this is where it all leads. To the rejection of all structure and purpose, all the ways the powerful keep us down. The freedom of no meaning. But now, all that is lost."

A laugh burst from Emberly. "You haven't changed. You didn't get what you wanted, so it's not fun anymore. You act so passionate, but your passions are as deep as my toenail. You won't grow up."

"What does 'growing up' mean? Does it mean compromising until I no longer know myself? That's your path, not mine."

"Your people deserve to know what you tried to do."

"They wouldn't understand. Let's not forget, I know a secret of yours that's just as damning."

Emberly trembled. "You are scum. And a coward."

"I'm a coward?" Rayan cried. "I've fought for what I believed my whole life. You ran off to the army to hide."

"I joined to redeem our family after you disgraced us."

Something struck the door, an impact like a boot. It seemed both Emberly and his brother had accepted the violence that would soon ensue. They kept arguing, ignoring the noise outside and the screaming child.

"Is that what you think Mother and Father care about?" Rayan cried. "Reputation? You joined because you crave others' approval more than anything else in this world."

"You had already left us when you committed the crimes that sent you here. You chose a life of murder and terror."

It was Rayan's turn to laugh. "You really don't see the irony, do you?"

Someone outside yelled for Rayan to come out. Other voices rose in agreement.

"Your friends are here," said Emberly. "They don't sound happy."

The two men listened. The mob sounded as large as the one Rayan had faced yesterday.

The captain continued, "Maybe I'm tired of hiding the truth. Maybe all our secrets should come to light. You could tell the people outside that I freed you from your cell."

Rayan's eyes widened. "You'd kill us both. Your people would want to kill you as much as mine already want to kill me."

"Still. Maybe I'm tired of it all."

Rayan leaned back. "Try it. When we were boys, you followed me like a faithful dog. It's about time you made a decision on your own."

"Fine." The captain stood and walked to the door. He was reaching for the knob when Rayan told him to stop.

Emberly turned to find his brother's gun pointed at him. He relaxed his shoulders. "I expected as much."

"Step away from the door," said Rayan. "Stand against the far wall."

Multiple fists pounded on the door. Voices raged and cursed. They were close to breaking in.

Still holding his pistol, Rayan folded his note using his free hand and the tabletop. He put it in a pocket of his ragged vest.

His face had grown dark and vicious. "I will decide. Only me."

Putting his gun on the table, he strode past Emberly and opened the door.

The noise outside was so overwhelming it drowned out the baby's cries. The man at the front of the surging crowd froze in surprise, fist raised to knock again. He stepped back, unsure what to do now that he had found his quarry. Those behind him were bolder, advancing on Rayan but not quite closing in.

Rayan paused in the doorway for an instant as if to speak. He stepped into the crowd.

Emberly watched as the mob engulfed his brother, pulling him this way and that. Rayan shouted, trying futilely to make the people hear something. Whenever he freed a hand, he pointed at Emberly.

The captain took the pistol from the table and stepped outside. He fired the weapon into the morning sky.

He had been an idiot to think this would restore order. Some in the crowd bolted, others crouched or threw themselves down, still others scrambled for their weapons. Rayan, suddenly free, fell like a sack of dung. The calmer and better-armed members of the crowd quickly held Emberly at gunpoint.

When the screams subsided, the captain shouted, "He's my brother. If there's justice to be done, I will do it."

"Will you indeed?" shouted one of the armed men. "Will you carry out the sentence we decide?"

"Not at all. His fate is up to me."

"Like hell."

The captain gazed at Rayan, who was still on the ground, collecting himself. "I promise to judge him fairly."

"I doubt that," the man said. "Family is family. You'll let him go."

Emberly lowered the gun to his side. "It's my right."

"By what law? You're a long way from Ronia."

"By your law, the law of the wild. I have a knife in my belt. I will fight anyone who disputes my right to Rayan's life."

The man's face contorted. "We're his victims. His life is ours."

"Don't just say so. Fight for it."

"We won't need any of that," called Belith, approaching. She walked with dogged resilience, teetering against her cane. As the crowd's attention turned to her, she announced, "There will be fighting enough for all of us very soon."

Arriving in their midst, she looked down at Rayan as if she had scraped him from her boot. "I might've known you'd be here. I should've burned this place down when you left." She nodded to the hut. "Let Captain Emberly choose. He lived with *this* longer than we did. And for Goddess's sake, someone see to that child."

The armed man said, "But, Sister Belith, he'll release him."

"So be it. The jungle can have him. He may die there far more miserably than here."

"He could make it back to the gateway," the man countered. "He could tell the Ronians we're here."

"That doesn't matter. We've lost this place, my friends, no matter what happens. The wraiths will come soon, probably this very night. If we hope to survive, we'll need multiple favors from the captain and his company. Our former enemies."

35

— · —

EMBERLY

WORK HAD ALREADY BEGUN when the brothers left the camp that morning. The convicts had inherited many axes and hammers used by the fallen prison's work details. The ringing of blades being sharpened and the cracks of rocks being split followed Cyril and Rayan into the twisting trees.

Rayan walked in front with Emberly's gun at his back. "How far will we go?"

"I don't know yet," Emberly said.

Rayan sighed. "Damn it, Cyril, it's not a hard question."

"Quiet," warned the captain. He needed time to think.

"If I escape, no one has to know," said Rayan. His tone remained maddeningly conversational. "Just decide where."

"Keep your mouth shut, or I'll decide to shoot you."

"I won't. Why should I? It will end the same for me regardless."

Emberly did not answer.

"Do you have something else on your mind? A question, maybe?"

"No."

"I could ask why you bothered saving me from the mob if you meant to kill me."

The captain could answer that at least. "You're a part of my family. I couldn't let you die like that."

"So—you meant what you told those animals back there? You would have fought them?"

"Is that hard to believe?"

Rayan was momentarily quiet. When he spoke, his voice had recovered its jauntiness. "I've thought of a question. You could ask me why I didn't tell them your biggest secret. I could have shouted it after the crowd calmed down."

Emberly scoffed at that. "You tried. No one listened."

"I didn't, Cyril. Truly. But I betrayed you in another way. When the crowd took me, I panicked. I thought I was ready to face them, but I wasn't. So I told them what you offered the wraiths in the jungle in exchange for letting us go."

Emberly took a deep, heavy breath.

"Your man, Robir, figured out the first symbol you drew in the dirt but not the other ones. The skull-shaped one especially intrigued him. I think I know what it said."

"You've made your point," Emberly rumbled.

Rayan could not resist sadism even when admitting wrongdoing. "Those symbols were invented by desperate soldiers, surrounded by dead comrades, ready to offer the wraiths anything..."

"Say it, then!" Emberly shouted.

"Can you bear to hear it?"

"I wrote it, didn't I?"

Rayan stopped and turned. "Then say it yourself."

"I offered the wraiths bodies! Is that what you want to hear? I told them if they let us leave to attack the prison, we would give them our dead from then on. Fuel for their ceremonies. I was lying, and I never would have done it."

"And the night you left the waytower. You planned to buy safe passage from the wraiths." Rayan nodded as the pieces fell together. "You were planning to offer your dead from the swamp."

"There was no other way!" Emberly yelled. "I would have arranged for the wraiths to steal the bodies somehow. My men would never have known. No living person would have been harmed!"

He stopped to breathe.

"What does that make you?" asked Rayan. "Are you any better than me?"

"I don't... Yes. Yes, I'm still better than you. Also, I'm holding the gun."

Rayan glowered.

"Are you satisfied?" asked Emberly.

Rayan looked down. "No," he admitted. "I still regret what I did. I've faced death before, but when that mob grabbed me... I wanted to escape more than anything. I wanted them to take you instead of me. You must admit, the convicts wouldn't have been happy to hear what you'd offered the wraiths. Neither would your men, and some of them are turning on you already."

Emberly was silent for a moment. "I never would have done it."

Rayan sighed. "Fortunately, we'll never know. No one heard me. I didn't come to my senses until you fired the gun."

The captain sighed. "What do you expect me to say?"

"Nothing. But I'm sorry."

Emberly bit his lip. "Why haven't you said that before? You never apologize for anything or even admit you're wrong. Not sincerely, anyway."

"Don't I?" Rayan thought aloud. They'd had this conversation before, and it always amused him. "I suppose, early in life, I became accustomed to being right."

"Why not admit to being wrong when it happens? It's all anyone wants."

Rayan stepped forward so the pistol pressed into his chest. "You know very well that isn't true. If honesty was all it took, this would be a different world."

"You've tried lying. And look where you are."

"Do you listen to yourself?" Rayan gasped. "My lies pale next to yours."

"My biggest lie started with you! You squawked to the Ronians about how brave I was, and I've had to hide the truth ever since."

Rayan shot back, "I did you a favor, brother. One you took full advantage of."

"I wouldn't have begun it by myself. And now it's too late. I'm acting in a play all the time. I can't talk to anyone, even my wife."

Rayan spread his arms. "You chose it all! You could've told the truth—that the great convicts' revolt was your doing—and taken your punishment like a man. You still could. Why don't you?"

The captain's lip trembled. Mortified, he said, "I should have stopped it. I know I should've. Now I'm alone."

"That's what I thought. You are everything I am. The difference is, you're still a child."

Emberly bit his lip again, hard. Soon, it would swell. "Keep walking."

His brother's chest puffed. "No."

"Turn and walk. Now."

"What if I don't? You'll kill me either way, or so you claim."

"I haven't said that. But if you don't move, I'll have no choice."

Rayan shook his head. "You're pitiful. By the way, I have a parting gift for you. It's in my vest pocket. If you kill me before I give it to you, be sure to take a look."

Emberly's knees shook. Next to his lip trembling, it was the worst thing that could have happened. He answered, forming the words carefully. "If I release you, where will you go?"

Rayan's face fell. "Don't be cruel, brother. If you're going to kill me, do it."

"I'm serious." Emberly's voice was a little firmer. "Where will you go?"

Rayan considered it, perhaps for the first time. "I would make for the gateway towards Ronia."

"Even if you reached it, you would be arrested and shot."

"Probably. But miracles happen. Your secret would die with me."

Emberly was aware of everything: the coppery taste in his mouth, the sighing of the air in the trees. "Turn and walk a hundred paces. Do it slowly, and don't look back."

Rayan tilted his head. He was searching for the trick.

"After that," Emberly said, "you're on your own. Don't return to the camp. If you do, I'll kill you—if your old friends don't kill you first."

Nodding, Rayan reached into his pocket and fished out the note he had written in the hut. He dropped it into Emberly's hand.

The sun shone brighter through the trees, and Rayan squinted. "Suddenly, I don't know what to say next."

Seeing genuine feeling in his brother's face might once have given Emberly joy but no longer. "There's nothing left. We've each heard all the other has to say. You're wrong about us. We're nothing alike."

Rayan turned away. "Alike or not, brother," he began, but instead of finishing the sentence, he started walking. "Whatever you owe me, I owe more to you. You set me free." Finally, he called, "I'll give your love to—"

He fell. As he dropped, he grabbed a tree trunk, which crumbled in his hand, bringing the tree down. He lay still.

The gun had almost leapt out of Emberly's hand when he pulled the trigger. He had not held it properly. Perhaps he had hoped it would malfunction and the choice would not be his after all.

The sound was so vast that people in the camp must have heard it. Everyone would know, and when he returned, they would all stare at him, knowing.

He walked to the body, pausing halfway to steel himself. Standing over the thing, he tore off his cloak. He rolled up his sleeves but kept sweating. He tried to cry but could not.

A short time later, he found himself sitting next to it, hoping it would tell him what to think or how to feel. He put his hands on it, his brother, his family's ruin, and turned it over. He was looking at a marvelous facsimile of Rayan, accurate in every detail but still a failure, still wrong.

He closed his eyes and said a few words he could not remember later. It was time to go back.

36

—·—

ARUMIN

ARUMIN LAY ON THE cot in the late afternoon and hissed as Brin leaned over him, applying ointment to his chest wound. The substance still burned, and in the small room Belith had given them—its location secret to prevent violence—Arumin did not hide the pain.

"Sorry." Brin's voice was toneless as he unwound cloth to cover the wound.

Arumin blinked until the fog cleared from his eyes. "All the scum in that hole, and it still doesn't seem infected. But I've had worse if you can believe it."

"You're lucky you're important," said Brin coldly, finishing his work. "Staubel is short on supplies."

The bishop touched his newly bandaged chest. "At least it missed my face. Not that my looks are much to speak of anymore."

Brin set the cloth down hard, thumping the table. "What am I supposed to say to that? Would you like a compliment? Tell me so I can say it."

Arumin's face hardened. He straightened his body on the cot. "I forced that confession out of you because it was important. I was harsh, I know. But you failed me."

"And when you dragged the explanation out of me, in front of the monk and that woman, you learned I'd simply forgotten to tell you Shada was attacked. No trickery. It's just me, your ever-loyal servant."

"Yes, I heard your confession." Arumin was sure Brin was still hiding something—another reason for not telling him about the attack on Shada. But he had no idea what it could be, and more than anything, he wanted to stop fighting.

The news of the attack had terrified the bishop. In particular, the vial Shada had described haunted him. Whatever was in it had made the attacker confident he could cow the Lady herself.

The bishop could not help connecting the attack with the company's battle in the streets of Ronia. A group of Unheard terrorists had attacked the crusaders' column until a mysterious force of black-clad figures had overrun the Unheard and wiped them out.

Cut off from news from Ronia, the crusaders had most-ly assumed the black figures were a rival group to the Un-heard, maybe religious activists. They would likely never know.

But Arumin suspected their assumption was wrong. Those figures had been so capable and effortless. He had shot one of them by mistake in his rush to save Brin, as-suming the man was an enemy and pulling the trigger too quickly. The man's body had boasted yellow reptilian eyes of a kind he had never seen before.

And now, this attack on Shada. One man, in the mid-dle of the jungle, had thought he could enslave the Lady. Maybe he'd been a simple lunatic. The army had enough of those. But maybe…

He suspected he knew what puzzle these pieces be-longed to. It was a puzzle that few in Ronia knew existed. If Emberly knew of it, he had said nothing. Arumin, for his part, had not even told Brin about it. He disliked letting Brin see him afraid.

Brin coveted secrets, too, for the access they represented. He had pressed Arumin about whether more spies might be hiding in the company's ranks. To his own dismay, the bishop did not know.

Though Shada's news had alarmed him, Arumin's anger at Brin had passed quickly. He was too damned lonely to stay angry, and he grew eager to end their fight. But now Brin was angry, and he was the rare person whose anger Arumin, bishop of Huire's Temple, feared.

As Brin stood over him, Arumin asked, "Do you hate me now, too?"

Brin turned his head away. "What do you mean? Since you obviously hope I'll ask."

The bishop sighed. "You saw what the convicts did to me. How they hate me. I'm the monster that haunts their sleep, and who can blame them? One of them may come along and kill me at any moment. And Emberly's soldiers have heard all about my shaming by now. If any had forgotten what they learned in school—that I am the Coward of Caidfell, who ran during the re-volt—they won't forget again. I've been the bishop for so long, I hoped I'd outlived the commandant."

He poked masochistically at the wound and winced at the pain. "But the commandant is back, and I'm too old to outlive him again."

Brin huffed. "Why do you care? You have the Goddess. Isn't she enough?"

To his surprise, Arumin was not angry at the young man's defiance. It was just like Brin to say something wise while meaning it as sarcasm.

Arumin knew from experience that Brin's anger was wavering, and the bishop would soon win him over. He needed Brin's kind side now, so badly he might have begged for it. Everything else had gone wrong.

"I almost lost you," he said. "When that witch threatened you, I would have said anything to save you."

Brin huffed again, but the sound was at least half a sigh. "I know."

"This place brings everything back." It truly did. Arumin's mind turned like a mill wheel, churning up ancient things, and suddenly, he was saying them. "When we met, you were young, very young. Did I wait long enough to be with you?"

Brin stared. When he finally understood, his eyes widened, and he stammered as he answered. "The first time, I was already a man."

"I was old even then. I didn't force you, did I?"

Brin cocked his head. "Goddess, no. Is that how you remember it?"

"I don't know. It gets all twisted. I had everything, and you needed me..."

"Stop it!" Brin cried. "I don't like this side of you, filled with apologies. You treated me kindly, unlike anyone else. Now stop groveling." He put his hand on Arumin's.

The bishop said, "I'm not *that* bad." He repeated the words like an incantation, willing them to be true. "Huire cannot hate me. I do everything for her. So why is she letting everything fall apart? It all began in the swamp, when we almost drowned."

Brin looked down on him, his expression a mixture of pity and disgust. "You need to be strong now. I don't know what's wrong with you, but—"

"I know what you did," said Arumin softly.

He saw a flash of fear in Brin's eyes. The young man's tone was annoyed. "What?"

Arumin lay still, as if on his death bed. His voice gurgled from his throat. "When Belith held my head under water. In that dungeon. You would have let me die."

When surprised, the young priest was sometimes a poor liar. "No. That's ridiculous."

"Don't deny it. She wanted to know something."

"This is a waste of time."

"Fine, deny it. Don't even tell me what she asked. It doesn't matter." His hand shot out and grabbed Brin's wrist. "I forgive you."

He let the words sink in, watching Brin cast about for an excuse. He said it again. "I forgive you."

"All right," Brin spat. He shifted from foot to foot, almost dancing, longing to escape. He yanked his hand from Arumin's grasp. "No. I take it back. Don't forgive me."

"What?"

"I kept secrets from you. I almost let that hag kill you. You should be angry."

Arumin glared. "When I'm angry, you sulk."

"I know, but... that's only because you're so sad about it. Anger's a powerful thing, but you make it so... weak, somehow."

Arumin sat up, threw his legs over the edge of the cot, and watched Brin closely. "I simply don't understand you. What do you want?"

Brin folded his arms. "I'll tell you what I want. I want to feel safe. You may wish to forget the commandant, but I wish he was here. He got whatever he wanted."

Incredulous, Arumin stared. "I've made you as safe as anyone could. I took you from this place to a life of luxury. The price of that life is service to the Goddess."

"Believe me, I know." Brin held his gaze. "You never shut up about your Goddess. It makes me wonder which of us you love more."

The bishop's jaw dropped. Soon, he said, "Don't make me answer that. And she's your Goddess too."

"Maybe, but not the same way. Your obsession with service, it's brought us to this accursed jungle."

"What did you think a priest's life would be? It can't all be affairs with whoever catches your eye."

"I didn't know what it would be. When you took me, I was so young."

Silence. Arumin, stricken, touched his face.

"I'll ask again," said Brin. "Who do you love more?"

Arumin said nothing, but Brin must have seen an answer in his face. He nodded.

A knock on the door startled them both. When Brin recovered, he had a pleasant expression. "I'm sorry, Bishop. I spoke out of turn. Shall I get the door?" A curtain had fallen. His smile was cold and polite.

Arumin wanted to say something cutting, but despair touched him when he saw that smile. He merely nodded.

Brin opened the door to reveal Robir, one of the soldiers captured by the wraiths during Emberly's ill-fated nighttime search party.

"I have something to confess, Your Holiness," he said before either of the holy men could say anything.

The bishop had heard several confessions today. He would have preferred a boot to the face to hearing another damned confession. "Our vows excuse us from confessing. Be at peace, Private. I'll arrange a public confessing ceremony in the coming days, when there's time, so if you feel obligated—"

Robir interrupted. "It's about the captain."

Arumin halted. Something in the private's tone struck him. Robir had hung out Emberly's name like a piece of bait.

"Go on," said the bishop.

The man continued, "There's something I know that I should have told others, but I've kept it to myself. I tried talking to Brother Nor, but he hardly heard me. Him, who knew exactly what I was talking about. After we suffered so together, he should have been my partner in this. Worse, when he realized what I was talking about, he told me to tell no one else."

Somewhere in Arumin's tense, throbbing chest, excitement stirred. Robir's information was probably something banal, but the bishop had a feeling otherwise. "You've been through a terrible experience, more than the rest of us. I only wish Captain Emberly had consulted me before leading you out there. We are supposed to lead together."

"I'm afraid I'll never forgive Emberly," said Robir. He sounded truly afraid. "He let Private Keesin die in the jungle. Worse, he let him be eaten."

He shook his head. "I've told the others this, but... it's like they don't care. It's bad and all, they say, but this whole world is rotten. Now that Borna and Elisar are gone, it's like I'm alone." He tossed his hands up. "Why don't people want to fight evil when they hear of it?"

"Sometimes the full weight of a sin is only apparent to those who witness it," said the bishop. "Is that all you have to tell me?"

"No, Your Holiness. There's more that I haven't told. Emberly's got a secret."

"We'll work on forgiving Emberly together. You did the right thing coming to me, Private. Please, tell me everything you know." Hearing him out would hold off despair for a little while.

Robir nodded as if he hadn't needed the assurance. "It seems you're the only one I can trust, Your Holiness. You put the Goddess before all else."

37

SHADA

SHADA STOOD ON THE wall as sunset approached and scanned the brittle, wiry trees surrounding the field. The convicts had fought back the forest over the years, leaving an open area around the camp and the keep. They knew well to fear the trees and to stay in their enclave whenever possible.

Now the field swarmed with life. The captain was everywhere at once, directing soldiers and convicts as they cut down trees at the forest's edge and piled them in rows around the keep's walls. The convicts had suggested this, claiming the trees would burn like a heap of matches. A large amount of sap from other nearby trees would aid their ignition.

Following the lone gunshot that had echoed over the trees, Emberly had returned from the forest with Rayan's body on his back. He had said nothing about what happened, and no one had pressed him about it.

In the courtyard within the walls, soldiers grunted and cursed as they dug a large hole. They had reached an impressive depth in a few hours. Only a few could fit in the hole at once, and they worked in shifts, lifting buckets of dirt and rock to those waiting outside.

The attack was expected after nightfall, when the wraiths could take the best advantage of their speed and camouflage. Whatever the wraiths' grasp of strategy, they must have realized tonight was their best chance. Emberly and Belith's people would try to escape the next day. As far as the wraiths knew, they would make for the gateway to Ronia.

There was no time to fully plan or prepare. The men digging could only work as hard as their backs allowed. The people carrying wood could only scurry so quickly.

The convicts were demolishing their little town. They carried the canvas from the tents inside the walls, knocked down the flimsiest huts, and burned the sturdier ones. By common agreement, Rayan's hideout was first to go. Pillars of smoke reached into the stifling air—a warning to the wraiths of the offworlders' power, perhaps.

Against all advice, refusing any company, Sister Belith had hobbled into the woods to enlist the help of her tame wraiths one last time. She had returned hours later, sweaty and exhausted, to announce the wraiths would not be coming. Only one had appeared at their meeting spot to tell her that many had died in the fight, and the rest were in hiding, unwilling to throw their lives away.

While she was gone, some of the convicts mourned her foolishness in going into the jungle in her state. Even Drucin, among those closest to her, noted sadly that she was not herself lately. The sight of her bleeding and swelling from the plant's venom would not be easily forgotten.

Shada heard Nor call to her from nearby on the wall. Startled, she was glad he had announced himself before coming closer. He walked to her and turned to share her view, leaning on the parapet. His wrist was newly bandaged, but his bruises still showed.

She waited for him to speak. When she had visited him and the other holy men the previous night, her mention of Boots' attack on her had led the entire conversation astray. She could not imagine why Father Brin had kept that information from Bishop Arumin.

When they finally came to discussing Shada's difficulty with the Lady, the bishop had mostly reiterated what the Lady had already said: Shada must accept what she was told and only ask questions in line with that acceptance.

Arumin had been confident the Lady would return. So had Emberly when Shada told him the Lady was absent, though the captain had shown surprisingly little emotion at the news. He had said the Lady would not intervene in the battle anyway.

Shada wasn't so sure the Lady would return. This was not the first time a thoughtless word from Shada had driven her away, but this separation felt more eerily significant than the last one. Shada wished she at least knew where the Lady was. Maybe this was how her father had felt when she wandered off as a child: mostly scared but also a little angry.

As she spoke to Arumin, Nor had listened and said nothing. Maybe he was upset with her too. Like the rest of the company, he had risked everything to be here.

When he approached her on the wall, his first words surprised her. "The bishop is a fool."

"I'm sorry?"

"He was angry with you because he doesn't know how it feels to be in your place. No one does, of course. But I can see it's difficult."

Shada paused to adjust to his unexpected attitude. "For my life, I don't know why the Lady chose me. Maybe it's because she happened to meet me first. I thought I might do something good by joining this crusade, but I've put us all in terrible danger. Is it possible the Goddess made a mistake?" She meant the question to be a joke, but it tasted bitter.

"You ask questions. That'll get you in trouble with some people."

"I also lack faith."

"Faith is best if it's preceded by questions."

"The Lady disagreed." Without thinking, she had referred to the Lady as part of her past. The realization was chilling.

"I'm surprised by how she treated you. She tolerated all manner of foolishness from me."

She smiled at him. "Maybe I'm lying."

He looked embarrassed. She wondered if he had taken her last statement seriously, and she was embarrassed in turn. His blank eyes revealed as little as ever.

"No, I don't think so," he said. "Something else must be behind it. If we see her again, I hope we'll find out together."

He gave her a smile she could not return. His comment had reminded her the sun was going down and the trees would be thick with wraiths. She had never had to anticipate a battle or anything like one. A wave of stunning fear washed over her, and she clung to the parapet.

"I'm sorry," he said quickly. "I can't think before I speak. Not even with you."

"I'm fine," she said, though her voice betrayed her lie. She bent over the parapet, praying she would not be sick. If she fell apart before the battle even started, she would be more of a burden than she already was.

"We'll be inside, of course," Nor said, watching her with obvious discomfort. "The caretaker and the holy men are considered indispensable."

"Do you think we should be?"

"You are. I'm not so sure about the rest of us."

"Why me?" She did not hide her frustration. He looked at her until she continued. "Everyone is helping to get ready. Men, women, and children. But when I offered to help, they wouldn't consider it."

"Maybe they're showing reverence for your position."

"I'm no more important than anyone else. I know that, so how should this treatment make me feel?"

"It should—"

"Like I'm on the outside, looking through a window. And the window is even dirtier than usual."

He leaned on the wall and smiled. "Sounds like you're uniquely qualified for the job."

She had no answer.

"They may be showing your role too much reverence, but it is your role, Shada. The Lady insists on your safety, as much as you might wish otherwise."

"I thought I was ready for it, that I knew how it would feel."

"This won't surprise you, Caretaker, but I often feel like a loner myself. What's worse, I act like one, then I get angry about it." He laughed again. "So I might be the worst person to give you advice—"

"You're not." She interrupted again because the words were urgent. She put her hand on his arm. "It makes you qualified."

His eyes revealed as little as ever, but he could not hide his blush. "Then I'll give you advice I might not follow myself. Whatever happens to you, you're free to dislike it. Suffering toward worthy ends can be an act of service."

"I hope you're right. Because I'll never like this."

"That's true freedom."

"I just... When people see me treated like some kind of queen, they'll think it's what I want."

"Then they don't know you yet," said Nor. "What's important is your role, and your role lies in you. So you must protect yourself."

"I'll do that in exchange for something."

His smile returned. "What's that?"

"Keep yourself safe too. I'm certain you're as important as me. I didn't dive into that swamp to watch you throw your life away."

His smile disappeared.

She cursed her lack of sense. "Sorry. I shouldn't have mentioned that."

"Don't apologize. It was amazing. I've never seen anything like it."

She could not fathom that response. "If I'd been in your place, I would have nightmares forever."

"It's too soon to tell," Nor said with perfect seriousness. "Honestly, I've been through worse since. The wraiths tormented us. A little while ago, I refused to hear a man's confession."

"Are you allowed to do that?"

"No."

She raised her eyebrows. "Still, refusing a confession hardly sounds as bad as the rest of it."

"Bad for my soul, maybe. I refused a man to whom I was obligated so I could protect another man I don't like. The first man wasn't happy, and neither am I. I hope it was for the best. I believe in Huire and in our mission. When I refused the man, I told him people have a right to secrets."

"Well, it's true."

He nodded. "Listen... When you pulled me out of the swamp, you did more than save my life. I'm afraid to talk about it. Maybe someday."

She saw his hand on the wall and wanted to touch it. "I thought nothing but blood and death came out of that day."

"It wasn't the Lady who picked you," he said. "It was the Goddess, and she made the right choice."

The sun had disappeared behind the treetops. The soldiers in the hole kept digging. Outside the wall, arrangements were more or less complete. Despite the urgency, many people trudged along. Someone had collapsed from exhaustion, and their neighbor had moved to help.

Nor pulled a length of cloth from a pocket and unrolled it. "It's time."

Shada found hers, which had once been a long headscarf, and wrapped it around her face, covering her mouth and nose. Already, the light was dimming, and the wind stirred. A gust brushed past them from the direction of the fainted worker.

At the forest's edge, someone else had collapsed. "Nor," she said, and pointed. As she spoke, another worker dropped to his knees. Yet another fell as she watched. "Oh, no."

"That's it!" Nor shouted from the wall, "The wraiths are here! Get inside!"

Chaos ensued. Shada's heart pounded as if it would never need to work another day. But as they hurried off the wall, she was pleased to note that she was calmer. She was even a little giddy, and she clutched Nor's hand flirtatiously. He squeezed her fingers as they crossed the courtyard. He pressed too hard, and she yelped and giggled. He laughed too. She had not known he could really laugh.

They made it through the keep's doors as part of a crowd, children and people unable or unwilling to fight. The crowd's mood was odd. Everyone shuffled along, worried but excited and even a little jolly.

Her last glimpse of the outside world was Emberly's men around the hole. A foul smell came from there. They dug at a frenzied pace, and Shada laughed again.

As they approached a stairway leading down, she was happy. She had rarely felt so warm and comfortable, like the world was embracing her.

38

— · —

EMBERLY

WHEN NOR CALLED HIS warning, Emberly prayed he was wrong, that the wraiths had not come yet.

The men digging in the courtyard had found nothing so far, though they had dug deeper than Rayan's note said they should.

Their position was poor. The wraiths would scale the walls quickly. Soon after, the men in the hole would have to defend themselves. Emberly had given them a few guns, ammunition, and a tarp and ordered the construction of a wooden barricade around the hole. It consisted of stacks of wood, a smaller version of the ring that encompassed the keep's wall. When it ignited, it would protect the diggers as well as anything could.

Realizing the wraiths might leap into the hole from the wall, they had arranged to cover it with a round grate from one of the pits outside. They had leaned the grate against a nearby wall in preparation.

The first time Emberly read Rayan's note and realized what his gift was, a plan had come into his mind almost fully formed. But as his men dug deeper and found nothing, he read the note again and again, hoping to glean some new insight:

Cyril,

Don't be disappointed. This note is not my gift. That is buried in the courtyard of the keep, five paces in from the gate. No one has dared touch it since I put it there. Dig quickly. It's buried at least up to your head.

But now I must hurry.

This gift cost my closest friends their lives. Soon after, the rest sent me into the jungle for good.

I stole something precious from a wicked old king of the jungle.

Everyone thought I was mad, provoking him. But I wanted a final option for when all was lost. You'll find out.

Why did you free me from that cell? I suppose I'll never know.

I hope you'll spare me. If you don't, at least think of me when it all catches up with you.

Your gift is dangerous, and it's not finished killing. When you—

He stopped there on his last reading, tossing away the note when Nor's shout ignited a stampede toward the wall. There was no way to control the rush. The captain could only hope everyone remembered their assigned places.

Several people had fallen near the woods. First, he thought with an awful jolt that the fighting had already begun. When he realized the truth, it was hardly better. The wraiths must have released one of their concocted fumes into the air.

He lifted the cloth tied around his neck to his face and tightened it. He sprinted for the fallen.

Some workers had tied on their makeshift masks before the wraiths' vapor overcame them. The rags would not keep out the fumes completely, but they were better than nothing. These workers carried the less fortunate, staggering in pairs and alone. As he came closer, Emberly realized the victims were still conscious.

What was more, they were smiling.

Some stretched lazily on the ground, as if on a blanket by the sea. Others sat picking at the grass or staring in wonder at flowers. Those lucky enough to be rescued let others lead or drag them while they grinned at the sky or closed their eyes for a nap. Some laughed. Emberly heard someone whistling a tune.

He could only carry one. He decided on a young woman lying prone who was small enough to lift easily. Her arm had fallen over the chest of a burly man twice her size who appeared to be asleep. As the captain picked her up, she gave him a smile of careless beauty.

He ran with her back to the gates, jostling her awake. He laid her against a wall in the courtyard, where Lieutenant Roark barked commands and willed the scene's madness into order. Emberly's gratitude for Roark's presence knew no bounds.

Almost everyone who could still walk had crowded through the gates. As the noncombatants shut themselves in the keep, a dreadful calm descended. Emberly was pleased at how quickly the defenses were falling into place and pleased that this whole affair would soon resolve itself one way or another.

He realized, to his embarrassment, that his mind had wandered. He was still kneeling by the woman. As he rose to join Roark, she touched his arm. She said something soft and wistful that he could not hear. He bent close and asked her to repeat it.

"Where's Griff?" she asked.

He looked at her then at the gate and stood. There might be time for one more.

Dashing out through the gate, he found Griff where they had left him. A strange excitement stirred in Emberly, a lightness of mood, as if this race against death was merely an extra adventure he had stumbled into.

He sobered when he realized the man was even larger than he remembered, and Emberly could not carry him alone.

Should he kill him? Surely the man would prefer instant death to being torn apart in the wraiths' demonic ceremonies. But people were watching from the wall. What would they think if the captain shot one of their own?

"Fine then, Griff," said Emberly, and he began dragging the man.

As soon as he saw the gate, he knew it was impossibly far. People were watching him from the walls, and he realized he was the only conscious person outside. It was him and the wraiths, who might charge at any moment.

Feeling strangely lighthearted despite his certain failure, he turned back to his task. With one mighty pull, he slipped and fell, jamming his boot into Griff's crotch. Laughter erupted from him. He was a flea trying to pull a boulder.

He felt good about trying to save this man. He was also glad it was over. Maybe by trying, he had redeemed himself from some sin or other. One of the small ones.

Thinking about sin led him to think of the pistol leaping in his hands, Rayan falling.

"No," he said aloud. As he inhaled, he caught the faint odor of grass and soil.

A chill shook him.

He had forgotten the wraiths' vapors, which his mask could not keep out entirely. The natural, insidious giddiness that was filling him would soon lull him to his death. He remembered something Rayan had said—*the freedom of no meaning*—and tried to feel afraid.

The wraith's fumes affected people to differing degrees. When Emberly had been in the wraiths' captivity, they had affected him strongly. But then the wraiths had breathed directly into his face. The current assault was coming on the wind.

The captain could think of only one explanation. There must be so many wraiths in the surrounding jungle that their collected breathing produced enough vapors to alter the mind from a distance. If more than a fraction were brave enough to attack directly, the defenders' cause might be hopeless.

He wished the thought disturbed him more.

As dread and softness clashed inside him, a voice called to him from the gate. It was Belith. He did not think she was real at first, but she slowly grew larger. She was coming toward him.

Earlier, she had protested mightily when everyone commanded her to take shelter during the battle. In the end, her physical state had left her no option, and she had agreed. But here she was, coming to help him with a cloth wrapped over her nose and mouth.

He leaped up, managing not to fall again. With a final glance at Griff's face, its fractional smile hinting at pleasant dreams, he ran to Belith before she could hobble farther into danger.

When he reached her, she shouted and pulled his arm. He grinned to tell her she was right, they were in an awful lot of trouble. They hurried to the gate as quickly as she could manage. There, he sent her to shelter under the keep.

As the gates closed, he glimpsed once more the barricade of piled logs. Their defenses were small and amateurish, perhaps entirely futile.

He stifled a chuckle. This had all become terribly amusing.

Then the wraiths began to howl.

39

— · —

ARUMIN

BEFORE LETTING BRIN FALL asleep that afternoon, Arumin had made sure the young priest knew where to go when the battle began. The two of them would take shelter in one of the keep's underground cells with the children and those unable to fight.

Brin now slept, having pushed his cot pointedly across the room from Arumin's.

That was how the bishop left him.

Arumin had no plan except to go into battle. He wrapped his long hair in a cloth and exchanged his robe for the simpler clothes of Emberly's soldiers, altering his appearance as much as he reasonably could. Maybe, if he was lucky, the convicts he fought alongside would not recognize him.

He did not want a pitiful death—some convict shooting him from behind. He did not mean to throw himself into the claws of the wraiths, either. This was not suicide.

He would put himself at the front, fight hard, and let the Goddess take him.

The image of her striding through the swamp, come to take him to the next life, had not left him. It would never leave him. It had not been Shada, it had been *her*, and the more things crumbled and went sour, the more convinced he became that he had somehow missed the moment when he should have died.

Brin had missed his too, but Arumin must leave that to Brin. The boy would not listen now, but he would understand someday. He might even follow.

Meanwhile, if Brin survived the battle, he could make use of Private Robir's confession against Emberly for the sake of the crusade. Arumin prayed he would see that his duty lay there.

Tonight, when the alarm was sounded, someone would come to warn the bishop but would find only his assistant. Brin would know where to go. Arumin would be on the wall, giving the Goddess another chance.

If she declined to take him again, despair certainly would. It waited beyond the coming fight, hungry.

By the time someone cried out that the attack had begun, Arumin was waiting on the keep's wall. He was mostly relieved the wait was over. On climbing atop the wall, he had accepted a rifle, ammunition, and a torch.

He had thrown his cloak's hood over his face, and amid the bustle of preparation, no one had recognized him. It was a good sign.

Hearing the alarm, soldiers and convicts took their posts around him. The convicts had only the firearms that had survived the revolt and the years since. Those without guns wielded axes, primitive bows, torches, and other tools. The soldiers, being far fewer but better armed, spaced themselves among the convicts.

Arumin had chosen a spot on the wall farthest from the front gate. Near him were Private Merin and, more promisingly, Private Hulgar. There were worse places to be in battle than next to a giant. The two had been ostracized for their cowardly actions in the keep, though no official punishment had occurred yet. Merin had been clinging to Hulgar, who showed little care for what anyone thought.

Looking at the people around him, Arumin noticed with a surge of fear that he had forgotten to tie cloth over his mouth and nose to hold back the wraiths' vapors. He wanted to meet his end in his right mind.

His hands hesitated on the way to tear off his headscarf. His long silver hair would identify him to anyone with eyes. He was still frozen when a woman nearby shoved another scarf at him. She was armed with nothing but a shovel.

He put on the gift with a smile. Maybe he was in a different kind of story than he had thought. Gallobrethi fireside tales were full of incompetent, bumbling heroes who survived all manner of dangers despite their own banality. He might be one of those. An elderly, forgetful fool. He would be every child's favorite character.

He wondered where his newly jolly mood had come from. For a moment, he had forgotten about dying. Others on the wall looked the same. Their faces were covered, but their eyes smiled.

His amusement curdled when the wraiths howled. Their voices rose from the woods—many of them, so many. It was a dreadful hymn sung by a hoarse, tuneless chorus. Around Arumin, people froze, their eyes widening as the horror of that sound pierced their lighthearted mood. The wraiths were entering their blood frenzy, bolstering their courage to face the dreaded offworlders.

Orders came down the line for people with rifles to fix their bayonets. Everyone was to hold their fire until told otherwise. Arumin had not fired a rifle since leaving the army in disgrace. A good rifleman could get off three or four shots per minute. He chuckled at this statistic as he fumbled through the steps of loading his weapon.

Still, the howling went on.

Maybe he would not need to worry about reloading. If the wraiths were as fast and difficult to see as he had heard, the defenders might find no clear targets until the wraiths scampered up the wall and fought them hand-to-hand.

As darkness fell, the wraiths' song trailed off, replaced by the shivering wails of Caidfell's night winds. He had expected the attack to start by now.

His emotions had settled into an enjoyable hum of peace. Rather than the expected terror of death, he was curious to see how it would all work out. He detected similar renewed cheer in the faces of those around him—a feeling of openness to what the night offered. It was the wraiths' vapors, it must be, but that fact worried him less than he had expected.

He never got a chance to fire. Over the wind, he heard shouting from the front gate. He turned as rifle fire clattered, but the keep's shadowy mass blocked his view of the gate. The shouts became screams, and many voices joined in.

"Sounds like a mess," he said aloud. It was something his mother might have said.

Cries, grunts, and a few shots followed. The wraiths had surprised them, approaching the wall unseen. Everyone nearby shifted uncomfortably. But Emberly's repeated command held firm—no one moved. The wraiths might be attacking from the front to draw attention away from a larger attack from the rear.

As seconds passed, shots echoed from both directions along the wall. Someone loosed a flaming arrow, and the piled logs that encircled the wall caught fire section by section. The strange, brittle trees quickly ignited.

Shaking crazily in the wind, the fire spread along the barricade, approaching Arumin's spot from both directions. It passed him first from the left and stopped maybe ten paces to his right. The flame coming from the right stopped short, leaving a gap as wide as his arm span in the wall of fire.

Everyone cursed and exclaimed dully as if late for an appointment. Part of their defensive plan had failed. The wraiths might not touch or leap over a flaming barricade, but they could pour in and out freely through that gap. The flames would bewilder them less than Emberly had hoped.

But Arumin had seen no wraiths. Maybe none of them had seen the gap—yet. Someone should fix it before they did.

Deep inside, part of him whooped in triumph at the chance to die while trying to save the day. But most of him thought a walk would be a nice diversion.

He was only a little afraid as he threw his legs over the parapet, tossed his rifle down, and shoved off.

He had never jumped such a distance before. The ground struck him like a giant hammer, leaving him senseless and hurting all over. Reminded violently of his age, he tried to stand, but his knees gave way. People on the wall pointed and chattered like bird-watchers in a park.

Once he was on his feet, he was delighted that none of his bones seemed broken. But his ankles ached, and he limped toward the gap in the barricade. He had forgotten his torch, and he stayed near the wall, scared of being out in the open. It was the first real fear he had felt in a while.

The wind thrashed the flames. His eyes watered, blurring the scene. Were it not for shouts and gunshots from the wall, the wraith would have caught him by complete surprise.

He noticed its shadow as it sprinted at him. Realizing he had dropped his rifle in the fall, he ran, limping, back toward it. The wraith would pounce any instant, and he marveled that he was not more afraid.

Wild shots rang from above. A few people dropped torches for him, but they were too far away. He reached his rifle and snatched it up, his back aching as he straightened. The wraith swayed grotesquely as it closed in. A bullet had struck it below the waist, and in the firelight, something dark poured out.

With a howl, he thrust the bayonet at its chest. It jumped back, still dreadfully quick. He recovered with a wobble, knowing keenly how much stronger and faster he had once been. He thrust again, overreached, and the wraith grabbed the blade and pulled, heedless of pain. Arumin refused to drop the rifle, so it pulled him in close where it could slash him.

But the bayonet was loose from the fall. It broke away from the rifle barrel, and Arumin fell flat on his back. The fiend stumbled but did not fall. The bishop used his instant of grace to raise the rifle and pull the trigger. The trigger stuck fast.

Some people had visions from their lives before they died. Arumin, who did not remember life fondly, wondered why he had dropped his rifle from such a great height.

The wraith cast the bayonet aside. Shots rang from above. Arumin threw his rifle at the wraith, who slapped it aside as it came for him.

Someone roared, and the ground shook. Hulgar's colossal form squatted on the wraith. He had crushed it as he landed.

Though half flattened, the wraith still moved. Hulgar put his massive knees on its chest and took its head in his hands. His muscles trembled as he pulled in one direction, then another. Arumin, accustomed to seeing awful things, closed his eyes.

When the wraith was dead, Hulgar collapsed. He was unwilling or unable to move any more.

"No!" Arumin shouted. Standing, he stumbled over to the big man. "You've got to stand up. More are coming! Get up!"

Hulgar did not respond. The bishop kicked him in the ribs, and searing pain shot through his own ankle. He wondered how badly the man's fall had injured him. If he was bleeding inside, he might die on the spot.

On the wall, bystanders cheered their small victory. Others shouted warnings and pointed.

A second wraith had appeared around the keep's wall to his left. The gap in the flames lay to his right. The wraith cast a momentary silhouette against the fire. It vanished. The air shimmered. It was coming right at him.

His heart froze. He ran toward the gap in the fire, but dizziness overcame him. Heartbeats passed, and he found himself on the ground. He had fallen again.

With his first rush of true, electrifying terror, he willed himself up. He was close to the gap. He did not look to see where the wraith was.

The gap had been caused by a single bundle of tree trunks that lay askew and unburned, with neither end touching the flames on the neighboring piles.

People on the wall were shooting and loosing arrows. He reached the near end of the misplaced bundle, which was an arm's length from the adjacent pile. Once he moved it and saw it ignite, he would have to move the other end. He tried to roll it, but his feet slipped. Then he ran out of time.

A bullet struck the logs. From the corner of his eye, he saw the wraith coming. He reached into the flames, snatched up a large flaming branch, and spun.

The wraith was moving too fast to stop, but it changed course and dodged the fire as he thrust at it. It now stood at his side. He whipped the branch around in a desperate swing, but the wraith dodged again. The branch was too big to manage.

The wraith stepped in close. Arumin brought the branch up again, but the wraith's arm lashed out and struck it from his weakened grip. He watched the flame spiral away. He gazed into his enemy's eyes. He tried to see the human in there, as Brother Nor would have wanted.

The side of its head burst. It dropped.

He turned to the wall, wondering who had fired the miraculous shot. It was Private Merin. The man waved his arms wildly as people around him shouted and pointed to him. Whatever sorcery had made Arumin so carefree still gripped Merin and the rest. Except they were rapt spectators—it had not occurred to most to come down and help.

It was possible Brin was among them. Maybe he had been unwilling to hide.

Thrilled by his audience, the bishop let out a whoop and raised a fist. But their cries no longer sounded like cheers.

Alarmed, he went back to work. The bundle of logs was light enough that he thought he could lift it instead of rolling it. He squatted, knees creaking, and inched it toward its destination. He peered out beyond the barricade, and all other thoughts left his mind.

The night vibrated, a mass of shadows in frantic motion. Wraiths were charging in an endless tide toward the little gap in the wall of fire.

He heaved the bundle. It settled against the adjacent stack of wood and caught fire. He hobbled toward the other end, which lay outside the barricade. He had to move it to close the gap, or the enemy might still come through. If the fire got there first, he would not be able to touch it.

He reached the end and lifted it. Taking a small step, he stumbled and fell. Nearing the end of his strength, he forced himself up only to see fire swallow the bundle. He stretched an arm toward it, knowing he could not touch it again.

Another, mightier hand enveloped his. Hulgar dragged him through the gap, discarded him like a doll, and picked up the flaming bundle. With a squeal of agony, he shifted it and dropped it into place.

The wraiths struck the flaming barricade in a wave. Those in front could not stop in time, and the barricade shook and sparks showered with the collision. Some wraiths leaped back, while others tripped and fell into the flames. A few made it across, dazed and scorched. Through it all, they maintained their ghastly silence.

Hulgar picked up a discarded hatchet and attacked the pitiable creatures that had crossed the barricade. Arumin decided to help but quickly realized he was not moving.

His own tangled hair filled his mouth. At some point, his disguise had fallen away. The Goddess did not come for him like she had in the swamp, but that did not matter. She was with him again. Burned and abused, his body took command at last, and he slept.

40

— · —

EMBERLY

THE FIRST WAVE OF wraiths came quickly and silently after dark. The first cries told Emberly they were here, and the first shots were fired before he snatched up his rifle.

The men and women on the wall had been waiting for some time, lulled by the quiet. Emberly careened up the stairs as their shouts of surprise turned to fear and savagery.

He reached the top of the wall as the first wraiths sprang over the parapet. There were many more outside, and they moved too fast to count.

A wraith sailed onto the wall in front of him as if catapulted. Emberly had no time to think and no torch to frighten it with. He fired his rifle as it cleared the parapet, a dark ripple in the air. It bowled him over, smashing his rifle against his chest. For an instant, its weight crushed him, then it was gone.

As he glanced around in confusion, another wraith leaped over him. The courtyard had exploded with motion. The wraiths were inside the wall, and so far, Emberly had not even delayed them.

He roared and scrambled to his feet. Drawing his saber, he faced a wraith that had gruesomely dispatched the man next to him.

He slashed it terribly, but it attacked him with speedy indifference, parrying his next thrust with a gesture. He could not evade its embrace. It trapped his arms and tipped its face toward his.

Only raw fear let him do what he did. He grabbed its waist and threw his legs forward and his head back. His weight dropped, pulling the wraith forward, and they fell from the wall together.

They landed lengthwise in the courtyard, Emberly on top of his enemy. For a moment, the captain only knew he could not breathe. When the world came into focus, he saw the wraith shuddering in multihued agony as men bludgeoned it with boots and shovels.

A soldier lifted the captain under the armpits and dragged him somewhere quieter. As the man sat him against a wall, Emberly could speak again. He groaned, "Tell them to start the fires!" His voice sounded like an old man's. The soldier nodded and left.

The man had moved him to a part of the courtyard where the fighting had not yet reached. His company's wagons and beasts of burden were stored here in a stone enclosure. The animals brayed and fidgeted. On the wall above him, defenders milled about, peering down at him.

He could not afford to rest. The battle plan was in tatters. The barricade was a temporary defense and would soon burn away. He had intended to light it at the last possible moment to give the soldiers more time to dig up Rayan's gift. If a few crossed the barricade before it ignited, the defenders would hold them off. But far too many had climbed the wall and come inside.

He got up slowly and jogged toward the front of the keep. Peering around the corner, he saw the gate.

The melee continued on the wall, but the wraiths had overrun the courtyard. The defenders had managed to light the barrier around the hole, surrounding it with towering flames. However, the round grate that was meant to cover the hole still leaned against a nearby wall. Without the grate, wraiths could jump into the hole from the wall.

Several wraiths stood around the hole. Could they have guessed the object of the digging?

The diggers in the hole must be defended at any cost. But the wraiths would see him and attack as soon as he emerged from cover. In his fall, he had lost everything but his pistol with its single shot.

Moving as quickly as his pain would allow, he hurried to the animals' enclosure. The battle had spread to the wall above him, and the beasts were near panic. Opening the gate, he found his mount and led it forward. It nuzzled him in recognition, and guilt stung him.

He walked the beast out, closed the gate, and mounted bareback. He hoped the animal's nerves could handle charging across the courtyard.

He should have moved faster. A barrage of gunfire rang out from the wall. A man fell with a scream and landed among the animals, striking one across its back.

It was the last straw for the beasts. They burst through the gate in full flight, rushing toward Emberly on his mount. Emberly's animal took off, leading the charge between the wall and the corner of the keep.

The stampede rolled into the front courtyard. The wraiths froze. Though Emberly could not read their faces, he had been in their situation before.

Having lost control of his animal, he could only cling to its back like a barnacle. The wraiths fled, scampering up the wall.

As the herd neared the hole, the animals parted to avoid the flames. He had planned to halt the beast and jump into the hole from its back, but he could not stop it now.

He made an insane choice. As they passed the hole, he threw himself toward it from the animal's back.

He landed on the flaming wood, which crumbled. The animals raced past. Things became confused. Coolness brushed him and turned into unimaginable heat. He was in the fire. He rolled back and forth, out of his mind.

Someone hugged his leg and pulled him into the hole. He did not know he had been saved until someone shook him.

"Stop!" shouted Sergeant Orund.

Shivering, Emberly looked up at the diggers gathered around him. He had been waving his arms, but now Orund gripped them.

"You're fine, sir."

"Am I burned?" Emberly asked. He needed to know how bad it was.

"You're just a little singed, Captain," Orund said. "You didn't touch the fire for more than a second."

The men went back to work. Emberly patted himself all over. There was no charred skin, no flesh falling from bone. His clothes had started to burn, but the men must have patted out the fire.

He stood to find that the hole's rim was above his head. He noticed the smell at last. The hole stank like rotting meat. Two men, both convicts, stood outside the hole, beyond the flames. "You chased the wraiths out of the yard, Captain," said one, looking around nervously.

"Listen!" snapped Emberly, still shaking. "Bring the grate over here. You've got to close us in."

While they were gone, a great rumble passed by. The panicked animals had made a full circuit of the wall and passed the hole again.

The men returned, carrying the grate between them.

"Hurry!" said Emberly. "What's happening out there?"

The men stood as close to the flames as they dared and heaved the grate. It landed roughly, covering the hole and sending charred wood tumbling down on Emberly and the others. No one would be able to lift it from outside without standing in the fire.

"The fiends are everywhere," said one of the men. "We've lost a lot of people on the wall. Emberly, a few got into the keep."

The captain kept his composure. "How?"

"The windows," said the man. "They climbed right up and through the slits. Of all the things to forget about."

Emberly wanted to snap that he had not forgotten the windows, he had just lacked time to do anything about them. His entire strategy now looked like a dream.

The man shouted, "They're coming now!" Both men vanished.

Something moved on top of the wall. Emberly yelled a warning to the soldiers as a wraith leaped down and landed on the grate. Its arm shot through and cut his shoulder. He and the others wound up cowering in the hole as the wraith strained to reach them. The captain drew his pistol and fired.

The noise was tremendous. The wraith's arm kept swiping, but it was slower, and blood dripped from its claws.

On their knees, the diggers returned to work. The captain hoisted one of their rifles, pressed the barrel against the wraith's shaking body, and fired. Another staggering sound. The shower of blood left no person or surface untouched, though Emberly got the worst of it. The wraith died quickly.

As the men worked, the odor that filled the hole had grown until it was almost overpowering. This was good news. The diggers were getting close. But they could hardly work quickly while under attack.

Several wraiths arrived, leaping one after another from the wall. As they landed on the grate, he wondered if it would collapse. They all reached for him, maybe understanding he was the hole's most dangerous occupant. He dropped to the dirt to avoid their claws.

Unable to touch him, they went after his men. One set of claws caught Orund across the back. Another grabbed a man by the hair and lifted him as he screamed. Seeing this, Emberly jumped up without thinking. Grabbing the hand that held the man's hair, he pulled down on it with all his weight and sank his teeth into it.

The hand let go instantly and pulled out of Emberly's bite. But the captain did not duck fast enough, and a long arm shot around his neck and yanked him up, banging his head on the grate. It squeezed his neck, wiry muscles flexing, and he saw spots before his eyes.

Another gunshot, and the arm relaxed, letting him fall. He could not tell who had fired. His ears rang as the men fired their weapons upward. Blood rained on them all.

The attack ceased for the moment. Dead wraiths lay atop the grate. The men scrambled around, searching under everything. They'd had a bag of ammunition, but they could not find it.

"I'll look for it," said Emberly. "Keep digging."

They glanced at each other and obeyed. Emberly touched his face and realized it must be a mask of blood and dirt.

After scouring the hole, climbing over the men as they dug, he admitted to himself the ammunition might really be lost.

As he struggled to accept this, Orund spoke. "Captain, sir... did you really let Keesin die?" It sounded like a question he had been waiting to ask and that the others had been waiting for him to ask.

The captain's vision grew foggy. He wiped his eyes with his filthy sleeve, and they stung. He looked from soldier to soldier, meeting their gazes. Before he could answer, the real attack came.

A series of impacts rocked the grate nearly out of place. A forest of arms poured through.

Everyone dove again to avoid the claws. The men kept digging, now using their hands. Emberly had nothing to shoot with. He started swinging his fists. His punches landed ineffectually, and he roared with the desire to kill.

The swiping claws drove him down until he lay on his belly. There, he saw a bayonet in the dirt. Another lay nearby.

Grinning like death's head, he snatched the blades and attacked with one in each hand. His hands tingled with power as they swung at the wraiths' arms, slashing and stabbing ever faster. The arms kept striking at him. As some fell still and others withdrew, he began stabbing upward through the grate at the wraiths' feet, his blades leaping like pistons in some ancient engine.

Again, the attack lulled. More dead had collected on the grate, and any wraiths that survived had jumped atop the corpses of their comrades. The hole was a hellish mix of blood and dirt. The stench was intolerable.

The wraiths must have guessed what the men were digging up. They had recognized the smell. They had little other reason to try so hard to stop them.

The men had kept digging, undaunted, tossing the dirt to the hole's edges. Someone's fingers had touched a soft surface under the soil, and the men leaped on the find, pawing away like dogs.

His heart leaping, Emberly crawled to join them. Rayan had not lied.

The hole went dark. The faces of several wraiths filled empty spaces in the grate. The spaces not blocked by wraiths' bodies were filled by the faces of living wraiths, pressed close to the grate.

Their mouths opened, and they exhaled with a low sigh.

Emberly's pain melted away, and the tension left his shoulders. "Cover your faces!" he shouted. The soldiers tightened and tucked the fabric covering their mouths and noses.

Emberly's had fallen off somewhere. He found it somehow in the darkness and muck and tied it over his face.

He found a bayonet and got up to thrust it through the grate, but the wraiths were wise to this game. Each one pulled back to avoid the blade and then resumed breathing its poison into the hole.

The men clawed the dirt, hands and fingers bleeding. They began to giggle and bounce. Their struggle was becoming a lark, a game with death.

Emberly sat down. He had inhaled more of the wraiths' fumes than the others, and his mind buzzed with fascination at each sound and sensation. He pushed his thumbs into his eyes, trying to feel. His mind was fading.

He pulled up his sleeve and cut his arm with the bayonet. Exhilarating pain flooded his senses, leaving his mind clearer. The blade was filthy, and he could not distinguish between the wraiths' blood and his own.

The men cried out in excitement. They had uncovered the object. He smiled at their giddiness like a proud father, but he could only watch. Bothered by that, he drove the tip of the bayonet straight into his arm. It was only sensible.

The pain brought him briefly to the present, and he saw the men hoist up a large, oddly shaped bundle tied off with rope. They opened the bag, and out tumbled some decayed pieces of one of the giant leaves they had encountered in the swamp.

The odor rose by an order of magnitude. The leaf's smell had not diminished while buried, but it had grown sickly and rotten. One of the fragments must have come from the leaf's very tip. On it, ripples formed what was unmistakably a face.

A glow from the wraiths' faces lit the hole with a rainbow of colors. The meaning of the leaf was not lost on them.

The glow vanished. The wraiths were gone. Emberly's soldiers looked at him. He saw no judgment in their faces, not even Orund's. He loved them.

His pain had focused his mind, and he remembered to unroll the tarp. They huddled under it together and waited for the swarms.

41

BRIN

Still giggling, Nor and Shada reached the underground corridor that held their assigned room. An elderly woman beckoned them in from down the hall.

Children, wounded, and the elderly already filled the candlelit room. It had once held prisoners. Chains hung from the walls, and the floor featured a small well like the one that had nearly drowned the bishop.

"We're the last room to close up," the woman told them. "Wish we could lock the doors. These cells all lock from outside."

"Even closing it may keep the wraiths out," said Nor with a final chuckle. "They have no locks or doors where they live."

This was wildly optimistic, but it felt good to say and might ease the others' minds for the moment. Shada smiled at him, a broad, silly smile as if they had shared a childish joke. He returned the smile, wishing the wraiths' power did not lie behind it. That smile did more than anything to help him shake off the jolliness of the wraith's spell and come to his senses.

That and the memory of torture.

No one here had breathed the wraiths' vapors. People huddled together, whispering, embracing, and weeping. Confusion hung in the air, and Nor reviewed the plan aloud to bring some order. "Whatever happens, we'll stay unarmed. It's our only chance if they find us. Captain Emberly says the swarms follow the leaves—"

"It's true," said the old woman who had let them in. "The biggest trees know it. That's why they send the leaves. They want something destroyed."

Nor nodded his thanks for the contribution. A couple minutes of conversation, even about things they all knew, might keep them calm—him not least—as long as they did not dwell on the grimness of their situation. Soon, they would have to lower their voices to whispers. "Since we don't know when the swarms will come, let's fill the cracks around the door now. That'll keep out the wraiths' vapors too."

The woman wasn't finished. "He stole that leaf. Rayan, that bastard. From an evil tree. Those wiry trees out there are its children. They're taking over this jungle, hunting for that leaf."

This, Nor had not heard before. It sounded unlikely, but he would discount nothing here. "Well, we're putting it to good use."

"What is she talking about?" said a shaking voice. It was Brin. Nor had not noticed him in the crowd.

"Father Brin," he said, "I thought you were with the bishop."

"He left me," said Brin. He walked out of the crowd toward Nor, his lip trembling with each uncertain step. "He's gone. And those things are coming..."

Shada had been silent until now. She went to Brin and put her hands on his arms. "It's all right." She whispered soothing things.

"No." Brin shook her off. "Don't lie. You're lying."

The sight of a priest breaking down was too much to handle. "It's madness," the elderly woman cried. "Madness. Calling down these swarms. They might kill the wraiths, but they won't stop with them. They're coming for all of us."

Nor tried to sound reassuring. "That's why we have so many tarps and blankets—"

The woman ignored him. "That tree knows we took it now, and it'll punish us." She shouted to the room, "It knows!"

Fear rippled through the others.

Feeling the room's mood slipping toward panic, Nor whispered to Shada, "Help her," and nodded toward the old woman.

She obeyed.

Nor spoke to Brin in a sympathetic tone that did not match his feelings. "Father Brin, what's your favorite prayer?"

Brin stared at him as if he was speaking in tongues. "My..."

Nor glanced toward the elderly woman, who had eagerly accepted Shada's embrace. "What's the first one you can think of? Doesn't have to be your favorite."

It was clearly not a thing Brin often considered. He moved his lips, searching for a name. "I don't know what it's called."

"Say it for us."

Others nearby were listening.

Brin launched into the mealtime blessing. It was simple, very brief, and usually said in the presence of food. Nor joined him, reciting enthusiastically. He gestured for those around them to join in, and they did, softly at first, wondering if they were crazy.

By the time Brin finished, he had fallen to his knees out of habit. Nor kneeled also and said, "Again."

On the second and third recitations, almost everyone joined in. Their voices were low and tense but calmer.

Nor was about to gently interrupt and suggest blocking the cracks around the door when someone knocked.

Shada opened the door, and Belith limped in on her cane.

"I can't find anyone else," she said. She nodded to Shada. "Everyone who's not fighting has hidden."

Shada returned her nod, clearly glad to see the woman. She straightened and grabbed Nor's arm. "The Lady! I've forgotten her."

Nor shook his head. "But you don't know where she is."

"Her box is out there somewhere. That's her shelter. She might flee there."

"It's in my room," said Belith. "I can take you there. But Shada, it's useless." She looked guilty. "I've had it for a while now. I've tried to open it, to summon the Lady, but it was no use."

"Oh," said Shada.

"I should've given it back, I know. Useless as it is, it's important to you."

Shada nodded.

The woman looked old and sad. "I just... really thought I could make her talk to me." After a second's thought, she perked up. "I'll take you there now." The prospect of taking action seemed to give her energy.

"I would appreciate that." Shada glanced at her cane. "You've walked so far already, though. You can't make it like that." That was not true, and she clearly knew it. "Yes, take me there. Thank you."

Nor could not believe this. He kept his voice calm. "The Lady can protect herself."

"I know." Shada's voice revealed he had not moved her a bit. "But she'll be safer here. My place is with her."

"Shada..." Nor was momentarily speechless. "She wouldn't ask you to do this."

"She might not ask, but she wants me to. I think I've gotten to know her better."

"The wraiths could be anywhere."

She dismissed the danger with a shake of her head. "This is why I'm here. I have to do it, Nor. I've done nothing else for anyone."

He gave her a small, weak smile. "'Nothing else.' That's the biggest lie I've heard you tell. May I come?"

"No. Stay and do your job. You're a good monk, whether you know it or not."

She was right, but still, he fought. "The wraiths..."

"They can kill one of us as quickly as the next." The truth of the words seemed to surprise her, and she shook her head. "We'd better leave before I think too hard about this. I'll see you soon."

As they spoke, Belith had taken Brin aside. Putting an arm around his shoulder, she pulled him close and whispered to him. Maybe she sensed his fear and was comforting him. When she left him, he was calmer, but he threw his cloak over himself as if hiding from the world.

Shada nodded in readiness. Belith opened the door, and the two women left without another word.

When the door shut, Nor turned to see many eyes on him. "It's time to whisper," he said. "But let's keep praying."

They prayed in whispers, and he joined them. The words gained a soft momentum, and they continued without him when he stopped. Brin had touched his shoulder.

The priest's eyes were red from crying. "I'll never forgive him," he whispered. He clutched the front of his shirt in a bunch.

Nor almost asked who, but then he remembered. "You must."

"Why did he leave?"

"I don't know. Just remember, whatever it is, forgive him."

Nor returned to prayer, but Brin tapped him again. Tears ran down the priest's face. "Tell Shada I'm sorry."

"For what? You'll tell her yourself soon."

"Someone attacked her."

"I know." Nor was worried. Brin was barely lucid.

"I was... scared... to tell anyone," said the priest. "I delayed it. Stupid. But I have to keep *it* secret."

Nor leaned in. "Keep what secret?"

Brin shivered and looked away. "Nothing. Don't listen to me. I don't know what I'm saying." Remembering something, he spoke slowly and clearly. "Did you and Shada plan to keep me out of here? Me and Arumin, I mean. Did you keep the room you liked for yourselves?"

Nor glared. "What does that even mean? Of course not. Why would anyone do that?"

Brin appeared relieved. "I know. Don't listen. Stupid."

"You're all right." Nor patted him on the back, hoping it was true.

Someone screamed in the hallway, a gut-wrenching wail. Everyone in the shelter shared a gasp.

"Lie down," said Nor as soon as he recovered his nerves. "As if you're hurt. Keep praying, silent now."

The people obeyed, sinking to the floor, holding each other, lips still moving.

Scuffling and grunting followed the scream. The sounds seemed to uncork a bottle, letting the noises of battle filter in from above. The hallway grew quiet.

Nor stayed on his hands and knees, watching the handle of the door but afraid of the noise he would make moving to grab it. Seconds passed like weeks. His heartbeat sounded so loud that whatever was outside must hear it.

The doorknob rattled for a short time but did not turn. Then it turned.

He dove for the handle. The door whipped open and struck him like a club. His feet left the ground, and his back hit the wall.

He stayed conscious, as much as he wished otherwise. Falling, his body settled in a sitting position against the wall. There, he prayed and watched what followed.

The first wraith to enter found Brin. The priest had jumped up to help Nor and come face-to-face with the enemy.

It rushed in on all fours, an afterimage of smooth, strong motion that matched the gray of the walls. It stopped in front of Brin, halting its momentum faster than should have been possible. There it stood, wisp-thin except for a muscular upper body. Yet it was human.

Brin crouched, covering his head, eyes shut. He did not cry. Most others in the room still lay prone except for a few who had panicked and crowded against the back wall. Many sets of lips moved silently.

Nor had no breath after hitting the wall, but his mouth shaped words of advice Brin would never hear. *Quiet. Lie down.*

Brin started to obey Nor's wish. He sank to his knees, then his hands, breathing hard, still whispering.

Dark eyes regarded the priest. They lacked malice or benevolence. They lacked anything Nor recognized.

All the way down.

Brin shuffled like an infant, turning on his hands and knees until he faced the wraith. His eyes were wide, no longer blinded by fear. Full of intent. His pupils shook, taking in many things at once, and Nor wondered how many wraiths stood in the hallway.

Brin crossed his arms over his chest and bowed. He sank forward until his forehead touched the floor. His priestly robes bunched around him. He trembled.

Nor slowly realized what Brin had done. Lying prone had not felt safe enough. Faced with power that could destroy him, he wanted to gratify it.

His posture was not one of surrender but of worship. The words on his lips were a prayer but not to Huire.

Brin, no.

The perversity of the scene echoed in Nor's memory after he shut his eyes. He hoped he would live so this would not be the last thing he saw.

He waited, hearing no sounds of butchery. Finally, he dared to open his eyes. The wraith had gone, leaving the door open. The people in the room were beginning to raise their heads and breathe. But Brin still bent, head down and arms crossed in unholy adoration of raw violence.

42

SHADA

IT TOOK SHADA AND Belith several minutes to creep to Belith's room, guarding the light of their only candle. The sounds of battle were plain outside, but here, all was worryingly still. With each tap of her boots or Belith's cane, Shada expected the wraiths to descend on them. The rising and falling of her terror wracked her nerves.

Belith tottered along, holding a pistol Shada had not noticed until now.

They reached the hallway to Belith's chamber without meeting any wraiths. Here, several windows let the sounds of battle in to echo in the corridor. They reached the door at the end and shut themselves quietly inside.

In the bare room, they found the giant vine plant spread across the floor, its ugly potato-red bulk dragged out from under the cot. The young man who had fetched the flute last night must have had quite a struggle.

The room had one small window, making the fighting outside sound much closer.

Belith sighed despondently and pointed. In close to the plant's red bulk, its tendrils had trapped an assortment of objects in a permanent embrace. There, between a dagger and a makeshift belt, was the Lady's box, held by several thick, muscly vines.

"I should have known she'd get ahold of it," Belith said. "That's that."

Shada shifted from one foot to another. "What do we do?"

"We leave. You can't still want it."

"Of course I do." Shada put the candle on the floor by the wall. "It's why we came."

"Your Lady isn't inside it." Belith pointed to the box, clutched in tendrils. "Do you think she'd let that happen if she was?"

"Listen," Shada said. "The Lady needs that box. It's her home, and she's not here to get it. I ask her too many questions, I never say the right thing to her, but I can damned well do the right thing *for* her. It's all I can offer now." She looked at the box. "I'm not leaving without it. You know this... thing... better than me. So tell me what to do."

Belith was mournful. "You can't get it without getting pricked. To move the vines, you'll have to pull them. Unless you have an axe under that cloak." She swallowed. "Maybe not even then. She can be irritable when you come too close."

Shada thought about the vines in the swamp, pulling wagons off the road. "Does... it have a name?" She asked out of morbid curiosity and maybe to delay what lay ahead.

"No. She doesn't deserve that. You're right to call her 'it.'"

An idea occurred to Shada. "I'll use my cloak like a glove. It can't sting me through that."

"Maybe, maybe not. Anyway, she's got too many vines. You can't block them all."

"What about the candle? Let's set it on fire."

"It's one tiny flame, and she's too big. She'd hurt you in the process, worse than you would hurt her. She's strongest near her center." Belith pointed to a wooden brush clutched against the bulk. The plant had snapped it in two.

"You have a gun." Shada saw the weakness of that idea even as she suggested it.

"You'd hurt her, but she wouldn't give up the box. Plus you'd call the wraiths down on our heads."

Looking at the plant, Shada clenched and unclenched her fists. "I'm out of choices. I won't ask you to help. It's my fight, and you've given too much blood to this thing already."

Belith stared at her then at the plant. "You're not planning... What are you doing? Are you going to *wrestle* it?"

Shada did not answer.

"The pain will drive you mad before you pry the box away. If you're lucky, you'll only pass out after."

"That's what happened last time, and here I am." It was mostly true. Her hand still ached where the plant had stung her.

"The wraiths could show up at any moment. Am I supposed to carry you back? Look at me."

"No. Leave me in here, under the bed. The wraiths might miss me." Shada spoke quickly as she whipped off her cloak, racing to begin before fear could stop her.

"I won't allow it." Belith stepped between her and the plant. "You've given enough."

Mind aflame, Shada faced her.

Belith glared. "Will you fight me to get to her?"

"Give me another choice."

Belith bit her lip. It made her appear younger. "I can't, Caretaker. But I won't watch you throw yourself on that. When she's really in danger... I don't know what she'll do."

Still holding the cloak, Shada let it drop. She got an idea.

"Wait." She hurried to the cot. Tossing aside the thin mattress, which the plant's tendrils had filled with holes and furrows, she saw through the bedframe to the floor. There lay an assortment of items apparently pulled under by the plant. Amid these, she found what she wanted, a tangle of dark blankets that had once covered the bed.

"Listen," she said, yanking the thickest of them from the pile.

She quickly explained her plan. She and Belith took one end of the blanket each and stood apart.

"Ready?" said Shada. "We've got to be fast, before the smoke chokes us."

Belith shook her head. "This had better work."

They moved to the candle by the wall and dipped the blanket's center into the flame. The fabric caught fire quickly. Smoke gathered above their heads as the flame spread across the blanket.

"Now."

They hurled the blanket onto the plant. Crouching far from its splayed tendrils, they held the blanket's corners to the floor.

The plant struggled silently. Its vines flailed, slapping their boots and clothing. One brushed Shada's bare leg.

No stings yet. If Shada had thought the thing could feel, she could not have continued.

Something thumped under the blanket. In its struggle, the plant had dropped one of its possessions. "Soon, I hope," said Shada, encouraged by the calm in her own voice. The sheet would quickly burn to nothing.

From under the blanket came a clatter like the spilling of a junk drawer. A drinking cup rolled past Shada's feet. The plant's mass rose under the blanket, hoisted by its vines.

Shada fell. A vine had grabbed her leg and pulled as the plant heaved its lumpy red mass at her.

It struck her, then she struck the ground. She gasped for air and swung her arms blindly as the vine plant pounced on her like a hunting spider. Still covered by the burning blanket, it moved on inner vines as thick as a man's biceps. On its mottled surface, little barbs popped in and out of red skin, all of it wreathed in flames as it sank toward her face.

It stopped short of touching her. Belith had grabbed a trailing vine and was trying to drag the thing back. As Shada scrambled from under the plant, the older woman's legs collapsed.

The thing reared up on its vines and pulled Belith in. It leaped on her as the blanket fell away.

Shada thrashed, her body demanding escape, unsure of up or down. Through the gathering haze of smoke, she saw the window with its promise of fresh night air outside. For an instant, she would have risked jumping blindly out.

A gunshot shook the building. Shada found the floor and heard screams. Belith and the plant were rolling, the plant on top and unhurt, Belith beating it with her empty pistol. Shada pushed herself up and grabbed the blanket, still burning in patches. Unfurling it as she ran, she threw it and then herself on the plant's bucking potato mass.

Battered through the blanket by clumsy, muscular vines, she hugged the thing to herself and rose. Shaking like a strongman, she staggered backward, its shifting weight tipping her with each step, its tendrils a storm of bruising whips.

It was only a few steps, but they were the longest of her life. At the window, she heaved it onto the sill. One of its thick vines wrapped around her neck, but she ducked out of its grasp. Another climbed under her collar and stung her, the pain like a stab wound in her breast.

She reeled back a couple steps and charged the thing shoulder first. Its vines filled the window, pumping wildly but blind and clumsy. Its barbs stung her shoulder as it gave way, grasping at her hair and then falling out the window to the ground.

Shada didn't watch it hit. She sank to the floor, knowing they had no time to rest. After that gunshot, the wraiths would be on their way. She pulled herself up using the windowsill, and the night wind touched her face. She went to Belith.

The woman was not only alive but awake. She looked up at Shada, blood from all the stings dotting her face, neck, and hands. Breathing noisily, she murmured, "Good idea."

Shada gasped. "You're not dead."

"Not yet." Belith's face and chest were bright red.

"Let's go." Shada pulled her up and helped her walk.

They aimed first to reach the demolished bed, but one step told Shada they would not make it. Instead, she helped Belith to the wall and sat her there, opposite the door. She fetched the candle and a knife the plant had dropped. Finally, she took the next-thickest blanket from under the cot. With the swarms coming, they would need it.

Belith waved a hand, eyes wide. "Wraiths," she croaked.

"I know." In this maze of a keep, the wraiths might take minutes to find them, or seconds.

Shada had spotted the box amid the wreckage of the room, and now she picked it up. It was smaller than she remembered. A strange, ornate thing but only a thing.

Not only its size had diminished. She knew without opening it that the Lady was not inside.

"I don't know what I expected," she said aloud. "I suppose I thought she would appear when I needed her—again."

"She's safe somewhere," said Belith hoarsely. "That's what you wanted."

Shada hadn't really expected Belith to answer, but the woman seemed more awake, not less.

"Maybe part of me," Shada said. "The better part."

Belith shrugged. Her face was swelling and her breathing was labored, but her mouth bent in a lazy smile.

"You're going to live," Shada said, trying to sound confident. "That thing has bitten you before."

"Not this many times. It... hurts a lot, Shada."

Shada sat next to her and put the box down in front of them, making sure its door was closed. "Pray with me," she said.

They spent a couple minutes there, Shada pressing her head to the ground, Belith letting hers droop. Shada's thoughts were as muddled as ever. The pain of the plant's stings struck her with full force, and she breathed heavily. Tears dropped from her brow. She could only hope her effort to pray counted for something.

"Goddess Huire," she said finally aloud, "if we need the Lady's protection, or if she needs ours, I know you will send her to us." She ended her prayer without a goodbye. All needless words seemed stupid now.

She sat up and opened her eyes. The box sat unchanged. She opened the box, still hoping, but the Lady was not there.

That made everything real. She threw the box against the wall. It fell with a clang, undamaged. She screamed at it. It did not answer. Nothing she did mattered. She sat back next to Belith, chest and shoulder throbbing wildly, and listened to the scream's echo die away.

The door handle moved.

For an instant, she froze. The handle shook. She lunged across the room and caught it as it turned.

The intruder must be a wraith. It was too quiet to be anything else. It was much stronger than her, and the knob turned despite her effort. She released one hand and shoved the lock into place.

She backed away as the wraith beat on the door. The pounding soon stopped, replaced by terrific impacts as the wraith rammed the door with its body.

Belith cleared her throat and spoke in a distorted voice. "Won't hold long."

She was right. Shada trudged back to the wall and sank down next to Belith. Her energy had gone, and the pain of the stings oppressed her with every step.

The older woman nudged her. "Cheer up. Swarm might save us."

They sat. Each crash of the door sent a jolt of fear through Shada, but she forced herself to breathe slowly. "I should've brought Nor. But I wanted to do this myself."

Belith shrugged again. Her calmness made Shada want to shake her. "If he survives... got you to thank."

"It was idiotic."

"If you see him... don't say that."

"I thought that thing had killed you. But you're still with me."

"Like you said. Been doing this... for a while. Hurts a little less." As she spoke, Belith stared at a severed piece of vine on the floor near them. Several lay around the room, this one almost close enough to touch.

Shada looked at her. "You're an old fool."

Belith's laugh was half gurgle. Her speech was ever slower as she kept pausing to breathe. But her expression was impish. "Why not? Should be dreaming now. Having my vision."

"You can't be serious."

"S'stupid, but… maybe Arumin was right. Maybe it's a test. What if all it takes… is one more try?"

Shada looked at the vine fragment. Had it moved closer? "It has no more to give you. You've survived the worst it can do."

"Few ideas yet. Might swallow a piece."

The thought made Shada ill. "It doesn't work that way. Huire knows we're sorry. She'll forgive us, or she won't. It's up to her."

The door was splintering. Belith tossed her gun aside. "Almost forgot. Maybe the wraith will… judge us innocent."

Shada listened to the door. "More than one out there, I think."

Back in Ronia, winter would soon arrive. Once, years ago, she and her father had woken in an alley, partly covered by the first snow.

She traced the thought to its root and realized a few specks of dust or ash had just blown inside through the tiny window. They whirled in the air.

"It's here." She pulled the blanket to them and cast it over them both.

More specks glided through the window as the two women tucked the edges of the blanket under themselves, trying to seal themselves inside. They were pulling it over their heads when all of their attackers entered at once.

The door broke and swung wide. The wraiths blurred into gray shapes as they charged.

The swarm poured through the window like a giant serpent. It was creamy white.

The wraiths saw it but did not stop. Shada saw why. Another swarm was right behind them, rushing down the moonlit hallway. They vanished into the white cloud as the second cloud collided with it. The second cloud was bright crimson, and when the two merged in swirling fury, their mixture was soft and pink.

Before they overran her, Shada buried her head under the blanket. And waited. The wraiths could have reached them in a few strides, but they heard no more footsteps.

The blanket got heavier. Shada wondered if she was imagining it, but soon, it became unmistakable. As the swarm filled the room, it was piling on them.

Shada held as still as she could. Moving could open the blanket a little and allow something through. She had covered herself too quickly to get comfortable, and now her neck and joints began to hurt. The plant's stings burned. Aching and trembling, she felt an instant of pleasure at a cool touch on the back of her neck. Her other pains melted away, even the stings.

She held in a scream. The swarm was on her. Just a few specks, maybe only one. It had come in somehow, maybe through a hole in the blanket or by running down the wall at her back. It was colder than rainwater.

"It's got me," she whispered.

Belith found her hand and held it.

Shada was sure only one speck from the swarm had touched her. It was a tiny point of coolness on her neck. She was all right for the moment. But it would start soon, whatever it was, and she would endure it right here. With a steady voice, she prayed again, and Belith joined her.

43

—·—

SHADA

THE NEXT TIME SHADA opened her eyes, she gasped and looked around. Her heart raced against her ribcage. She was in the cot in her wagon, alone, and her sweat had soaked through her clothes. Dim light came through the window.

Before this moment, there had been only blackness and searing cold. The last thing she remembered was hiding with Belith under the blanket. Since then, she had been held prisoner away from the world.

Sitting up, she tried to gulp and winced. Her throat was stiff and dry. Her skin was grimy, and her face and ears itched. The spots where Belith's plant had stung her still ached a little. She stood slowly, her legs feeble and her knees ticklish under her weight. She walked to the door and opened it.

They were in a clearing in the jungle. The company's wagons stood in a circle with hers at the center, but she saw no one. The sky was twilight gray like the dusk or predawn. The wind moaned. A gust ripped the door handle from her hand.

This might be a dream. She stepped down and put her bare feet in the grass, leaving the door to swing and slap.

Nearby, the remains of a campfire shed strands of smoke into the wind.

Outside the circle of wagons rose a hulking stone ruin. Though shapeless, it had clearly once been taller, and it still held the walls and floors of many rooms. From it came the faint clangs of tools and shouts of labor.

Someone yelped in surprise behind her. Doctor Staubel stood wide-eyed with an armful of sheets and a canteen. "Caretaker. You've come back to us. I was coming to check on you."

Pleasantries were beyond her right now. "Where are we?"

He frowned. "A lot has happened. How long have you been awake?"

"A minute or two. What is this place?"

"That will take some telling. If you'll lie down again, I'll come back in a moment."

She shook her head. "I've been in there too long, thank you. How long have I been asleep?"

"It would be… four days. I can imagine your confusion. I'll tell you everything, but first, you must return to your wagon."

"Tell me this: is it morning or evening?"

"It's morning."

The young soldier's reverence for her position had collided with his voice of authority as a doctor. It was amusing, though she had enough sense not to laugh. The alarm she had felt upon waking was subsiding, and despite having slept for days, she was somehow exhausted. As curious as she was to know what was happening in those ruins, her bed was closer. "You win," she said, taking the canteen from him.

Nor came into the wagon a couple minutes later. Though he acted composed, his face flushed, and his breath was short. "I came as quickly as I could. The others will be here in a little while."

"One at a time will suit me," she said, smiling. She was learning to read him despite his empty eyes. "Will you tell me where we are? I couldn't get anything from the doctor."

He took a deep breath, gathering his resolve. "Of course." He glanced around for a place to sit then decided to stay where he was. "Staubel was coming back here, but

I told him to wait. I hope that's all right. He's got many patients to look after."

He smiled. "Where to begin? We've arrived at the next gateway, but we can't reach it yet. It's underground, beneath that ruin out there, and the only tunnel to reach it has partly collapsed. The men have been digging all day."

Shada's next thought shoved out everything else. "The Lady! Has she...?" She stopped, seeing the answer on Nor's face.

"There's been no sign of her," said the monk. "And no one knows what that means."

Shada resisted her creeping suspicion that the Lady really had left them forever. "How did you find the gateway without her help?"

"We followed Belith's wraiths. They came to help after all but only after the fight and only to show us the way. They led us here and disappeared."

"We won the battle."

"Yes, though it doesn't feel that way. When the swarms came, they were everywhere. They even came into the basement. We had to block the cracks around the door to keep them out."

"I'm glad you were safe. I don't regret going off without you."

"I do regret it," he said, and his face darkened. "I don't doubt you, Caretaker. You didn't need me there. But I am sorry I stayed in that room."

"Why? The enemy didn't find you, clearly."

"He did find us."

"I see," she said cautiously.

"Father Brin regrets not telling the bishop you were attacked."

"Oh." She had not thought about that in a while. "Is he all right?"

"He's fine. He's been angry lately." Nor licked his lips. "Pardon me, but I'd rather not say more right now."

"That's fine." She gladly dropped the subject. Whatever Nor's cause for upset, the wraiths must not have broken into the room, or he and Brin would probably be dead.

She felt stupid. Of course—the wraiths had tortured him. Then, instead of facing his tormentors in battle, he had allowed himself to be locked in a cell. Hiding would not come naturally to someone like him, even if it was wise.

Hearing his news had excited her, and her exhaustion had subsided. She wanted to get out of this cramped wagon, which felt too much like a cell right now.

She stood up. "Will you take me for a walk?"

A few minutes later, they stepped into the dig site. There, at the center of the ruins, the remains of a grand stairway led down into the bedrock. Partway down the stairs, the weathered rock overhead had long ago collapsed, blocking the passage with rubble.

The men dug in shifts, breaking the rocks and hauling them away. Among the soldiers were convicts from the prison, who must have traveled with the company. The work was back-breaking, and many of them limped along with minor injuries. Those not on duty lay strewn nearby, exhausted.

They all cheered when Shada arrived. She smiled and waved.

"They've been praying for you," said Nor.

Indeed, the men moved a little faster and swung their hammers harder.

Moments ago, Shada had greeted the men in Staubel's makeshift infirmary elsewhere in the ruins. Before the doctor chased her out, ordering her back to bed, she had glimpsed the range of injuries suffered in the battle and in the swamp.

Now, watching all the men hard at work while wearing bandages or limping, she said, "So many hurt. I'm amazed any of us are still here."

Nor nodded. "Emberly's plan worked in the end. When the swarms came, our people outside hid under collapsed tents and fabric and waited for daylight. The wraiths and swarms found some of them, and others suffocated when the swarms piled on them. Most of the dead on our side were convicts. Our soldiers had seen real battles before. Our company lost five, though more are hurt."

Shada gazed at the sky. "How can we continue like this? We've been gone from Ronia for a week, and we're already limping along."

"I don't know," Nor said. "The wraiths that came inside the barricade had it worse. Every swarm in the jungle attacked them. I hear the swarms looked like a rainbow, filling the air.

"More of those giant leaves landed near the prison during the fight. Several of those huge trees shed leaves to draw swarms to the battle. The whole jungle turned on us."

His brow furrowed. "Those wraiths went through hell. They died in all sorts of ways—melted, burned, shriveled into husks. Some, you couldn't tell what had happened. It was like the swarms fought over them."

He took a long breath. "Their faces are so different from ours. It's hard to tell and maybe foolish to hope, but a few of their expressions seemed peaceful."

"What's foolish about that?"

"That's not what I meant to say." He shook his head. "I meant... the Goddess accepts everyone. Even the Changed, like you and I—and the wraiths. They aren't *things*, though Ronia wishes they were. The ones who died... I hope some were open to Huire. The alternative is terrible."

"Are their souls your concern?"

"Of course." He looked surprised. "Nothing is more important."

"I suppose you're right. But I still think our own souls are our first priority." She lowered her voice. "Speaking of souls, how does the bishop feel about all this?"

Nor snickered, and she smiled. Her trust in him had been great to make that joke.

But his amusement was short-lived. His face fell as he answered. "The bishop has shut himself away. It's strange. He saved the battle, and the men think more highly of him since. But he's not seeing anyone much, even Father Brin. He knows better than anyone that we can't go on without the Lady."

"What now? Will we return to Ronia, do you think?" Shada wondered if the company could even survive a return trek through the jungle.

"The captain and the bishop haven't decided. They might know something I don't, but I doubt it. I don't think they're speaking to each other, really. Arumin is convinced that someone has betrayed their vows, hiding a sin or secret harmful to the crusade, and that's what has driven the Lady away. If she doesn't show herself today, he will hold a confessing ceremony tonight to root out everyone's sins. We'll all have to take part."

She sighed. "I hope I'm up to it. Whatever the swarm did to me, my sleep was not restful."

"I'm confused about that, Caretaker. Grateful you're alive, of course, but still confused."

"Why?"

"Well..." He smiled. "I was about to warn you that this might frighten you, but I'd forgotten who I'm talking to. Let me ask you something. What color was the swarm that attacked you?"

"White or red. White, I think."

"If I'm right, that one left a peaceful expression on everyone it killed. And it killed everything else it touched, Shada."

"Really? It barely touched me. Only one little speck. Maybe that's why I survived."

"One speck, and you were unconscious for four days. It was no ordinary sleep, either. You were cold, and your breathing was slow."

Shada tried to remember what her sleep had been like. She'd had none of the poisonous, wicked dreams she had expected from the vine's stings. The swarm's touch must have blotted them out.

She shivered. "Let's go sit outside."

Leading him back to her wagon, she sat in the grass by its door. She pulled him down gently by the hand. "You came to see me?"

He shook his head in disbelief. "Did you think I wouldn't?"

"It was nice when you called me Shada. I don't really know what a 'caretaker' is, and I don't feel like one."

"Did I say your name?" His mouth rose into a smile that quickly faded. "I shouldn't have done that."

"Why not?"

"It's not appropriate. For someone... in my position."

He spoke kindly, but his words left a hot little ball of embarrassment inside her. As it sat there and she realized its implication, the ball grew hotter.

He had finally sensed her interest in him, and it went beyond what his position would allow. She had blinded herself to the ridiculousness of it. Now, he was inviting her to see it in the gentlest way possible.

Taking interest in a holy man, of all men! Expecting that a man of integrity like him would surrender his principles for her. And in the midst of all this death, to pursue something so trivial. She had never thought of it that way, of course—and that was the problem.

Her thoughts rushed by in a blur, faster and faster. Maybe he had tried other, subtler means of fending her off, but she had missed them. It was her loneliness, it must be. Here she was, surrounded by strangers, on a faraway world.

His words had caught her off guard, and she had no answer. As the two of them sat there and the silence between them grew longer, the hot little ball turned red then orange and finally white. She rushed to catalogue all their interactions, what she had said and done, how much she had actually implied, and how he had answered.

It was too much. She pulled together a conversational tone of voice and changed the subject. "What will happen to the convicts? They can't keep living in the jungle."

"No." He sounded unconcerned with what had just occurred, and she did not know whether to admire or resent him for it. "The battle has renewed the wraiths' fear of offworlders, but that can only last so long. Most of the surviving convicts headed back to Ronia. They're mainly children and families. They hope for mercy from the Ronian authorities."

"You sound doubtful that they'll get it." To her relief, her words sounded normal.

"It's not that. I'm not used to associating Ronia with mercy. Actually, I think they've got a good chance. They mostly weren't active during the revolt. Some of them weren't born yet. To his credit, Emberly wrote a letter describing how they served Ronia in battle and saved the crusade. He even got the bishop to cosign it and seal it."

Shada felt lighter on hearing this. "The public will be on their side, I'm sure."

Nor nodded. "Not all the convicts wanted to go back. The ones you saw working in there are some of the more notorious. They don't have much hope of mercy, so they'll travel with us until they find a new home."

"Did..." Shada paused as a pit formed in her stomach. "Belith. Did she...?"

"Belith died in the keep, Caretaker." Nor delivered the news without hesitation, though a shadow passed over his face. "We found her next to you. Her people burned her body. They do that with their dead, so the wraiths can't get them."

Shada swallowed. She wished she was in the wagon, where the light was dim. "I shouldn't be surprised," she managed to say. "She was hurt so badly. Still, though... she didn't seem capable of dying."

"I can tell you, she looked restful. Satisfied."

He leaned toward Shada and took her hand. It was an awkward set of motions, but it showed a willingness to forgive. His calloused hand was warm, and she was glad.

"Now that you're up and about, you're going to have other visitors."

"Yes. I'd better go inside. Please, come see me again."

That got her another fleeting smile. "Yes, Caretaker."

His boots brushed the grass as he walked away.

The world spun as she stood up, from conflicting emotions and from lying down for four days. As the day began and the night winds died away, the sounds of work rang more clearly from the ruin. The men must have started early. She stepped up into the wagon.

She jumped when the Lady spoke. "Shada."

The Lady was nowhere to be seen, but her voice was clear. Shada asked, "Where have you been?"

"There were things I needed to do, and you needed to reconsider your attitude toward me. Have you?"

"Yes. I've reconsidered a lot."

"I hope so, Shada. If things had continued as they were, our relationship would have changed."

The idea terrified her. Being with the Lady was uncomfortable, but now Shada knew how much worse her absence was.

She said, "I'll show you you're wrong about me."

"You will have a chance soon, child. This is a very important day."

44

—·—

EMBERLY

EMBERLY STAYED IN HIS wagon that day. The only people he saw, Roark and the sergeants, came and went, sensing they were not welcome. His back still hurt from his fall off the prison wall. His bandaged arm stung where he had wounded himself.

Something grew inside him. It was in his head, in his chest, and in the room all at once. He summoned it against his will.

He longed to speak casually to someone, but the thought of asking for that embarrassed him. So he turned inward and made himself busy. Unwilling to leave the wagon but scared to be alone, he would even have settled for Arumin's sparring and scheming.

He had spoken little to the bishop in the past few days, ever since Nor told him one of his men had attacked Shada in the waytower. Emberly had been trying to account for a missing soldier whom no one had seen since that night, and the monk had related the story Shada had told him and the other holy men.

Emberly had gone to Arumin in a rage, demanding to know why the bishop had not already reported this to him. Arumin had raged right back, demanding to know why the captain had taken his men on a mission from the waytower while the bishop lay upstairs, asleep and unaware. Emberly had replied that he needed no one's permission to command his soldiers, and the argument had only intensified from there.

It seemed Shada's attacker, who had tried to steal the Lady, had been working for someone. None of Emberly's soldiers had been close to the man, most regarding him as strange and hard to get along with. They could only speculate why he had done what he did.

His employer's identity was a separate issue, and Emberly could think of no comforting possibilities. The perpetrators of separate attacks on the temple and on the Unheard in Ronia were still unknown, and his imagination connected these events with the attack on Shada. Again, all speculation.

Since he knew nothing more, he had agreed with Arumin to limit knowledge of the attack to those who already knew. Emberly would only tell his lieutenants and sergeants. No use draining his men's tenuous morale with paranoia about secret agents among them.

As usual, thinking of Arumin soon led Emberly to think of Brin. But that thought had become much easier to endure. He had seen the man's face enough recently that he no longer attached it to the pale, frightened boy's face in his memory. Brin the child and Brin the man were different people now, and waves of emotion no longer greeted the sight of the man's face. Father Brin seemed to look at Emberly more easily too. For these things, the captain gave thanks.

He gave thanks again when Merin and Hulgar stepped into his wagon, though the business ahead was grim.

The room was a tight fit for the three of them. This was mostly because of Hulgar, who stooped. Merin fit himself into the remaining space like a puzzle piece.

Emberly took his time before speaking. "Thank you for coming. Now that we have a moment to breathe, I want to talk to you two. I've heard you are heroes." He put a hint of grave sarcasm on the last word.

Hulgar did not react, but Merin's face brightened. He said, "Thank you, sir. The men have been kind to us, sir."

"Don't thank me yet." He looked at Hulgar. "How are you feeling, Private? You've been acting strange."

Hulgar seemed more alert than he had since they left Ronia. "Better, Captain. Had some nightmares is all."

Emberly nodded, hiding his surprise at the baldness of the admission. A Ronian soldier must care little for others' opinions if he admitted to being bothered by bad dreams. "I'll be glad to leave this planet. And you, Merin?"

The private looked uneasy. "I feel better, sir. Since the battle, the men have treated me differently, like I belong."

Another uncomfortable admission: loneliness.

Merin stared at the floor in a boyish manner that embarrassed Emberly. "I'll be honest, Captain. I've dreaded this moment."

"I'll be honest in return," said Emberly. "You should feel more than dread. You should feel shame. You betrayed all of your comrades."

Merin's mouth opened.

The captain continued. "Did you think acts of courage had erased that? When you opened the doors of the waytower, you risked everyone's lives—the holy men, the caretaker, even the Lady herself. You should indeed dread facing me, a man you betrayed."

"Sir, I—"

"Do you know who you should dread more? Dread your fellow soldiers, who know they can't trust you. Dread Lieutenant Roark, who won't forget that you attacked him. Dread the Lady and the Goddess herself, who sees all and judges all. She'll forgive the sins of everyone on this crusade, but only if you keep your oath."

"Captain, we had no choice. The doctor says—"

"No choice? Did the swarm move your feet and force you to flee the waytower? Did it grab your arm and force you to open the tower's doors?"

"No, but—"

"And you, Hulgar. Did the swarm press your hands into fists and force you to strike an officer?"

Hulgar stood silent and unmoved.

"Unless the answer to all of these is yes, you chose to turn your back on the cause to which you're sworn."

He glanced between the two men. "I spoke to Doctor Staubel. His excuses for you make me doubt his judgment. So you were tempted. You were afraid. I have no tolerance for cowards or the weak.

"So your actions in the battle impressed the men. Congratulations; you did your duty. You fought the enemy. When their excitement dies, do you think they won't remember your betrayal? Trust isn't rebuilt easily.

"If you want a place among them, here's what I would do. Starting now, devote your whole selves to being the best, the bravest, the holiest men this army has ever seen.

Put the Lady herself to shame, and perhaps you will earn your way back."

His anger had taken hold as he spoke, and now his breath was short. He stopped and waited.

"Yes, sir," Merin replied in a small voice. He shrank, and his eyes fixed on the floor.

"Hulgar?" Emberly said.

The private rumbled, "If Lieutenant Roark has words for me, he can tell me himself."

"He will," Emberly snapped. "He has my permission to deal with you as he sees fit. I would take one of him over twenty of either of you."

He leaned forward. "The next time some mystic force compels you to commit treason, if you can't bring yourself to resist it, your standing order is to kill yourself. Do it quickly, before you put anyone else in danger. Now, get out of my sight."

Merin left in a daze. Hulgar, unmovable as a boulder, waited a second longer. But soon, he lumbered out.

Emberly watched the door shut. He faced the small desk in the wagon's rear and stared at its surface. He cupped his hands to make a tunnel around his eyes, blinding himself to everything but the grain of the wood. He could not avoid the thing inside him, but he would try.

He heard footsteps near the closed door. They sounded as real and solid as any other noise. This time, he was determined not to turn around.

A smell reached his nostrils. It was sweet and nauseating, a rush of air from another place.

The footsteps halted behind him. "Look at me," said Rayan.

"I won't. I know now that you aren't there."

"You must look, at least."

The captain clenched his jaw. "You won't be there. If I keep looking, you will never stay away."

"Things are different now, Cyril. I'm here, whether you believe it or not. I have nowhere else to be."

Emberly gave in. He turned slowly, his hands over his face, peering at the floor.

He saw an upright pair of boots and the bottoms of trousers. Both crawled with insects. The captain exhaled and gulped.

A ghostly white hand reached into his field of vision. Its fingers touched his chin, and the smell of death filled his nostrils. The fingers tugged gently but insistently, turning his face upward. He resisted.

"Come on," said Rayan. "You've come this far."

Emberly let his face tilt up toward his brother. Part of Rayan's jaw was missing, taken off by the captain's bullet.

Rayan's words came from his opened throat as clearly as if they'd come from an intact mouth.

"My Goddess," Emberly whispered.

"What did you think I would look like?" asked the pale visage.

"I..."

"Yes?"

Emberly's throat was dry, and his voice was desolate. "I gave them your body. They burned you."

The face glared. "No. Not me. After you told them about my bargain with the wraiths, they left me out, hoping the wraiths would eat me."

"Forgive me."

"Forgiveness isn't mine to give anymore, brother, for anything you've done. You missed your chance. I could only forgive you while I was here."

The captain crossed his arms and shivered. "Then... what do I do?"

Rayan tilted his head in resignation. "You can make it all better, I think. But it's not my place to say when. You'll know when the time comes. Meanwhile, you must start working toward it right now."

Emberly nodded eagerly. "Yes."

"Good. Now... Should I leave?"

"No. I'm alone here. Stay."

The thing that had been his brother pulled its remaining face into a half smile.

Emberly shut his eyes. He had to steel himself to look again.

The thing said, "Very well. You need me, Cyril. You always will." It took the captain by the shoulders. "I should tell you something. I love you, brother."

It opened its arms to Emberly, who slowly accepted its embrace with a tearful smile. Its stiff arms squeezed him, and he felt heat deep inside it. Blood flowed anew from its face, warming Emberly's shoulders, running down his chest and back.

"Thank the Goddess you're real," he said. "I thought I was crazy."

"I'm real, and I won't leave again. I promise. You're going to need me more than ever. You'll need the wisdom of a killer."

45

THE CRUSADERS

THE COMPANY GATHERED INSIDE the circle of wagons as night fell and the wind started singing in the trees. A few men moved Shada's wagon aside, leaving a roundish open space with a new, billowing fire protected from the gale.

The soldiers sat with their arms around their knees like children. None lay about or joked. The convicts had retreated out of sight, as the confessing was only for soldiers, but the quiet beyond the wagon circle told Arumin they were listening.

Everyone hushed as the bishop stepped in front of them. He stood with his back to the fire, which would give his silhouette a flaming aura. Brother Nor took a customary position behind him and to one side.

The bishop had privately ordered Brin to stand by him also, but the young priest slouched against a nearby wagon wheel instead. Their few conversations lately had been cold and formal.

Arumin ached. His chest stung where the swamp plant had slashed him. The rest of him ached from his leap off the wall and his struggles with the wraiths and the convicts. His skin, like everyone's, was gritty and sweaty from several days without washing.

But he betrayed none of this as he cleared his throat to address the assembly.

"The Lady has not returned." He glared about. "Someone among us has caused this."

Nervous energy buzzed among the company.

"Had we kept our vows," said Arumin, "the Goddess would have forgiven our sins. But we may have lost that chance. The Goddess does not forgive the outright rejection of her will.

"One of us, maybe more than one, has driven her away. They may have done this deliberately, in an act of premeditated evil. Maybe even a pact with demons. We shall find out tonight.

"For tonight, we lay all our sins bare."

He flicked his eyes to Captain Emberly, who stood in the back. The captain's arms were crossed, and his face was grim. Maybe he suspected the bishop was planning something.

Near Emberly stood the caretaker, quiet and unobtrusive as ever. The bishop had already examined her closely on the night before the battle. He had reviewed her conversations with the Lady again and again, seeking the one misstep or bit of disrespect that had driven the Lady to disappear for so long. It must have occurred, but nothing the woman reported sounded sufficient.

Arumin doubted she was lying, but something did not add up. He pushed down a darker concern: his private confusion at the Lady's choice of that naïve young woman. Why, with so many more capable, worthy choices available?

Nothing good could result from such pondering. He ignored the questions, though they continued to gnaw at him. It was time to begin.

"One by one," the bishop said, "each of us will kneel before the fire. There, Huire will question us. She will speak through me. When my turn comes, she will speak through Father Brin. Speak only when chosen to speak, and only in direct response to questions. Any of us who lies or omits the truth gives his soul irrevocably to the dark. Nothing could be worse. The public shame of admitting wrongdoing pales in comparison."

He spread his arms, robe rising like wings. "In speaking truth lies the hope for salvation of everyone touched by this fire's light."

A dreadful silence had fallen. The soldiers' faces glowed in the firelight, cold and afraid.

Arumin gazed over them all. "Who will speak first?"

The silence held sway for a few long moments. The bishop had opened his mouth to threaten the assembly when a brave soul finally volunteered, coming to the front and kneeling before the bishop. He was a private whose name Arumin did not know. As the bishop questioned him, guided by Huire, he quickly determined the man's sins to be bland and anonymous.

When he dismissed the man, others volunteered to follow. Arumin spoke to these a little less harshly. His criticisms seemed to cut them more deeply than before. His actions in the battle had raised him further in their esteem than he had realized. Before, they had feared his authority and position but held mostly contempt for the man behind it. Now, they showed him respect as well as fear.

He waited through several insignificant confessions before stroking his beard with his left hand.

Robir was ready. His hand shot up. "I have something to confess, Your Holiness. Something terrible."

No one else had announced themselves this way. Soldiers looked at Robir and at each other, but no one talked. Arumin risked another glance at Emberly. The captain's face was stony. His hand cradled his chin.

A few men had raised their hands before Robir spoke up, but they lowered them as if deferring to the man's urgency. Robir stepped in front of Arumin and kneeled.

"Your Holiness, I have sinned." He did not wait for questioning. "I have a secret I should not have kept."

Arumin assumed a tone of angry surprise. "By tolerating an unjust secret, you have lied to all who should know it. What is this secret?"

"It's a military secret."

Emberly's hand fell from his chin.

Arumin frowned. "The military has good reason to keep secrets. Why does this one warrant telling?"

Robir set his jaw. "The conflict is long past. No one can be hurt by this confession... except those guilty of throwing away the lives of Ronian boys in a secret war."

Regardless of the wind, his words echoed. Robir was a quiet man, not known to speak frivolously. The men leaned forward. No one had expected a confession of such magnitude, and they wanted to know more.

Nodding once, Arumin feigned tentative approval. "Go on."

"I believe Ronia secretly invaded Caidfell after the prison revolt."

The men's silence held but only barely. Outside the circle of wagons, convicts murmured. Emberly had become a statue.

Arumin had warned Robir that he must appear skeptical. Letting his mouth fall open, he said, "That's an incredible claim. What evidence do you have? Speak clearly so all can hear you."

"I can't do that without revealing the sins of another present. Someone who knew all this, maybe even led the secret war."

Everyone wanted more. Had Arumin forbidden Robir to continue, the others would have dragged it out of him.

Now, to lay out the evidence, bit by damning bit. Excitement fluttered in the bishop's chest. "Who?"

"Me!" called Captain Emberly.

—◆—

After admitting his guilt, Emberly listened as the bishop's edict of silence gained a thousand tiny cracks. Gasps and curses filled the air. The convicts, who already knew of the war, waited.

The bishop's lips froze on the word *who*. He trembled with outrage.

Confessing ceremonies were rare, but every Ronian knew how they worked. Interruptions were not tolerated, not even if one participant knew another was lying. Participants must wait until the holy man serving as confessor called on them to speak.

Confessors treated speaking out of turn as a virtual admission of some hidden guilt. Emberly shuddered inwardly.

He should have expected this plot of Arumin's. He should have dealt with Robir sooner. Left alone, the man's resentment had festered, and he had a willing partner in the bishop, a predator who loved the smell of blood. Now, Emberly would pay the price for his failure—a fight for his career and maybe his life.

An image came to him: the man from his dreams, the stranger made of little facets of glass. The man was here to watch Emberly crumble. The captain began to shake. As he struggled to shut out the man's gaze, he pleaded silently, *Who are you? Tell me what you want!*

He saw Rayan. His brother stood behind the fire, wounds glistening, visible only to the captain. The ruins of his face curled into a smile.

Emberly breathed in deeply and paused. He waited until silence resumed around the fire. They waited for him to speak. All centered around him.

The bishop had stayed calm. Whatever his goal, he would not achieve it by exploding. "You?"

"That's right." Emberly raised his voice, addressing everyone. "Shortly after the prison fell, the Ronian army sent a force to Caidfell to retake the prison. It failed."

He let the words sink in. He half expected the bishop to cut in, to try to maintain control, but the old man waited and watched. After all, Emberly might be hanging himself. "The revolt had dashed the army's pride. Public sentiment was against further action on this planet, but the army believed a quick strike could overwhelm the convicts and win back the planet.

"Someone, somewhere, thought the victory would boost Ronia's morale even more if it came as a surprise. So they kept it secret.

"The jungle obliterated the invading force. Our soldiers never even fought the convicts. The planet and all the life on it rejected the assault. The army hid the affair, as you've probably guessed. A struggling empire could hardly stand to hear it."

He raised a pair of fingers. "I participated in two ways: first, the army consulted me on the invasion because of my experience. I advised against it, for all the reasons we've encountered the past several days. Second, I kept the secret. It was my duty."

He paused again, listening. Silence greeted him, but the mood underlying it felt surprisingly favorable. Maybe they understood if not the army's decisions, at least his position within them. Maybe they appreciated his honesty, late though it was.

"Another thing," he said. "After we lost Private Keesin in the swamp, the wraiths took him and killed him. They devoured him in one of their heathen ceremonies. I refused to rescue him, and I would refuse again. That's because it might have cost the lives of everyone with me."

He swallowed a lump in his throat. "If I could trade places with Keesin, I would. Since I can't, I'll pray in his memory and in the memories of everyone we've lost in this damned place. Please do the same. And pray that, if we must set foot on Caidfell again, we will do it only briefly, while traveling home."

He let the silence stretch long enough for any rabble-rousers to stir up trouble, but none did. He spoke again as Arumin opened his mouth. "Anyone with more questions for me on these subjects may come to my wagon. Anyone, officer or enlisted man. I admit, I'm relieved to talk about this at last."

Rayan watched. Emberly took a deep, satisfied breath. His voice was strong, his memories clear. No stranger, no man made of glass could use them to hurt him. Not as long as he had family.

He stared at Private Robir. The man had been kneeling the whole time, facing the bishop. Emberly could not see his face, but Robir's disbelief at the conversation's direction radiated from every line of his body.

"As you can see," said Emberly, speaking to the back of Robir's head, "most military secrets are nothing enjoyable. Most aren't even interesting. Many are sad and burdensome—a fallible organization full of fallible people hiding their failures. But that doesn't mean they have no purpose." His voice hardened. "Revealing them publicly is stupid and reckless and shows an absolute—"

Robir shot to his feet and marched toward the captain. "Why, you..."

"Private! Halt!" cried Arumin.

Robir obeyed. He faced Emberly across the assembly, shifting his weight from foot to foot, seething with rage.

"We have heard Captain Emberly's confession," said the bishop. "If he has any more, he will deliver them kneeling before me, like anyone else."

Arumin's eyes blazed, but his mind must still be clear. Emberly's sin was grander than most, but the company had failed to show the outrage the bishop had obviously expected. Arumin would not take dramatic action without support, whatever his reasons for doing so.

"No," said Robir to the captain. "You won't get away that easily. You got two good men killed outside that tower."

Emberly met his gaze. "Borna and Elisar died doing their duty."

"They died for you. So did Keesin. They all died so you could meet in secret with your worthless brother."

Under the wind, the captain heard gasps.

Though Robir spoke to the captain, he shouted so all could hear. "You didn't meet him by chance. You knew he was there."

"Nonsense. I couldn't have known that."

"You knew because you've been talking with him all along."

Those words carried over the wagon tops and struck Emberly in the gut. "What?"

"I don't know how, but you were in league with him. You had business together."

"Mind your tongue. What kind of—"

"Did he get in your way?" Robir's eyes gleamed. "Is that why you killed him?"

The silence began crumbling. Mutters arose. Most were surprised; some were hostile to Robir; some were supportive of him. Arumin might have stopped them as he had halted Robir moments ago. But this exchange had caught his interest, and he watched, his eyes barely concealing his excitement.

Emberly waited to speak, wrestling with his fury. Above all, he must control his temper. "How dare you?"

Robir looked around at the others. "He's got it all worked out, doesn't he? Hides behind his duty while chasing his own ends. Again and again. I'm not the only one who remembers Gallobraith."

Indeed, he was not. The muttering sank to a hush as the company was washed in memories of horror.

Emberly ground his teeth and considered his options. He recalled the pistol at his waist and considered the consequences of using it on his own man.

Everyone had accepted his killing Rayan because most had wanted to do it themselves. Harming one of their brotherhood, let alone killing him, was utterly different. Especially here, far from any authority. Without Arumin's support, Emberly was on his own.

He could order Robir flogged or beaten. His men would probably obey. Or he could stand and defend himself from these accusations. So far, he had done the latter, and to his wonder and terror, he was losing ground.

"You remember it..." he said slowly, "because you are alive."

"How many aren't?" Robir asked. "And all for your secrets. You must've been scheming with your animal of a brother since the prison fell, at least."

His eyes swept his assembled comrades. "So many killed then, too, in the revolt. How is it that only the captain survived?"

Emberly shut his eyes. His self-control hung by a thread. His voice wavered as he gave the same reason the convicts had given Ronia for sparing him. "Bravery."

Robir's voice softened. "And those who died, Emberly? What would you call them, if not brave?"

"Stop." Emberly heard his teeth grate. His hand twitched by his pistol. "Address me as your captain, or I'll make you regret it."

"That's enough!" called Arumin, startling everyone. "Captain, have you forgotten you are confessing your sins?"

"I have not, Your Holiness." There was no escape. He would have to tell the truth or face damnation.

"You must confess. Now."

"No. This has to end," said Nor, stepping forward.

The bishop whirled. His eyes were wide. "That is not your decision, *monk*."

Nor did not begrudge him his anger. To interrupt a confessing was not done. For a fellow holy man to interrupt must be beyond even Arumin's long experience.

A few nights ago, in front of another fire, Nor had been choked by a creeping, stalking silence. It still roamed out there beyond the firelight. But as Robir's attack on Emberly proceeded, it had withdrawn its hands from its throat. Maybe it knew moments of mercy. Maybe it recognized necessity.

"The decision is made for both of us," Nor said. "This ceremony has become a crusade in itself."

The bishop was lost for words. Nor pressed ahead. "The Lady is gone. Getting her back is all that matters. We won't do that by dragging every last sin out of everyone here."

Arumin's voice was cold and deadly. "How else can we bring her back, Brother Nor?"

Nor looked past him at everyone assembled there. "We pray!" he cried. "And we go on. Once we open the tunnel to the gateway, we know which way to go. Forward.

Whatever's on the other side, we've got to trust her and trust Huire—trust that when we really don't know the way, they'll tell us. They already got the wraiths to lead us here."

In the instant of quiet between sentences, Nor sensed something. Over them all, not in the sky but maybe behind it, someone watched them. A face he remembered, maybe from dreams. A face of glass or crystal.

Suddenly, he feared the quiet that would descend when he stopped speaking. "We must have more faith," he said.

Luckily, Robir answered at once. "Let us go on, then. But only after justice is done."

Nor shook his head. "We'll find no justice here."

"We can make it. There is a rot among us. To serve our Goddess, we've got to dig it out."

"Have you examined yourself, Private?" Nor faced him. "Think about what the wraiths did to you."

Robir's face darkened. "I've thought about it already. More than anyone here knows. It's one more crime of Emberly's."

"Do you hear the hate in your voice?"

"You were *there*!" Robir screamed. "We went through it together, monk. Now you act like it was nothing, like I'm some weakling."

"I said nothing like that."

"You didn't have to. You wouldn't even hear my confession!"

The soldiers rumbled like a dark storm cloud. The bishop stared. Holy men could deny a sinner forgiveness, but to deny him the ability to confess at all was forbidden. Nor was stunned. He had not realized until now how his refusal would look to an observer.

"You had committed no sin," he said. "You wanted to conspire and spread rumors, which are sins in themselves."

"Rumors." Robir spat the word. "Wise with words, aren't you, you housebroken savage?"

Anger overcame Nor in a flash. "Maybe we can't trust your word. Maybe those wraiths cracked your mind."

The quiet of the night shattered. Several soldiers rose, shouting at him, outraged at his implication that their comrade's mind was broken, that his story of torture should be doubted. First among them was Sergeant Orund, red-faced and anxious to defend a good Ronian boy from this enemy of the empire.

Face-to-face with Orund, with others crowded behind, Nor cast out a prayer. Huire must know that if he died now, he would never solve Abbott Cadmon's quandary—not that he had made any progress. He wondered where his abbot was now. Probably scribbling at his desk, caring too much for the world.

This must be exactly how Cadmon had feared Nor's life would end.

———◆◇◆———

Brin stepped between Nor and the outraged soldiers before he realized what he was doing. He screamed at them to stop, saying no single word but rather a jumble of words mashed together.

The volume of his cry brought Sergeant Orund up short. Into the lull in angry voices, Brin shouted, "Huire is watching you."

Orund stopped and stared daggers at him. Brin looked past him, scared that meeting his eyes would make him angrier. Shada stood out in the crowd. She had started toward the confrontation, but Brin, to his sorrow, had gotten there first.

"I'm saving your life," he told Orund, relieved at the strength in his voice. "Twice now, you've nearly raised your hand to a holy man. Huire may forgive your sins, but that won't stop her from striking you dead where you stand."

Orund glared. The others, packed behind him, advanced no further.

"Father Brin," the bishop rumbled, his face pale. "For you, of all people, to interrupt this ceremony..."

Brin spoke over him. "Now, listen. We all lie. We all have secrets. We all do things we're ashamed of. We have before and will again."

He thought of himself kneeling on a stone floor, worshipping a monster. Praying for its mercy. He did not love the wraiths or feel sympathy for them. But they were so powerful.

"I know you do shameful things, priest," said Orund. "Or do you think we don't notice?"

A chill like cold rain passed over Brin's face and chest.

Orund saw the effect of his words and smiled. "Don't you know? Everyone sees it."

"Silence," said Arumin. In their many years together, Brin had never heard his voice so icy.

Orund stepped back as if he had touched a hot stove. In his rage, he must have forgotten that the secret he threatened to reveal did not only involve Brin.

The bishop's tone, combined with his authority and new esteem in the company, were an intimidating combination. "Your Holiness," said Orund. He seemed pained to speak those words immediately after his crass insinuation.

"Get away from Father Brin," said Arumin. "Whatever you think you know about him, forget it if you hope for Huire to forget your actions this night. Say no more about it, ever. Idle speculation is no excuse for spreading lies."

"Yes, Your Holiness."

"Sit down."

The sergeant nodded. Confused and deflated, he stalked to the back of the assembly. The men behind him, bereft of their leader, glanced at each other and meandered uncomfortably out of the way. No one spoke Brin and Arumin's secret.

It was too late, of course. Anyone who somehow did not know what Orund had referred to would learn soon. The knowledge hung thick in the air.

Humiliating as the moment was, Brin was almost relieved. He had briefly wondered if the sergeant knew about the vial he carried. Of all the reasons Brin had to feel guilty—most recently, worshipping the perverse child of an alien god—the vial and the mission behind it were the last he wanted Arumin to learn about.

When Belith had returned the vial to him in the cell, imagining she was redeeming herself for tormenting him, he had felt both enormously relieved and as if a millstone had been tossed onto his back. His terrifying secret had returned. The Lady had killed his potential assassin, but the possibility of others in the company made Brin too scared to toss away the vial willingly.

Then there was Arumin. He told himself he no longer cared if any secret of his hurt the bishop, but he certainly feared the bishop's wrath, the punishments he could inflict.

Maybe that was why Brin had saved Nor from that small army a moment ago. He was grateful to the monk for keeping some of his secrets. Such vulnerability was painful, so he resolved to ignore the feeling as best he could from now on.

The bishop glared at Nor then at Brin. The young priest looked away. He would never forgive Arumin's abandonment. He could not forgive it, whatever Huire might think. She would have to understand how weak he was. As long as Arumin pushed Brin for forgiveness, Brin would keep punishing him.

As Brin stood before the assembly, heart still pounding, the bishop cleared his throat. "Huire's will must be done, no matter the opinions of her children. To leave this ceremony unfinished would disregard the ritual she handed down to us."

"Bishop..." Captain Emberly began.

Arumin's head snapped round to him. "And it would disregard the seriousness of sin."

Brin saw the bishop's eyes meet the captain's. Emberly froze, unable to escape. Arumin's voice hummed with righteous energy.

"Cyril Emberly, I summon you."

"I have spoken to the Lady," announced Shada.

The words took a moment to sink in.

Everyone turned to her. Arumin asked in a voice hushed with urgency, "When?"

"Just now," she replied.

It was true. When the bishop summoned the captain to confess, the Lady's voice had come to Shada's ears, hidden from everyone else: "It is time."

Arumin was caught between deference and pride. "Caretaker, this ceremony is critical. We cannot spare ourselves the—"

"Please sit down, Bishop."

Arumin stood in shocked silence. He weighed his options. With everyone waiting, he obeyed.

"No one will be spared," said Shada. "Our lives will catch up to us even if Huire forgives our sins. But the reason for this confessing has passed. The Lady has returned. To me."

Whispers spread into the darkness beyond the fire.

Arumin was visibly bursting with questions. But he only said softly, "Praise Huire."

The Lady had said nothing else to Shada yet. Perhaps she sensed her caretaker did not need help. Shada went on, "The Goddess's forgiveness depends on the Lady's. The Lady will forgive us on one condition."

"What condition?" Arumin asked.

"A show of faith," she told them all. "I will go through the gateway, alone. On the other side, she will appear to me. I will bring her back."

The thought had filled her with dread ever since the Lady had revealed it to her. Whatever awaited through the gateway, the Lady still would not intervene to save her from danger. If the next planet was anything like this one, a single wrong step might get her killed.

The bishop managed to appear stiff and reverent, however much he was reeling on the inside. The captain's face was solemn.

Arumin spoke first. "That isn't possible yet. We haven't finished digging."

"The men have created a small opening in the rocks, haven't they?"

Let Arumin wonder how she knew that—if the Lady had seen it or if soldiers were speaking to her.

"Yes," he said, "but it's not wide enough to pass through."

"I'll manage. It's only me."

Even at his most confused, the bishop's eyes could still pierce. "We will do as the Lady wishes."

"Hold on," said Emberly. "We don't know what's through the gateway. Surely the Lady doesn't want you to face danger alone."

"There will be no danger," Shada replied. "She told me so." She hoped her voice conveyed more confidence than she felt.

He frowned. "Have you actually seen her or only heard her voice?"

"Captain!" the bishop cried.

"I haven't seen her," Shada admitted. "But I have no doubt she spoke to me."

"You've been through a terrible ordeal," said the captain. "How can you be sure you really heard her?"

"Emberly, you have no right to ask that," said Arumin.

"Why not?" Emberly snapped. "Your Holiness, this isn't right. This woman was at death's door for four days. What more can we ask of her?"

The bishop raised his voice in turn. "It's not a request, and it doesn't come from us."

"Yes, that sounds right," replied Emberly derisively. "The Lady has suddenly returned—only not completely. She must test us yet again before she'll *truly* return."

Arumin whirled on the captain. "What are you implying, Emberly? Perhaps you do have something more to confess."

The captain's eyes darted around, then he sighed. "Caretaker, I'll ask again. How can you be sure the Lady spoke to you?"

"Do you doubt my word?" Shada asked. She was grateful for the captain's protectiveness. She had thought he cared little about her except as another person he was charged to protect. But his doubts about her mental state touched deep fears inside her, fears of people thinking she was insane and, worse yet, of their being right.

Emberly pressed his lips together. "Not your word. I doubt your health. You often speak privately to the Lady, and I've believed what you tell me. But you've just come back from the edge of death—and you haven't even *seen* her. You can't be surprised that I doubt you."

His hands tightened into fists. "Especially when you're planning to crawl alone into the bowels of the planet and hurl yourself into another world!"

His voice reached a furious pitch. "This cannot go on! I forbid it! Robir is right—too many have died."

Catching his breath, he composed himself. "Your Holiness, continue with the confessing. We'll have to put our hope in honesty."

Shada opened her mouth to protest more strongly, but Nor beat her to it.

"Captain, wait," he said. "We have to trust her. That's all there is to it."

The monk looked around. "We've all seen the Lady act through Shada. You remember what happened in the swamp." He met Shada's eyes, and she suppressed a smile. "These are signs, Captain."

Stepping among the crowd, he approached Emberly. "We can fear for her, but we have no right to stop her. It's her job to know if what she sees and hears is real. Our job is to watch and pray she survives."

Emberly looked at Shada, and his chest rose and fell.

"I'll be back soon," she said.

46

SHADA

NO ONE SAW ANY reason to wait. Underground would be no brighter in daylight.

The opening in the rocks was smaller than Shada had envisioned when the Lady described it. She left her dignity behind as she wriggled through like a worm. The men could not pass her a torch until she was inside, so her entry was like crawling into the womb of night.

Inside, the air was still, and every scrap of noise resounded from every surface. As a soldier had warned, she found herself on a treacherous slope. Under her feet were rocks of all sizes, some of which moved or tumbled. Down the slope, regular folds of shadow showed where the staircase emerged from the rubble.

The descent needed all her attention, so she turned to say her goodbyes. To her relief, Nor had pushed his way to the front. His face filled the opening.

"I won't be long, I hope," she said.

He smiled. "Go on. We'll be watching for you."

It seemed he had forgiven their misunderstanding, though Shada doubted she would ever forgive herself. What lay ahead of her dwarfed all else in importance.

Clambering down toward the stairs, she slipped and fell a few times, saving herself by fingerholds from a bone-breaking tumble. Fine, slippery dust covered the rocks, reminding her of the gritty dirt on her skin. She wondered if Nor was still watching.

The stairs proved crude and uneven. They were also small, built for legs and feet smaller than hers. This made walking oddly laborious.

As she descended, noises came from the murk overhead. Things chirped. Once in a while, something larger shifted cautiously. This cave could have hidden openings.

The stairway ended in a stone wall of large, ungainly stone blocks with a doorway so low she had to duck through it. To either side, handholds led up to a small platform above the doorway, with slot-shaped windows cut into the wall.

Following the Lady's instructions, she chose the straightest path: through the doorway. On the other side, the air changed as the space around her grew. The walls and ceiling were too far away for torchlight to reach. "Lady, are you here?" she asked, her voice alarmingly loud.

No answer. Fighting panic, she clung to one thought: the only thing worse than taking one more step forward would be going back and telling the others she had been too scared to go on.

She took a step then another and another. A second wall emerged from the gloom, this one with no visible openings.

She followed it to the left. Soon, she realized it was curving away from her.

It kept curving, and she followed. Her terror matured into horror. If the wall made a full circle, she would have no idea when she had passed her starting point or what to do next.

A faint glow appeared. Her old eyes in the world above would never have seen it. But it grew.

It grew until she reached its source, a doorway in the wall twice as wide as the last one, with more handholds and a platform. Through it, the glow was bright enough that she barely needed her torch. Close in front of her stood another wall, parallel to the last one, with a doorway off to her left.

Through that doorway was another parallel wall with another doorway. This pattern repeated several times.

The illumination was bright as day. Passing the last barrier, she staggered back with a cry, shielding her eyes from the light.

When her eyes adjusted, she saw a gateway as tall and broad as a Ronian temple. On the other side was perhaps the brightest day creation had ever known.

Sun-bleached land met a blue sky in a flat line, like a floor meeting a wall. The breath of this unknown world touched her as the gateway sighed warm air.

Putting her torch aside, she stepped over the threshold. Baked sand crackled under her feet, and she shivered in the heat of a new sun.

The flat horizon stretched all around, appearing to fall away in every direction. Coming from the close confines of the cave, it was dizzying, as if she might fall in any direction and roll forever down a mountain with no bottom.

She sank closer to the hard, dry ground. From this safer stance, she noticed breaks in the shining horizon. Objects rose here and there, columns of enormously varied dimensions with round or pointed tops. Their colors also varied greatly. Some were dark like little pits of night.

She focused on one of the closest. It was wide and gray, and a swath of ground around its base was dark. The dark patch shone in the sun, stretching and receding.

The object was a gateway, as were all the rest. The darkness at its base was water, surging in waves from the world on the other side.

"Hello!" Shada called. Her voice disappeared in all that space. "Lady, are you here?"

The breeze was the only answer. "Of course you're not," she said.

Some of the gateways appeared close enough to reach on foot before the sun cooked her. She wondered what waited through that watery one. A lake to sit and relax by? A raging sea to drown in?

She walked away from her gateway and into open country, far enough that her gateway shrank almost to the size of the others. Turning slowly, she realized she could leave the crusade behind and never come back. A universe of worlds to choose from.

Some might kill her. Some might be paradises. Somewhere out there, one might offer her a home. Whatever happened, it would be because of her own choices. She would be free. The service into which she had been forced, which had driven her to risk her life, would be a distant memory.

But she would be alone. The Lady needed her. The crusade needed her. And she needed them.

Nor had said something about true freedom—it was the ability to dislike what you were called to do even as you did it. Everyone was obligated to others. Your life was not your own, not completely.

She had taken a few steps back toward her gateway when a dark point on the horizon caught her eye. It moved and grew. When she looked straight at it, it swam in front of her eyes. Hoping to see it more clearly, she focused on another, larger shape near it.

This larger shape demanded her attention. She realized it was actually far away, farther than the speck. It appeared massive because it was.

It was immense. She was surprised she had missed it before now. It was a tower-shaped structure overlooking the desert.

Her skin crawled. It was something out of antiquity. It had to be. Humans could not build such things without the gods.

Meanwhile, the moving point had divided into many points. They were still growing.

"Oh, no."

She ran for the gateway, but searing pain stopped her. Something burned in her throat, in her ears, on her skin. She bent as the feeling ran up her body.

Something poured out of her mouth and ears. It came off her skin too—the grit and filth she had felt since waking rose like steam and gathered, humming, in the air.

The Lady formed in front of her. The humming congealed into words. "Hello, Caretaker."

Shada coughed and spat.

"We haven't much time," the Lady continued. "Someone is riding this way."

"Who are they?"

"I don't know, child."

"But you've been here before! You led us here!"

The Lady stared at her, eyes blank.

Shada heard the hostility in her tone. "I'm sorry. I'm scared. You're right, we should go back."

"We will. But first, I must congratulate you."

"Why? What did I do?"

"You've done so well, Shada. Caidfell held many trials, but you survived them all. Your latest victory came just now."

"Do you mean... all the terrible things that happened on Caidfell... did you make them happen?"

"Not at all. But when you defied me in the prison, I stopped offering my guidance for a while. You had resisted the Goddess's will so often that I wondered if I had chosen the wrong caretaker. I needed to know how devoted you were, if you would give up without my help.

"You didn't. Not only that, but you entered this new planet by yourself. Finally, given all these gateways to choose from and all the worlds behind them, you chose to stay with Huire's crusade."

"That's why you made me come here alone." Shada's mouth went dry. "Arumin was right. It was all a test. Everything."

"You're not the only one who's been tested," the Lady said. "Recent circumstances have tried us both."

Shada glanced at the approaching figures. They had little time to argue.

"I don't believe you," she told the Lady.

The Lady's humming rose in pitch. "Be very clear, Shada. What do you mean?"

"I don't believe you planned any of this. You admitted the Goddess hasn't spoken to you." Her face burned. "You're not in control. You might remember the general route we're to take, but when it comes to knowing what Huire wants, you're as lost as me. You just won't admit it."

The Lady's voice wavered. "You lied to me, child. You told me you had repented for your defiance."

"I considered it. But you've convinced me I shouldn't. Since we're both lost, why can't we work together? We could do the Goddess's will—together."

The Lady paused. "What has changed in you?"

"What do you mean?"

"Something I feared has come to pass. The admiration of others has gone to your head. Perhaps those visions you received inflated your self-importance."

"What? No."

The Lady loomed closer. "Perhaps that crystalline man in your visions was a demon sent to corrupt you."

"My visions stopped! I don't even know if he's real."

"Perhaps he sensed your potential for pride."

"No, it's nothing like that. I just—"

Shada jumped as the Lady reached for her. "What are you doing?" she gasped.

"I am a piece of the Goddess," said the Lady. Her voice had lost all emotion.

"I know that," Shada cried.

The Lady reached again and again. Each motion was slow enough to let Shada dodge it. The Lady drove her backward. "You believe you are my equal."

"No!"

The next hand swung a hair faster and knocked Shada down. She scrambled to her feet as the Lady reached again.

"Stay away!" Shada cried. "Who are you?"

"I am who I say I am."

"Please. Those riders will be here soon. If I don't leave now, they'll catch me."

"Then they will catch you."

"I've got to go back to my friends."

"'Friends'? You are too close to them."

There was nothing else to say. Shada turned to go.

The Lady swooped down on her with terrible speed. She struck the backs of Shada's knees like a solid object. Shada fell, barely catching herself with her hands, but the Lady swept those from under her.

Her cheek hit the ground. Dust filled her mouth. The great cloud that was the Lady funneled down her throat. Shada snapped her mouth shut, but the Lady flowed into her nostrils and wrenched her jaw open.

Once she had mostly hidden inside Shada's body, the Lady spread across Shada's face and into her ears, all one filmy surface.

From inside Shada's ears, the Lady spoke. "You have forced me to do this."

Thrashing, Shada reached into her mouth, but there was nothing to grab or pull.

The Lady said, "If only I'd known what you were like. I had hoped for a guardian and companion."

Shada could still speak, barely. "No, you didn't. You wanted a slave."

Then she could not breathe. The Lady formed a solid lump that blocked her throat like dried tar.

"Doing this also hurts me," said the Lady.

Shada rolled on the ground. Faces appeared to her, especially her father's. She saw him comfortable in the Temple's care, eating the apples she had given him. Thinking of her often but not grieving, she hoped.

"Killing can gratify when the cause is righteous. I learned that when I held that man in the fire to save you. But I want you to live."

Shada could hardly listen. Her world was a storm of spots and colors and need.

"That man wasn't the first. But I've only killed out of necessity. And I won't give up on you, Shada. If you wish to continue with me, to do my bidding, cross your arms over your chest."

She released a little air into Shada's lungs. "Let us pray together."

The ground shook as the riders approached. Shada crossed her arms and brought her face to the ground. She didn't understand any of this. If the riders killed her, the Lady would be alone on a strange planet. What could the

Lady desire so badly as to risk that? She had nothing to gain except...

With her face pressed against the cracked dirt, Shada gurgled, "I'll obey you."

Air rushed into her lungs like a mythical flood. Each breath was vast, stretching her chest. Her hands fell to the ground, limp.

"Goddess Huire," said the Lady, "come into us and strengthen us. Forgive us, and me most of all. For though your mercy is endless, mine is not."

Mounted soldiers surrounded them in a flurry. The men carried large guns and rode on tall beasts with hooves and swishing tails. There were many of them. Ranks of legs reached back as far as Shada could see. One man dismounted and approached her.

Shada had fallen to the ground as a free woman. She rose a slave, captive to her latest master, this one the most dreadful and powerful of all.

She stumbled. The man saw and ran to her.

His cheerful blue uniform was layered and ornate, something a soldier wore in a parade, not in the field. He smiled handsomely and spoke, but she couldn't understand a word.

She replied hoarsely in her own language. "My name is Shada."

His smile never faltered. "Welcome, Shada," he said, speaking perfect Ronian.

Stunned, she said nothing. The language was spoken across many worlds and called by many names. But here, beyond known space...

"What god do you worship, Shada?" The man asked the question as if it was perfectly normal.

The Lady spoke in her ear. "You must remain as anonymous as possible. Say you worship no god. Answer quickly."

The man noticed her hesitation. "You must tell the truth."

"None."

His face froze. A murmur ran around the circle of riders. "Remarkable. Where do you come from that you know no gods?"

"Don't mention Ronia," came the whisper.

"A place not worth speaking of," she told him. "It is far away and doomed."

If her evasiveness bothered him, he did not show it. His smile returned, faint but warm. "You've traveled a long way, plainly. But your journey is over." He spoke to the others. "Make our new friend comfortable."

Her insides tightened. A pair of men dismounted and strode past the others. They wore all black, and their slitted eyes shone a wicked shade of yellow.

The uniformed man turned back, his smile burning like the sun above the desert. "I'm glad you've come, Shada. You've entered a realm of splendor and power. We have only one god." He pointed to his head. He offered her his hand. "You will soon count this as the luckiest day of your life."

To continue the quest, read *The Kingdom and the Power*, book 3 of the Liturgy of Worlds, on sale here:

https://books2read.com/thekingdomandthepower

If you enjoyed this book, I would hugely appreciate a review wherever you got it or on Goodreads. Writing just a line or two helps me immensely!

Want a free short story set in the Liturgy of Worlds universe? Join my mailing list! Titled "A Monster's War," the story tells of the day the Lady came to Ronia—and it stars her caretaker, beastly warrior that he is. Check out the preview below. Plus, as a list member, you'll get the latest news from me, behind-the-scenes updates, media reviews and recommendations, and more!

Join my newsletter at nathanhartle.com for this free story!

The folk of these realms call him "Beast."

If only they knew he is their savior.

Filled with shame after a cowardly act, a giant warrior with a wolf's face sees one last chance for redemption: he must return a lost goddess to the city of her birth.

If she reaches home, she will remake the world. An age of light will dawn. But she is sick and weak, and she needs a protector.

Only Beast can help. If he triumphs, evil and darkness may disappear forever... and his shame will end. If he fails, he will lose his life and soul. Every step of his quest will be perilous—in these lands, Beast's size and appearance make him feared and hated.

But they also make him mighty.

"A Monster's War" is a quick adventure in the Liturgy of Worlds epic fantasy series.

⸻⬦⸻

Preview of A Monster's War

(Beast, the Lady's caretaker, is confronting a gang who have abducted the Lady...)

Beast strode toward the man, his pace steady, not quite promising violence.

Larky stood his ground as his men fled. At the last instant, he fell back, knife drawn, but Beast's arm shot out and grabbed him by the shirt.

Hoisting him off the ground, Beast looked him in the eyes and growled a promise. Larky shouted, and something stung Beast's leg.

A tingle raced like wildfire down to his foot and up to his hip. Something was terribly wrong, and he spun to watch several feathered spikes lodge in his leather breastplate. There stood several of Larky's men, holding thin pipes to their mouths.

For a sliver of an instant, he froze. They had poisoned him. Rather than fight openly, rather than seize combat as a chance to show honor and courage, they had used trickery and deceit. And they had won.

It was the epitome of civilization. He could never win against it. He could not even resist it—not without doing things the only way he knew. He disobeyed his goddess.

With an almighty roar, he charged the men, ready to kill them all...

"A Monster's War" is *only* available by signing up for my newsletter. Sign up here: nathanhartle.com

ABOUT THE AUTHOR

Nathan Hartle lives in North Carolina, USA with his amazing wife, son, and two cats who are kind enough to share their house.

Though he's had many, many jobs—travel agent in Bangkok, hostel clerk in Morocco, construction worker in Washington, DC—writing fantasy and science fiction is by far his favorite.

He believes storytelling is a service to others and a sacred act that honors Creation. Good stories let us glimpse eternity.

Keep up with Nathan by following him on Facebook, Goodreads, and BookBub.

www.ingramcontent.com/pod-product-compliance
Lightning Source LLC
Chambersburg PA
CBHW051306190726
48290CB00001B/31